33 Bits

Jane Bash

Copyright © 2009 Jane Bash
All rights reserved.
ISBN: 1-4392-4850-8
ISBN-13: 9781439248508

For additional copies:
www.Amazon.co.uk
www.Amazon.com
www.BookSurge.com
KINDLE Edition at www.Amazon.com
Cover design by © Pamela Wessel, Photographer

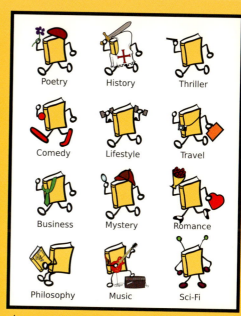

Discover the Secret Lives of Books...

I'm a travelling book. Go to **www.bookcrossing.com**, enter this BCID, and see where I've been. Then help keep my dream alive. **READ & RELEASE ME!**

BCID:	841-8568739
Registered By:	Liza Jane
Where & When:	1/11/11

 bookcrossing.com™
the karma of literature · free and anonymous
©2001-2010 bookcrossing.com

I would be remiss if I did not thank the following for the generous spirit and variety with which they contributed to this project.

University of Birmingham, UK
Wallace Holmquist
Steve Thorne, PhD
Dennis Davis
David Poe
Mandy Facer
Dennis Jacks
Ginger Mills
Jennifer Reynosa
Carolyn Holmquist
The Teapot Ladies
Lionel Matthews
Alice McDaniel
Stephen Boyd
Rick Vincent
Vuepoint IT
Goldmasters Jewelers
Louise Parsons Matthews
Pamela Wessel, Photographer

Preface

I played travel companion with my husband on a business trip in Birmingham, England. Meandering the streets of the famous Jewellery Quarter, I found nothing of interest for my customarily voracious appetite for gemstones. But inside a pawnshop, I was struck by a strange energy, emitting from the far right corner of the room.

"What's in that tray?" I asked the shopkeeper.

"Nothen fer sale. It's scrap metal we am melten," he replied in his Brummie accent, with disinterest.

I felt a sudden panic rise up in my mind as the item called, no, *screamed* at me to save it. I felt the sudden nonnegotiable urge to rescue whatever work of art was going to be melted down. I offered to buy whatever was in the tray across the room. He reiterated that it was not for sale. I became desperate and hysterically pleaded with the man to part with the object. He finally gave in to the "lunatic American." The Brummie sold the lump in the tray to me for the weight of the metal.

Once out of the shop, I finally was able to carefully inspect the work of art that *screamed* to be rescued from the horrible fate of being washed away forever with other metal items. It was not a piece of art, after all. It was a woman's life, encoded on an incredible bracelet of thirty-three charms, detailing a journey through life in Europe.

I wept.

The spirit of this woman's life was so powerful that it inspired this story. All charms referred to in this re-creation are the actual artifacts from this woman's adventures.

I have personally attempted to wear her bracelet on only three occasions. Each time, the bracelet broke off my arm. This is strange, according to Goldmasters in San Antonio, who keep all my fine jewelry intact. After all, it is a sturdy, link charm bracelet with no weak spots.

I think *she* calls to me. I think she wants her life story to be rescued. It still screams to be listened to, to be found by her family.

So, as you read, listen...

33 Bits of *Charming Etta*

Chapter 1 – Charmed	1
Chapter 2 – Family Love	19
Chapter 3 – Flight Mantras	27
Chapter 4 – Sojourn Saint	41
Chapter 5 – Double Deck Luck	47
Chapter 6 – Irish State Coach	57
Chapter 7 – Break for Tea	63
Chapter 8 – Grain Thief	71
Chapter 9 – Lucky Purse	79
Chapter 10 – Coffee Hour	89
Chapter 11 – Sheepish Intent	103
Chapter 12 – Splitting Hares	115
Chapter 13 – Prince Charming	127
Chapter 14 – Charming Princess	141
Chapter 15 – Empanada	155
Chapter 16 – Key to My Heart	167
Chapter 17 – King George IV Diadem	177
Chapter 18 – Imperial State	189

Chapter 19 – Tower Bridge	207
Chapter 20 – Open Country Carriage	221
Chapter 21 – Italian Horn	235
Chapter 22 – Hammered Urn	247
Chapter 23 – Gondola of Love	259
Chapter 24 – Swiss Skate	271
Chapter 25 – Castle Harewood	279
Chapter 26 – German Cross	291
Chapter 27 – Edelweiss	299
Chapter 28 – Garden Boot	307
Chapter 29 – Stork	317
Chapter 30 – Leprechaun Luck	325
Chapter 31 – Swiss Cowbell	335
Chapter 32 – Fork in the Road	345
Chapter 33 – Equestrian Luck	357

Prologue

Grace waited impatiently in line, clutching the carry-on with both hands. Her proximal awareness was heightened with news of the attacks in London. The hair on the back of Grace's neck was on alert as her eyes swept the other shocked people around her waiting to check onto various flights. Was Al-Qaeda in Madrid? Of course they were. They were everywhere. Grace just wanted to get home—quickly.

She shifted the bag onto her left arm while collecting her documents from the international flight desk. The clicking sound of the boarding pass being printed distracted her for only a moment, when a hand firmly grasped her left wrist, causing her to drop the carry-on. In terror, Grace whirled around to view the culprit, wanting to scream with fright, but then she was silenced by the vision of a stranger with fire in his eyes.

"Where did you get this?" the man demanded with a wheezy restraint in his voice.

Chapter 1
CHARMED

∽ 1974 ∽

Etta was old for her twenty years. It wasn't that she intimately knew this desert and all its hidden treasures already, even in her dreams. Rather, the desert knew *her* too well, and it seemed tired of her customary presence. It had taken her virgin skin and made it middle-aged. It had mercilessly cracked her nails and calloused her frequently bare feet. It had baked her skin and bleached her chestnut hair.

In the formative years that Etta spent in the Arizona desert, she embraced the remote solitude of the valley and its inhabitants. She enjoyed the company of the horned toads and lizards as she hiked a dusty path across a small span of desert to the A. J. Bayless grocer where she worked.

Her mother, Martha, worried about this second child who wasted her academic talents, choosing instead to enjoy the social monotony of the local patrons as she bagged groceries. Money did not appear to motivate Etta. Martha and George Johnson had never known money and, quite frankly, did not understand how to position their children to acquire it.

Even years after George moved on without his family to greener terrain and younger company, Martha expected that neither Abigail nor Etta would ever overcome the loss of their father. She was overtly nervous that Etta had not yet found an acceptable suitor and that she curiously spent much time alone in the desert. The matriarch herself detested Phoenix, having been deposited there after a cross-country move for that worthless husband. He had left *her* when the girls were still in high school.

Martha was unsure what her daughter Etta did in the desert, but she was unwilling to brave the oppressive, dry heat to check on her anymore.

In the partial shade of a mesquite tree, Etta penned her thoughts into a journaling notebook she carried as a sort of self-help project. In that, Tuesday's entry, Etta wrote on the topic of exploration.

It is mine to know the hundred shades of brown.

The expanse of valley and the sweat of my brow.

My adventure is in the smell of wet caliche and small stone.

The sight of rattlesnake beneath the ocotillo.

In this regal saguaro field there is brother roadrunner.

Hiding too are javelina, waiting for the passage of the sun.

I know much of this place, and yet I am of few years.

I was given this knowledge as one who stops to hear.

Though this world is vast and much in it to learn,

I seek adventure out of common borders, I yearn.

Etta laughed and scratched through several words she was unhappy with.

༄

Etta strolled down the dusty path, past the ranch she had worked at shoveling manure and exercising horses through her school years. She briefly paused to acknowledge one of the especially needy older mares. "Fine lady you are, Indira." With that nurturing nose rub, off she strolled through the dry brush to work. A content whinny sailed into the wind behind her.

She made it to the grocery store just as the time clock turned over with a loud click. *Whew, nothing like being really ON time,* Etta thought to herself.

The store manager, Mr. Brown, asked with the familiar fatherly tone, "Are you entering the Lucky London writing contest? I can't imagine you would pass up a chance to win a vacation to England…"

Etta cut him off, attempting to curb her enthusiasm. "Yes, sir. I saw the notice on the bulletin board last week. With a few weeks to work on it, I should have an entry."

Semantics and rhythm intrigued her, and this was an important start. It was a contest of terrific odds. Etta was aware of her competition. Those who had talents would not enter such a contest as this. Those who had no ability to write would contribute one entry. Etta would fill the contest boxes to swelling. This, she felt, would give her a fair advantage.

"Do you know who put up the money for this one?"

"Mr. Bayless, I suppose. Maybe he thought it would be an opportunity to distract us during the annual Fourth of July rush. You're on the schedule for the Fourth."

"Yeah. I had President's Day off, so I figured it was only fair to volunteer for Fourth of July this time. Besides, it'll be slow enough, I'm sure I can fix up an entry."

Mr. Brown shook his head and laughed out of pity, or hope, for his overqualified bagger.

For Etta, this was not unpleasant work. Though she had earned an associate's degree in secretarial work at Phoenix College, she had few needs and required a minimum pittance for her selfish wants. She loved the regular customers who never read her name tag but called her by what pleased them. Her nametag read Etta, though she answered to any other derivative the local Mexican or Native American inhabitants would offer. She would even answer to "honey," "darling," or "sweetie pie," which came flowing out of the exaggerated drawl of the community's sole Texan, Mrs. Edwin Earl Busch.

"Etta, Etta, gota geta fella!" her sister teased upon entering the store.

"Oh, Abigail, back off the dead horse!" Etta playfully returned. Abigail hugged her younger sister and strolled up the bakery aisle seeking fresh tortillas for their mother's enchiladas.

Upon her return, Abigail inquired, "Are you going to Chuck's barbeque this weekend? He really wants you to meet his new lady."

"Well..." Etta tried to be polite. "Chuck seems to have a new girl he is serious about every few months! I suppose I'll go, though. He does make the best steaks this side of Texas!"

Etta and Chuck had been pals since second grade when Etta had beaten him at every single athletic event during the school's annual field day. He was walking home in tears when Etta ran up behind him. She instinctively apologized. For what? She did not know, but they were forever friends afterward.

"OK, I didn't tell you this, but he wants to introduce you to a friend from church named Norman. Chuck thinks you two would really hit it off!" Abigail's eyes pleaded before she maneuvered the shopping cart toward the canned goods aisle.

Etta just shook her head and returned to work carrying her notebook and pen. Etta kept her precious journal within close reach of any new idea she could pen between the endless bags of groceries. She overheard Mrs. Edwin Earl Busch discussing the Lucky London contest with Mr. Brown.

"You know, Billy, I'm not sure that your patrons would appreciate a trip to England. Ed Earl and I traveled the United Kingdom one summer, and it was not for the common..."

"Mrs. Busch, I'm sure *anyone* would appreciate an opportunity to travel outside the country, especially if it's on A. J. Bayless!" he retorted with the heat rising up his neck. Bill attempted to conceal his tone and the irritation he felt toward this regular customer by changing the subject.

Etta was surprised to feel a tear escape her eye socket and fall from her customarily brave eyes onto the brown grocery bag. Thankfully, Mrs. Ed Earl was too self-absorbed to notice that "the girl who never cried" (a reputation Etta earned in several boxing bouts during her school days), was reduced to inaudible tears. Her voice was steady enough for Etta to excuse herself from bagging duties for a powder room break. Thankfully, Mr. Brown remained unaware of the effect Mrs. Ed Earl's comment had on Etta.

Behind the toilet stall door, Etta felt the world descend upon her for the very first time. She realized that she had indeed outgrown her family, job, community, and even the very things that grounded her in this life. The tears steadily came down her cheeks as Etta resolved that she *was* worthy to explore the world. Resolving that she would submit entries in every A. J. Bayless store in the city, with as many entries as she could create, her final thoughts were to emerge from the powder room with no evidence of her private breakdown.

∽

Etta pored over the contest rules. She read them over and over to prevent any disqualification issue with an employee entry.

LUCKY LONDON!

Presented by A. J. Bayless
Do you long for the adventure of a lifetime?
Now is your chance to win a two-week trip to London, England!
Just tell us in five hundred words or less why YOU
should see a queen!

Rules for entry: Each form must include applicant's name, address, and phone number on the reverse side of the submittal. One entry per envelope, please. Family members of, and managerial A. J. Bayless employees will be disqualified. All entries must be received by August 6, 1974. Grand prizewinner receives roundtrip airfare, accommodations, and a transportation sum in the amount of $200. One runner-up will be selected from each store for a second-place cash prize of $100. Four winners from each store will receive a third-place $25 gift certificate to be redeemed at any A. J. Bayless grocery store. All entries must be original, unpublished work of the applicant.

Well, they never restricted the number of entries. They didn't regulate how many stores you could enter either. Etta schemed, plotted, and dreamed the most effective entry strategy.

In a painstaking effort (since she possessed neither a typewriter nor quality penmanship), Etta worked several hours each night in the local library. The rotating troupe of part-time clerks staffing the center always offered similar questions about her perceived task and its apparent tie to some educational pursuit. Etta returned very little explanation or response to what she considered to be an invasion of her private endeavor.

After the third week of the grueling, self-imposed schedule, Etta borrowed her sister's sun-faded but dependable Buick.

She drove from store to store, ensuring that the varied entries would be delivered directly into the hands of some ranking A. J. Bayless assistant grocery manager. With each delivery, she offered a stack of entries in a curiously mismatched assortment of envelopes that she scrounged from her estranged father's box of office supplies. The mismatched envelopes had genuinely been part of Etta's scheme to not be disqualified for having multiple entries, despite that fact the rules did not explicitly state, "One entry per person."

Billy Brown enjoyed attending district meetings. His store was equipped with only an employee break area. The district office was in downtown Phoenix on an upper floor of the luxurious Luhrs building. The corner office faced the visually powerful, soul-recharging, mountain view of Squaw Peak on the north and the infamous Camelback Mountain to the northeast. This elevated view always made Billy feel just a tad more important than his daily responsibilities of the store in the northeast desert region. He was there, early as usual, to secure his seat with a view of the mountains.

"Mr. Brown, I don't believe I will ever live to see you come to a meeting on time!" the vice president's secretary offered. "Even though you drive the furthest, you always seem to be the first one to show."

"Blame my Midwestern roots that dictate being on time is fifteen minutes too late," Billy replied accompanied with a laugh, which he realized afterward revealed his anxiousness to enjoy the company of Rita, who was reportedly hired for her looks rather than her skills.

Rita showed Billy into the conference room, which was adorned with the familiar crystal water pitcher, eight beautifully cut glasses, and tool-punched leather A. J. Bayless trademark coasters. Rita poured Billy a glass of water and set it on a coaster in front of his favorite chair. He found these items were the only things that interfered with the table's lacquered reflection of the coffered ceiling and Arizona native décor. He also pondered whether Squaw Peak or Rita, seated behind the French doors, offered a better view.

Billy stood with his hands in his pockets, surveying the skyline. He paused longer on the image of Camelback Mountain a lovely imposition on the horizon. The rugged colors were sharp in this private, clear moment, and Billy could actually make out some of the boulders from his vantage point. Squaw Peak evoked a different emotion since Billy knew this one intimately through his various hikes up her sides. It was one of those precious "visionary" spots you can distract yourself with when work becomes mundane or intolerable.

After the fifteen-minute reflection time, other managers arrived, greeting their A. J. club members with firm handshakes, slaps on the back, and jokes about the weather. All managers wore the customary short-sleeve shirt with a tie and suit coat. It was not as practical to actually wear the suit coat as it was important to arrive in one and remove it before the temperature got the best of you.

Billy was aware of his position with the managers. His store was ranked sixth out of seven in sales. But he defended the store in his mind with the understanding that his most loyal customers supplemented their diets with cuisine originating from unnamed yard animals, small gardens, and the occasional prickly pear patch, which he could attest made a delicious jelly or syrup.

Mr. Philip Davenport was always on the fashionably late side, arriving at "quarter-past the managers." Billy felt fortunate to work under this new VP who possessed people skills. "Gentlemen today may be one of the most entertaining meetings this year. I wiped the agenda clean to focus on selecting a winner for our contest. Keep fairness in mind. Don't look at the back of the entries. They have been screened down to your store's top five. It is my hope, gentlemen, that we can all agree on one first-place entry per store for the hundred dollar bills and the best of those for the grand prize. Agreed?"

Nearly in unison, the seven men communicated verbally and nodded in agreement to the task at hand. All understood the remaining four entries they judged from each store would receive a twenty-five-dollar A. J. Bayless gift certificate.

The room fell quiet as the managers read each one-page entry. Mr. Davenport left to attend to a brief update with Rita and returned to the head of the table after twenty minutes had passed. By this time, the men were actively seeking each other's counsel on which entries deserved to be first for their stores. Three entries were clearly superior, and the other four took some discussion. Once they selected the final seven entries, the real work began. Each manager read his store's entry while Mr. Davenport studied the words and thoughts of the hopeful.

It was tough to differentiate a clear winner. A few were funny topics, but one was stone serious. Two were pleasant verse. And then a clear winner emerged. The northwest location entry read like a travel ad for the *Arizona Highways* magazine. The author wrote with delicious sincerity about loving the desert and how the colors of the Phoenix sky could compare to the colors of London. How the cactus blossoms could contrast with the shapes of the lush English gardens. It was poetic, reflective, and deep. All agreed that this was their winner.

Mr. Davenport watched from behind fingers clasped at his chin. He was pleased that this was such an easy process. Mr. Bayless's transportation department would work directly with the winner after a personal visit from Mr. Philip Davenport, accompanied by the corporate photographer. This would, in fact, be wonderful media for the dominant grocer of the valley. The winners were turned over to Rita, who would record the contact information and coordinate the production of the poster for each store. The second-place stacks would be returned to the stores for processing. Each store's accountant would take care of the gift certificates.

The managers cleared their piles into manila envelopes, closed their folios, and extended farewells. Of course, the coats predictably would last only until the elevator door closed behind them. It was a great way to break that awkward silence in an elevator, removing one's coat.

Rita collected the finalists' papers and cleared the conference room table. She walked slowly back to her desk, surveying her next paper duty, and then she stopped short. She called out in an unnatural tone, a tad too loud for appropriate office volume, "Mr. Davenport, we have a problem!"

Martha and Abigail weeded the terrain of the unconfined yard. It was rather difficult to discern what was yard and what was desert. The barren, dusty space spanning in all directions from their home contained many undeveloped lots. The Johnsons had chosen this one because it nurtured several mesquite trees. Their closest neighbor, at present, was twelve acres away, more or less.

The sun beat down on their necks, and the triple-digit heat roasted them slowly from the outside. An intrusion drove up what appeared to be a dirt driveway in a luxurious Cadillac with shaded windows. It was a welcome interruption as the Johnsons didn't get much company during the summer months.

From the passenger seat, a fine-looking man emerged, standing over six feet in stature, with an athletic cut body and a head of full, wavy brown hair.

"Good morning, ladies. Is Etta Johnson here?"

Both women looked at each other with raised eyebrows and the same feminine thought wave. In unison, their eyes exchanged, *Could it be that Etta met a man who would wear a suit on a summer day? Could it be that Etta is interested in* men?

"Ladies...?"

Martha broke the strange silence with an awkward noise, clearing her throat before offering words. "Etta's not here right now."

"I am very interested in seeing her today if possible. Is there a better time to stop by?" the man questioned impatiently.

Abigail offered, "Etta should be back around five this evening. Can we tell her whom to expect?"

Martha looked with surprise at her daughter, who had never been prone to using the word "whom." She then noticed two other men in the vehicle. A driver waited for the exchange to be over, and another man in the backseat was leaning forward in an impatient gesture.

"Look, if you have an issue with Etta, can we at least prepare her for your arrival?"

The man's tone revealed increasing frustration as he replied, "No, thank you. Please don't let her anticipate anyone. I prefer this to be a surprise."

Martha studied her options. There are good surprises and bad surprises. The calculated odds, using family track record, prepared her wicked imagination for something horrific. To make matters worse, Etta was unaccounted for, somewhere in the desert. It was an off day, so she could be hunting for Indian pottery, hiking Squaw Peak, or just sitting in the shade, writing in one of those notebooks that seemed to manage her thoughts.

"Agreed," Martha snapped. She abruptly turned her back and stormed purposefully off to the backyard so she wouldn't press or aggravate the issue further.

Abigail shrugged her shoulders and watched the man load back into the car. The car drove off, leaving swirls of light brown dust clouds behind.

༄

Martha and Abigail were visibly nervous when Etta came in. She had only been gone for a few hours, and yet they seemed far too interested in her recent whereabouts. That in itself was strange because Etta had always come and gone as she pleased, without regard for the family agenda.

Martha carefully started, not wanting to seem too nosy. "We had a car full of men here looking for you this afternoon. They were driving a nice car and had suits on. Is there anything we oughta know about?"

Etta was a bit put off by this notion. "Are you sure they wanted me?"

Abigail interjected, "They wouldn't tell us anything. Seems kinda strange that they couldn't tell us why they needed to see you."

Just then, clouds of dirt disturbed the rising purple and blue hues of sunset as a vehicle approached once again.

"That's the car!" Abigail screeched, extending her arm in a pointing gesture that was neither subtle nor customary of her ladylike behavior.

Emerging from the car, a gentleman of perhaps thirty stood, fastening buttons on a dark blue suit and an impossibly white shirt with a European tie and shined shoes. Etta thought it was funny to wear shoes like that here. She watched the dust settle on the top of those shoes, slowly erasing the sheen as he introduced himself to the anxious family.

"Ladies, I am Philip Davenport, vice president of the valley's A. J. Bayless grocery stores. This is Martin Patterson, our advertising manager, Marion Allen, photographer, and Bill, come on out here." Mr. Davenport waved a hand toward the man emerging from the darkened backseat of the car. "Bill Brown is the manager of your local A. J. Bayless store."

Martha didn't want to be rude, but this was obvious information to regular customers who had a family member under Billy's employ. "Sir, just what do you need?"

"Are you Etta Johnson?" Mr. Davenport inquired of the only young lady he had not met in the group.

Etta was smiling so broadly her face just may have cracked at both edges. "You are here about England, aren't you?" she inquired with audible anticipation.

"As a matter of fact, I am…"

"Are you sending me to London?" Etta screeched in an inhuman, excited sound.

"Yes, Etta, you won our contest."

Like a bullet escaping the barrel of a pistol, Etta shot off in a run, kicking up dust in a wide circle around the guests and her small family. The photographer, Marion, had great difficulty capturing an image of this wild woman who had just learned she won a vacation.

She was hysterically crying and screaming and carrying on so much so that her mother was provoked into her long-forgotten parental duty of child management. "Etta, stop that! Please come in so we can discuss this proper."

Etta continued her yard dance in a wide circle, which appeared to be settling more into the dance rhythm of a Navajo powwow. Even her cries and screams evolved into having a particular cadence. She circled the yard eight or twelve times before surrendering into the house to take her chair in the kitchen. She didn't feel like her back side was touching the chair so much as she was floating just above the padded seat. Her brain was tingling with the joy that was circulating rapidly through her body.

Etta didn't hear much of the conversation after that. She was vaguely aware of the flashes caused by Marion's professional photography equipment. But she was absorbing it all in deep, beneath human contact, in a place she customarily reserved for times of solitary reflection in the desert.

She vaguely felt her hand sign an award document in a signature that wasn't quite her own. Etta didn't hear the details, only her family's reaction to them. The manager in the brown suit seemed unfamiliar, with his unnaturally business-like demeanor she had never seen conducted in the store that employed her. It was a glorious fog of events played out as if she was on some other euphoric planet.

The working relationship between Billy and his employee was never exposed during the exciting events. It was established that Etta was in no shape to be reckoned with. Some of the documents were left with Martha to review with her daughter once Etta could calm down and gather her wits.

The car drove off with only Abigail to watch them disappear into shades of the progressing dusk's grays and browns.

༄

Billy returned late that night after a small group of his coworkers dispersed. He was pleased to find Etta close to the edge of rational after they allowed her a couple hours. "Etta, I'm not sure you understand the weight of what you've achieved here. You not only won the trip to England, but you won four of the seven stores' top entries. *And*, you won eleven gift certificates, to ice the cake. That'd be four hundred dollars and two hundred and seventy-five dollars in groceries. I really underestimated your skills. When you return, would you be interested in working in our advertising section? We could really use your talent, and there would be a significant pay increase."

"Mr. Brown, I'm actually going to England! I have absolutely no memories of anyplace besides here, and I'm going to England!" Etta was clearly fueled by an adrenaline rush and was unable to either articulate her thoughts or respond to the promotion offer from her beloved manager.

"Well, this check is the combination of the monetary awards, and these are your store gift certificates. Can I see Martha for a minute?"

Etta excused herself from the suddenly brighter kitchen. It was as though her disposition had changed the color of the walls from beige to sun-kissed yellow. Even the old kitchen table appeared to clear itself of routine piles housed on its workspace.

Martha came in to greet Billy in her favorite Sunday dress, which fit pretty well considering she'd purchased it over a decade ago. The glow of her face accentuated the pink bouquets of flowers on the sturdy fabric. "We can't thank you enough for all this! It's such a surprise!"

"You bet! I just don't think she grasps the big picture. Can you talk to Etta about working in advertising once she floats back into her body? I gave her the check and certificates, but I don't think she should come to work tomorrow. She may need some time to get over the shock. I don't think she has her feet back on the ground yet. For good reason..." Martha and Bill shared a hearty laugh.

"I think she should go to the downtown office tomorrow. Here's Rita Ortiz's number. She works for Mr. Davenport, our vice president. She'll help Etta walk through all the requirements for the trip."

Martha collected the business card. "Wow! How can I thank you?" Martha began with a softened edge to her voice. "Etta will have quite an experience. Frankly, it'll be a life-changing experience for her."

༄

Etta borrowed Abigail's car and drove downtown to meet with Rita. She dressed in her most conservative appearing sundress with a coordinating jacket. She stepped out of the car and reviewed the lessons from her charm school class many moons ago. "Stand up straight, look people in the eye, walk with grace and poise." She was feeling attractive today, an attribute Etta rarely shot for.

Without moving her chin down, she noted that the entry carpet just before the regal entry was dust free. Her eyes surveyed the double glass doors without so much as a tilt of her head. It was beginning to feel like a social game as the doorman greeted her with genuine interest. As he opened the door, Etta felt his eyes follow her while the ceiling seemed to vault before her into an enormous atrium. She paused for a moment and looked upward. She soaked in the art, textures, and fabrics of the lush furnishings. She meandered over to the elevator, which opened on cue with her arrival. Out stepped Martin Patterson, who looked directly at Etta, yet he said nothing.

"Good morning, Mr. Patterson," Etta offered warmly with a genuine smile.

Martin appeared puzzled. "You are?"

"Etta Johnson."

"Oh, I didn't recognize you! How are you? Are you here for reservations or for professional purposes?"

"Both. I want to go to the personnel office to find out about job openings and will meet with Rita about the trip, too."

"Well," Martin said, pausing in hopes of delaying the moment. "I hope you do join us. And have a really wonderful trip. You sure earned it."

"Thanks. I'm pretty excited about getting all the paperwork complete. They told me to get a passport. I've never flown before, so I'm a little nervous about that."

"I fly a few times a year and really enjoy it. The clouds outside the window relax you, and watching the ant-sized houses just fade away as you increase in altitude... There's nothing like it. I still find it thrilling."

"It was nice to see you again, sir. Maybe we will work together in the future?"

Martin watched her enter the elevator, amazed that she was the same person Philip Davenport had recently introduced to him as the contest winner. He genuinely hoped they would work together.

The elevator doors parted to reveal Mr. Davenport's large office suite. Etta observed a beautiful desk, which appeared more a fine piece of wood furniture than a working desk as she knew one to be. It was topped with trays that contained piles of projects, nevertheless appearing organized and under control. To her left was a conference room visible through two French doors. She could see the mountains through the conference room and realized why Mr. Brown liked to come here for his regular meetings. The tone of this stately office, in this imposing structure in the valley, flashed quickly into Etta's realization as a place where she would really enjoy working.

With deliberate courtesy, Etta made eye contact with the secretary, whose name was announced on a brass, horizontal placard. "Good morning. I am Etta Johnson for the nine o'clock appointment."

Etta had alternately practiced "*I am Etta*" and "*My name is Etta*," deciding at last that "*I am*" sounded more businesslike. She attempted to draw on skills she learned a few years ago in college. She offered her hand when the beautiful, statuesque woman stood to reply.

Rita stood, offering her manicured hand and the obvious, "Hello. Rita Ortiz. I work for Philip Davenport, the vice president of sales." This sounded a little stilted. "William Brown from the northwest store told me to expect you."

Rita was not prepared for Etta's polished appearance after hearing Marion's description of the photo shoot. Marion had described a wild, unkempt person who appeared awkward in her God-given stature. What Rita saw was a young woman of poise and grace. She was unnaturally erect in her posture, making her appear downright regal. Her tanned skin was made up softly with pale hues that revealed her naturally beautiful features. She was dressed in nice clothing with sensible shoes. Etta sported turquoise earrings and a matching necklace, but no rings. This surprised Rita, who had achieved her engagement ring at only sixteen.

They pored over papers to fill out, laughing when Etta confessed that her nickname was short for Henrietta, her maternal grandmother. Rita had just assumed that Etta was short for some Spanish derivative such as Loretta, Glorietta, or Doretta. It was a common misconception as the name was rare in the western region.

༄

Two miles away from where Etta was making trip arrangements, Martha and Abigail were shopping at Forty-Second Street and Camelback in Goldwater's department store. They dressed up for the event, feeling in a celebratory mood on the hunt for the perfect gift for the surprise party. Etta was a tough shop. She was a simple person with few needs. Abigail meandered to the jewelry counter to gaze more for herself than Etta. The clerk overheard a discussion about their challenge to hunt down an appropriate gift.

"May I help you with something special?" the clerk inquired of the two.

"My daughter is kind of like a desert hare. She's going on a trip abroad, and we need a going-away gift for her. But I don't think you'd have anything for her. She doesn't like jewelry much."

The clerk countered. "Of course we do! The new low-key statement is the gold charm bracelet. She can purchase charms on her trip as a tangible memento."

The ladies faced each other and exchanged a surprised look. "Gosh, that's a great idea!"

Martha responded thoughtfully, "Yes, perhaps, but Etta only wears Hopi Indian silver. Do you think she would want gold?"

The clerk interjected, "We have silver, madam, but if you are searching for something special, silver is too common. She can select charms in gold or silver, but gold will hold its value better as a fine jewelry."

Martha paused for a span of time that felt like five minutes. She finally turned toward the clerk and simply asked, "Can you please show us those gold charm bracelet designs?"

Chapter 2
FAMILY LOVE

The house was cleaned from spick to span, and Abigail had arranged streamers and balloons to decorate the small living room. Martha made a cake using a recipe she had not visited in perhaps ten years. It miraculously rose to the occasion as a dessert, worthy of the honor as the dining room table centerpiece. They both elicited the help of Mrs. Busch for the arrangements since she had the most experience of anyone in their community at throwing grand parties.

The barbecue grill was emitting swirls of sweet mesquite smoke and was anxious to meet up with the slabs of meat that were forthcoming. Even though the neighbors were acres away, they could smell the anticipation. They invited all of the neighbors, a few church members, and old friends to the surprise party. Etta would not be leaving for a few weeks, but they realized time would pass quickly before her departure.

Chuck was the first to arrive, and he was carrying a small gift and a slab of beef from Simson's butcher shop. Chuck was a regular, and Simson always reserved the choicest cuts for him. In exchange, Chuck appreciated that the elder Simson always had an unspoiled, white apron, despite carrying any given variety of raw flesh.

Martha was more than happy to allow Chuck to take over the grill. It was a skill she never learned from her former husband and, quite frankly, had no interest in acquiring. Chuck had taught himself the art of cooking on Martha's grill since his own family would not allow him near anything with a flame. The ladies at the Johnson home were eager guinea pigs, never criticizing the outcome as Chuck gradually honed his barbeque skills. The sisters were grateful for the dinner company, and he was forever grateful to play with fire.

Martha deposited Chuck's gift on the table where Abigail had arranged a lace tablecloth and two family gifts. Already the aromatic steaks were teasing the occupants of the house.

Etta was bagging groceries for customers who exhibited a new appreciation for her. Nearly everyone had seen her photo featured for an entire week in the *Arizona Daily Sun*. The advertising had paid off, at least in Billy's store where customers were swayed from the newer Safeway store back to old faithful A. J. Bayless. Etta was a local celebrity, and she played the part quite nicely. She had begun to invest in a new wardrobe for not only her trip to England, but also for the job change, which appeared inevitable upon her return.

The new duds had a way of changing Etta's entire demeanor with customers. They were surprised to engage her in intelligent conversation while the checkout clerks rang up each item's price with quiet accuracy.

Shifts seem to pass more quickly with the new pleasantries of her customers. Each person seemed to enrich her by a small margin and collectively, so that when she returned home, she felt increasingly more intelligent. Her confidence was at an all-time high, and she felt ready to step out of the country, alone.

The time clock slammed the tiny inked record of her shift's end onto the thick timecard. How she hated the sound! It was an enslaving sound that seemed belittling and unnecessary. Perhaps it seemed that way even more so now as her thoughts turned to getting her documents and papers in order for the trip.

As she walked home, the dust seemed unnaturally settled, and her smart new leather shoes appeared fairly clean. They also felt broken in now after several days on her feet. For that, she was grateful.

While passing Lenny's ranch, Etta noticed two new fillies, but she also registered the visual absence of her favorite old friend, Indira. Etta climbed the first rail and hollered into the lunge pen to one of the Mexican hands, "Where'd you put up Indira?"

The ranch hand reported back over the fence, yet he maintained eye contact with the horse he was working. "Colic... *muerto ayer*."

Etta hopped off the fence and felt an invisible hand slap her across the face so hard that tears welled up and flowed out of her eyes. Perhaps it was better it was not a long illness for her equine friend. The horse had had a lovely life in her evolution from racing, to showing, and finally to retiring as a petting horse for timid new riders. Etta groomed Indira countless times during her employment at the barn during high school. Even now, she could sketch every unique mark by memory. She could visualize every hair on her muzzle. In fact, she could now sense the familiar feel of the horse's warm neck on her side. Etta silently mourned Indira's passing.

Farther up the road through tear-blurred eyes, Etta perceived a problem. There were cars all around her house! Theirs was not a very social residence, so this was surely cause for panic. Etta raced up the path kicking up dirt, no longer aware of her new shoes, wondering what calamity had fallen upon her mother or sister. Arriving at the mailbox, her chest heaved huge breaths in and out as she paused in a numb shock. The balloons attested to the lack of an emergency at home. For this, Etta said a prayer of thanks, wiped her eyes, and kicked some of the dust off her shoes.

Chuck spotted her first, and led the "One! Two! Three! Surprise!" in unison with thirty-four supportive friends.

"Surprise, honey," Martha said, her face beaming.

Abigail offered, "Good luck, and bon voyage, punk!"

The room swelled with pleasant conversation and food. Chuck helped to serve the beef with pride on his face. Guests filled their plates with Navajo tacos, prickly pear pad salad, and a large assortment of other local delicacies reserved for special occasions such as this.

"Whoa! Thank you, Mrs. Busch," Etta reacted to the leather passport holder. The gift wrap fell to the floor to be counted with the beautiful wrappings from dozens of gifts Etta would enjoy receiving this day. Abigail collected a snippet from each wrapping to add to the gift register she wrote for her sister. She could tell Etta was nervous. Though her smile was genuine, there was an absence of Etta's customary steadiness. Abigail expected this gala would feel a little over the top since the Johnsons were generally not big party people.

The travel suit her mother bought looked fine with the new shoes. After Etta had opened all the gifts, one gift was reserved during the joyous commotion. It wasn't until the next morning, as Etta was leaving to address the passport papers, that she noticed it beside a donut-filled plate on the kitchen table. The room was partially cleaned up, but occasional remnants of the party remained as cheerful reminders of the love shared with Etta just yesterday.

"Mom! What's the box in here?" Etta yelled across the house.

Abigail yelled from the back bedroom, "Wait! Don't open it yet."

"We didn't want you to open this one 'til we were together. Abby, hurry up! Etta needs to get to town." Martha referred to anywhere with a two-story building as "town."

Abigail sashayed into the room looking like a million bucks for an eight o'clock desert morning. "You better be careful with my car! Go on now. Open it."

Etta opened the first layer of wrap and saw the Goldwater's department store logo broadcast across the silver and gray box. She was aware this was no common gift as the Johnsons rarely stepped foot in the highfalutin store. Etta paused and walked into the living room, followed by her beloved family.

The box top was pulled away to reveal a jewelry box in black velvet. The top of the box opened to a sturdy gold link charm bracelet with a small filigree heart charm hanging from one side.

Etta's eyes teared up, and her voice choked out words of gratitude. "Thank you so much. I can't believe you did this… all this. Gosh, thanks so much…"

Martha, Abby, and Etta entwined in what looked like a schoolyard huddle with their arms around each other. This silence lasted for only a few moments when a very strange mood caught them off guard. The women began to bawl in unison. Three women, in a very small living room, overcome with emotion at the prospect that luck was favorable for once. Etta's personal luck, which she had worked so hard for, was a turning point for the family. This single achievement would bring the Johnson name into vogue conversation from apartment, to ranch, to luxury home in the "Valley of the Sun." This single opportunity was about to change many lives.

༄

Flash! The camera captured a unique image of an exotically beautiful young woman for a passport. Papers changed hands, money transactions were tended to, and the photographer could not erase the sight of the young woman from his mind.

Who was she? The black and white image haunted him. The woman sat regally in his chair where many others had sat before. But something about her was very different from his regular passport studies. The air about her made him pause to appreciate her demeanor and appearance. He wondered just what adventure lay in store for this rare young woman.

༄

Etta carefully packed her bag through the week, attempting to organize her life into a small suitcase for the trip. Would she have enough lipstick? This use of regular cosmetics was rather new to her, and she was not yet cognizant of consumption rates for the various powders and face enhancers in tow. But she sensed that she needed to look her best.

She had acquired a new habit of playing with her gold charm between the middle finger and thumb of her right hand. Though she could not feel the intricate lines embossed on the beautiful heart, she had actually engraved their pattern into her visual memory. She played with the heart and spoke softly to herself, questioning whether she had enough undergarments and socks for the trip. After surveying the contents for the umpteenth time, she secured the bag and installed the address cardholder on the handle of her bag. She was as ready as Etta could ever be.

Abby brought the suitcase to the car and put it in the trunk. It would have fit in the backseat, but she felt she should make a bigger deal of this departure than normal. Martha sat in the passenger side of the front seat, and Etta sat in the back. They drove silently to the Phoenix airport to the sounds of news radio. Etta watched the blurs of browns and shades of gray pass by her backseat window. She was excited yet anxious about the long journey. She had never traveled alone, nor had she ever been on a plane. Now she was doing both, across an ocean she had never seen. *Oh no,* she thought, *how can I do this alone?*

Mustering a brave face, she hugged her mother. She hugged her sister and pinched her on the arm. "I'll bring you both goodies in a few weeks."

"Right...surely, you're going to have so much fun you won't want to come back. Do be careful."

"I will, I'll try," retorted Etta who then flashed the Girl Scouts' sign with her right hand in the gesture of "scout's honor."

Martha had little to say to her precious daughter. It was a long way, and she herself was unsure how safe overseas flights were. Nevertheless, it was an enviable risk to take, and she was thrilled that they would share in the experience, if only vicariously.

Chapter 3
FLIGHT MANTRAS

The buzzing noise from the Boeing 707 tamed Etta's fears. She didn't feel nervous anymore. In fact, she felt quite comfortable sharing takeoff with the other 178 passengers. The journal—her security blanket—rested on her lap. The pen was quick to record her preliminary thoughts.

The notion of traveling abroad had never occurred to me as the child of a working single mother. You know, barring any Wild Kingdom *programs featuring exotic animals from far distant lands, I never paid much attention to geography. Yet, just this week I was given provision to travel to England. Sounds lucky, right?*

Amazing! I am here. I am on my way!

JANE BASH

I recently learned I had a chance to go to the mythical United Kingdom that so many of my friends had dreamed of visiting after high school. None of us did. It was a delicious want, though.

The glamour of our adolescent-colored wishes seemed plastic and artificial. But deep down, I really, really, really wanted to go to report back to my family and friends. (Nobody I know has been there except Mrs. Edwin Earl Busch and her Ed Earl, whom we refer to as "Figment" because we don't know if he really exists.)

I petitioned God that he understand it was a special opportunity that would enrich my writing someday. Then I felt guilty for asking. How flattering I could be so irreplaceable that I didn't deserve to take off from my bag station to find some wings. So, I petitioned earnestly that if I had the opportunity, it would be a reward for my generous service (and really inadequate pay). I think it's time for change. This proves it.

Today! It's my reward! Armed with a free airline ticket, I have quite nearly willed myself on this trip. It's quite remarkable when the body clicks into severe desire how many simultaneous tasks a person can accomplish. In three days, I single-handedly organized life, as I knew it, to run in my absence. I delegated various activities and the chore management to various people who would take over while I'm gone. And now, I'm gone. I'm free, and I'm gone.

The hardest part about getting on the plane was the sadness I felt over the death of my horse friend, Indira, and I will really miss my mother and sister as I see this new world with my own eyes. How I wish it were fare for three...

I have a mantra. My brain screams, "I'm on vacation! I'm on vacation! I'm on vacation!" It helps distract me from the smoke coming from the third person to my left. It must be a queer flaw that I hate the smell of cigarette smoke but kinda enjoy sitting next to a person smoking to collect that funny feeling in my head. My private meditation is interrupted by a baby squealing eight seats in front of me on this wide airplane. Wide, but not wide enough. I wish I could stretch out. My legs feel thick, sore, and heavy.

My father would have a fit! He spent his life trying to get lucky without working at it. I have come to believe that luck takes really *extraordinary hard work. He wasn't willing to work, so he split. He's long gone. Who knows where? And I don't care.*

I really need to pay attention to what is around me. I have become so focused on details. Like what I see outside the window. It's a tag on the wing that sports "Hoist Flap" . Really, I thought hoist denoted an individual was needed such as, "Hoist me that paint bucket, will ya?" I wondered who would hoist the flap on that wing?

"I'm on vacation, I'm on vacation, and quit fixating!" I yell to myself in my very loud mind. The passengers around me all seem to have quiet minds. They look peaceful, relaxed, and comfortable. I am too excited to be comfortable. Yahoo!

A man two rows up was explaining to the girl sitting next to him that she should say "Britain" not "England" when referring to the region. I wonder about this. I do not want to offend anyone...

Etta determined that flying was not all that bad and that she rather enjoyed the sensation. The stewardess crew on board were the most beautiful women she had ever seen. Their makeup was very sharp, almost doll-like, and they all seemed to be slightly shorter than she was but certainly with shapelier figures. They all appeared content as they attended to the cargo of passengers.

Etta observed their professional airline dresses with flowing European scarves attached by various ornate pins. She made a mental note to search for a dress of this cut when building her wardrobe for the new position back home.

There were two airport layovers where Etta stretched her stiff torso in the privacy of the ladies' room. At each stop, she bought a newspaper and absorbed it as if she had actually enjoyed a vacation through the city. The flat photos in the various sections of each paper came into a three-dimensional vision in Etta's mind. The backgrounds in these newspaper photos were rich in visual detail, telling much of the problems and progress of each area.

The passengers waited patiently with their tickets to board the flight over the Atlantic Ocean. A good share of these people looked at the entry with some trepidation.

When the line was halfway into the tunnel, Etta stepped up to surrender her ticket. She slid down into the seat, preparing for the long flight. Whether it was excitement or exhaustion that lulled her to sleep, she could not tell. When she woke, Etta collected herself to explore the airplane.

One of the pilots came out of the cockpit for a smoke. Etta knew this only because she walked up through the first-class section to stretch her legs and observe what "luxury" might look like on the scale of an airplane. It was lovely, there up front. They had larger seats with interesting appearing hors d'oeuvres on little china plates. Several people had crystal wine glasses with assorted colors of beverages.

The pilot was engaged in a conversation with a burly man in a pinstripe suit near the front. The men laughed louder than what Etta thought was necessary. Whirls of smoke filled the air between her and the pilot. He gazed her way while still talking and actually stammered on his words. Etta was aware enough of the conversation to note this, and she interpreted this behavior to be their notice that she was out of place from the "regular" section of the cabin.

Captain Elvin Ernest Blackwell felt himself stammer on his words as he saw the extraordinary young woman approaching him. He had been out of the military long enough now to have sampled the various women he might consider dating for more long-term aspirations. *That is one striking bird,* he thought to himself, and he breathed the cigarette smoke deep into the bottom of his lungs.

Captain Blackwell was confident enough, but when he caught her eye and then stammered for a moment, he innately felt she was out of his league. When she turned to disappear through the curtain to the middle of the plane, it was confirmed in his mind. He actually forgot where the conversation was going with the other fellow, so he snuffed out his Camel and excused himself back to the cockpit.

In daylight, Etta could view the horizon and where it met the ocean far below. She wondered if one could see whales from this elevation. She felt as though she should feel anxious about this journey, but she wasn't anymore.

There were foods to be sampled and drinks to be consumed. There were newspapers from many states and magazines that Etta had never read (or heard of). The flight in itself was a learning experience. And she soaked up everything she could between a few unfulfilling naps.

The Boeing landed at Heathrow Airport just as the sun began to rise on the horizon. Etta was stiff and groggy from the extended time in the narrow seat. At least she had some shut-eye to recharge her battery after exerting so much adrenaline in the name of anticipation.

She overheard two Englishmen speaking about the airport and paused to enjoy their accents as well as the historical elements of their discourse.

The distinguished bearded gentleman offered, "I worked here when it was the Great Western Aerodrome in World War II. We had only one runway, and the only terminal here was an army surplus tent. It was frigid cold! I had great difficulty recording the cargo coming in on the aircraft carriers with my bone-cold numb fingers. My bum was numb for two months!"

The leaner man with the leather briefcase laughed and retorted, "I was here when the queen herself inaugurated terminal two and the tunnel to town. We had good heat for her appearance!"

Etta's bag was easy to spot. Her sister Abigail had assembled a hideous pompom with orange and purple yarn, which attached to the handle of her suitcase. Abby anticipated that her sister would not lose luggage with a profound pompom on it. She felt under-packed as most of the people on the flight were collecting three, even four bags from the luggage claim belt.

There were wonderful shops beginning to open their doors for business and illuminating the ceiling lights. Etta spotted a jewelry store with a wooden sign announcing, "Manchester Jewellery." She paused when she saw charms in the front case.

After taking note of her gold charm bracelet peeking from beneath her crumpled sleeve, the elderly woman asked genuinely if she could show Etta anything. There was a small airplane in gold that Etta decided to add to her bracelet after surviving her first flight. The woman offered to attach it if Etta was willing to wait. Etta sat with her suitcase beneath her feet and dozed off as the grinding sound of the jewelry tools announced the progress.

She dreamed in British accents with strange story combinations and lingual noise, which didn't make sense but were nevertheless entertaining because of new sounds. A gate slammed, bringing Etta back to consciousness with a confused feeling. With fresh orientation, she cleared her blurred eyes to study the beautiful new charm on her bracelet.

"That's a lovely piece, that is," the woman stated.

"It was a gift from my family to record my adventures here," Etta responded, afterward, expecting that the woman certainly did not care to know her personal history. On the contrary, the elderly rounded clerk was quite interested and engaged Etta in a delightful conversation, which lasted nearly an hour through several customers' purchases.

It was time to earn her wings. Etta had to locate the National Express Coach. She was aware she had to get from the airport to the bus terminus in London, called the Victoria Coach Station.

"Excuse me," Etta said attempting to interrupt the employees at the airline counter without appearing rude. "Can you tell me how to get to the National Express?"

Another conversation began as the Brits appreciated Etta's accent. "So, where you from, love?"

"I'm from Phoenix, Arizona. I'm here visiting London for two weeks. How can I get to the bus?"

"Have you got a place to stay, do ya?" an agent inquired.

"Yes, I have a bed and breakfast place lined up. I have never stayed at a bed and breakfast before. What is it like?"

"Well, you get a fair bed but not your own bath. You have to share that. They serve you baked beans, eggs, and potatoes for breakfast, and the rest of the day you eat on your own."

"Baked beans? For breakfast? We only eat those for supper," Etta remarked to the chuckle of the attendants.

It then occurred to Etta that these people were engaging her in conversation not because they were interested in what she had to say, but rather in how she spoke. Her dialect and accent intrigued them. She politely excused herself and made a mental note to not speak so much unless spoken to.

Etta found a taxi to take her to the bus terminal. Her body was in a substantial fight with her brain as the wooziness of the jet lag began to kick in. She realized that it was approaching afternoon by the sun, although at home it was five thirty in the morning. Her body felt as though she had been awake all night despite the fact she had slept off and on through the flights.

Etta purchased her ticket, put her bags below, and then boarded the large coach. She was so exhausted by this time that she fell asleep immediately in the high back of the window seat.

༺༻

Etta woke briefly to recognize there were others around her. She was aware only that several people disembarked with the assistance of the bus steward. She fell lazily back to sleep into what seemed like a dark, warm abyss.

When Etta was shocked into consciousness, the steward was clearing all passengers off the bus. She expected the drive was awfully long for the trip into London. It was dark as Etta allowed the other passengers to pass her off the bus. She stood patiently in line to collect her bag.

The pit of Etta's stomach dropped, and she felt as though she had been punched. The compartment was empty! Etta swallowed hard against the hysteria she felt, knowing full well her return airline ticket, most of her money, and her new wardrobe were in the suitcase.

The bus driver and bus steward spoke rapidly with a Brummie accent too thick for Etta to understand. They looked worried as they quickly went back into the bus to search the overhead compartment and discuss the issue. When they returned slowly, the steward slowed his proper speech and lowered his voice in sympathy.

"Look, you don't have any luggage, and you don't have a ticket for this bus. I don't know what happened here, but you sure are not in London. You are in Birmingham."

The tears washed over Etta's eyes as she attempted to digest this horrible hand of circumstances. She numbly filled out the paperwork for lost luggage and fell limply into a seat in the waiting room in shock.

A serviceman in an American uniform approached her and knelt down on the floor to catch her eye. "Miss, I heard about your predicament. Do you have friends near?"

Etta let the words spill so fast it sounded like one long breath rather than the sum of the parts of her sad discourse. "I won this trip to London, but I don't have my ticket home because it was in the suitcase. All my new clothes from the bon voyage—I have never had a bon voyage before. The clothes were in there. I did not want to be pick-pocketed, so I put most of my money in the bag, too. In my—well, I can't tell you where, but it was in there, too. I don't have my money or my clothes, and I am in the wrong city! I didn't study the geography of the United Kingdom. I only studied about what to do in London. I was supposed to be in London! It was supposed to be lucky London for me, but…" Etta was unable to continue as the sobs overwhelmed her.

"I think I can help you. My name is George Lockley. What's your name?"

The sound of another American was somehow reassuring despite sharing a vulgar first name with her detested father. Under regular circumstances, Etta would not have been so bold as to converse so frankly with a stranger, much less a soldier. But the desperate situation gave her cause to relax her safety standards somewhat. "I'm Etta Johnson."

"Today's not a total loss. My aunt lives here, and if you would be so inclined, I can take you to her house and see what she can do to at least get you out of the old clothing. I can catch the next bus back to base."

"This is my new clothing!" Etta responded defensively.

"If you don't mind me saying so, you smell as though you must have had a long journey. Really, my aunt will help you out."

"What do you mean I smell like a long journey?" The tone of her voice rose, nearing a shriek. She had forgotten herself, and the entire room now understood the scope of the problem with the American.

The bus steward cut into the conversation with a knowing smile. "You all right then, there, lassie? You seem a bit manky."

"No! I'm not all right! What the *hell* do you think I'm going to do?"

The bystanders quickly dispersed, and Etta was acutely aware that she had managed to offend and clear out an entire room full of people with her father's favorite shock word. She resigned herself to audible sobbing, and the tears kept coming like a river from "the girl who never cried." With her head down near her chest, Etta now recognized that she was emitting a pungent smell and supposed George had meant well in getting her changed into fresh clothes. How much more humiliating could this become?

The National Express driver and steward left without another word, and George gave the teller his aunt's phone number in the event the bag was located. He exchanged his bus ticket for the following day and hailed a taxi for the short ride.

※

Margaret Grace Kendall was a patient listener. She heard the full story with the pre-saga in its entirety. She nodded and sympathetically listened, but she asked few questions. Her nephew George was a character. He always seemed to have trouble dropping upon his feet. Margaret expected that growing up at her sister's home in Texas, George must have been the child all the strays would walk home with.

The full story was laid out across the living room like the sad air of a family in mourning, but the sadness was hers alone. Margaret and George were mere spectators with no vested interest in the complicated mess she was in. A most hospitable Brit, Margaret showed Etta the tub and linens with which to freshen up. Margaret herself was a large woman, but she managed to find one of her daughter's dresses. Though not very fashionable, it was close to Etta's size.

George and Margaret discussed business in the parlor while Etta washed two days of wear, the monetary advantage afforded by the contest winnings, and the entire London aspiration right down the drain. It was a therapeutic shower correcting that feeling of "being rode hard and put up wet," as the rancher Lenny would have said.

The flowered, lace-trimmed dress had hoped it would someday return into style, but alas, that had not come to pass. But as luck would have it, Etta's figure would make the dress appear trendy and fresh once again.

Etta was extremely grateful to find some of the new makeup in her oversized satchel purse. She made herself up the best she could, and her eyes appeared to have recovered from the tears. When Etta emerged from the ladies' room, Margaret and George had everything planned out for her in the belief she probably could no longer think this through herself.

There would be a telegram to her family explaining the situation. Mrs. Kendall would take Etta to a ladies' shop for clothes, and they would enjoy tea. Etta could stay in the guest room for a week and look for work or await money to be wired to her from Arizona. Margaret did not want to appear nosy and was relieved when Etta revealed the monetary contents of her purse. It was helpful to know just what she was up against. Yes, the money would need to be changed at the bank, also. You could not exchange dollars for pounds on the same day. The small bank required you leave the foreign money in a non-interest-bearing account until a bank in London could verify the money was authentic. The bank would call the Kendalls once the money was clear to exchange. Some town banks were just not equipped to exchange foreign currency on such short notice.

George and Margaret accompanied Etta through various stops in town and assisted her in completing the barrage of tasks. Etta began to realize the scope of their generosity as she began to feel less helpless, though not entirely in control. She was unable to complete the task of the SOS telegram. She could not bring herself to admit that she had created such a magnificent blunder. Instead she sent the following:

CHANGE OF PLANS <STOP> IN BIRMINGHAM ON ADVENTURE <STOP> ETTA <STOP>

Etta did not allow George and Margaret to view the change in the message. She wanted to work this out for herself. She had managed without much for so long that she should be able to work things out. The trouble would be how she could ever get enough money for the return air passage home. She chose not to worry about that and resigned herself to studying what she could do to earn money in the interim. She would have enough money on the exchange to buy a set of clothes, food, and her telegram. With Margaret's good graces and the loan of several pounds, Etta would get through the week and pay her back when the money exchange went through.

At tea in a small shop, Etta actually saw George for the first time. She studied his bespectacled eyes and found them kind. This went a long way in forgiving him for sharing the same name as her father. She watched him exchange pleasant conversation with his aunt and decided he was devoted to his family. His crisp uniform revealed his penchant for neatness, and he was not hard on the eye, with sharp features and neatly trimmed hair. He had a movie-starish cleft chin, which accentuated a strong jaw line.

She learned George's short genealogy through the course of conversation. He was the nephew of Margaret. George's mother, Elizabeth, was Margaret's sister. Elizabeth had left Birmingham in her twenties, finding her destiny in America with a sailor named Ralph. He was clad in an American naval uniform when they met, which Elizabeth found extremely attractive at the time. George had followed in his father's military footsteps, though opting for the army, leaving a younger sister and brother at home in Texas.

Etta felt comforted in the tea shop. She realized that despite the fact she was indoors, she was surrounded by familiar brown hues. There were wood floors with cracks of deep brown from decades of cleaning. The wall panels were a lighter brown with many wooden objects adorning them. It was as if she was in a deco desert. The tea soothed her as she became increasingly more rational.

Margaret took Etta to a thrift store, which raised money for the care of orphans in a region Etta was unable to commit to memory. There was a dress and two tailored suits, which fit as though they must have been ordered just for Etta. The tags confirmed that one owner had donated all three outfits. Perhaps there were more? The women searched the tags on the slacks in hopes of finding more items the lady would have donated. They uncovered one pair of slacks and two crisp cotton blouses. Etta was amazed that clothes as lovely as these would be so gently worn and given up. It was a splendid bargain, and she now had clothing to locate a decent job.

When they returned home, George's uncle Harvey was waiting. He had learned about the houseguest over the phone but devoted only scant interest in the details of why the American had come into such need.

Introductions were made, and Harvey Kendall excused himself for his routine pint at the neighborhood public house.

Before Harvey returned, Etta bathed and fell into a long, dark slumber. Instead of rousing her for a six o'clock dinner, the Kendalls and George decided to let Etta sleep.

In the morning, Etta was surprised to find herself still wrapped in towels. She realized that she had fallen asleep, but she was unclear what day or what time it might be. She dressed and came downstairs. Margaret was visible out the front door in the garden. The rest of the house sounded empty. George had left for the bus terminal, and Harvey had gone to work.

Chapter 4
Sojourn Saint

Etta noticed a whatnot table at the entry to the beautiful, small home. On it lay her precious bracelet, only it appeared to be more ample. When she picked it up, she noticed that a new gold charm dangled happily from it. The circular coin had a man's figure with a staff engraved on one side. It was crudely attached, but it appeared sturdy enough.

Etta was admiring the coin when Margaret came back into the house. "I see you found your bracelet. That's Saint Christopher. He is a patron saint for travelers. I thought with as much bad luck as you have had, you certainly need a little heavenly luck."

Etta's mind wound back to her youth when she remembered her father on more than one occasion saying, "I'll be lucky this time!" To which her mother would protest his wasting precious family funds with, "Luck is what you earn when you work hard."

Etta's head was still bowed studying the bracelet, and one tear escaped her feeble attempt at control. It fell, as if in slow motion, splashing onto the planked wood entry. She was so touched with this precious gift that words escaped her. Thoughts escaped her also. She felt only pure goodness in this blessed home. Etta managed to choke out, "Thank you," and Margaret understood.

Margaret's dear sister had written many years ago describing the first weeks in America when she was alone and lost in a great big city. It felt good for Margaret to reciprocate the good will the Americans had bestowed upon her sister.

Etta's jacket was cleaned and returned sans the "aroma" that George had so candidly pointed out. She tightly wrapped it around herself as the reality of the forty-six-degree October morning slapped her desert face and hands with a freezing, smarting sensation. Margaret offered Etta a scarf for her journey around the community. Etta advised her that she would be exploring alone this day.

"Would you rather meet me at the Garden House for elevenses, or later at four?"

"Isn't the Garden House a pub?"

"Yes, but they have brilliant tea before the locals come for their takeaways or dinner."

"I guess I thought the pub was a bar. I mean, isn't that where Harvey gets his beer?"

"Oh, I see. I don't take bevy either. No, the pub serves as a second home for the community. We watch football and rugby on the telly sometimes. We eat, have tea, and take a pint there, too. I suppose you can say it's our home away from home."

"Can I meet you at fourses then?" Etta asked, trying desperately to fit in.

Margaret corrected her with, "We'll break at four then." Her giggle communicated to Etta that "elevenses" did not translate to four in the afternoon.

"You know where you are then, lass? You know how to get about?"

Etta smiled warmly in affirmation.

◇

Etta stepped though the screen door and into Birmingham. She was Dorothy in the *Wizard of Oz* just coming into the land of Technicolor. It was breathtaking! Aside from the fact that the weather felt very cold to her skin, Etta was surprised she had not noticed the remarkably beautiful setting that her literary effort rewarded her with. She supposed she had been too distracted by the calamities of the past forty-eight hours. She absolutely must capture the events in her journal!

There was a suspicious absence of dirt. Everywhere there was organic moss or manufactured material, but absolutely no dirt at all! Stone streets, grass lawns, and the skyline jagged with buildings were all very different from the graceful meandering of the outline of her mountains back home. And the color! Technicolor so vivid the town exploded into what felt like her most vivid dreams. She had never remembered dreaming in color before this moment of awakening. Her childhood had been colored in hues of browns and muted orange or red. Soft heaven colors flowing across the desert spilled down onto the walls of the simple adobe and brick in her neighborhood back home.

What Etta saw before her were brick or wood slat homes with gardens overfilling their allotment with greenery hanging over the edges of the beds. Though it was cold, there were flowers of every type, strong, erect, and appearing very proud.

She started on foot in her attempt to find a job with no passport or work papers. She expected it would have to be a cash job, perhaps a position too menial for the community labor pool. Etta found confidence in the fact that the opportunity in Phoenix would be a new and exciting one once she could earn enough money for the airfare home.

After Etta had applied for hire at several neighbor shops, she noticed the botanical gardens on her trek to the supermarket. They were having some exhibition, and the doors were open to the public without fee. What luck! Etta meandered the grounds and enjoyed natural specimens from the world over. As she entered the desert exhibit, she was shocked at the sad spoilage of plants that had too much water and not enough light. A docent strolled in and commented on the misfortune that the cacti expert had been in a terrible accident, which entailed a long disability with question of whether he would work again.

Etta commented on the problems with the environment and asked if they were seeking temporary help. She filled out the necessary paperwork and included the temporary phone number at Margaret and Harvey's home. She was fortunate to be interviewed on the spot by the chief botanist.

"Miss Johnson, I don't see where you have any experience working with gardens or plants. Can you explain what makes you feel qualified to work with us?" The proper Mrs. Ingle was aware she needed help, but she was unwilling to be too generous with this information.

"I have lived in the desert region of Arizona in the United Stated for the better share of my entire life. I have studied and understood a vast variety of cacti and what it takes to make them content in their surroundings. And quite frankly, yours are very sick, even on the brink of death!"

As they talked, Mrs. Ingle was pleased this young woman would refer to cacti as precious little souls who felt something. She seemed passionate enough, but she could not risk too high a payroll for such a novice. "Miss Johnson, I will give you a trial employment of two weeks under our entry wage. If you prove yourself, we will consider paying you more. If you are unable to improve the situation in the cactus room, you will be terminated. Is that understood?"

Etta rather appreciated this woman's frank demeanor and responded with enthusiasm. She was given a brief orientation before being sent off to anticipate her new opportunity.

Walking the stretch back to the Garden House, she found several *Room to Let* signs and paused to tour several. She would be hard stretched to pay for one, but she felt determined not to abuse the kindness of the Kendall family. Her favorite prospect was one she could not tour. Her knock went unanswered, but the little sign said much. *Room to let. Must be tidy. No tobacco, alcohol, children, or pets. By the week or month.*

Etta walked backward on the street, gazing up at the elevation of the tiny, two-story home. It was crowned with a chimney pot, which quite resembled a chess pawn. The shingled roof was in good shape, and the brick structure was trimmed with lace privacy curtains and cheerful flowerbeds.

Margaret met Etta for tea and was delighted at Etta's fortune in finding not only a temporary job, but also in her initiative to search for a place to live. Her instincts had been correct about Etta. She was glad George had come to her aid. Margaret was certain there would be no phone call from the bus station in regard to Etta's possessions. She expected that vagabonds at some stop along the way had stolen her case. It was unlikely it would ever be returned. But Margaret was certain that Etta possessed the gumption to work it out.

Various local patrons filed in to converse quietly about town happenings and daily news. The atmosphere was surreal to Etta. It was as if the entire town stopped and paused to reflect. What a wonderful opportunity! Etta regretted not having her journal. With the pleasant company, Etta would have had a plethora of inspiration.

Slate boards mounted on the walls marked with chalk announced everything that would have been on a paper menu back home. Again, Etta felt surrounded by comforting shades of dark brown woods. The tables, floors, walls, and accents were wood, and the tables were set with surprisingly little elbow space. Everyone seemed comfortable with themselves and others in their shared space. Even when people knocked into her chair or bumped into her, Etta noticed that they exhaled a quick, curt "Sorry." But this was not a sincere apology so much as a knee-jerk reaction, overused because of how frequently people were in close quarters.

Margaret's black tea was weakened with milk, and Etta ordered an herbal tea, but she requested they hold the milk. The hostess looked puzzled, but she complied with the request. What a relaxing, fragrant potion. It filled her nose and warmed her throat. Etta was pleased, too, that in the air of conversation, nobody was overly interested in her accent. They were too absorbed to expend their curiosity on the American in their presence. They would know soon enough who she was and why she shared their tea.

After their meeting, Margaret walked with Etta back to the "tidy" home she had hoped to tour. The landlord was home. She stood only four foot ten in stature with an added inch from the heel of her shiny, black lace-up shoes, which were protruding from beneath her full smock. She was an elfish, elderly lady with deep smile wrinkles, which, even at rest, were contagious.

Chapter 5
DOUBLE DECK LUCK

Etta anxiously moved her small collection of articles, acquired through the graces of her accidental British hosts, to the ten-by-ten room she would "let" from Geraldine Bonneville. Geraldine sported a cheerful disposition and was generous in the negotiation of terms. Etta had no money to put up as deposit, but she would be collecting her wage weekly and would offer a double rent during the first month. Thankfully, the room was unattractive, a tough sell. It provided only occasional income for her landlord. Geraldine was grateful for the security of a tenant and an additional sum of money, however small. Etta did not need much room. What Etta did need was a better plan.

The twin bed slept well enough, and the cantankerous alarm woke Etta with a start. It was her first day of work, and she was anxious to rescue the cacti and succulents. The pathetic efforts of the substitute caretaker had caused a few precious specimens to die.

Etta showered, dressed in her best thrift store suit, and fastened the gold bracelet on her wrist. She engaged in a new morning ritual. She paused for a moment to pray for a safe return home and for the safety of her family while clutching the links of gold. Although she was not Catholic, she also looked at Saint Christopher's image and spoke to him in a familiar, conversant tone.

"Saint Christopher, you, my little man, are in charge of getting me through this journey safely. Please let me earn enough to pay my way back home." It occurred to Etta that this conversation somewhat resembled a prayer, and even though she believed in worshiping God, she convinced herself that the discussion with St. Chris was merely deep-seated hope.

The walk to Birmingham Botanical Gardens was cool and relatively short. Etta arrived ten minutes early, which was customary for her family. She was greeted not by Mrs. Ingle, but by Larkin Ladimore, her new supervisor.

In the seconds that Etta sized up Mr. Ladimore, she found him to be tall and quite elegant. Larkin sported deep, brown eyes and a dark chocolate complexion, interrupted only by a pink birthmark exposed slightly over the collar of his starched shirt. Larkin extended his hand gently Etta's way.

"Welcome, Miss Johnson," Larkin began.

"Please, call me Etta."

"All right then. Sorry. Etta, we have a difficult situation with your payroll. While we are unable to provide you with an official paycheck due to your alien status, we are able to supply regular consultation fees, which are collected through grants and donations. This could last for three months or a year. We just don't know. But your charge must be proven in two weeks, according to Mrs. Ingle."

"Will I need an account, or will you be able to pay me in pounds?" Etta questioned, realizing that she would need a sponsor in order to open a bank account.

"We will draw a check for you, and Kelly will cash it here in the trinket shop, adjacent to the gardener's flat."

"Thank you for all your help. Where can I find you, if I need anything?"

"Whatever you require must be submitted in writing and delivered to my office. Are you aware of any needs at the moment?"

"I know I will need several large heaters with fans to dry out the soil. It's way too wet in there!" Etta reported, armed only with mere, preliminary findings.

"All right, then. I will arrange their transport by this afternoon. Good luck then."

With that, Larkin turned on his brown loafer heel and walked down the corridor toward the orchids. She was impressed that he appeared young for a supervisor, and yet the lines of his clothing and demeanor suggested that he had invested at least some years to acquire this comfort level with his position. He was a refined looking, trim man, someone Etta thought it would be pleasant to converse with; she could imagine Mr. Ladimore filling her ears with proper English and his wonderful accent.

Into the Fantastic Cactus Room. Etta nearly choked! The humid air and dark black soil at the base of the plants were contributing to a quick rot. The normally easy-to-care for rat's tail and peanut cactus appeared to be tilting, wilting, and in general, dying before her eyes. She bolted back into the Larkin's office without even knocking.

"Larkin! We have an urgent situation here! I need a truckload of lime and sand. The soil is muddy, and we have to get it dried out immediately, or you will lose the entire room!" Etta projected the words desperately, through wild eyes.

Larkin was impressed by her urgency and recognized the reaction was substantiated from experience, something he previously was unsure she possessed.

"I'll get right on it. Oh then, I'll get a jumper and blouse you can use straightaway. I will have two trousers and another blouse by afternoon. Mind you, those glad rags may be a tad much. I'll find you a suitable uniform."

Etta excused herself, changing into the pullover blouse and overall jumper with the garden logo on it. It would certainly serve her well, being significantly cooler than the blouse and jacket she wore. She removed her coat and tucked the blouse into her skirt. It would be tricky work today. She felt more pressure than vanity, removing several towels from the ladies' room to kneel on while she worked with the soil. She forgot herself in this public place and removed her bracelet, placing it over her ear for safekeeping.

A golden barrel cactus's small companion was the first casualty. The sorry sidekick was brown and gooey. She cut back into the main root and carefully removed any infectious contact from the main plant. The onlookers who recognized her obvious error of judgment in work attire must have found her quite a sight.

Larkin was a man of his word and was able to get the soils delivered by the time Etta had cleared the roots and removed several wheelbarrows of soil. It was apparent that the last caretaker for the room thought the soil too light, and they had mixed loads of rich dark soil and then soaked it to a dangerous pH level.

Larkin looked in on Etta briefly. He was tremendously impressed with her personal call to action. What a funny sight Etta was with her bare feet and her knees resting on paper towels, digging into the dirt in her "mannish" jumper! Her derriere unabashedly rocked with the rhythm of the hand raking Etta accomplished in the beds. Even with the gloves, a random thorn would pierce through, causing a familiar itchy, stinging sensation.

With the new soil mixed in the top foot of sediment, Etta cranked up the heaters and two spotlights she managed to sweet-talk from the rotating exhibits super. She absentmindedly grabbed the bracelet still hanging over her ear and prayed.

"Oh Lord, I really need these to recover. Help me know what to do to make them thrive. I really, really, desperately need this job! Please help me fix this so I can stay for a short while."

⁓

The return home went purposefully slower than her earlier power walk toward the gardens. She had cause to gaze skyward as efficiencies competed with structures sporting far superior ornamental facings. The crowning jewels on each building, in Etta's eyes, were the curious chimney pots. She surveyed a vast variety adorning the sky as she passed through the middle-class neighborhood with the still curious absence of dirt.

The chimney pots varied in shape and texture, yet they achieved the same function. She imagined the hearth smoke curling from the pots up into the beautiful blue sky. Sometimes there were rows of these pots, which appeared in boring conformity, until one comically different chimney pot would break the visual chain.

Etta's favorite chimney pots thus far were those that resembled chess pawns or crowns. They appeared rather dignified at the top of the brick buildings. Red brick, like red canyons back home. Etta imagined these brick walls as muted red hues enveloping her in the canyons of middle Arizona. She would hear echoes of coyotes bounce from wall to resident wall.

Jolted back to reality, Etta recognized she had ventured too far and was out of familiar territory. She vowed that at first opportunity, she would learn the community around her. The mindless sojourn had been good therapy, but after a full day and the intense efforts to save the Fantastic Cactus Room, as well as preserve a job, Etta did not need to concern herself with any safety issues of the rapidly approaching evening.

⁂

Outfitted in a becoming new uniform of trousers and an embroidered blouse, Etta spent the week gingerly caring for her spiny, adopted cacti. By Friday, the environment appeared to be stable enough to remove the heaters and heavy fans. Only one heater remained in constant use. Etta began stage two of her strategy to nurse the cacti. Larkin ordered the gallon of surgical alcohol without question as Etta appeared to know what she was doing. Section by section, she swabbed down the abnormal spots and discoloration on her precious plants with the alcohol.

Etta had been exposed to simple insect control early in her youth when her mother had started off life in the desert with an indoor Joseph's coat. The alcohol would get rid of mealy bugs, which would pierce the pods and suck the juice and life from a healthy cactus. It also seemed to deter mites and scale insects if attacked head-on. Trouble was, you had to be careful not to get too much alcohol on the plants, or they would become irritated. Etta was patient. Etta was persistent. She had single-handedly protected the entire room by week's end. As a final precaution, Etta fumigated the edges of the room away from the cacti bases with Malathion. She even drew a line across each doorway so the bugs would be warned not to cross over her line. She was aware the maintenance workers would intend to come in to mop up, so she posted a sign for them:

DON'T DISTURB THIS ROOM UNTIL MONDAY!!! THANKS – ETTA

The small sum of money Etta had originally changed into English pounds set her up with food for the week. Once paid, after surrendering a fourth of the double week's let and Margaret's generous loan, she was surprised to have a little pocket money.

Etta left the money in an envelope on the kitchen table. So far, Geraldine and Etta rarely crossed paths. From evidence of the living room photos, Etta surmised Geraldine's five children, twenty-two grandchildren, and an odd collection of lifelong friends must keep her pretty busy. Etta had not met any of them, and she wondered what large-family dynamics would feel like.

෴

Saturday morning, before the first pickup, Etta braved the bus stop. She had grave difficulty with simple tasks such as crossing the street. With the traffic raging in the opposite direction from her usual orientation, she was nearly hit several times by passersby in their small, roundish cars.

When the brilliant red double-decker bus arrived and slowed, Etta was able to read her destination on the sign. *Smallbrook – Queensway* was where Larkin recommended she find her shopping and breakfast. She soaked in the details of her experience as if in slow motion. Her coinage, now easier to use as familiarity sunk in, slipped down into the transparent chamber beside the driver. She ascended to the second level in order to appreciate the fresh experience and the view. Etta sat down alone in the front of the second level with only two rough-looking boys in the backseat. They were after effect, challenging one another to use profanity to a more shocking degree than the other.

The boy with the long bangs interjected, "Shove it up yer fleekin' arse!"

After which, the other mop-headed boy retorted, "Cowin' hell! I wouldn't back yer - Hey! What you gawkin' at, y' mare?"

After the exchange, Etta tried not to make issue of descending to the crowd more to her disposition. The view was not as good as the second level had been, but the experience was greatly enhanced.

Departing the bus, Etta was pleased with herself for not uttering a single word. No one would have suspected that she was a stranded American in search of her community.

Etta passed a tourist shop named Piper's, with a knick-knack-filled window of charms. She eased in and indulged herself by purchasing a gold double-decker bus for the bracelet. Although it was an indulgence she would sacrifice for until her next payday, she reminded herself that this charm bracelet was a record of her travels since she had neither a film nor a movie camera in her possession.

While patiently waiting for the installation of her new charm onto a link, Etta soaked in the magazines with a hunger to understand British culture. She observed the lines of the models, the clothing, and hairstyles, even makeup trends despite her feelings of abhorrence to makeup in general.

With the remainder of her monetary lot, she made the decision that breakfast out was far too indulgent for the week. She settled on grocery shopping in the supermarket. The Tesco supermarket was superior to the neighborhood shop, but it was still only two-thirds the floor space of her own employer back home.

The aisles were laid out the same although the manufacturers were mostly all foreign to her. Heinz beans! Now there was a can she knew! Chuck always used Heinz when he barbecued. The label was much less crowded with words, instructions, and nutritional information. Rather, the bold HEINZ was large and obtrusive against the teal colored label. Etta bought one just to see if the British beans had the same flavor as the American Heinz.

Etta's favorite purchase was a breakfast cereal sporting a wonderful picture of a man in a kilt. It was an oat product that Etta could take or leave, but she was intrigued by the vision of the well-endowed, muscular man on the box. Birmingham proved to be an area where the norm looked like the kids in her youth taunted with remarks such as, "Beanpole!"

The English men seemed slim and elegant compared to her huskier neighbors back home.

This comparison quite possibly was exaggerated by the fact that Etta stood taller and prouder than was customary for her. She also wore heels, something she would not have been caught dead in at home. After all, shoes in general were an accessory Etta wore only for work. Etta was transforming on so many levels that people admired her for the presence she offered a room, not just for her notoriety as a foreigner.

Chapter 6
IRISH STATE COACH

"Etta, I'm amazed at the overget of the cacti house," Mrs. Ingle said. "They look healthy and happy! Well, as happy as an *Astrophytum myriostigma* might be. Straightaway, you will be allotted a fifty-pound increase to your base fee. The moneys appear to be quite solid, so I expect you will be secure in labor for at least the year."

"Mrs. Ingle, I am so grateful for this opportunity. I am really enjoying the opportunity to work here and listen to the customers. It's very good for me to soak in the local culture."

"Local culture? You make us Brummagemites sound like foreigners!" Mrs. Ingle said curtly, and when the door closed between them, Etta let out a hearty laugh and audibly said to nobody in particular, "You *are* foreigners to me! But I *love* it here anyhow."

"I heard that!" retorted Larkin, who inconspicuously snuck up from the rear. He smiled, communicating to Etta that he was not offended, but rather he was entertained by the comment. He strolled through the office without another word.

Etta then calculated in her mind what the increase in pay would do to decrease the number of months she would have to stay here. After work, she sent another telegram to her *family now that she had a better plan.*

HAVE JOB <STOP> STAYING IN BIRMINGHAM SOME MONTHS <STOP> LETTER SOON <STOP> ETTA <STOP>

She walked down the cobblestone street off Hagley Road to the post office, intending to write a letter to her family. But in the store window was a simple cardboard sign with letters written in marker announcing, "CLOSED DUE TO DEATH IN FAMILY."

As inappropriate as it was, Etta laughed aloud, knowing full well that a government establishment would never close in Phoenix. Then the humanitarian side kicked in, and she was genuinely remorseful for her disrespect of the dead. She touched the links on her bracelet and offered a prayer on the spot.

The most curious piece to her touch was the new installation of Queen Elizabeth's Irish State Coach. The wheels on this charm did not turn although Etta's fingers wished they might. She sincerely appreciated her mother and sister's gesture of providing her this bracelet to collect her memories. She really had not bought any items a normal tourist might. But for now, Etta was not a tourist. She was a contributing member of the Edgbaston section of Birmingham, England. Somehow, it did not feel right collecting tourist trinkets from where you live, even if under temporary emergency circumstances. Nevertheless, Etta would allow herself to buy these charms as a record of each event she encountered in the area and touring about.

Returning home, her eyes gazed skyward, enjoying the variety of chimney pots now working in unison to direct the smoke toward the heavens. Etta stopped at the local pub, the Garden House of Edgbaston. She was curious more than she was thirsty. She soaked in the brown wood feeling again, pretending she was at home surrounded by various hues of the desert, only in the darker range of the color scheme.

The walls contained slate blackboards filled with menu offerings, including a variety of items that Etta had never heard of, some which raised an eyebrow like "spotted dick" or "bangers and mash."

Across the room, she heard a familiar voice call her name. She could see by the curly headed vision of the black man across the room that it was Larkin with a few pals she did not recognize. He had already consumed a few pints and was flushed and cheerful in his demeanor.

"Etta! Why don't you let us parker up fer a tank? We have bets in the football game, and I am thinking that the bluenoses will collect. Yes?"

To which his companions booed him and his soccer team.

"Lar! If they do, I bain't a gooin' a work Monday," slurred the blond, portly man on his left. Etta had understood him to say football, but once she observed the game of interest, it was one more difference she would have to digest.

"Well, boys, I don't drink. But thank you just the same."

All heads turned to Larkin first.

"You harboring an American, Lar? What else you hiding from us, huh? Give us a clean way fer 'er, Etta, we 'ave a crackin' time."

Perhaps more out of sport than authentic interest, Etta pulled a seat up to the booth. She noticed the different issue with space once again. The five of them were sharing a table that at home would serve only two. When people knocked elbows or arms, nothing was said, nobody noticed.

Etta felt adventuresome. She ordered a "hot hob," which turned out to be hot gammon on a baguette. They served "hot chipped potatoes" on the side, which resembled potato slices more than American chips. Etta did not want to seem rude and refrained from asking for any form of condiment she normally would have enjoyed with a supper like this. The sandwich really needed mustard and mayonnaise. The wedges could use some ketchup, in her opinion.

"Er, don't want a pint?" Pete invited through his overtly impaired gaze.

"If you don't mind, a soda pop will do."

The conversation was pleasant, though silly at times. Etta enjoyed the company of these guys as much as she had enjoyed Chuck's company at home. She recognized an interesting change in herself. Instead of reporting to the guys what it was like *at home*, she carried the conversation about the goings on of the past few weeks in the location of her current adventure. She did not seem to miss home so much and was appreciating the social exchange, despite the fact her dinner companions were very drunk.

One of Larkin's compadres, John, stood up, nearly toppling the table. He had been married young, divorced recently, and held onto the wedding band as a security blanket. John stood tall and held the simple gold ring up for all to see.

"There's no lections of lovering tonight fer me!"

"Sit down!" Larkin sternly ordered, peering to the sides of the room to gauge how deeply to be embarrassed by his drunk companion.

Lar let Etta sniff his beer, and she found it to be extremely pungent. It was not a habit she would easily, or willingly, acquire. She was fascinated with the variety of colors in the glasses. Some of the clear steins shown reddish and some were so thick brown, you could not see through the glass.

It was nice to have company more her own age to converse with. Although she did answer simple questions at her post in the cactus room, it wasn't the same as pure conversation with the men.

The neighborhood was safe enough, but Larkin felt better walking Etta back to her place. "Afore ye go!" he bellowed into the wind and to anyone within earshot. He had difficulty keeping up with her pace as Etta's path was far straighter than his own.

Mr. Ladimore offered a strong handshake, so unlike when he first introduced himself. Etta thanked him with reciprocal strength in her shake and offered an appreciative, warm smile. Larkin paused on the stoop, collected his bearings, and walked on.

Safe inside her small room, Etta lay across the bed on her stomach, the position reserved for studying in her youth. Geraldine would be either asleep or out visiting family overnight. It mattered not. They were both comfortable with the arrangement, and the lines were clear about safety and security. Geraldine was unwavering in her rules regarding, "No men, no bevy, no manky, no tobacco." Reviewing the lecture in her mind made Etta laugh. Trying to get her point across using Brummie language just felt so strange coming off her lips.

As Etta considered spilling her heart onto the stationery, she paused to assess if it would be wise to record her experience without censor. Should she save face? She was acutely aware that she had to write carefully as this letter could potentially be passed to a great many people in her hometown. She had much to say. She had much to refrain from elaborating. She chose severe censorship, sprinkled generously with optimism.

Chapter 7
BREAK FOR TEA

Etta broke for tea and carefully edited the contents of the letter she intended to send to her family. She took small sips of black currant flavor, not really enjoying so much as following what was expected at that time of the day. The fruit tea was strong, having been steeped too long. She had asked them to hold the milk, but even so, she was not yet comfortable enough to ask for honey or sugar to assist the flavor.

Etta had purchased a teapot charm to commemorate blending in daily during teatime. It was a lovely ornate teapot with a tiny lid that opened on a remarkably small hinge. It was quite ceremonious the way the British took tea. It was a pause in the day to celebrate what had gone right and review what to improve. For some, it was a social break from the intense activity of the day to speak of nothing and meet with people for no real agenda other than rest. Stores closed for tea; busy people stopped for this pause. It was one of the finest customs Etta had discovered thus far.

The men at the table to her left in the garden tearoom spoke in quiet tones about the impressive Victorian conservatory called the Orangery. The couples on her right had visited the Tropical House as evidenced by the brochures on their table. Etta peered down at the garden logo embroidered on her blouse and appreciated the efforts of the entire staff to make this a special place to visit.

The room was filled to capacity with all tables full except Etta's. An elderly lady with a lovely wool hat approached Etta for a space.

"Excuse me, miss. Might I join you? I'm afraid there are no other seats in the pavilion today."

"Certainly. Please have a seat."

"Ah, an American. My deceased husband, Joseph, God rest his soul, worked with several American apprentices in the Jewellery Quarter. He provided a peg for the men to learn the metals trade. He earned more from sharing the trade skills than he could have earned in the labor of producing his designs."

"What do you mean by a peg?" Etta asked, hopeful that it was not an inappropriate question.

"Yes. The peg was the artisan's bench with tools. With such competition in the Jewellery Quarter, a peg was hard to come by, but my dear Joseph would sponsor Americans because they already had the money to make a start of it. It's tough, the Quarter."

"Where is this Quarter?"

"Do you know where the Birmingham Assay Office is?" the woman inquired.

"No. I'm afraid I have not ventured out beyond my neighborhood. I live off Vicarage and am sort of stranded."

"How curious! My name is Greta. And you are?"

"Etta Johnson."

"If you don't mind my inquisition, how did you come to work here, if you are stranded?"

With twenty remaining minutes to invest in conversation on her tea break and an interested ear, Etta detailed the adventures of the past weeks. She was specific with the courtesies extended by the Kendalls and Mrs. Ingle, who gave her a job despite her unproven expertise. She was surprised at her own amazing fortune as she shared the preliminary bad luck in Britain after winning the Lucky London contest in Arizona.

Greta remarked, "My word! You weren't supposed to be here at all? Do you know how rare it is to have foreigners come to this area? We just assume travelers come to our industrial town for familial purposes."

"I had expected that. I try not to talk in public too much because people are surprised to hear my accent. Or is it my lack of a British accent?"

The woman laughed.

"Etta, I live rather near here also. This Saturday I am hosting a dinner social at my home. Would you like to come and meet some of the neighbors?"

"That would be wonderful!" Etta replied. "What does one wear to a dinner party, if I might ask?"

Greta did not appear taken aback by the question, but she was privately surprised and impressed that the young foreigner was interested enough to want to fit in. "It would require you wear a dress. Not too short and not floor length either. Nothing bright or bold in color. Heels, but not the pointed trend that will sink in turf. A felt hat would be lovely. Gloves are optional, but perhaps a dab more color on your face."

Etta was thrilled with the prospect of attending a local social activity and with the woman's frankness. It would be wonderful to meet people outside her work environment. As it was, she had not yet been successful in acquiring friends in the gardens. Most employees were suspicious of her for enjoying work with the cacti, which was an area most thought undesirable and unattractive.

Etta left Geraldine's phone and house numbers with Greta and excused herself back to work.

Greta sipped her tea and studied the holistic image of Etta in her mind. She had acclimated so quickly in an urgent situation. She had to be admired for her ability to work it out herself and not run to family for help. That strong character impressed Greta, who had single-handedly built her own fortune without the assistance of her dear husband or vast family. Perhaps one of her sons would enjoy Etta's company. Greta had not shared with Etta her collection of children. Greta had three single sons and one daughter, who directly emulated her mother's successful entrepreneurial prowess.

Yes, Greta agreed with her quiet mind. *Etta will be an interesting addition to this social.*

Customers strolled out in an orderly fashion feeling somewhat more content. Etta had not seen the departures this day, but she recognized by now the change in disposition of the customers recharged for the second half of their day.

༺༻

The Cactus and Succulent House in the garden was landscaped as a rocky desert. Though plants were collected from all parts of the world, Etta was empathetic enough to care for her drier-region plants with success.

The glasshouse no longer possessed the dangerous visible humidity clouding the ceiling panels. The leaf succulents were more erect and trimmer than they had been with the overabundance of water forced upon them. The stem succulents were now free from the scar of pests who attempted to overtake her plants with no leaves. The sclerophytes were back to their tough, scrubby stature as well. Etta doctored the prickly pears with great interest in the hope that someday they would bear fruit for her to prepare and share with the garden staff.

The temperature was now right on the money. Etta did not measure it, as she had been unable to methodically translate the Celsius to Fahrenheit yet. But she could feel it on her bare skin with such precision that within two hours, she could feel the temperature increase and the humidity decrease to the preference of the precious plants in her care. Her extremities intimately knew the minimum temperature. It was when the wrinkle lines became not only visible, but she could feel them by running her index finger along the back of her hand. The humidity was equally easy for Etta to resolve. To Etta, high humidity felt quite similar to having her arms covered with dress nylons. It was an irritating sensation to her body, but she was getting accustomed to the regular humidity of Britain's climate. When the glasshouse was dry enough, her skin felt the comfort of heat rising from the hair on her arms. The feeling of being slowly cooked returned to her skin's surface, and she was very pleased with the familiar feeling of home.

She monitored the plants, soil, insects, and thorns carefully and now had difficulty justifying her salary. It became redundant work. There was an abundance of downtime, which she was unable to fill with authentic labor. She did treat herself to exploring the grounds in the guise that she was retrieving something. On these occasional outings, she would carry something in her arms that was related to her Fantastic Cactus Room. While feeling somewhat guilty for attempting to pull English wool over their eyes, she was delighted with the quality of the establishment in which she worked.

Etta knew only a few of the staff by name and fewer still by the areas of their charge. But it was a pleasant place to work, and Mrs. Ingle and Larkin were both exceptional people to work for.

Etta's favorite spot was a re-creation of an old British meadow. The native plants thrived in the small plot, emulating what used to be a common sight in the agriculturally rich countryside. She was intrigued over time, observing the area gradually succumbing to seasonal changes. She silently wondered if she would see it in the spring.

The most offensive place in the gardens was the Tropical House. The area, which simulated the lowland region, was hot and humid, two companions that made Etta physically nauseated even amid the marvelous collection of paw-paw, lotus, and ginger plants.

The largest glasshouse in the garden surprisingly did not have a proportionally larger staff to care for the plants. The Palm House contained ferns, bird-of-paradise, and fragrant orchids. Though the humidity was significantly higher than in her own room, she was not so uncomfortable as to refrain from enjoying this section. Etta especially enjoyed the variety of orchids that lived either on the trees or right in the rich, dark soil that quite easily could have killed her own precious plants. The melodic sound of the central fountain in the palm room relaxed her.

The only sections of the garden that puzzled Etta were the Historic Gardens. Having not been immersed in history in her school years, she did not understand the Roman, Medieval, or Tudor Gardens to their fullest offering. Visiting these areas made Etta feel ignorant.

The many outdoor gardens ambled on, invoking a quiet, reflective, even spiritual experience. Etta took note to begin investigating the fowl of the area, as her bird-watching opportunities were excellent at work.

For the most part, Etta was careful to keep her garden uniform as clean as possible. She felt she had done well with what she was given. And in all practicality, she despised the thought of the replacement cost and what sacrifice that might represent.

❦

"Hello, Harvey, is Margaret there?" Etta inquired into the rudimentary telephone in the foyer of Mrs. Bonneville's home.

"Well, how are you getting along, Etta?" Margaret's warm voice sailed though the phone lines and into her right ear.

"I am doing really well. The job has been a real godsend, and I like my room here. I have a favor to ask. Are you up for a shop Saturday morning?"

"I would love to! What is the occasion?" quizzed her former hostess.

"I have to find a dress suitable for a dinner party. Accessories too! I met this woman named Greta Colmore in the tearoom at work, and she has invited me to a social this weekend. I'm afraid I have never attended a function such as this and need coaching, too."

"Oh, Etta, you are a resourceful one, aren't you? I'd be happy to help you about gitten yer best bib and tucker. Wouldn't want you to appear ragged-arsed now. By the way, do you know *anything* about Greta?"

"We talked for a while, and I suppose I didn't learn much about her. She asked me many questions, though. She got an earful about my adventures of the past few months!"

"Oh, my dear, Greta is one of the largest benefactors of the Birmingham Botanical Gardens and Glasshouses. And she is one of Edgbaston's wealthiest women. Her husband was a Spitfire pilot with the Royal Air Force Fighters in World War II. Harvey and I were invited to the party as well. He attended Sunday school with Joseph Colmore as a tot. Joseph was as common as we are. That is, until he married Greta. Then he was all kippers 'n' curtains!"

"Gosh, then I should feel rather lucky to have been invited at all! Can you help me then?" Etta's words escaped her mouth with a hint of rude persistence.

Margaret forgave this as an American character flaw and replied, "Certainly! I need 'glad rags' as well. We should plan to be in town when shops open. We have many wares to seek."

"I have one more favor to ask…"

Margaret expected the worst, having heard this plea many times from her own children.

"Can I tag along to the party with you, then? I really hate going places alone, and it would be nice to arrive with a group."

Margaret was more flattered than put out. They had acquired a quick bond of friendship that rose above Etta's desperation, Margaret's age, Etta's citizenship, and Margaret's casual British manner.

"Absolutely. In fact, you are welcome to sprightle up at our home. I'm sure you would not mind borrowing some facial color or accessories there, too."

"It's a date! I will meet you at eight o'clock sharp, then?" Etta enthusiastically asked.

"We will see you then. Goodnight."

The lonely tone of the terminated phone connection didn't feel so bad this time, and Etta began counting her fortunes.

Chapter 8
GRAIN THIEF

Friday afternoon, after allotting for necessities, Etta treated herself to a new charm from the gift shop. The spiny hedgehog seemed to personify how she felt—tender on the inside and yet guarded on the outside. It was linked to Etta's bracelet just before it was time to lock up for the evening.

༄

The letter in the Johnsons' mailbox was pleasantly plump. Abigail and Martha had been anxious for news about Etta's adventures in England. They had gone to the main library to look up Birmingham and found it in the West Midlands section of England. This was a curious place because it was reportedly an industrial town. Why would a tourist venture into an industrial town? Etta was never conventional; all recognized that in her character.

The Johnsons almost hated to go into town anymore, having become something of celebrity status in the community. They could go nowhere without encountering uninvited questions regarding Etta's whereabouts and activity. It was tough. They knew nothing. Why did such a homebody travel out of London to stay after the two weeks? What could have provoked her to want to seek such unfamiliar circumstances?

The one who received the most information was Billy. Martha felt it necessary to advise him of her delayed return and change of plans. He was as curious as they were.

Chuck was not curious. He was worried. He knew his childhood pal well enough to recognize deep down that she was in trouble. Half of him wanted to make the trip there to see what was actually going on. He waited anxiously for news from Etta, but he put on an awfully good act to her family about his concerns. After checking his bank account and anonymously phoning a reservation agent in nearby Glendale, he was frustrated to admit he did not have the reserves to fly there to investigate. He additionally was not strong or secure enough in his budding relationship with Kim to convince her that it was brotherly, not romantic concern.

Mrs. Busch quizzed the family with deliberate disinterest in her tone. She knew what it was like there. They did not. She recalled what a fairy tale it could be. They did not. She suspected it was a man—a man not unlike the fruit vendor she had great lust for on their second trip to London. It was a pretend affair, actually, one that happened only in her mind. The fictitious encounters had on many occasions spiced up her love life with Ed Earl. It was a delicious, impractical affair. One Mrs. Busch expected the youthful Etta to be enjoying at the moment. Only, perhaps, for real.

In the security of their home, Abigail and Martha were anxious for the news. They delayed their gratification by pouring a glass of sun tea. They set out the glasses on either side of the letter and collected their nerves with a ridiculous pouring ceremony. They sat down opposite one another, and Martha opened the envelope. She handed the letter to Abigail to read. From the folds of a multiple-page letter fell a postcard of Birmingham. It was a canal boat resting on the water. It was a photo that they expected from romantic Italy, not the industrial section of England.

```
Dear Mom and Abby,
    I have had a wonderful time in
Birmingham! I met some really great peo-
ple, too. The first person I met was a
man named George. He was really helpful
and introduced me to his aunt and uncle.
The Kendalls are British. They helped
me find a place to stay since it was such
a lovely community.
    I have a job! Can you believe it?
I happened to be visiting the botani-
cal gardens, and they needed a cactus
keeper. They hired me on the spot! It's
not a glamorous job, but it will pay for
further adventures here.
    I rent a room that's the same size as
my room at home. Only, it's very sparse,
with only a dresser and a nightstand
with a lamp. But the landlord is a self-
proclaimed "tidy" person and is very
kind to me. Geraldine's home is within
walking distance from work and from the
bus stop.
    I took a double-decker bus into town
to get some groceries. It was not as
wonderful as I had imagined, but I am
not opposed to taking a tour on a bus
like this at some point.
```

I have taken every opportunity to add to the charm bracelet you gave me. So far, I have added the following pieces to the heart you gave me:

- Airplane - commemorates the long flights and layovers
- Traveling saint coin – a gift from the Kendalls
- Double-decker bus – hope for more interesting trips
- Queen's carriage – she has several (maybe another?)
- Teapot – I actually *have* been drinking tea each day
- Hedgehog - from the hedgehog preservation society, a cute, spiny critter (there used to be a bounty on them for grain theft)

I don't wear it to work as much. I have a uniform for the "Fantastic Cactus Room," which was not all that fantastic when I got there. They had added in black soil and tons of water. They nearly killed off all the little guys in the entire collection. I faked my way through the soil correction but was pleased that I knew what to do for bugs, temperature, and humidity.

I wear beige pants that are the weight of jeans, but they look like dress pants. And the button-up blouse is white cotton with a nice collar. The logo is a fountain, and it is embroidered above the garden name above the right pocket.

I like it. I look professional. I am trying to learn the proper names of my plants so I can help more people who visit. As it is, I hardly speak. I do *not* want people to be interested in my home in Arizona instead of my glasshouse here at work. An American accent in this area is a real oddity. I wish I had taken foreign language in school. I could really use German or French here!

Tell Chuck the beef here is *horrible*! It's tough and stringy, and everyone overcooks it! I miss his cooking. But I have found American baked beans, at least.

A wealthy lady who visited the garden this week invited me to a dinner party. As luck would have it, she invited the Kendalls also, so I'll go to the party with them. I have to pick out a dress, heels, purse, coat, and maybe gloves.

At this comment, Abigail looked up from the letter, and she and her mother laughed at the image of Etta all fussed up. This was a side neither of them ever saw, even at formal school dances. Etta always balked at the line between casual and unacceptable. Abigail returned to the letter.

There is an area I hope to visit soon in town called the Jewellery Quarter. No, I did not spell it wrong. They spell many words here differently like "labour." Anyway, the Quarter is a section of town with blocks and blocks of jewelers who create and sell the majority of goods for the entire country. I want to find a

```
charm from there. The bracelet was a won-
derful idea! Thanks! Thanks! Thanks!
   Thank you both again for the great
party and the bracelet and all. It has
been a great experience so far, and I
will try to write more soon.

                          Love and kisses,
                          Etta
```

The letter had created more questions that it had answered, in Martha's opinion.

"So, do you think she is dating George?" Martha asked Abigail.

"I think so. Sounds like she is going to the party with him, his aunt and his uncle."

"She must not have liked London at all! She didn't say anything nice about it."

"Nothing at all."

Martha allowed herself a deep sigh and raised her eyebrows. She spoke slowly, as if searching for each word somewhere in the abyss of a new Webster's Dictionary. "We have…some news…at least." She folded up the letter and copied the address onto two envelopes—one to send and one to copy to the next envelope she would send. It was a quirky method of keeping addresses—that was true. The letter-sized envelope took its place in alphabetical order in the front of the envelope box where the addressed ones had overtaken the blank ones in quantity.

Henrietta Johnson
Agustus Road 133 - Edgbaston
Birmingham, West Midlands B15 3TR
Great Britain

Into the desert, news of Etta's adventures spread like wildfire. Mrs. Busch was pleased that her notion was correct about Etta being distracted by a man named George. Disappointing though, he was living with an aunt and uncle. Must be a real loser. She felt Etta should have done better than that with such an opportunity. Chuck was somewhat comforted by the news but wondered about what horrible thing could have happened to Etta in London. He remained privately suspicious.

Martha returned news of the friends and family, knowing that it would take weeks to get to her daughter. She did not write as many questions into the letter as she had originally planned. She was just grateful for news. She did ask Etta for the phone number. Maybe she would splurge and call her daughter.

For now, Martha could rest easier having some news, even if it was a few weeks old. She wondered how the party went. She hoped to see a photograph of Etta in her party attire. The thought made her smile.

Chapter 9
LUCKY PURSE

At 7:43 a.m., Etta waited outside the Kendalls' home. She watched her breath form a thick cloud resembling cigarette smoke. Her hands, shoved deep in the pockets of the wool coat, were partially frozen to the second knuckle. The tips of all of her fingers had succumbed to the cold, and her desert blood was obviously thin. The purchase of ornamental and functional gloves would be required this day.

Etta noticed the cold had an immeasurably negative effect on the entryway as the autumn garden wilted helplessly against the onset of the cold months.

"Etta!" yelled Margaret as she ran through the foyer to open the door. "Why on earth didn't you knock?"

"Well, I was early...again. Sorry," Etta replied rather sheepishly.

"Come along in here and warm your toes. Let me grab the keys. Harvey!" And then with a little more screech and force she yelled again, "Harveeeyyy!"

A muffled reply came from somewhere in the house behind one of the closed doors. After a few minutes of hunting him and collecting his keys, they walked down the cobblestone drive to the little green car.

Unbeknownst to Etta, there was a third person who required a shopping trip this day—Margaret's lady friend from church, Mimi. Hers was a nickname so deeply engrained that nobody remembered her real name aside from her darling husband.

Mimi's house was only two blocks away from their trek to town. When Mimi stepped out of the house, age dictated that Etta take the backseat out of courtesy. Etta sat behind Margaret, the driver. The trouble was that this seat would have been behind the shotgun passenger seat in America.

It was so visually confusing that the simple ride to town turned into one of the most nightmarish experiences Etta had had in many years.

Mimi, trying to be polite, was talking to Etta and was turning around to maintain eye contact. This, from the perspective of Etta's brain, was the driver neglecting the wheel to talk, and she grabbed protruding elements of the car's interior in a desperate effort to minimize the crash they would surely have. Cars were flying right at Etta! Then she snapped back, realizing that Margaret was in front of her and driving. So, she moved over behind Mimi, not to be rude, but to reduce the tricks on her visual perception. That did not work at all! Now she had offended Mimi by her assertive move out of eye contact to take the seat behind her. Margaret now turned briefly from the shotgun position, which was actually the driver's side, to view what was going on in the backseat.

Traffic was busy this morning, and vehicles flew by in both directions, allowing only a smidgen of following distance. The oncoming traffic from Etta's perception were all in the wrong lanes. The shotgun passengers were the drivers, and oh! It was all too much.

Etta hysterically yelled, "Stop the car!" After which Margaret swerved the car off to the left, which appeared to Etta to be into the oncoming traffic lane. It was all confusing, frightening, and at last overwhelming to Etta, who'd had enough. Etta urgently escaped through the door behind Mimi. The panic rose over the top of her esophagus, and she threw up right there on the sidewalk.

Mimi stared out the window a second and then quietly commented to Margaret, "Sees then, that's about 'er barror ennet?"

Margaret was quite upset at the vision of her guest dry-heaving over a pile of fresh vomit on a resident's walkway. She shut down the engine, shifted the car into first gear, and set the brake as Harvey had methodically taught her. She carefully approached Etta, not quite collecting the words needed to complete a full statement.

"Hey there…What…?"

Etta peered over to her by cocking her head from a bent-at-the-waist position. Her face was ghastly white, and her eyes were puffing up from puking her breakfast. There was a slim trail of fresh ooze running down the front of her coat and a dribble of drool trying to escape the corner of her mouth. That was the first time Etta was unable to respond to Margaret. Margaret did not know what to do or say, so she got back into the car and sat silently with Mimi for nothing short of six minutes.

With great deliberation, Etta crawled back into the car. She grasped the side and back of the car once again and quietly pleaded, "Can you please take me home for a moment?"

Margaret neither questioned nor responded but simply drove back the six blocks to Etta's flat. Etta slowly lifted herself out of the car and met a freshly awakened Geraldine on her way back in. Mrs. Bonneville smelled the vomit and noted Etta's haggard expression and thought the worst. She raced outside to catch red-handed the culprits of whatever wild night Etta had experienced. But what she saw was quite surprising.

"Atcha! Good to see you! What the hell happened to the girl? 'Er's got a right cob on 'er over samming!"

"Mimi, Geraldine. Geraldine, Mimi. I have no idea! We just drove not five blocks, and she went collywobbles! She was acting rather odd and hopped out of the car and tossed her breakfast on the walk."

"Is she pissed?" Geraldine inquired in a rather undignified manner.

"No, we were just going out for a shop in town. I don't know what to think." Margaret turned back to look at Mimi, who was as dumbfounded with this young stranger as she was sympathetic to her dear friend Margaret.

After a minute, Etta returned with a heavy sweater, having abandoned the coat, which reeked too badly. She had brushed her teeth and washed her face too in hopes that she would not appear as ghastly as she felt. She tried to collect herself and slowly descended the stairs.

The three ladies stood expectantly near the car, waiting for Etta's comment.

"Forgive me. Driving in England is quite hard on the eye still. Shall we give it another try?"

Margaret noticed that Etta had tried to conceal a plastic bag in the pocket of her sweater, perhaps so she would not have to scream at her to stop if she felt the desire to toss her cookies inside that car. She really, really hoped this would not happen because Harvey was quite particular about the way his car was kept. He would notice any lingering stench, dropped pastry crumb, or hairline scratch on the auto. Vomit would be unforgivable, and he would surely feel compelled to sell the car.

Etta climbed back into the car, but she selected the middle of the back bench so she could see out the windshield. This she expected would assist her in becoming accustomed to the traffic pattern. Mimi had resolved not to talk to her at all! After all, what could she say?

Etta endured what seemed like several hours of traffic torture, though in reality it was only eighteen minutes. While she was able to keep down the half glass of water she allowed herself while cleaning up, she was unable to control her sweat glands, which were alerted by the "fight or flight" response. She chose to fight her physical responses, and her body responded with a strong sweat production on her brow, palms, and under her arms, where she was now mortified to actually be able to smell her own odor. Oh, this was just not going well at all!

After the silent drive into town, Margaret parked in a lot across from a block of shops with various offerings. Etta peeled her aching grip from the door and carefully stepped out of the car onto shaking legs. The walk did her good, and soon she felt her footing again.

Once inside the friendly doors of Lemmings, Mimi sauntered off to hunt down her outfit for the dinner. Until this time, Etta was unaware that Mimi was a guest as well. Margaret tried to act casual, but Etta knew she was still shaken up by the preliminary events of the morning.

Etta tried on many ultraconservative looks before settling on a wool dress with a matching suit blazer. It felt warm enough.

"Oh, Etta! You can't wear that! You look like a mim-mucking 'er does!" Mimi interjected in her neighborhood dialect.

"What would you suggest?"

"What color is yer fur?"

"I don't have a fur or even an evening coat," Etta responded.

"Well then, let's start with a coat and work your way back in. Miss! Can you please help this young lady find a coat that's suitable for a dinner?"

Etta wasn't sure if she should be grateful or embarrassed.

The shop maiden found a lovely blue coat with threads of black running in a sparse pattern near the cuffs and collar. It was a terrific, trendy color that Etta thought she could pull off with her height. She was taller than most women she met, and while she didn't intend to command attention, it was allotted to her due to her natural and statuesque beauty.

"We'll be putting our prices up next week when we get the new lot in. This really is a swell tag," the lady attempted to persuade. "Do you need the matching stick an' rag?"

"No, thank you." Etta didn't want frivolous accessories such as an umbrella until she was a good bit ahead on her finances.

As it turned out, there was no need to coach Etta; she was now "working her way in," as Mimi suggested, by surveying the selection of dresses that would match the shell. There were two, really. One was a black fitted dress with a round collar. Although the dress was youthful and fit beautifully, she recalled Greta advised against black. The second dress was the same shade of blue as the coat she selected, only there was black trim on the three-quarter-length sleeves and the hem. After trying on both dresses, the elderly women could not agree. She tried them both on a second time, and they could not decide between the two. In the privacy behind the dressing curtain, Etta re-counted her money from the wad of English pounds in her pocket. She had hoped to find a new charm today in town, too. Gold charms were an investment that would cost more that the fine coat she wanted. If she was really careful on the other accessories, she might be OK. And if it did not work out, she could always return…

"Etta! Which one will you take, dear?" Margaret asked.

Etta had a flashback to Mrs. Busch calling her "dear," though Margaret made it sound far more endearing. "Actually, I am going to buy them both!"

She possessed only other people's clothes and her work uniforms until this shop. It felt like a defining moment, having found apparel that fit and was hers alone.

Mimi had found a nice suit with warm brown colors as well, but the commissioned clerk was obviously more pleased with the three items Etta purchased.

The three ladies enjoyed the window dressings of several shops along the way, pausing to soak in the latest fashion for the fall season. They entered a few stores, which yielded nothing but pleasant conversation.

The ladies struck gold when they went into Panache. The store was crowded with goods, and the merchandise was cramped together so much that customers could not look through a rack of clothing but one person at a time.

Margaret immediately found the right autumn dress, tawny in color and the perfect length. She cooed with delight from inside the dressing corner. There was no space for a fitting room, so the owner had used a space behind a stack of boxes by which to fix a sliding curtain. A two-way mirror stood just the other side of the boxes, and Margaret's two shopping companions "ooed" when they saw her in the dress as well.

Etta found an elegant black leather purse with a wallet that matched quite nicely. She had used her pockets up till now to store money. That had made her feel awkwardly masculine and uncomfortable. Instead of purchasing evening gloves and protective wear, she settled on a pair of blue gloves that matched her coat. She chose to be bare-handed during the dinner. That was not too much of a crime. Etta had nice hands that she groomed particularly carefully because of her job. Etta's nails were shaped nicely on her long, slender fingers, and the gold charm bracelet would be a nice accessory with the new black dress. With these purchases, Etta ascertained she had enough left over to comfortably find her shoes and a new charm.

Margaret and Mimi had equally good fortune in this store, completing most of their required purchases inside. On the checkout counter, Etta noticed a stack of small papers reproduced with an advertisement of 50 percent off any clearance item of choice at Jasper Jewellery. She took one of the ads. Her shopping companions were drunk with shopping success, willing to make any detour within the next several hours they had budgeted for the hunt. There was no contingency plan. None of the ladies had anything in mind to wear to the event, and they were delighted to have completed such a quick, successful shop.

The detour to Jasper's was Broadlands Shoe House, which Etta comically envisioned to be a shoe house for portly, oversized men. The selection proved quite different with a vast array of beautiful shoes from all over Europe. The selection for Etta's size was regrettably small. But she managed to find a nice, all-purpose dress shoe with a youthful, stylish heel and a sturdy back.

Mimi and Margaret decided to wear shoes they already had. "After all, my fat feet will be under the table most of the affair, anyhow!" remarked Mimi.

Jasper Jewellery had but a scant selection of charms in gold. There were several cases of silver charms and chains. There was one case of exotic gold, which appeared to be Indian in origin.

Etta held out the coupon for the bespectacled man to see. "What do you have in mind, miss?"

"I would like a charm, but I don't really see any I like. Do you have others?"

The Englishman was courteous and looked diligently through his newly received trays for more charms. "I'm afraid I have only these three and what is in the window."

The three were also unattractive, but after exiting the store to take a second look at the display, Etta saw a lovely handbag. She asked to see the charm, and it had a tiny clasp that opened up to reveal a small hollow space to conceal miniscule items. She was instantly drawn to it and purchased it at the advertised discount with free installation to boot. He was quick to attach and secure the charm to the collection she had started.

This little purse charm had a special feel as it represented several profound experiences. It commemorated her first horrific drive into town in a little green death machine. It marked the first time she bought her own clothes in England. And it balanced the bracelet links perfectly because the charms were now spread out around the bracelet. She absentmindedly played with it as a prayer of thanks came to her heart that she was not killed in an automobile accident during her pursuit of locating an appropriate evening dress.

She was only slightly able to bear the return home as she slowly became accustomed to driving on the left in a very, very small enclosure. Mimi was the first drop.

"Ta-ra a bit!" she called back from the front door.

At six forty-five in the evening, Harvey pulled up to Etta's. Margaret went to the door and knocked. She expected something special of Etta due to the basket of facial colors she had sent with her after their shop. "Special" was a gross understatement. Etta was nothing short of stunning in her fitted black dress with her hair swooped into a French twist. Her facial features were pronounced with 360-degree eyeliner and shadow at the top. Her lovely cheekbones were more apparent with the rouge, and she had fabulously balanced lips, accentuated by the dark red lipstick.

Etta felt a little self-conscious, unaccustomed as she was to wearing much makeup, but she felt confident that it improved her appearance somewhat. She was pleased they were early. She had been ready to wait out the last fifteen, as was customary for her family.

Margaret greeted her with a hug. "Etta, you look smashing! If I had my wits, I'd have fixed you up with George before he went back to America."

Etta remarked, "The face color really helps. Thank you for lending them to me. I suppose I should break down and buy my own kit. Have you heard anything from George?" Etta thought about the man who rescued her and this generous family who continued to assist her. Etta was surprised that her visual memory of George was fading, and without seeing a photo of him, she could not conjure up what he looked like.

"George is on a temporary duty in California. He just proposed to his high school sweetheart. My sister Elizabeth said he'll return home so they can marry next month. That way so 'ers able to join him for his next duty tour which, with any luck, will be here!"

"Oh, that would be wonderful!" Etta replied genuinely. She had no feelings for George other than deep gratitude.

"Will you be OK then in the car?" Margaret asked in jest.

"I have been working on that," Etta explained with a furrowed brow, "and I will sit in the middle with a security bag. Would it be too much trouble to ask Harvey to take it easy on me?"

"Of course not! That's why *we* were early this time!" Only the women laughed.

Chapter 10
COFFEE HOUR

Harvey pulled up to a grand estate. He stepped out onto the middle of the cobblestone street. Etta was puzzled until she noticed the man in a black uniform and driving cap motion for the keys. He opened the doors for Margaret and Etta and drove off.

"Where do you suppose he is going?" asked Etta to no one in particular.

"They have a bare lot behind that section of trees to park all the guests," Harvey replied, knowing the routine.

Etta observantly watched another uniformed man appear with the same cap to collect the next car.

Her eyes were drawn to a grand entry with a colorful profusion of blooming plants that seemed out of place with the climate cooling as it was. The stone home was surrounded by modest homes of brick and thus appeared stately and regal in their midst. The estate was an amazing surprise to Etta, who had never seen this sort of mini-castle in her travels to work or town. It was appropriately hidden on a block, irregular in shape so as to provide some semblance of privacy for the family.

As they entered the palatial, grand hall, Etta coached herself to keep her head and eyes level. She had been taught at the trade school to not seem too impressed when a business client exposed his assets. She lost composure briefly on a smile when the butler bowed down in a gesture of accepting her coat and gloves to check. Watching those before her, she realized that one did not thank the help at this affair. Despite this observation, Harvey shook the butler's gloved hand and thanked him for taking items from Margaret and him.

The trio meandered about the home, greeting people they knew and introducing a few to Etta, too. They wandered clear through the home and into the luxurious outdoor annex where a pool house was sparkling clear, even in its seasonal disuse. The flower den enveloped a conservatory, with wonderfully comfortable seating. Plant arrangements soothed the mind and eye. A quartet of strings entertained the ears with melodic, classical ensembles.

The terracing was cobblestone, irregular in construction, flowing from one area to the next. It was a wonderland, but it was cold. They returned into the comforts of the estate to converse politely with their fellow guests.

"Ah, Greta! Lovely to see you!" Margaret enthusiastically offered.

"I'm so glad to see you, Margaret, Harvey. And I recall our tea, but what was your name?" Greta's tone was not offensive as much as curious.

"Etta. Etta Johnson."

"Ah, yes. I'm delighted you are here. There is someone I wish for you to meet. Excuse me a moment."

With that, Greta danced across the room in her deep blue gown, which floated after her with its short train. Without time for so much as a change of topic, Greta floated back toward them, this time with a young woman in tow. Upon her return, a beautiful pointed shoe with a coin on the toe resembling a bejeweled crown was exposed from beneath Greta's gown. Etta was conscious not to look down to observe these details too closely.

"This is my queen bee, my only daughter. May I present Binny. Binny, this is Etta Johnson, the American who works at the Birmingham Botanical Gardens and Glasshouses."

With a sideways tilt of her head, Binny closed her eyes and then stood back erect before offering her hand to Etta.

"I am delighted to meet you. Do you know that Lana Ingle speaks quite highly of your work with the succulents?"

"Pleasure to meet you as well. Thank you. Actually, I don't have the opportunity to speak to Mrs. Ingle that often."

Binny laughed and threw her head back so the sound reverberated from the ceiling and back to them. "She would never offer her first name to keep a sort of power over you. She really is a pussycat. When you see her next, try calling her Lana. You'll be surprised at how sweet she will be that you took an interest in her. She really is unfulfilled, if you catch what I mean, and she enjoys personal attention regardless of her overt intensity."

"Thank you. I will give it a try," Etta responded, surprised to hear such private details about her boss.

Binny took Etta by the arm as perhaps American teenage friends might walk school halls. She guided her away from the adults toward a group of men of various sizes, shapes, and levels of alcohol consumption.

"Boys, this is Etta. She attends the fabulous cactus room. This is Thomas, my middle brother, and Josiah, his colleague.

This is Jeremy, my younger brother, and his neighbor, Arthur. And this is my eldest brother, Joseph."

There was a chorus of British "Hellos!" with one exception. Joseph. He appeared stern and drunk.

"Pleased to meet you all," Etta offered gracefully.

"You're not a Brum, then?" Joseph spit forth into the air in front of Etta's nose.

"I...I don't understand what you mean," she offered softly so as not to antagonize the situation.

Arthur came to her rescue. "You aren't from Birmingham, then? Your accent is a loud introduction to us, indicating that you're a foreigner."

"Oh, let her be, you!" Thomas spoke with a slight slur.

Jeremy and Josiah stood by helplessly, watching from voice to voice, unsure of just when to interject or intervene.

Before they could offer anything at all, Binny ta-taed them and swept Etta toward the grand staircase. Outside one of the beautifully carved doors was a sitting area. A wonderful wood-framed window overlooked the middle level of the trees outdoors in their various shades of autumn color. The harpist was audible from this vantage point, providing a soothing backdrop to the conversation.

"I should have given you the gossip first, Etta. My brothers are all eligible, though you would want for none of them. Truth is, if I might be so bold, I am the only one who has made a mark yet. Just like my mum. And now they meet you, a successful botanist, and it just kenched their pride."

Etta was bewildered to have received such misleading hospitality. Since she had neither contributed to, nor fed the notion of her social class, she decided to see how far this would go.

Binny sure was a chatty one—not at all professional in the way Etta had been trained back home. It was sure nice to have company closer to her own age for a while, though.

"I formed up a re-creation company for tourists. Kind of funny, actually. I met a couple from Sweden who really loved our draft horses' brass. They were so curious about the history and production of such objects and how they were used. I figured tourists would be fascinated by our past. I constructed an open-air experience to preserve our heritage for our kinters and travelers, too. What smarts is that I'm in the Livery Companies of London. My brothers are quite envious of that."

"Sounds like a great idea. But what's a livery?" Etta asked, believing it to be along the lines of equestrian in nature. She was hoping for an abbreviated answer.

"To be in London Livery, I had to come up with a unique activity. The old ones like the Cordwainers were established in the thirteenth century. You can't cross over anyone's toes. Since Founders was established already, this seemed the right thing. It's a very big deal, really. I had to build over a hundred in my employ, sustain it for seven years, and participate in charitable and educational funds. Mum really helps me there. She has a right mind for business, and she passed it onto me. *I listened!* And so it is that I chartered in the livery with Historical Preservation as my offering."

Etta was surprised that with as much as Binny could talk, she had time to soak in a mother's entrepreneurial coaching. She observed Binny's high energy escaping through her toes as she nervously pumped her leg back and forth over her knee. Though they were close to the same age Binny had already achieved greatness and a company legacy. Etta had achieved being stranded. It struck her as funny, and she started to laugh. She laughed so hard that Binny thought it was something she said and looked puzzled. Etta had not let go since she had come into this predicament.

"Binny, you are really something. I can't believe you have achieved all this. What comes next for you?"

"I have thought about taking the stage and booths and creating a museum or taking it on the road—er—across the ocean like a historical circus of sorts…"

"No, no, no! I mean what do you do with you? What brings *you* joy?" After the words escaped her lips, she regretfully recognized the boldness of her line of questioning. Binny's eyes teared visibly, though not enough to spill onto her cheek.

"I want a man. Some lovering! I want a family, too."

"I didn't mean..." Etta attempted to recover her error.

"No, that's all right. I need to step away from myself sometimes and check on reality. Gosh, nobody ever asked me what brings *me* happiness. I don't think I know that yet. But I remember witnessing happiness. When I was younger, before Father died. It was in me mum's eyes. She was so busy and remarkably successful in her time, and when she looked at him...that was joy. He was so common, and she was so glamorous. But Daddy brought Mum joy. I want that, too. Trouble is I'm a lummox with men. I haven't dated, really."

"Me neither. I can't say I had the same experience, though. My folks were not compatible. Dad left us in a bad way," Etta admitted with a faraway look.

"Gosh then. I'm so sorry! Let's roll some male company and see what we can fish up, then?" Binny perked up as she attempted to lighten the mood. It was strange how quickly she felt a bond with Etta.

Etta followed Binny down the stairs, watching in slow motion as the hem of her brown silk dress crawled gracefully down the stairs before her. Before entering the social masses now congregated, Binny turned to face Etta and stated eye to eye, "We must club!"

Etta did not know what clubbing was but understood this to be something Binny was serious about. Etta felt a strong social connection with Binny immensely appreciating her disposition and enthusiasm. They were separated in the crowd, and Joseph approached her again. The visible kindling of a fire came into his eyes, and Etta's female warning sensors were on alert. She chose to play this carefully.

"You, you don't even know your own history. You don't even know where you are, do you?" Joseph hissed.

"Hello again, Joseph," Etta attempted to approach on neutral ground.

"Do you even know who belongs to the United Kingdom, Yank?" he challenged.

"Well, if you ask me, I would respond, do *you* know who Yanks are?" Etta devised a puzzle for him to work through.

Joseph recognized a quandary, but it seemed too easy. He surrendered quickly to her, and she replied, "Americans are Aztecs, Incas, Navajos, and Inuit." With a lofty chin and confident demeanor, she continued. "We, of the fifty states, are either New or Native American. So, Americans are far older than the four-hundred-year history of the United Crowns of Scotland and England, *your* precious UK!"

Thomas and Arthur approached and let out a joint sound, "Whooooa!" and then erupted in laughter at Joseph.

Joseph's stupor was visible as he attempted to reckon this thought through his impaired processor. The puzzle diverted him, and his attitude slightly mellowed just long enough for Thomas to sweep Etta away to the foyer.

"I'm so sorry about Joseph. He really takes his liquor seriously," Thomas offered.

A small bell was audible above the conversations, and everyone came to a hush. They gathered in the grand hall, where Mrs. Colmore was perched midway up the staircase, looking regal and beautiful.

"Ladies and gentlemen, we have much to be thankful for in this year of our Lord. I wish to welcome all to our home, and may you accept our friendship as much as we have treasured yours. Please congregate to the dining hall."

With that, she floated gracefully down the stairs. With hands on both ornate handles, she opened the twelve-foot doors that revealed an enormous room set with a table spanning the entire length of the room. The wood walls were warm and adorned with all fashions of fowl and animal trophies. The natural theme was interrupted with large, beautiful vases decorated in themes of hunting, flora, or fauna. Ornately carved eighteenth-century furniture with fine detail decorated the room. Carvings spilled down the arms and legs of the chairs standing at attention for each guest.

Delicate bone china, sturdy silver utensils, and several services of light crystal covered a long span of white linen. The attractive visual presentation made it difficult for Etta to contain the gasp building in the back of her throat. She felt especially fortunate at this moment. The beautiful plates were hand painted with a foxhunting scene, and she noted particular accuracy in the muscles of the horses, suspended mid-jump over a fence. Etta fought an awfully strong urge to turn over the plate to determine the china maker.

But as they took their seats, Etta was at a loss. Margaret and Harvey had sat opposite Mimi. Unbeknownst to Etta, Mimi's husband had bowed out of the affair after refusing to wear the only appropriate dark suit he owned. She was unaccompanied this evening.

Binny was three seats to the left of a group of dignified elderly guests. There was a church leader of some sort in his black cloak and white collar to Etta's left and a group of younger people to the right of Joseph. Yes, Joseph had drawn the seat to Etta's right—a very vulnerable place to be at the moment. It was a stroke of luck, and Etta was reminded about her family's penchant for polar sorts of extraordinary luck, good and bad. The vicar remained standing after everyone else had been seated. Etta strained her neck to watch his eyes survey the guests. Joseph appeared very uncomfortable in his placement.

Once the gracious host had taken her seat, the vicar offered a thankful dialogue to God in the mother tongue of proper Queen's English. To Etta, it seemed remarkably devoid of any spiritual feeling. It felt more like a speech to a group of royal knights rather than a petition to the God she knew. So she silently tossed in her own pithy American grace, knowing that her Heavenly Father was cognizant of *her* deep gratitude to Him.

Being seated nearly in the center of the room, Etta could not count the number of guests seated at the table. From the looks of it as she surveyed the table, attempting to be unimpressed, she estimated around fifty adult guests.

In came the eight kitchen stewards in long, black tailcoats with white gloves and silver trays containing the first plates. As luck would have it, there was a small announcement next to each setting detailing the wine and cuisine service for the evening.

Etta surveyed her cornmeal oysters with pickapeppa rémoulade while her proximal table guests were waiting for their first plates to be set. The first white wine was delivered about the same time Joseph offered his first kind word of the evening.

Joseph slurred a remark to the wait staff behind his chair. "Kindly tell William that the rémoulade is remarkable tonight."

Apparently, the recipient knew the gig and returned to the kitchen prior to setting out his tray of wine glasses. He was smiling when he reentered the room—a good sign that the compliment had perhaps begot another.

Joseph laid off Etta and engaged in neutral conversation about the goings on of the lord mayor of Birmingham, who might make an appearance even if briefly toward the end of the evening, as was his custom. He enjoyed Mrs. Colmore, but he did not want to mix too closely with her guests, who were always reportedly the neighbors, not the dignitaries he preferred to surround himself with. But there was a historic obligation here, and his attendance was necessary.

The guest across from Etta was Molly. She was Thomas's girlfriend. Though she did not live in Edgbaston, she was well known among the circle of Greta's offspring's friends. She spoke patiently to Etta about what she was experiencing, offering explanations on customs, education, and community interests. She really was quite helpful, enriching the experience for Etta.

By the second first plate, snapper turtle soup, accompanied by a fresh wine service of a different flavor, Joseph was participating in the conversation with interjections or elaboration.

With the third first plate, reportedly dandelion salad, Joseph was sobering somewhat and engaging in original communication with the dinner guests. Jeremy and Josiah, seated several seats across and down the table, were relieved to surrender their watchful service of their brother, so he would not embarrass the family (again). He seemed to be tolerating, no, enjoying Etta's proximity.

The second plate, lamb with rosemary, arrived with its select wine. Etta, unaccustomed to sitting so long, experienced two sensations. Her extremities began to feel numb and disjoined. She was ever so worried she would drop a utensil or tip over one of the series of crystal set before her. She also felt a sickening rise in her stomach as the foreign aroma of the lamb sailed up to her acute nostrils. She knew quite assuredly that she would be unable to partake of this delicacy.

The pumpkin gratin side would be priceless in saving face. She gently and carefully hid half of the lamb under the pumpkin and enjoyed only half of the side dish with her nostrils closed off to avoid further contact with the sensationally pungent aroma. She thirsted for a simple glass of water as the wine selections remained full in front of her plate.

Her ploy worked. In the winds of fine conversation around her, it appeared that she ate only half of her side and half of her meat. Surely, this would not offend anyone.

After the plates were once again collected, there was a lapse in food with a coffee service and wonderful conversation with the vicar and the couple across from him. Etta discreetly motioned the help for more water and politely declined the coffee. Nobody was rude about the fact that the American herself was a conversation piece. They engaged her in topics safe to participate in intelligently.

The finale was presented on the ornately engraved silver trays. Etta was impressed that the gloves on the waiters were all still as stark white as they had been with the first plates. The dessert trays sported French holiday logs topped with meringue. Having not downed the last course, Etta was comfortable in her dress while those around her seemed to shift from side to side occasionally to make room for just one more bite while warding off a broken zipper or seam.

Etta searched her memory for a moment in her life that could compare to the outstanding flavor of any one of these courses, sans lamb. She came up with a sole experience at her own bon voyage. Mrs. Busch had brought a marinated heart salad to her party. It was comprised of palm, artichoke, and other exotic plant hearts Etta had never heard of. It too was a culinary marvel.

As the final plates were collected onto the silver trays, Chef Kuck emerged from the kitchen. Greta stood and introduced her head chef to her guests. "Ladies and gentlemen, may I present the brilliant palate behind our dinner this evening, Master Head Chef William Kuck." With that, the room erupted into a standing ovation, and Chef Kuck was pleased, smiling and bowing to the masses and waving both naked hands at his captive audience.

The several hours that passed had been good for Etta and Joseph, who had achieved peace—or at least what appeared to be mutual apathy. Jeremy and Binny approached Etta in the dining room as others meandered back out into the common areas to converse and enjoy more music.

"So he backed off you, did he?" Binny quizzed.

"Yes," sighed Etta. "I suppose I'm just not his type."

"Not his type?" Jeremy asked in an octave slightly too high. "You likely scared him to death. You are exactly his type. Not his type. I'm glad he quit being such a tosser to you now."

"Yeah, well..." Etta started her comeback thought, but she was interrupted by Binny's enthusiasm.

"Come on, Etta. We need to club! Please come this Friday. Say you will. We'll bring the boys along."

"We can tote you around," persuaded Jeremy.

"*Only* if Joseph stays at home," Etta tentatively agreed.

Etta provided her phone and the location of the house. It would be really good for her to find people her own age for company. She had never been terribly social, but perhaps it was time to come out of her shell.

Weariness numbed the terrifying experience of being a passenger in the car. Etta enjoyed the swirls of nighttime colors in the town lights they passed as she was deposited back at Geraldine's home.

༄

Etta invested hours recording every detail from the evening into her journal. Her memories were still acute, and she was undoubtedly enriched by the conversation of the evening. She fought sensations of sleepiness in exchange for recording even the slightest impression from the glorious evening.

༄

Dear Mom and Abby,

I know I just wrote you, but I could not wait to tell you about the party. It turns out this lady is really well-to-do! I mean she had car valets, butlers, a chef, and a great staff to wait on us. The mayor of the town stopped in for a courteous hello.

Mrs. Colmore's kids are great. She has three sons and one daughter. The daughter takes after her mom, a real go-getter. She has already built a company that demonstrates the old trades and enacts the traditional English methods. Do you think people in the US would pay to visit trade booths? They show you how to forge brass and work horseshoes and weave cloth and so much more!

I don't care for her older brother much, but I like her other two brothers. One may join us next weekend. Binny and I are going dancing next weekend. They say, "Let's club!"

Anyway, the house was huge, grand, and decorated like a palace. There were so many things to see that it was really hard not to gawk at it all.

I have been so filled with visual stimulation that I wrote for hours in my in my journal. I keep adding to my bracelet. The latest is a coffee urn. It will remind me of that wonderful, six-course dinner at the Colmore estate.

I have decided to stay here for Christmas. Maybe I will come home next summer or so. It depends on how things go. There is still so much to see and do! Please do not send a gift. I will not send one home either. When I come home, I will bring all kinds of treasures from Britain. Do you think that you would like to come visit me here? I know the airline would be very expensive, but with all the people I have met, it would be a wonderful experience.

Why haven't you written?

Love and kisses,
Etta

Abby folded up the letter and put it back into the envelope so her mother could enjoy it when she returned home. She started answering the question aloud.

"Well, Etta, we have not written again because we expected you to return. We expected you to throw in the towel and come home. We thought maybe you would even come home with George and announce you were engaged. Etta..." Abby looked thoughtfully at the envelope, "we really didn't think you'd want to do it on your own. Be safe there on the other side of the world." With that she kissed the envelope and placed it lovingly on her mother's bed.

Chapter 11
SHEEPISH INTENT

True to her word, Binny phoned. For Etta, it was exciting taking a phone call at home. Being secluded seemed quite natural, but in the eye of this tornado of adventure, it seemed ungrateful, if not a pathetic condition of social apathy. Etta needed to get out.

They ping-ponged topics back and forth. It was a forty-minute temporal investment, and both women felt sure that the fresh companionship was genuine. They agreed on Friday, ten o'clock at night, Disco 21, with Arthur and her brother Jeremy. Binny was correct in assuming her brother Joseph was interested in Etta. Etta dug her heels in deeply, reminding Binny she had agreed to the dance night only sans Joseph.

At eight o'clock, Etta began the transformation ritual between her small bedroom and the bathroom mirror, which had better lighting. Of course, Geraldine selfishly stole fifteen minutes, quizzing Etta on her whatnots, details, and contingency plans. She warned (as always) for Etta not to partake of the bevy this evening.

Etta enjoyed the attention and her new comfort level wearing cosmetics suggested by Margaret. It was not so bad wearing makeup here as it had been in the desert, where one's face felt like melting wax. She felt no such sensation, but she noticed she received more eye contact from the guests at Greta's party. Maybe she could slowly break into such a habit as regularly wearing makeup.

Her freshly trimmed hair still looked kissed from the harsh Arizona sun. Her nails had grown nicely despite the work at her garden job. She outlined her lips and eyes and darkened her brows, lashes, and cheeks in the mirror. She was pleased with the image peering back, assisted by the fresh new makeup assortment she invested in at the neighborhood chemist shop.

She put on her "tights," a term that still caused her a chuckle, and promptly broke her nail clear through. Hoping the injury was high enough on her leg, she attempted to patch the nylon with the same winter red nail polish she had already applied to her fingers and toes. It left a bloody-looking mark on her thigh, but it appeared to hold her stockings without further runs.

She was now very pleased to have purchased two dresses to match the beautiful winter coat. Etta selected to debut the blue dress with the black trim on the sleeves and hem. She wore borrowed pearl accessories with the gold bracelet. Her hair was nearly dry now, and before she had a chance to fix it up into place, she heard a high-pitched honk from outside. Etta grabbed her blue wool coat and new leather bag, completely forgetting her gloves and bobby pins.

"I'm going out, Geraldine! I'll be in early in the morning. And I promise I won't be drinking. See you later."

An inaudible response came from behind the bathroom door, and Etta felt no obligation to wait for a clarification or any moral check on her evening. It was only difficult sometimes to let a room from a lonely widow.

Etta rushed to the small, black Mini resting in the street, protected from the cold in her warm, wool wrap. Binny was driving, Jeremy was shotgun, and Arthur sat in the backseat. Etta paused for only a moment, remembering her fear of riding in English traffic. Behind the windows, Binny picked up on the pause as the men could not. Her take on the pause was that Etta was expecting to sit in the front, so she promptly instructed her brother to let her in the car and join his friend in the back. Etta was not privy to the misguided conversation and prayed momentarily to the God the vicar does not talk to. It started rather as a prayer, but it wound up an earnest petition for vehicular safety.

"Hello then, Etta. I had to take my brother's car. I don't like driving mine in that parking lot."

"Hey, everyone," Etta started, and then she caught herself in this unaccustomed, rude slang. She perceived her friends noticed the slip, too. She also ascertained that Binny must own a splendidly fine car since the one they rode in was nicer than cars her sister or mother ever owned. Etta herself had not owned a car yet. She had not been able to justify the need for one, and she did not aspire high enough to manage to afford the upkeep and cost of having one.

The conversation was lively, and the opportunity to ride in the front seat felt much safer. Etta equated the experience more to riding on her first bus trip instead of the disastrous shopping experience she was likely to never forget or be forgiven for.

She recognized some landmarks as they entered the city. It was nice having a sense of where she was, even if she wasn't certain of the direction. At home, Etta could navigate three hundred and sixty degrees with her various mountains. She never learned the cardinal points of the streets. Instead, she memorized the names and directions of each mountain and allowed herself to be drawn toward them when on any excursion. It was such a different notion of driving that she was unsure if she could navigate the new city she lived in, should the opportunity ever present itself.

Arthur and Jeremy hinted that they would take their own table so other women at the club would not mistake the two couples as having come together. They would manage to hook up a few times to negotiate their departure time and to relay any updated gossip.

Arthur lamented, "Joseph couldn't help himself. He would chivy Jeremy about coming, right out the door and into the car if I hadn't played interference. You know, Etta, he really does fancy you."

"He has a most ungentlemanly manner of demonstrating that! Jeremy, sorry to assign you as messenger here, but tell your darling brother there is not a Sam's chance in hell that I would consider his accompaniment," Etta stated quite matter-of-factly.

Arthur squeezed his head in between the ladies into the front seat of the small car and turned to study Etta's face. "You *are* serious, aren't you?" he asked with genuine curiosity. She sat back while Jeremy mumbled to himself, "Sam?"

"Serious as a heart attack!" Etta responded, and the trio erupted in laughter at the expression.

"How horribly irreverent!" Binny squealed between bouts of uncontrollable laughter.

There wasn't actually valet parking; however, when the doorman recognized Binny stepping out of the car parked conspicuously near the door, blocking traffic, he hopped over to her and demonstrated visible familiarity. "Good evening, Miss Colmore. Pleasant to see you in town for a change. I'll watch your keys, then."

The twenty-somethings stepped from the car and approached the door in the order of Arthur, Jeremy, and Etta, followed by Binny, who had handed several pounds to the doorman for his overtly irregular service to her.

Quite out of the blue, Binny gasped dramatically, and all three turned back toward her. "What the blooming hell are you sporting, Etta?" she spat angrily.

The comment was audible to several couples on the outskirts of the foursome. They logically were drawn around Etta to witness what the issue was.

"Etta! This is a *disco*! Haven't you ever been to a disco?" Binny quizzed intently after finally noticing what attire the beautiful blue coat concealed.

"I, ah no, I haven't. No." Only then did Etta understand the reason for Binny's drama as she watched the incomers shedding their coats. The men and women were dressed in glittery, satiny, polyester funk. Etta's lovely wool blend dress was way off the *worst prepared* list.

"We just can't have this," Binny said shortly. She faced the guys again and said, "*You* two, carry on. I will find you again inside in a few hours for an update."

The two silently complied as Binny abruptly snatched her keys back from the doorman.

"Do you want me to get the—"

"No, thank you, I will collect it myself." She promptly cut off the doorman's innocent question.

Once back at the Mini, Binny was breathing heavily from her intense jaunt back across the parking lot.

"I'm really sorry, Binny. I didn't realize what you all were wearing under your heavy coats. I just didn't know what to expect, so I dressed up," Etta attempted to explain.

"Oh, I just can't believe you wore *that*!"

"Now come on, Binny. It's a nice dress. You can't say it's *that* bad!" Etta said defensively.

"It's just all wrong. The whole look is wrong! You can't go in there looking like that, or you will never live it down.

These people are come-backers. You will know the entire floor once you're here a few weeks. I have the cursed ability to draw attention here, and you would be ruined if we passed through those doors." She sighed. "What say you we catch a coffee instead tonight, and we can work on your disco wardrobe another time?"

Binny was increasingly calmer, and she continued with more forgiveness in her tone. "I know a lovely restaurant we can go have a chat and some borrachos."

"What?" Etta asked, looking at the new friend she was certainly unable to predict.

"You know those little drunken cakes. They're made with sherry and served over oranges." There was that sigh again.

Etta feared she would lose this interesting friend before their friendship ever progressed past the foreigner/hostess relationship. Nevertheless, this time she willingly complied, knowing Binny was right. She had unintentionally ruined the evening before it had begun.

By the time they arrived at Circo, Binny had calmed considerably. She handed her keys to the valet, and they approached the doors to the Spanish restaurant. The décor was curious to Etta, who knew nothing of Spanish food, but she equated it to Mexican food in her mind. Spanish mixed with Indian blood populated the Mexico she knew. Therefore, Mexican food would have originated from Spain. At least, that was Etta's logic.

The establishment was crowded with a colorful collection of patrons. As demonstrated by the variety of ethnic representation in the room, this was apparently a hip place to go for dinner. Now their roles had changed. Etta was fashionably outfitted for Circo, but Binny stood out like a sore thumb. When she removed her coat, Binny exposed an outrageous outfit for the patrons to gaze at. The polyester, large blue and yellow paisley pattern with poetic, billowy sleeves was clearly over the top for this crowd. Her belled black slacks toned down the overall look somewhat until they sat down at the table. Nevertheless, Binny was confident and undaunted by her conspicuous attire.

Binny was familiar with the waiter, indicating she was a regular here, too. Etta could not understand how Binny achieved her community notoriety with her primary residence in London. Wherever they went, it seemed people bent over backward for the famous Miss Colmore.

The handsome waiter with the jet black, slicked hair waited patiently while Binny produced her serious, on-the-spot oration. "Luis, this evening it is my duty to expand the minds of the traditional sector of our community. I am modeling the latest fashion from the Paris night scene for your guests to enjoy. See the line of the cuffs here?" she said, extending her arms for him to survey the buttons and unusual cut of the sleeves. "Mark my words—you will see upscale attire like this seep into dining wear in the next few months."

"I see. What may I order for the ladies?"

Binny's arms descended, and her hands folded into her lap. Without so much as a glance at the menus he handed them, she replied, "I'll start with a red Montilla wine, *flamenquines de cerdo*, *mejillones a la vinagreta*, and *pulpo con cachelos*." She handed the menu back to the waiter.

Etta eyed him and slowly responded, "I have not had an opportunity to survey your menu. Do you mind if I keep it here a spell? I'd like a 7UP."

He wiped his meticulously clean hands over his stark white apron as a gesture of nervousness. His crisp black suit with the white shirt restricted the rest of his body. His pose left a rather serious impression. "Not at all, madam. Please enjoy."

"Luis fancies me," Binny stated matter-of-factly. "You aren't still ravished, are you?"

"No, it's just that I have never eaten in a Spanish restaurant, and I don't even know what you ordered! I thought it would be fun to see what they offered for the next time I eat here."

"I see. I hope you don't mind my ordering for us. It is sort of a bad habit I have, taking charge. Or was it charging? I don't know, but I hope you don't mind. Don't you want a drink?"

"Not at all," Etta honestly replied. "I appreciate anything you can offer with culinary or social issues. Truthfully, I don't drink at all. After the shock of my error, I'm really glad you didn't let me into the club tonight. I'm really sorry about that."

"Think nothing of it. I'll check back with the boys after we finish here and swing you home before I pick them up. Sorry you didn't get to dance, anyhow."

The white linen on the tablecloth made the service of dishes appear more ritzy than they actually were. The blue glass chargers beneath the plates were items Etta had never seen set at a table. It was a nice method of catching crumbs before they hit the tablecloth. It made the table appear smaller, though. All the tables were positioned quite close to each other, demanding the wait staff carefully maneuver the floor, sometimes sideways.

When the bottle was set at the table, Etta expected to see the printed name of Montilla on the wine label but noted rather that it *came from* Montilla. It had a bitter strong flavor, and since Etta did not drink wine anyway, it would be difficult to down even the first small portion.

Etta excused herself from the table to wash her hands. As she crossed the room, she felt a curious wisp of air as if someone whispered into her left ear. She peered left and then right, but she could not locate the origin of this strange sensation. She felt a chill rise from her lower back ending at the base of her neck. She had never perceived a sensation as soft and true as this.

She washed her hands and experienced the unique sensation of already having passed into this bathroom before. Etta knew these patterns painted on the walls. She had seen the carvings on the stall doors. She even recognized the feel of the Egyptian cotton finger towels. Here she was, on the verge of something very significant, though she found herself quite alone in this bathroom. Maybe she had snapped. Maybe it was the stress of being stranded and the overwhelming change she was forced to endure in her supposed adventure. Some days it was her adventure, but at dark moments, it was also her nightmare. She felt strangely alone. A horrifically creepy feeling set in, and she quickly returned to the safety of the table with her new friend.

Etta's brain tingled as she listened to conversation, predetermining what would emanate from the lips of the person at her table. She had heard this conversation before. It was recorded somewhere in her brain, in the depths of her memory, and it was playing as a rerun television show might.

Binny excused herself to wash up, and Etta sat at the table in a strange, gray mood of anticipation. As if in slow motion, her eyes spied the tables all around her, and she conspicuously caught a few eyes looking back at her. She watched Binny traverse the carpeted dining room and the many eyes that followed her. One set of eyes did not follow her.

She had difficulty in this surreal state not overtly staring at the man emitting such curious attention. In a flash, she saw his sideburns were longer than average. His wavy black hair was shiny, tamed back by a solution unlike the greasy look sported by their waiter. The Spaniard's brown eyes surveyed the huge aura around Etta and then zeroed in on the target eyes. Their eyes locked across the room, and there was a certainty in his expression that he felt this energy as well.

His olive brown face was unblemished aside from the small mole on his cheek. She blushed and broke the direct chain of energy, ashamed at appearing so interested or so curious about this man in her personal déjà vu.

The spell broke with Binny returning to the seat opposite Etta. This blocked the view and the wave of the spell that connected the two pair of eyes. Unbeknownst to Etta, the waiter had already delivered multiple plates of tapas and condiment items right under her nose during her moment of distraction. Etta hoped that she had extended the courtesy to thank him but could not recall. How strange. The brain tingling returned and then faded.

Binny pointed to one plate and reported, "This little fried delicacy is a gypsy pork roll. The other is Galician octopus, and the one close to you is mussels vinaigrette." She quickly added, "Bon appetite!"

These were not items that Etta would have been brave enough to order on her own. She read the classic tapas list of almonds, olives, and potato omelet, all listed bilingually. There were fried tapas, cold dishes, and hot tapas, too. She read on the menu that she was, in fact, an *extranjera*, or foreigner. Setting the menu aside, she began to sample the unusual plates and found all to be palatable except the pork rolls. Funny thing, too, since that was what she had predetermined to be the safest culinary item of the three selections.

Her body was back to normal, but she wondered why she had had such a strong experience. Etta opened her mouth to share, and then she consciously closed her lips after a warning signal in her brain deemed it too sacred to offer aloud.

Conversation and her first foray into Spanish culture proved she was entirely out of her element. The décor and foods in no way resembled what she knew of Mexico. They set their napkins onto the table after finishing the "drunken cake" with coffee. It was midnight, an hour Etta rarely experienced "alive," being an intrinsically geared morning person. "Strange how people eat their dinner so late in this establishment. Most fine dining rooms would have closed a few hours ago," Etta calculated. Seeing the sign near the cashier, she realized they would not close for another two hours.

Though Binny and Etta had conversed on a broad plethora of topics, Etta remembered nothing of the conversations. Burned into her recall were the architectural details, the cuisine, and the brown eyes she sensed were burning her back as Binny and she made their way to the door.

The two collected their wraps from the coat check and paid the bill with a stiff tip for the attentive, professional waiter. Binny set a box intended for Etta onto the counter as she waited to be queued to surrender her parking ticket. It appeared to be a ring box with small ribbon carefully fixed to all six sides of the box and erupting in a puff of ribbons at the top.

Binny explained, "Mum told me about your bracelet project. I thought you might need a little woolie to remind you of your Colmore friends. I have wool makers on staff who shear, card, spin, dye, and then weave it for the tourists. It's quite fascinating, really. I hope you can pay us visitation very soon."

Etta carefully opened the box, which contained a darling little horned sheep. The charm was formed so the curly wool coat ran from the sheep's upper leg up over the head and back.

"Oh Binny, what an unexpected surprise! A lovely evening after a tragic beginning, and this? It's absolutely the loveliest memento. Thank you *so much* for everything—for the whole evening."

"You're welcome. Come now, the boys will be wondering what's up with us. *You*, my dear will stay carside while I go hunt them down."

"Understood," Etta responded as her laughter rang through the air and made its deposit into the ears of the Spaniard with the powerful eyes. His ears tingled, and he bowed his head over his clasped hands as he rested his elbows on the table in front of his empty espresso cup.

Once the women collected the Mini, they waited while a street sweeper slowly performed his duties across the street they wished to enter. A pedestrian swaggered on the pavement, obviously returning home from some pub. They turned left and accelerated just after the "Reduce Speed Now" sign posted on the straightaway.

True to her word, Binny parked way in the back of Disco 21's parking lot and left the heater on while she, alone, entered the club to hunt down the boys. Etta studied the curly sheep and watched her breath form in small clouds in front of the collar of her wonderfully warm coat. She wished now she had brought gloves.

Surprisingly, Binny emerged through the sea of cars with both Arthur and Jeremy in tow. Apparently, the scene was weak, and they had not enjoyed many prospects. They gave up and drank a few before resigning themselves to calling it a night despite the fact the club stayed open until six in the morning. While they appeared sleepy, the ladies were energized.

Safe in the privacy of her bedroom, Etta worked through the evening keeping the pencil busy. The notes from the evening seemed unreal, even strange. Etta then spent an restless night tossing and turning under a light sleep. Her stomach was upset from the rich food consumed so late at night, and her mind was troubled with confusion and weird, short dream sequences.

Chapter 12
SPLITTING HARES

While not excessively spiritual in nature, Etta felt compelled on Sunday to return to a solemn, quiet study of scripture. She felt physically and emotionally exhausted from the fitful night. Geraldine had up and left before six to visit family, and while she was cognizant of her departure, Etta was unable to drag her body out of bed until eleven. She shuffled across the house in her pajamas, resolving to stay in them all day and work on laundry tomorrow or Tuesday night. That threw her schedule off somewhat as she had but a limited supply of clothing and undergarments to wear.

Into the small but formal parlor, she hunted through the three walls of cabinetry, filled to the ceiling with wondrously varied books. These bookcases and Geraldine's literary habit shrunk the room by good measure, but she didn't entertain in the room, anyhow.

There was an order to the books that Geraldine had briefly explained to Etta early in her tenancy. She could not remember what the system was, so she just foggily ran her eyes across each shelf with her head cocked to the side to read the titles of the select hardback, paperback, and antique literary pieces in the surprisingly large collection.

She found several books on various religions, but those did not interest her. Etta aspired to find the *source*. She found an elderly family Bible, quite oversized and with hand-colored illustrations, which would help fulfill her quest. Never having read the Holy Book cover to cover, she did not know where to start. In the past, she played a spiritual lottery with her deity by opening to five random pages, which she would study in earnest for secret messages. More often than not, she found a passage or section that pertained to her issue. This was a tough bill today with the issue at hand being simply "clarity."

The first lotto she turned to was in 1 Corinthians 12:8–10. Etta studied the list of spiritual gifts. She pondered wisdom, knowledge, faith, healing, miracles, prophecy, discerning of spirits, speaking in tongues, and the principal of love. She marked this place, but she was unsure how this had anything to do with clarity. Not knowing where she could locate bookmarks, she substituted five facial tissues to mark her scriptural journey.

The next tissue landed in the book of Acts 18:3. She was certain that the tent-making occupation detail had little to do with clarity.

Tissue three was secured between the pages containing Hebrews 13:1–8. Harsh as it read, Etta was curious about angels that may walk among us "unawares." Then a faint hymn memory slowly emerged into lyrics in her mind as if the one begot the other.

Give the winds thy fears; Hope and be undismayed; God hears thy sighs and counts thy tears; God shall lift up thy head. Through waves, and clouds, and storms, He gently clears the way; Wait thou his time; so this night soon end in joyous day.

The pilgrim hymn seemed as spiritual as scripture, and it filled her heart with an intense hope.

Tissue four found Isaiah 40:31, which itself she knew as a hymn from her childhood church home.

But they that wait upon the Lord shall renew their strength; they shall mount up with wings as eagles; they shall run and not be weary; and they shall walk, and not faint.

Etta hummed aloud the tune she had memorized in her youth.

The final tissue marked Revelation 17:5–7. Etta was disgusted by the image of the drunken, bloodstained harlot, and though it did not seem relevant, she left the tissue on this page as well and reviewed the five sections again, trying to be open for any wisdom. None assuredly came, so she returned the Bible with the marked scriptures back where she found it, feeling insatiably curious and unfulfilled.

With the run of the flat in Mrs. Bonneville's absence on this cold November day, Etta reclined in the formal chair in a most peculiar fashion. She swung her legs over one arm and propped her back on the other arm with her head resting against the back of the chair. It felt as if the chair was coddling her like a child. She played with the hem of her pajamas in a numb, meditative state for nearly an hour. Then, for no apparent reason, she began to cry. First came large tears pouring down her cheeks, progressing to muffled sighs, followed by full-blown wailing and sobbing. She cried until there were no more tears and her head banged in a rhythm that she might have enjoyed dancing to last night, but at the moment it was disabling and painful.

She dragged her exhausted body to the loo and sat on the pot for what was an unnecessarily long time. When she stood and flushed, Etta studied her puffy, distorted, face. It appeared red, worn, and damp, much older than her years.

Too much. She returned to her little room, with her little dresser and cozy little bed. She pulled the covers several feet over her head and curled herself into a fetal position, where she instantly fell asleep. This slumber was heavy, dark, and devoid of thought. Etta did not often experience this state of consciousness; it was probably like what a boxer might feel when knocked unconscious. It was darkness, pure and true.

She could blame one toe for waking her from the hard sleep. It was the only part of her body not hidden beneath the covers of the warm, safe, cavernous haven. From the fading sunlight cast upon the closed curtains, she estimated it to be nearly dusk.

Etta had slept away the day, and even the flannel pajamas were weary of the demanding duty imposed on them this day. She heard no one—a good sign that she would be alone with the house until Monday. Apparently, the homesick feeling, coupled with no communication from home, had significantly intensified her sad mood.

She stripped and placed her clothing into the wash. There was only time for one load, so she combined several fabrics into a load and washed it delicately in the hope that no dye would run and no article would shrink. She sat alone in her bedroom, shivering naked beneath the covers in a poetic temperament. Etta pulled out her trusted and constant companion, the journal. The fabric tumbled and washed while Etta wrote and wrote. She poured her thoughts and expressions through the writing instrument onto the pages, pausing only to put the clean clothing into the dryer. She wrote until the load needed ironing and folding and her arms were spent.

Fearing the worst, she pensively retired to bed. Her body celebrated the rested state she gave it with rewards of calm, tranquil rest and peaceful dreams.

༶

On Monday, Etta continued her work routine, caring for her cherished plants. They somehow comforted her with feelings of "home." It was so cold outside that she had to monitor the temperature closely, especially during crowded times when many guests visited in a short period. The double doors brought in a frigid deposit of air that endangered the plants nearest the entrance. Etta was protective of her charges but especially enjoyed showing the children her treasures during their field trips.

Etta had extracted a number of small offspring and transplanted them into red clay pots that only especially good children (that would be *all* children by her definition) could look at close up with Etta's tool kit. The collection of tools Etta requested of Larkin was an easy sell. He loved the direction this inventive skit might take.

Lana had warmed up to Etta considerably since she began to address Mrs. Ingle by only her first name. She was delighted that Etta did this privately and never in the company of other staff, which could perhaps diminish the control factor over the other members at the botanical gardens. Yes, Lana was pleased with Etta's work with the children also.

Monday, Lana came with a school group to observe Etta's tour. She spoke in a kind voice, from her knees, being sensitive to the height of small children. She opened the colorful toolbox, which was actually a delightfully gaudy makeup storage box. She asked one child to use the tweezers to pull off a spine from a potted baby barrel cactus. Etta pulled out dark black paper and showed all of them with the strong magnifying glass the hooked barb on the spine, to which the children responded with a chorus of, "Ooo!"

She let another child puncture an aloe vera plant with an eyedropper and pull out a small amount of pulp. Etta added the "magic chemical" from the chemist's vial (sugar) and a little liquid from the apothecary jar labeled H_2O. With some foresight, Etta always picked a "fall guy" in the school group. The last boy or girl who entered her exhibit, feet dragging with boredom, would be selected as the "fall guy." Etta quickly gave the child private, top-secret instructions before allowing him or her to rejoin the group. After the "solids and liquids" were combined with the eyedropper of aloe vera juice, it was poured into a clear glass. Then, she pulled the "fall guy" forward and invited him or her to drink it. The small children wrinkled their little noses and shook their heads, saying no. The child would then drink the "potion" and pretend to faint to the newly padded floor. The children would scream and gasp until the fallen child popped back up and yelled something to the effect of, "Ta-da!" to which the group would squeal with delight. The finale was educating children on the health benefits of eating specific cactus parts.

Lana was impressed with Etta's floorshow and knew that it helped sell field trips. Word spread in the community that the Birmingham Botanical Gardens and Glasshouses had brought in a female specialist all the way from the American desert to care for their prized exhibit. While Etta knew this to be a gross exaggeration, she went along for the ride, knowing that the increase in children's attendance could have a direct impact on whether they could continue to fund her "consultant fee" grant without the burden of national working papers. The American Embassy had granted her a replacement passport, but Etta wasn't motivated to secure a visa. Etta hoped it would take only a short time to raise the airfare funds required to return home to her family and maybe a new position with A. J. Bayless.

Etta took her break in the gift shop, surveying artificial flowers and discounted last-of-summer merchandise in hopes of cheering her potentially sad disposition. She selected a bunny charm for her collection to anticipate spring. When she stepped forward after the two authentic customers, Kelly refused her bills, stating, "You yav asked for nothen at all, so keep yaw munnoy. Consider this a perk of the job. Alrooight then?"

Etta was grateful for the token of her colleague's good will. Clerk Kelly even offered to mount it for her. The curly sheep was in Etta's pocket, so it too was installed onto the triple links of the sturdy gold charm bracelet.

In the rare privacy of the empty room, Binny's description of Lana was confirmed to be accurate. Lana would discuss intimate matters with Etta in the hopes of working through her particularly broad range of marital issues. Etta, being the good listener she was, simply asked target personal questions that led Lana to answer her own quandaries. Though she was a bright woman, Lana seemed to overestimate Etta's scientific and psychological talents by a significant margin.

With a late night required of her only rarely, Etta enjoyed the time in quiet reflective work. On this particular evening, Etta replaced the babies that had outgrown their pots with new little offshoots. She packed up her tool kit and turned off the light behind her. All of a sudden, she recognized the moon through the glass ceiling and the soft descent of snowflakes gracefully dancing to the ground. She raced back into the room and swung open the two sections of the tool kit to pull out the portable microscope. She raced outside with a glass slide in one hand and the microscope in the other. She allowed only a moment of exposure for the glass slide. She set it in the microscope and ran back into the doorway to illuminate her room.

For the first time in her life, Etta witnessed the wonderful world of snowflake architecture. The flakes melted quickly, and Etta responded by working very fast. She dried the slide on her hip and stuck it again into the snowfall for a second look. She watched the amazing forms melt before her magnified image. She repeated this many times before packing it in for the night. How she wished she could photograph such wondrous patterns!

Regrettably, Etta had played far too long, and the streets were dark, icy, and extremely cold. Still on foot, Etta carefully hiked back through the snow, feeling the extra exertion expended on the pre-shoveled walks. It was sort of like hiking in sand. What beauty there was in this approaching wonderland. There would be more snow to come.

She understood now why she was having such dark moods these November days. While most of her life she enjoyed many hours of sunshine feeding her soul, she now got just shy of two hours of daily sunshine. The depravity of sunlight soured her. She must find a way to combat this.

⁂

There was a note taped to her door when she returned late that night. But she was preoccupied with the task of shedding her coat, gloves, and newly acquired thrift store snow boots in the foyer. Winter demanded additional undressing time for this rookie.

Immediately thereafter, she collected the note. It was a message to phone Binny at a number she did not recognize. It was long distance, and Etta had never requested such privileges of her landlord. She pondered this and walked into her room, where she found a letter propped up on her pillow. Mail! It was the first piece of mail she had received. She leaped across the room onto the bed—not really an impressive feat due to the size of the room—and snatched the letter.

She ripped open the envelope with the edge of her finger, smearing a drop of blood on top of the correspondence from procuring a paper cut on the crisp, cream stationery.

Dear Etta,

We miss you! We were surprised that you were going to stay and wondered if that had anything to do with your friend George. Did he accompany you to the dinner?

Chuck is going to marry Kim in January at Saint Luke's Catholic Church, and he wondered if you would be home by then to help out. Now that you wear a Catholic medallion, does that mean you are going to join the Catholic Church? He has talked about going to England on his honeymoon.

What is London like? You haven't said a word about it. And what are you eating? I can't believe you are living on baked beans and shoe-leather beef!

Billy wondered when you would be back because they can't hold their marketing job opening forever. What do you want us to tell him?

We wish you would come home for Christmas. We certainly can't afford to come see you. I wish I could be a mouse in your suitcase, Etta. I wonder what you see each day.

Be happy, be safe, and come home soon.

Love,
Mom

Hi Sis!

Thanksgiving was really different this year without you. We didn't even make a turkey. We bought a turkey loaf but then ended up going to Sambo's for dinner. Neither of us ordered turkey, anyhow.

My car broke. Expired. Deceased. We buried it. So I bought a foreign car. It's a Datsun. Chuck helped me pick it out 'cause they are built well and never break down. It's not new, but it was in good shape except for the interior roof. The owner maintained the car well, but he smoked like a chimney! We have used a few buckets of Lysol but still have not removed the stench.

Kim's really jealous of Chuck. She thinks he has something for you because he asks us how you are all the time. When he told her he was hoping to go to England for their honeymoon, she hit the roof! They didn't talk the whole weekend. I don't think you will see them there.

Is there any reason for us to come see you? I mean, is it all that wonderful? I don't know where we could get the money, but we could sleep on the floor of your room or something.

I'll sure miss you for Christmas. You know me. I already have your presents bought. I'll save them for when we see you. I miss you a lot. Mom is still pretty sad you want to stay, but geez, what a lucky duck you are!

Do tell more about your George. Sounds tantalizing. (Send under separate cover, please.)

Love,
Abby

Etta chuckled at the confusing tone of the letters and resolved to clarify many things when she wrote next. For now, she clutched the letter to her chest, closed her eyes, and said to nobody, "Thank you!"

She felt the charms resting on her chest and visualized the rabbit. Etta searched for the new charm between her fingers, thinking of the privileged state of hibernation. *If I can just make it till spring. If I can just make it though the dark months,* and she completed the thought with a sigh.

Etta couldn't possibly call this late. She would use the pay phone to contact Binny the following day. A long-distance phone call was a courtesy she could not bring herself to request from Geraldine.

Chapter 13
PRINCE CHARMING

Binny woke up in her mother's home with a wicked headache. It was common for her to have access to a glass of table wine, but during the course of last night's dinner, she had consumed her share, Etta's share and then some. Ow. Ouch. She sought the aspirin on ginger feet, appreciating now why Etta did not drink.

Her mum was obviously worshiping at this hour, and as irreverent as it seemed, Binny herself was not interested in maintaining her membership in Edgbaston. She had not heard the phone ring, but she found the message the downstairs maid collected and taped to her door. Ouch. It hurt to even look at the letters. She put the note in the pocket of her robe and carefully set her head on the pillow in hopes the chemicals would more rapidly flow though her bloodstream provided this horizontal position. She dozed an hour or so and awoke with a buzzing brain, which, though not completely comfortable, seemed a vast improvement over the former sharp pain.

Binny rolled over and heard a crunching beneath her. She furrowed her brow and carefully reviewed the prospects. Oh, yes! It was the phone message in her pocket. She recognized neither the name nor the number. The maid had indicated "urgent" on the carefully written note.

Binny stared at the clock, knowing that it would breach any courtesy to phone before ten on a Sunday, but when the clock announced it was just shy of three in the afternoon, she expected it would be acceptable after all.

She carefully dialed the rotary for each number, letting the mechanism freely return to its position before the next digit. On the other end of the connection, the phone rang not nearly to the end of the first tone when an anxious voice picked up the line.

"Hello?" quizzed a male voice.

"Good day, I am Binny Colmore returning a morning call."

"Thank you for attending to my message. I am Roberto Luis Fernandez, owner of Horizon-Tech. We met the second Saturday of November at the Lord Mayor's Show at Guildhall."

Despite a morning-fresh brain, only slightly buzzing at the moment, Binny could not locate that file. She detected an accent, and a business call on a weekend at her mum's home was highly unusual.

"Mr. Fernandez, regrettably I do not recall the privilege of meeting you last month. On what may I blame the pleasure of your call to me?" Binny loved to play men, and fortunately, it came almost effortlessly, providing great leverage in her successful business ventures.

"If you might indulge me, I'm not sure how to explain this to you," the caller began, revealing most certainly that his accent was Spanish in origin.

"Sorry. Let me take this call in the office. Would you mind holding, or would you prefer to phone back?" Binny asked with piqued curiosity about what business opportunity he might propose.

"If you don't mind, I would be pleased to phone you back in a quarter hour," he stated with an increasingly shaky voice.

"All right then. I will prepare for your call, Mr. Fernandez."

Binny set down the heavy black receiver and went up to the small office. Though extremely cold and windy outdoors, the heater was working well, thank God, and she draped her luxurious embroidered silk robe over the back of the leather office chair. Sitting down, she recalled the treasured childhood moments when she would run into her father's office (the smaller of the two in this estate) and cozy up to him, attempting to form her first letters. She smiled at the memory and relished in the familial comfort the old chair still provided for her.

From the desk, she removed a yellow legal pad, fading with age since few people used this office or supplies anymore. The fountain pen within her reach contained a red cartridge, which would have to do. It was just such an awful color—the color the teachers would humiliate her with during those fitful grammar days.

Ah yes, *those* days. The days she wanted not to recall when she took her 11+ examination. She had been decreed "grammar school material," while her brothers were all "upper school secondary" placements. Maybe that's why she learned to be the scrapper and her brothers just assumed the world owed them. She loved all her brothers but resented that she was not entitled to their same educational benefit. They tried to sell her on the "same but different" line, but Binny would not buy into that notion. The red ink represented the magnification of humiliation for not making the cut to "upper school secondary."

Returning to happier thoughts of her father in this office and the items on the desk that he had handled, the phone suddenly broke the spell. She let it ring once for effect and then picked up on the second ring. "Binny Colmore," was all she said, knowing who the caller would be.

Silence. "Uhm, is Joseph at the house?" asked the forced, youthful-sounding voice on the line.

"No." And Binny hung up the phone. She didn't need to be so rude, but Joseph made bad choices in girls, and no doubt this was another waif he met last night. *Maybe we should have dragged him along, even with Etta's disapproval,* she pondered. Etta was a real catch, just what he would need to pick him up by his bootstraps. Trouble was, Etta didn't treat Joseph like the god he thought himself to be.

When the phone rang again, Binny answered with more reserve. "Hello?"

"This is Roberto Fernandez. May I speak with Miss Binny Colmore please?"

"This is she."

"You answer your own phone?"

"Not usually. Although I don't keep paid staff at me mum's."

"Ah, I see." Now Roberto felt self-conscious for calling her at her holiday home.

"What can I help you with, Mr. Fernandez? And may I ask if this is business or pleasure?" Binny quizzed into the sleek business phone.

Roberto began tentatively. "This week while I was dining at Circo with two prospective clients, I saw you dining there with a woman I recognized. I quite understand this is very forward of me, but can you tell me just who you were dining with?"

"And just what affiliation do you share?" Binny responded with a fairly harsh tone, feeling hurt this call was not about *her*.

"None," replied Roberto honestly. "It's just that I had seen her before, and I wanted the opportunity to be introduced to her. Unfortunately, my negotiations precluded that, and I've been unable to sleep because I regret not approaching your table." "Hmm…" Binny allowed him room to clarify the request or hang himself.

"If you do not feel comfortable telling me your association with her, would you at least tell me where I might have passed her company?" he asked, feeling the reservation thickening on the line.

"Have you actually met this woman, Ricardo…"

"Roberto Luis Fernandez."

"OK. Yeah. Have you met her, or what?"

"Please understand, Miss Colmore, I am not some Joe off the street. I have reputable company interests and run among many of the same social links as you. So you have no reason to withhold some biscuit, so *go* on!" Roberto's voice shook with anticipation and a hint of frustration.

"Fair enough, Mr. Fernandez. But I will ask that you do *not* tell her how you found her. The truth is, she is a botany specialist of some sort at the botanical gardens. That is all I will offer you since this is not a business venture. You may introduce yourself if you want to meet this woman."

"Is that the Birmingham Glasshouses?" Roberto asked, with hope returning to his voice.

"Yes," she replied flatly, hoping he was not a perv or something. *If* he was who he claimed, she knew of the company as she had recently solicited bids to automate her accounting system. It seemed a safe wager, especially if Etta could not blame the introduction on her.

"May I ask what section she works in…and…ah, her name?" Roberto hopefully requested.

"No and no. I'm sorry, sir. I believe you have enough to introduce yourself if you are still so inclined. And do I recall we have your bid for payroll services at the Historical Preservation of England?" she asked, nearly as an afterthought.

"I believe we have collected some of the data, but if my memory serves me, we saw fit to trawl a bit more before submitting our written proposal."

"I see. Well, again, please respect my request for anonymity. My interests do not expand to social introductions, you understand," Binny stated with a hint of "don't you dare cross me" attitude.

Roberto accurately read the tone and fully intended to honor the request. No entrepreneurial connection between the two women appeared to exist. Roberto decided he would take a look over the bid for Binny's HPE account personally, in an attempt to repay what she clearly did not feel comfortable sharing.

Before work Tuesday, Etta received an early morning phone summons. Geraldine announced the call loudly. Etta didn't mind since only one phone call per month was an extremely big deal.

"Hello, Etta, this is Binny. I just wanted you to know I had the best time this weekend, and I have to get back to London for some accounting issues. I wanted you to know how to get a hold of me so if you make it to town before I get back to Mum's, you can hunt me down. These numbers are private ones, so don't be intimidated by my secretary. She handles my personal, not professional, calendar. She's a *dream* coordinating airplanes, commuter trains, or pickups."

"That was great, but I hope next time I'll actually make it into the club!" Etta added, bringing laughter on both ends of the line. "When will you return from London?"

"Hell. I don't know. Maybe I'll take Christmas holiday there."

"You know your mother would love that!"

"You should come to London. It's wonderful before Christmas. We can shop for the family. You can find a *special* gift for Joseph, too."

"Yeah, that's a stretch! Well, thank you so much for changing your plans the other night. It's been such a pleasure."

"We'll have some fun in town. Here are my numbers…" Binny proceeded to provide Etta with all her contact information, which in itself was impressive.

Not wanting to be totally outdone, Etta gave Binny her mailing address as well as her work phone and extension. Etta knew she could not take calls at work, but she was banking that Binny would never phone there.

Etta left the house in a chipper mood, ready to face the gray sky and the dismal moods of light-deprived people. It seemed to her that her excessively bright cactus and succulent house cheered people immensely, providing she could captivate them for at least a fifteen-minute exposure. She secretly plotted her "light therapy" by honing her interpersonal skills and slowing her pace of conversation. It seemed to work well, and though it was an admittedly loose social experiment on patrons, she felt there was a notable change in the behavior of those people under her artificial sun therapy.

Roberto sent a telex to his office in Barcelona and announced he would not be returning until Thursday, but only if all else went well in his *negociaciones*. He then phoned his Birmingham office and asked them to hold the Historical Preservation of England bid until he had the opportunity to scrutinize it. They complied without question.

Leaning back in the hotel room wing chair, he felt his heart palpitating excessively while the minutes slowly passed.

He had invested several restless nights haunted by the magnetic spell of those *ojos verdes*.

The gardens would be open soon, but it was not soon enough for a tormented man. Roberto skipped his breakfast and strode to the front desk, whereby the concierge jumped on the phone, knowing the routine. Mr. Fernandez was a regular tenant. He spent more time in the hotel than any other guest. Sparse communication was demanded. He preferred to keep to himself. If he approached the desk, he needed his driver. It was actually the general manager's driver, but when Mr. Fernandez beckoned, it was *his* driver. If he approached the restaurant, the maitre d' had to alert the kitchen to pull out his special request menu, prescribed the first year he was with them.

The driver was waiting at the curb before Roberto buttoned his winter coat. He stepped onto the curb, and the driver hopped out and to the back door, opening it with a courteous, "Top a da mornen, Mr. Fernandez."

Roberto nodded. "Botanical Glasshouses."

"Ood that be the Birmingham Botanical Gardens?"

"Yes, thank you," Roberto retorted with an air of impatience.

"Yes, Mr. Fernandez. The driven toyme wull be approximately fifteen minutes."

This tradition was another Mr. Fernandez expected. His time was a precious commodity, and he selected his commuting projects based on the anticipated arrival time of any given jaunt. Suspiciously, he carried no briefcase this day. He was not known for being the exploring sort, but the driver dared not ask the purpose of this outing, nor did he request the return time. Henry knew that he would be summoned—even out of his bed, at times—to go somewhere to fetch this important client. Not even the general manager would make a request like that.

Though not rewarded with gratuities, Mr. Fernandez occasionally treated Henry to tangible items he would not ordinarily buy with the family budget. He called them "business leverage." He would say to Henry, "I have a gift for you." To Henry, it mattered not that he would acquire these items because Mr. Fernandez didn't like them. If a business deal had been procured, there was a chance Henry would make out with a logo pen set, cuff links, or maybe a leather blotter for a desk he would never own. Nevertheless, Henry and his family enjoyed the surprises and luxury of the various effects he was offered.

"Radio, sir?"

"Not today. Thank you, Henry."

Henry was always pleased when Mr. Fernandez called him by name. Sometimes he would slip, feeling too familiar with the man. If he made a simple comment of conversation, Mr. Fernandez would suddenly act as if he had never met the driver. How dare he speak on equal ground!

Since traffic was exceptionally light that morning, they arrived early, and the garden would not issue tickets for at least twenty minutes. Henry was afraid to ask, but he was aware of this morning's six degrees Celsius temperature. He wisely chose to stay in his driver's seat and not say a word. In the years Henry had chauffeured this man, he had never seen him without music, work, or even paper in his hands. But this time, he was totally engrossed in looking out the window. Henry waited patiently for his cue and kept the heater running.

A busload of young students from the neighborhood walked mitten in mitten across the parking lot, led in the front by their teacher; pulling up the rear was a parent volunteer.

When the children stood in front of the gate, the window opened, as if by magic. That's all Roberto had waited for. He opened the door.

"Let me get that, sir!"

"No need. I have it. I will phone later today."

"As you wish, Mr. Fernandez."

Out of habit, Henry stepped out of the car and closed the door for Mr. Fernandez.

Roberto waited patiently to get in after the collection of children. Patience was not a virtue that Roberto had successfully cultivated. Today he would try very, very hard to be patient, to select his timing wisely, and not to ruin this opportunity.

Gardens are not a terrifically popular place in the winter, and there were only a few elderly people queuing up the line behind Roberto. He summoned them in front of his place to gather his thoughts.

Ticket in hand, Roberto began to get nervous. Maybe this was a very bad idea. How would he know what to say?

Roberto explored the outer grounds, making fresh footprints in the snow. Roaming the barren grounds helped him to find more nerve than when he arrived. He walked back indoors, exploring the drawings in the gallery at leisure, though still alert for the statuesque vision of the woman whose name he did not know. Pausing in the Palm House, Roberto found himself enjoying the collection. He could not remember the last time he slowed down for anything, much less exotic flora in the winter. He clucked audibly and sat on a bench for a short while, just looking around the room in solitude. When he heard the children coming closer, he gave up his seat and moved on to the other glasshouses.

Through the tropics, passing impatiently though the orangery, and approaching the cactus and succulent room, he felt the pit of his stomach tumble in a ferocious moment of nerves. He saw the woman he sought through the glass. She was right in front of him, in the room alone. She was in a standing position, pulling her brown hair back into a ponytail. Yes, her hair was brown. It was sun-bleached, appearing at first glance as if it were blonde. She had a glove in her mouth, and to his surprise, she wore a uniform. The temperature difference made the windows cast a distorted image on the contents of this glasshouse. He was absolutely certain it was her. Roberto turned on his heel and left.

Etta had a quiet morning, entertaining only one school group and a few elderly people on whom she knowingly experimented. When it was time to break for tea, she strolled into the gift shop to see which cheerful stuffed animals still remained in the toy pile. The Friends of the Glasshouses women's group, which Etta knew Greta Colmore was serving in some official capacity, had delivered some new fundraising books for the shop. It was an unwritten law that if an employee borrowed a book from the shop, he or she would use it carefully and return it to be sold as new. Therefore, she would be careful not to force the spine open.

When she sat down in the pavilion to enjoy her fruit tea, she felt a strange feeling overtake the back of her head. She loosened her ponytail slightly, but the tingling ran from the base of her neck up to the crown of her head. It was the return of the strange sensation she had experienced with Binny that night.

She searched the room for the origin of this queer perception but found none. Few people were enjoying teatime, and she tried to distract herself with the illustrated pages of the borrowed book. Only, it was as if she was unable to view the pages, for her eyes saw through the body of the book to a prominent, standing figure. Startled, she turned all the way around in her seat but observed no one in particular. Nevertheless, her heart beat wildly, and the urgency of this familiar energy became unbearable. As if time slowed to a snail's pace, a quiet whisper rushed past her ear. She knew he must be there. She slowly turned to look behind her, and he approached from the rear, cradling a cup of coffee.

"Oh my," Etta said breathlessly. "It's *you*." And her brows rose in curiosity.

"I think I know you," Roberto countered, relieved her revelation confirmed that he was not imagining this amazing power.

"I saw you at that restaurant..." Etta looked directly at the magnetic power in those brown eyes, which drew her in from across the room at last viewing.

"No, I think I know you from before." Roberto felt an amazing energy from this woman, which defied all ideas about lust.

"I don't think that's possible. I'm from Arizona," Etta said, thinking her words sounded stupid.

"May I sit down and join you?" the man asked, recognizing the sudden weakening of his own knees.

"Why, of course. Please."

Etta was intrigued by a hint of a Spanish accent, which sounded so different from the Spanish speakers from Mexico.

"Arizona. Where is that?" he asked, noting that she was an American by her strong accent.

Etta responded nervously with an unnecessarily long answer. "Arizona is a state in a diverse region in the southwestern part of the United States in North America."

Roberto extended his hand. "I am from Barcelona, capital and seaport city in the northeastern region of Spain."

Etta reached across the table and remarked in words that seemed to be replaying from a dream, "I am Etta Johnson."

Roberto took her hand in his and replied, "I am Roberto Luis Fernandez."

He kissed the top of her hand softly and looked back into her beautiful eyes.

Etta's body warmed like electricity zapping from the back of her hand to all her extremities. Her chest actually ached from the amassed energy.

Roberto had obviously felt the lightning as well, and he tilted his head ever so slightly and smiled warmly, crinkling the corners of his deep eyes, and he said, "I am so pleased to find you."

There was no suspicion or question to this comment. Etta felt the same. It was so awkward that this moment would happen in a place where she was entrapped by the dictates of a work schedule.

"May I see you this evening?" Roberto wished vocally in her direction.

"Of course!"

Before her head would explode through the pavilion ceiling, she posed the invitation. "Would you walk me to the cactus room?"

"Of course."

He stood, offering his hand. Neither noticed that the cups of coffee and tea left on the table were full.

The walk back to her station was long and laborious. Her body trembled with the amazing familiarity of this man with whom she had just entrusted her name. Etta was instructed to never introduce herself to patrons by her last name. It was a security issue, one that she followed her gut to breach.

At the door to the Fantastic Cactus Room, the spell was broken with the intrusion of a retired couple enjoying the collection.

"Until then…"

Roberto lifted her hand out of eyeshot of the visitors and kissed it softly.

"Then!"

Etta felt the same rude interruption of the spell being broken.

Approaching the doorway, she watched him disappear around the corner. She took a deep breath, and as she did, he stuck only his head back around the corner and smiled again. Etta burst into laughter; he motioned with one finger to quiet her, and then he slipped away.

Etta returned to her job, unable to wipe the joy from her beaming face. It was an hour before she realized there was no time, no place, no arrangement. That was all right. There was faith.

Chapter 14
CHARMING PRINCESS

Henry was called back to fetch Mr. Fernandez. But first, he was instructed to return to the garden to wait for Etta. He didn't know what she looked like. Mr. Fernandez said he would just *know*.

As employees keyed out and walked past the gate, he parked on the curb as instructed. As promised, it was an easy pick. Etta was an oddity. The woman emerging from the building was tall, slender, and had the regal carriage of a princess. Her darker skin revealed she was not of British stock. How curious. She strolled out as if she were on her way.

"Pardon me. Are yoo Miss Johnson?" Henry knew the answer.

"Yes," Etta stated with anticipation. She did not know how to ask what was transpiring here, but she saw the black limousine with darkened windows parked on the curb. The man addressing her was outfitted in an evening suit, of sorts. She wondered if he was Roberto's personal driver. She became self-conscious, not knowing if she could fit in with the wealthy people she had recently been introduced to. They had obviously amassed a fortune. The upper echelon was foreign to her. What could she discuss? She knew nothing of their ways, means, interests, or manners. Etta tried desperately to hide her panic.

Henry watched the woman with interest. Her movements were deliberate and confident. What a smashing lady Mr. Fernandez had found! She paused on the curb, apparently awaiting the briefing, and Henry complied.

"I yam instructed ter folloo yoo ter yaw hume an' wait until yoo miskin dressed for dinner. I wull deliver yoo ter the Circo in Beeermigem where Mr. Fernandez wull wait yaw arrival. Weege car moy I folloo?" Henry asked.

Etta felt really vulnerable now, exposed as true as a bum in some cold alley. She had no car, no home, and barely any wardrobe to call her own. It was over before it had begun, in her mind. Her eyes began to fill with tears.

Henry had survived a teenage daughter and knew the panic signals girls gave off. He equated the tears he witnessed to his daughter's, and his fatherly radar reported these were not tears of joy.

"If I moight be so forward, lass, what did I soy ter startle yoo?" Henry said using the most patriarchal, kindly tone he could muster.

"I have made a big mistake," Etta started, with her forehead contorting into the furrowed wrinkling of pre-sobbing. "I can't do this! I'm just a gardener!"

"Miss Etta, skeet at me. I werk at the Holiday Hotel as a driver. I knoo yoo mun be bamfoozled by this. Let me fill yoo in," Henry said, quite boldly for his position, and he stepped away from the door of the limo. "Let's walk for a jiffy. What d'ya knoo of this date, Miss Etta?"

"I know nothing!" The first tear fell and froze on her cheek in a painful invitation to the winter wind, which also whipped at the length of hair behind her.

"I saw this man, and I thought I knew him, but that's not possible, and he showed up today, but I don't know how. It's all so intense. It's all so confusing. There is this…I'm just…This is just all wrong!" And now several tears escaped despite the amazing control she willed in order to maintain her tone.

"Okoy then. Yoo doe knoo Mr. Fernandez, but yoo feel strongly for him, d'ya?" Henry recounted to the best of his intuitive ability. He walked her across the brickwork to the cluster of trees that partially blocked the wind from the two unlikely conversationalists.

"I'm not in his class. I'm not even in your class, sir. I am stranded here and am trying to get back to America by working at this garden. I don't even have papers!" That was the truth. That was painful, and she couldn't choke back the first four throaty sobs. She struggled to keep the rest back.

"Ah, missy, that's where you're wrong. Class is 'oo yoo represent yerself. Class is what yoo does for others in yaw breathen space. Yoo yav enough class, an' yoo need ter flaunt it. If yaw heart is true, an' yaw efforts am class, then it don't matter what these bloke yav ter offer. They wull yav ter earn *yoo*."

Etta's head cocked to one side, exposing a damp line intersecting a rosy, chilled cheek. "You think I can fake *this*?" she asked hopefully.

"Missy, I don't fink yoo yav ter rubbish anythen. Be yourself, an' yoo wull charm anyone. An' yaw secret is bostin with me. I yav a code ter folloo. I wull instruct yoo on me code, an' yoo mun observe others around yoo ter break their code, too. *Class* wull draw them, *charm* engages them, an' yaw *code* wull endear them...ter commit."

That made total sense to Etta. Class, charm, code. Now she had a game plan. Now she had a strategist willing to share the logistics of the classes. Maybe she could engage in this remarkably difficult dance. The smile spreading from her eyes through all of her facial muscles indicated to Henry he had rescued another lost sheep. It felt good to be Etta's confidant. He opened the door for Etta, and she entered the lush interior of the manager's car.

Henry left the privacy window open and coached her on the nonverbal behaviors he was trained to respond to. He detailed whom she would directly and indirectly address, as well as issues of eye contact. He explained in detail about the ranks of who's who in an estate using secondhand information from his widowed sister, Lilly, who was on staff with a Staffordshire manor house. Her employers flaunted their wealth, so Lilly was a lively addition to family get-togethers with stories she shared about the goings-on in "that Peyton Place," as she referred to it. Henry generously passed on everything he could offer this young woman for a chance at a better life. He understood the wager to be a hefty one. Perhaps he understood this even better than she.

Henry pulled up in front of Etta's let and instructed her to never allow Mr. Fernandez to follow her home. He instructed her to warn him, "It would not be appropriate," and that should end the matter. He continued to coach her while parked in front of the house, where the vehicle quickly drew the attention of nosy neighbors.

Henry was in no hurry, but Etta was very uncomfortable with all this unsolicited attention, so she requested he return in two hours.

Etta applied her newly perfected "evening look" after a relaxing bath. She had replayed the tape of Henry's instructions over and over in her mind, visualizing what it would be like to perform these acts of ignoring people who were kind enough to wait on her or serve her. Henry explained that was a custom and that these people would not be offended by her behavior but rather would expect it of her. It was becoming clearer, but putting these behaviors into action may take some time. Especially the eye thing. She was quite accustomed to drawing people in with her eyes and then engaging them in conversation.

She slid into the black dress she had worn to Greta's dinner party, aware that Roberto had seen her in the blue dress already. Etta was grateful for the lining in these dresses as she did not own a proper slip to accompany her underclothing. After tonight, Roberto would have seen her entire closet of dress clothes. How would she ever pull that off? She had some time, some places to hunt, and some arrangement forming with her newly developing problem-solving talents. The tights with the red polished hole at the thigh would have to last just one more evening. Saturday, she would have to get to town to invest in details. Etta would not ask Margaret for her company on this trip. She would not understand the urgency in Etta's demeanor.

She checked her image in the mirror and practiced a new style with her hair in the remaining half hour before the arranged pickup. She loosely secured a ponytail and used wisps of braided hair to dangle as a second tail. It was not as becoming as the vision she had in her mind, but she heard the doorbell and, in her innate urgency, forgot that help was to wait for *her*. She took the entire collection of braids and wrapped them securely into a bun. Etta flew down the stairs with bobby pins still between her lips.

Henry stood in the doorway and shook his head. "We need ter werk a lickle mower on the manners. Don't let anyone see yoo ert of yaw own room until yoo get that 'finished look.' Remember, doe address me unless yoo miskin certain that naaa un can see yoo or hear yoo. The boss's missis told me that on me driv' with 'er."

"The boss's wife? Roberto is married?" Etta bristled.

"Naaa, lass. I werk for the hotel Mr. Fernandez lives in a bostin share of the year. Ee 'as business in other countroys an' owns sum techno-gizmo place eya. Me boss is a Brum; I driv' for the gaffer. Ee lends me at beck an' call as a courtesy for Mr. Fernandez's patronage."

Etta's shoulders relaxed back down, and she put the last bobby pin in place. She had no idea what her hair looked like in back, but it would be out of her face, which was the whole point of the hairstyle. Soon she would have to learn that vanity was more important than function for this new turf.

"Are we picking up Roberto?" Etta asked, still having trusted there was a plan, though nobody had let her in on one.

"No, I dropped him at Circo before I picked yoo up frum werk," Henry began, intending to share more had Etta not interrupted him in both speech and thought.

"You left him there for the past *three* hours?" Etta demanded, feeling horrible that she had kept him waiting.

"Trust me, missy. Mr. Fernandez is a busy geezer. Ee 'as a woy of busyen himself wherever ee is. I knoo."

"Humm," was all Etta could respond, still not sure how this would go. She sat back and was pleased she was not carsick at all with the lights streaming at her in the traffic. This was a real treat—her first limousine ride, and it was for a first date. People overtly stared at the vehicle, wondering what famous person passed them. Could it be Ringo? Royalty? The Duke of Westbourne? Little would they ever suspect the passenger was common, stranded Etta from Oz.

With the darkened windows and the window opened between them, Henry continued to give Etta tips for the evening. Etta was a quick study and rehearsed his suggestions in her mind with events and people from back home. Chuck and his fiancée played the role of the other couple, yet she had nobody to play Roberto. So she conjured up Ed Earl for his part. Not a pleasant thought, but it was a necessary one to practice her manners. She drew the line on that image when Henry detailed what was an appropriate upper crust departure with the silly sounding cheek kissing. Etta had never seen one, couldn't visualize it, and rather didn't know if she could pull one off.

Circo came all too quickly, and Etta's nerves were on the edge of her finger and toenails. She thanked Henry immensely for his efforts to help her. He had given her his solemn word that he would not reveal what he had learned about Etta to Mr. Fernandez. He had *not* said he wouldn't share the chronicles with his own family, who delighted in the adventures of their family patriarch, vicariously playing out this otherworldly life with the people he came in contact with.

Henry went straight for the curb and stepped out to take her door while the doorman sat waiting his turn. The doorman took her by an elevated hand and escorted her into the dining room, where she was picked up by the maitre d' to seek out her companion this evening. She didn't need visual confirmation, for she felt the energy calling her from a private room opposite where she had sat during her first Spanish dining experience.

Suspiciously, this side room was empty except for the table awaiting her, but the dining room was filled to capacity and there were people waiting. She assumed Roberto had some type of monetary power over these people as well.

Roberto did not need to see her approach, for he knew she had arrived when the whisper flashed past his neck as Henry arrived in the parking lot.

He instinctively stood, even before he saw her approach. Roberto cleared the table of several hours of unfruitful attempts at work and clasped his hands behind his back. When Etta entered the room, she was the most elegant woman Roberto had ever been in the company of.

She was stunning. Her curious, erect posture and sensual gait contradicted her classic attire and amazingly unique coif. Even her makeup could not detract from those eyes. Those green eyes had a death grip on his heartstrings, and he could not imagine how the recent series of strange events could take place in his rather routine world.

Etta was drawn across the room more as a floating motion than the movement of her own feet. Roberto's eyes drew her to the table, where he stood gallantly waiting for her. She let go of the arm that escorted her and extended her hand to him. He took it and reached for the other as well. Drawing them both up, he kissed both of her hands, and Etta flushed, relieved now that she was being indulged in this private room.

Etta felt something she could not deny. She was in love with a stranger. She felt this emotion reciprocated as well.

Without so much as a kiss, Roberto had fallen in love with the foreigner the evening his business negotiation was ruined by her electric presence.

Roberto's first glass of wine offered only surface "get-to know-yous." The second glass of wine came with the *ensaladilla de mariscos* that Etta selected from the waiter's recommendations. Etta continued to decline the waiter's wine offerings. He was good to allow them ample time between his service.

From two opposite parts of the world, two people came together and melted with heat as sure as colliding stars. For despite the differences in their national customs, worldly condition, and personal aspirations, they were meant to meet somewhere in time. This was the time. The stars had found each other and aligned. Tonight Etta and Roberto shared the notion that they individually, and jointly, experienced the start of something very raw and exciting. Destiny.

Dinner was simply a sideshow to the main event. Etta played listener more than conversationalist, revealing facts but not depths. Roberto learned about her family makeup and the city from which she came, but not of their circumstances and challenges. He learned of her college experience, but not her tenure bagging groceries. He learned about her garden position, but not her plight.

Conversely, Etta learned about Roberto's privileged upbringing, the family, and the extended units of assistance. He knew his nanny far better than he knew his mother. The collection of servants got credit for grooming him for manhood since his father was busy with his *politicos*. His tutor received credit for the solid foundation of knowledge that brought him to Cambridge University. *Papi* gave Roberto a set purse by which to establish his business interests. He had wisely split the money, organizing a company in Birmingham, which at the time was appropriately nicknamed the "workshop of the world," coupled with interests in the city in which he grew up, Barcelona. Roberto felt obliged to emulate his father's philanthropic contributions by providing support, service, and income to both of these communities.

Etta unabashedly studied details of Roberto. His hair was wavy, and his eyes were soft. The wrinkles around his eyes revealed he was older than Etta was. Still, his hands were soft with groomed nails, explaining he knew no labor. His collar was so stiff that it nearly appeared uncomfortable to Etta. When he crossed his legs, Etta could see socks with intricate patterns run out of the highly shined leather dress shoes. Although the toe was more pointed than she was used to seeing on men, they were as "elegant" as a man's shoe could be.

Roberto studied and fingered the charms on Etta's bracelet. He was fascinated with it, not having seen women in his circle wear such unfinished works. He thought it very bohemian of Etta to wear a "work in progress" and promised he would add *un amuleto de oro* upon their next encounter. She did not elaborate on her private talisman, the purpose for each trinket, or how holy a thing the bracelet was to her. It was her only tangible connection to home. The charms were not spaced evenly anymore with the recent addition of two new pieces. The unbalanced weight was what turned the bracelet every so often so it never really appeared to be the same. She loved that. Etta also appreciated that it was an evolving collection.

Roberto studied Etta, not suspecting her challenges in life. Roberto recognized that she carried herself in a manner that turned the heads of many in whatever room she commanded. He wanted her right then. He wanted to know she felt the same. He was pleased that she found no fault with his Spanish accent or in the long orations he gave to explain his insignificant, specific thoughts. He wanted her before someone else discovered this rare gem.

The three-course dinner and dessert was a wrap, but neither Etta nor Roberto was willing to call it an evening. They decided to stroll, a brave inclination considering the bitter weather.

They collected their coats while the restaurant manager himself saw the couple out the door. Etta noticed several details that impressed her. While Roberto never actually spoke *with* the waiters, he was never unkind or demanding. During the final course, he had made special efforts to hand tips directly to the various servicemen who waited on the table. He offered a generous tip to the chef when he made a special appearance to check on the couple's main course. And he left a final tip with his bill. The behaviors Henry described were accurate. *Be neither attending, nor rude. Just be a woman of grace,* she thought.

The change in color of Etta's cheeks was apparent even through her makeup. She was bitter cold and struggled to manage her body temperature to remain on this wonderful date with this sumptuous man. She could fight it no longer when she lost most of the sensation in her feet and realized she was in danger of falling at any second, not knowing just where her feet were stepping.

Roberto did not want it to end either, and he found a corner pub to shelter them from the cold. He took her upstairs where it was warmer, but the service was slower.

This turned out to be not altogether a bad thing, and they were treated to several more hours sipping their coffee and cider, uninterrupted.

The awkward part Henry had warned Etta about raised its fearful head and came to pass as the late hours shifted into the early morning of a promising new day.

Henry was summoned from his bed to pick up his regular guest and the lovely lady he felt fond enough of to help negotiate this challenging course. Knowing what would happen, he brazenly asked, "Where may I drop you, sir?"

To which Roberto responded, "Return the lady home, Henry."

Henry could infer by Mr. Fernandez's tone that he was in good spirits and would be able to be approached tentatively.

Etta chimed in first. "Roberto, it would be inappropriate for you to escort me home at this hour. Please have Henry drop you off. Then I will return home."

"Are you certain?" asked Roberto, feeling that he really did not understand enough about her culture to question such a puzzling arrangement.

"Yes," Etta stated, unwavering in her tone.

"Home then, Henry. Please close the window for us."

"All right then, sir." He responded with the hint of a yawn that only Etta detected.

With the window up, they were afforded total privacy for the first time since they cast their eyes in the direction of love. Roberto was afraid to ruin the moment and proceeded with great caution. Etta was aware of the level of privacy this opportunity provided, and she asked Roberto, "May I kiss you?"

Roberto did not answer. He stared into her eyes for a long pause before he leaned over and positioned her more in front of his chest. He held her face in his hands, and he gently kissed her on the lips. His hands moved around her shoulders, and she encircled him with her arms. She stated the obvious.

"I found you."

"Don't ever let go," he replied.

And with this kiss, they traversed deeper in affection, caressing side to side in the smooth dance of expert lovers.

All too quickly, they arrived at the hotel. Roberto kissed Etta once more on the lips and held onto her bottom lip for just three seconds more before Henry let him out. Roberto slid something into the man's hand. Etta believed this to be his tip. Henry closed the door and returned to the driver's seat on the right side of the limo. He opened the window and asked simply, "Oo did yoo does the'er, Etta?"

The big sigh. "It went well. I am so grateful to you for your coaching. Promise me you will teach me more. I obviously have many things to learn!"

Henry said, "Consider this yaw finishing class." He chuckled, knowing he still had much to share with this woman, who had proved herself to be a promising subject to break through those tightly bordered classes. "See yoo soon, Miss Etta," he called after she approached the door of her residence.

Etta glanced at the clock on the way into her room. She skipped the shower, figuring she would have to get ready for work in four hours anyhow. For a morning person, Etta was alarmingly bushy tailed, so she went about trying to clarify some of the confusion at home.

She plopped onto her bed with her tablet propped on the pillow as she wrote.

```
December 1, 1974
Dear Abigail and Mom,
    I'm so pleased to hear about Chuck
getting married. No, I can't come for
that. Tell Billy I have to respectfully
decline the invitation at this time be-
cause my future is uncertain here.
    Now is the best time for you two to step
out of the desert. You have lodging here,
and all you need is a plane ticket. I can
```

tell you in countless ways why it would be fun to come to England. The canal boats, music, the afternoon tea, chocolate, and the gardens! Always gardens and plants and green! It would be a life-changing opportunity for our family. I rather like living here.

Etta put her pen down a moment, thinking that especially now she really, really enjoyed living here with an interesting situation fast developing. She chewed on her pen and continued.

I never went out with George. He has a girlfriend, and though he helped get me settled in, we have no interest in one another. But I did meet a man this week from Spain. Roberto is ridiculously successful but a wonderful, thoughtful man, too. Funny thing is that, though I have not known him very long, I feel like we have a lot in common.

We went on a nice dinner date, and I hope to see him this weekend again.

I won't tell you much about London yet, but I plan to take more time some weekend before Christmas with my friend Binny. We tried to go to a disco here one night, but it didn't work out. She went back to London, so maybe we will try that again next month when she comes home.

I have sporadic bouts with my journal and have had much opportunity for reflection. No poetry to speak of. Just observation and experiences right now. My mind is almost on overload from new experiences and sensations, and I could fill books if there were more hours in a day.

I wrote and created a little floor show for children at the garden. Teachers really like the educational benefits. I find it's great practice working with the little ones.

The children always say I talk so funny! Yet I hear people say things like, "I'll just snatch a bacon butty in a High Street caff." And they think WE sound funny! I am getting much better not laughing aloud when I hear such strange expressions. I have quite an ear for the local dialects. I don't know the difference in where they come from, but I can tell if they aren't from this Birmingham area.

I am thinking about buying a camera so I can show you a few important buildings and people I cannot fit on my charm bracelet. It would be nice to put photos with my journal notes, too.

I do wish you would save up and come here very soon. Maybe I can send some money home to help with the tickets?

                    Love and miss you,
                    Etta

Etta folded the letter into the envelope and set it on her lap. Staring at the walls for a few minutes, she replayed the visions that she didn't share with her family. She reviewed the activity of the week and retrieved her journal. Pages and pages, and then sleep finally came.

Chapter 15

EMPANADA

The cold and the brief slumber made Etta sluggish at work. Every motion took considerably more energy than usual. After the first hour, she eased into a slower pace and decided not to tax herself. She turned to check on the vulnerable plants near the door and discovered an enormous red rose with predominant thorns resting next to the door. She smiled, thinking that somehow, someone snuck in while she was working. An hour later, another long-stemmed rose appeared inside the door. She didn't catch the culprit. Another hour passed, and she waited and watched. Nothing. She returned to work and heard the door and a quiet scurrying. There was a third. She stepped out into the cold but observed no one suspicious and certainly could not sense Roberto in the proximity. When she returned inside, there was yet another!

At irregular times now, roses were appearing just inside the door, but the person delivering surely must be very quick, for she could not catch the person in the act. When she was ready for tea, she located a large vase that would hold the ever-growing bouquet of aromatic flowers. Returning to her glasshouse, she caught the culprit red-handed. It was a small child with a plaid fabric cap. He didn't appear to possess sufficiently warm clothing, so Etta invited him in.

Etta squatted to her haunches and asked, "Who sent you here?"

"A man," the boy replied.

"What is the man's name?" Etta teased, knowing the answer.

"Larkin, like a bird," came the surprising answer.

The boy dropped the last few roses to the floor and ran before Etta could quiz him further.

Etta hunted for Larkin with many questions in her mind. He had been very clear with her that he was not interested in her romantically. She had never led him on—or had she?

Larkin wasn't in his office, and he wasn't having tea. Nobody had seen him, and Etta was beginning to pull her hair out with frustration over the peculiar situation she found herself in. Etta began to return to the glasshouse after spending her entire break on the hunt for Larkin. The shop clerk, Kelly, interrupted her journey.

"Etta! Cost ye cum in a minute?"

"What's going on? Have you seen Larkin this afternoon?" Etta asked, trying to catch her breath.

"Naaa. Sorry. I was asked by a well handsum geezer ter deliver this ter yoo before yoo caggy werk todie."

"Really...," Etta said with genuine curiosity.

She opened the box and note right there in front of Kelly. The box contained a charm for her bracelet in the half-moon shape of an empanada, in the likeness of those she ordered last night. The note said it was to commemorate their first date. It also said that nobody in the Jewellery Quarter knew what an empanada was. He had one custom made in the same method as a real empanada, only using toothpicks to mark the edges where the fingerprints normally were. Etta did not have her bracelet in her possession, or Kelly would have installed it on a link right there.

The note concluded with the news that Roberto must leave for Barcelona Thursday morning, so he desperately wanted to see her before his business meeting concluded that evening. The question was where? When could he send Henry for her? The phone number he left was not the one he had provided to her during their lengthy conversation about how difficult it would be to get a hold of him.

She thanked Kelly and went to Larkin's office. He was still not back, so she took the liberty of using his phone and sitting in his chair. She reached Roberto with one phone call to a receptionist, who patched her through to his secretary, who then put her on hold for a few minutes.

Etta had gotten a little too comfortable during the wait and positioned herself with feet propped carefully atop the various desk papers. Lana stepped in, expecting to see Larkin.

"My, my, Etta, this office does look good on you!" Lana said, teasing her.

Etta smiled and exaggerated the image even more by leaning further back, crossing her legs, and stretching, feet still rested on the Larkin's neatly organized desk.

"All you need is a cigar!" Lana excused herself, laughing right out into the hall.

Finally, Roberto was on the phone. He was curt and obviously in the middle of something, but there was urgency in his voice to settle on a time and place for her. OK. It would be five thirty, in work clothes, at the Digbeth fish and chips.

Etta managed to close up shop before speaking to Larkin about the beautiful and unexpected bundle of roses. "Rats!" she scolded herself. She had forgotten them at work! She spent more time there than anywhere else. It would be hard on them being in the hot room overnight. Maybe she could hike back to work and move them to safety. She jogged back to work, and her lungs angrily demanded Etta slow down in the thin winter air. Etta's sides ached, so she walked with the security guard back into the glasshouse and placed the vase of roses in Lana's office for the evening. She jogged back to the house, where she had no option but to change her sweaty shirt.

Henry fetched Etta from the house, noticing that her hair was a mess and she had not reapplied her makeup. His brow changed to a vision of scorn, and he was visibly disappointed in what he saw. "Lass, are you trying to stomp on a field of four-leaf clover?"

Etta was taken aback. "What do you mean by that?" she asked, with a hint of inappropriate attitude in the tone that emerged from her throat.

"If yoo expect ter be treated loike a princess, yoo yav ter *be* a princess. Yoo absolutely can't goo ert looken loike a hag."

"A hag?!" Etta replied in shock. "Do I look that bad?"

"No, Miss Etta. It's just that yoo skeet worn frum the doy, an' it is be'ah ter mek the gaffer wait for his supper, than ter throo crumbs on the table."

"So it's better to be late, than to go as I am?" Etta asked, realizing that this new way of thinking about time, place, and presentation was really going to be tough.

"Yes, love. I wull wait with yaw roid, if I moight be so bold."

Etta retreated to the house, realizing that her new shirt smelled sweaty also. Though Etta's sense of urgency made her want to rush through her wash, she fought the urge with a slow shower, replaying Henry's comment over and over in her mind. She recalled how, as a desert rat, she never worried about looks. She thought nobody else did, either. Perhaps she was wrong. Maybe she would have dated more if she had fussed up more. Cleaned up, dressed up, made up. She was embarrassed and confused. How many fields of four-leaf clovers had Etta already stomped on?

She wore simple slacks and a white shirt but restyled her hair in a bun and applied work makeup (which is to say, less than dinner makeup). She wore her thrift store winter coat. Apparently, Henry approved, for he said she was lovely and drove slightly faster than normal, which was nerve-racking for Etta, who had not ridden in limos enough to know how safely they would take corners at these speeds.

He dropped her off at the corner, and Roberto emerged from the shop with Cadbury cocoa for her in his mitten-protected hands. He was in casual clothing, but he was as striking as ever.

Etta studied Roberto's deep brown eyes and relaxed brow. She watched his smile bring forth symmetrical lines of joy around his eyes. His broad shoulders and trim waist were unmistakable even beneath his coat. Etta nuzzled up to Roberto's neck and drank in his scent. She kissed him and felt the hair on his neck bristle with excitement.

"Hello there," was all she said. Roberto was momentarily speechless.

The snow was falling, and the wind blew harder. The customers did not mind eating from the cone-shaped papers filled with fried fish and potatoes.

Roberto was out of his element somewhat, but he enjoyed being in Etta's company. The relaxed manner of eating on your feet was a challenging feat for Roberto. Other women in the shop were eyeing him, and Etta felt pleased to be his date. Roberto watched the other men eyeing Etta and felt warm knowing that he had the prize of this room. They made a lovely couple. A striking couple. When they were together, their energy was infectious.

"Fishy breath," Etta teased.

Eventually, the fish house gave way a little elbow room. They were facing each other with scant more than a foot between them to eat and visit on their feet, the elevated table between them.

Roberto glowed and smiled with his lips closed over a mouthful of the delicious street food. Now *this* was a real treat for Roberto, who equated it to home cooking. Etta was anxious to cook for him, but it would never happen in Mrs. Bonneville's home. Maybe when Binny returned they could double date in her mother's kitchen? They could prepare and serve dinner to their dates. Etta realized this was pretty middle class in thought. Perhaps Binny didn't know how to cook. She supposed wealthy people did not cook for recreation.

Roberto wanted to be near Etta. His heart had ached to be with her. Now, the bad news. "Etta, I have to leave for Barcelona. I won't be back for a few weeks."

The bomb dropped the news back into her ears, and it sank down into the pit of her stomach. Somehow she thought magic would keep him there. She was not ready to give up this amazing feeling even for a few days. It was a pivotal phase of their relationship, and it was developing all too naturally. What would separation do? Then, with her cursed or charming lack of restraint, it escaped her mouth.

"But…I love you." There it was. It came out unchecked and premature, in Etta's opinion.

"*Ay*, Etta, *mi amor…querida* Etta, I love you also. I have to go. Will you be here for me when I return?"

Although Etta had not understood exactly what he had said, she did recognize the word "amor" a few times, which was promising. Hearing the word love in two languages seemed comforting.

"I will be here. Can you return any sooner?" Etta pleaded.

"No, I have to stay for a conference and for work. I may be back just after Christmas."

"Will you be here *for* Christmas, Roberto?" Etta inquired, with his name rolling through her anxious lips.

"No. I will be home for Christmas. But we will celebrate together," Roberto replied, adding whatever consolation this might afford.

Etta had finished dinner, and her fingers were still greasy. She wiped them the best she could on the paper cone. Roberto was finished with his food though he had not tasted much of it. Oblivious to the crowd around them, Roberto took Etta's hands in his and kissed each finger tenderly. Etta felt the warmth flow deliciously through her body. He took Etta by the hand and out into the cold. They washed their bare hands with clean snow and then stood wrapped tightly around each other, waiting for the car.

When Henry arrived, Roberto was too quick for him, and he opened Etta's door as the car rolled to a stop. He instructed Henry to drive past Victoria Square so they could enjoy the sights. And he requested that Henry raise the privacy window.

Etta sat with her back propped against Roberto's chest. His arms fell around her and rested in Etta's lap, holding her hands. She was fully aware of his excitement to be there, in this moment, with her. She felt a certain glow about them both.

How easy it would be to leave with Roberto right now, Etta thought.

How difficult it would be to take Etta with me right now, Roberto thought.

Roberto adjusted himself and rested his hand in Etta's. Etta didn't want to break the spell and studied every physical connection between them. She was comforted by the arm that caressed her. Etta's right arm moved around Roberto's neck, and he responded with a deep, loving kiss.

He rolled her over and asked, "Etta, will you…?"

"When the time is right."

"Etta, I, ah…have to leave."

Etta was disappointed, for she could have kissed and caressed all night in his arms. Her body rejoiced beside him. The cloud of warmth surrounding them was one of the truest feelings she had experienced in her life. She was certain Roberto felt the same. She also suspected that people in their proximity would feel this soul-deep affection.

Etta was very content snuggling against Roberto's strong pectoral muscles. He wrapped his winter coat around her body. He wondered what it would be like being with this woman who had so quickly, and so deeply, affected him. That wish would have to remain unfulfilled, for now. What was important was they found each other within the expanse of infinite time and space.

Roberto knocked on the window. Henry opened the privacy glass between and asked, "Yes, Mr. Fernandez?"

"Take us home now," he responded. The request was vague enough for Henry to assume that the first drop would be the hotel so Roberto could prepare for his meeting. Etta was dropped next so he could hear the update and offer more instruction to her.

When the limousine arrived at the Holiday Hotel, Roberto seemed surprised. Etta leaned in and kissed him deeply. "I *do* love you, Roberto. Please call me while you're gone."

"I'm *in* love with you, Etta. But you have to know that in order for us to work together you have to let me run my affairs without distraction, or I will never be able to arrange time with you."

He kissed her softly on the lips and then kissed her eyes where he saw tears spilling down her face. "May time pass quickly," Roberto wished to Etta, God, and anyone within earshot. His eyes misted, but he willed the moisture from forming into tears.

Henry pulled out of the lot and left the window open. He complimented Etta on how well she had appeared to conduct herself. She let Henry know how much she appreciated his observations since she did not have a father to call her own.

He gave her only a few pointers, knowing that he would not see her for the next few weeks. Etta asked if she could call him if she had questions. Henry provided Etta with his home telephone, but he insisted she announce herself so the wife would not be worried. Of course. He was first a husband, next a father, and now, a social skills instructor.

She watched the driver pull away and disappear into the snow. Etta was fascinated with the snow. Unlike the raindrops that fell down, snow flew about. The flakes would catch a breeze and sail in irregular patterns across the sky, and when they landed, they shone like diamonds. When it was cold like tonight, Etta could count on a mesmerizing hike to work through the fields of white gems glistening in the morning. She loved watching the snowflakes wisp about her as if they danced in her presence. *"Be* a princess," she would now regularly coach herself. Her pretend snowflake subjects would rejoice around her regal shoulders.

Back in the warmth of Geraldine's home, Etta surrendered her outer clothing and retired to her room. She counted out the money she had saved after her rent and food expenses. She had managed to sock away sixty-four pounds and a jar full of pence that may add another seven to that. It wasn't much in a boutique, but she had found some great clothing at the thrift store. She would need to "dress ahead" now, anticipating more outings of a different sort with the man who said he would like to *provide* for her. Those were not his exact words, but she thought she knew what he meant.

She lay back on her pillow, resting her head against her cocked right arm. Etta thought about the cheesy stories she had heard regarding "love at first sight." She contemplated the physical sensation of being in love. She reflected on how this amazing, magnetic feeling begot such intense feelings for Roberto. She wondered which comes first, love, trust, or lust? Etta decided it must be love, for the thought of making love with this irresistible man had not occurred to her until this night. She felt a deep-seated moral obligation to stand her ground and wait until she was married. Judging by Roberto's family history, she felt sure he would comply, being of a goodly upbringing.

Etta fell asleep in her clothing and woke in the middle of the night, sensing that across the city Roberto was just turning in after his meeting. She could feel him long for her. She sensed his lonely struggle with sleep in the hotel room. Etta hoped deep in her heart that Roberto also felt her presence through tonight.

Thursday morning Etta strolled past the half-timbered home she had admired months ago with its fabulous gardens. With the snow creeping up the base of the home, entirely blanketing any sign of a living yard, it appeared rather like an enormous troll home. It didn't look any more real than a spotted toadstool yard ornament.

Etta passed through the admission door with Larkin, and she asked him straight up, "What's up, Larkin? I thought we were buddies."

"Whatever do you mean?" he innocently responded.

"What's with the roses? I mean, I am really grateful for them, and they are really beautiful, but why now?" Etta searched his eyes for answers.

"Oh, I understand. You are mistaken, though. I wasn't the one to send you the flowers. I was only instructed on how to have them delivered. I was too busy with vendors yesterday, so I hired a boy to hang around and fulfill this duty," Larkin explained.

"Ah, then Roberto sent them," Etta confidently stated.

"No. Just a neighbor. He seems to fancy you."

Larkin enjoyed saying just enough to ruffle her feathers.

"Just who sent them, then?" Etta demanded as her tone announced she was becoming impatient.

"Sorry. Won't tell you that. Sworn to secrecy, I am."

That was that. He would not be swayed; Etta was incredibly curious. Larkin fancied himself holding the upper hand.

Etta collected her vase from Lana's office, where the first four flowers delivered were fully open. The remainder looked freshly delivered since Etta had delayed getting the collection into a proper vase and out of the heat. She chose to display them in the coldest corner in the cactus house entry, where they would be flushed with a winter chill each time the door opened. They were beautiful. How terribly puzzling.

Chapter 16
KEY TO MY HEART

Etta was carefully folding a mixture of soils around her plants by hand, attempting to regulate the pH level. In solitude, Etta preferred the position on her knees, getting intimate with the soils. The close-up smell of her work was great comfort to her, and she remembered days of journal writing under an ocotillo's partial shade with the occasional horned toad pets she kept. Too bad she could not add lizards and friendly snakes to her room. She would love the added burden.

"Special delivery!" Roberto's sensual voice resonated from the door behind her.

Etta shook her head and laughed. "Why do you have to find me butt up in the soil?"

"I rather like your behind view!" he responded as she blushed and whirled around.

"Hey there. You wanna get fresh with me, do ya?" Etta swung around quickly, grabbed him around the neck, and planted a lingering, deep kiss on Roberto that instantly weakened his knees.

He couldn't wait to return from Spain to his little filly. She exhibited such promise. Etta proved by her comments that *she* would dictate the pace of their relationship. Roberto rather liked this refreshing quality in a woman. It certainly was unique, compared to the by-the-book, homemaking-minded habits of the Spanish women he had grown to know.

Self-consciously peering down, he noticed that Etta had rubbed soil onto the front of his suit. His brow furrowed, knowing he did not have time to replace his clothing.

Etta immediately recognized his concern and explained to him, "It's like Tab, Roberto. Don't worry."

"What do you mean, Tab?"

"Tab is a sugar-free pop that we drink in the States. When you spill it, it doesn't stain because it doesn't contain sugar. It doesn't dry sticky for the same reason. So if you have children at a party you treat them to Tab; you don't have to worry about spills because they evaporate. The soil in here is not damp or rich. You can just sweep it off." Etta opened the buttons of his suit jacket and blew directly onto his jacket and shirt. She pulled a small paintbrush from her tool chest and swept the dirt right off. Sure enough, he was fresh and unspotted.

Roberto was surprised with Etta in her element. She was a different, spirited woman in the Fantastic Cactus Room—so hippie, so free with herself. He spotted the red roses, and the heat rose up his neck, making his tie feel as if it was tightening.

"Where did you get those?" Roberto asked coldly.

"I actually can't tell you," Etta responded, entertained that she witnessed this jealous, protective streak in her new boyfriend.

"You mean you *won't* tell me?" he continued, sounding a little more harsh.

"No. I mean I can't tell you because I don't know. A young boy delivered them for some fan, and I have not heard from anyone, nor do I know who sent them. Besides, when I do find this generous person, I will inform him that I am dating you and am not interested. Is that all right with you? I mean, I can't prevent what I don't know, right?"

Roberto grabbed her, allowing a distance between them so he would not have to test her Tab theory again. He kissed her on the forehead and slowly responded, "I suppose not."

He pulled a lovely silver box out of his pocket and gave it to Etta.

She opened it to reveal a charm in the shape of a key. There was a finely constructed hinge on the edge of this one.

Roberto demanded, "Open it, Etta."

Etta pulled the folded skeleton portion apart to reveal the four-word message. She read it aloud, amazed at the intensity of the personal sentiment engraved to her: *"Key to my heart – RLF."*

She was aware he did not want chest-to-chest contact with her soiled front again, but she did lean into him with only her arms and gave him the warmest hug she could muster without sharing her morning project. "Aren't you pleased I don't work with manure in my glasshouse?" Etta teased.

The morning's good-bye lasted four full minutes.

Etta felt emotionally stronger with this good-bye. She would make it work. If he had to sacrifice to be away from her to run his businesses, then she would support him and make it easy for him. She knew this would please him. Etta was pleased with his thoughtfulness. *After all,* she clarified to herself, *charms are for the living, while roses are for the dead.*

She worked a few more hours in solitude. Without the door swinging open, the roses did not get their cool reprieve and wilted in a sad, unfulfilled position. She removed her gloves and pulled all the petals off the stems. She placed them in a garden pot and brought them into the gift shop. She had the bracelet with her and now two more charms. Kelly felt a little envious of Etta for having two suitors. She did not have any at the moment, and her position in the gardens was much more public. It didn't seem fair. After all, Kelly greeted *all* the patrons. As she installed the next two charms on the gold links, Etta complimented her.

"You do such fine work, Kelly. Have you ever thought about creating jewelry?"

"Actually, I yav. I cawn afford the materials, though," Kelly confessed.

"Really..." Etta had a brainstorm. "Would you be interested in being an apprentice in a shop that re-creates traditional gold and silver smithing?"

"It sounds interesten. But where ood I werk?" Kelly asked, cheering some that Etta had such confidence in her.

"The problem is that it's a roving job. You would be based in London, but they travel and set up camps in other cities also."

"Gosh, that sounds excitin'!" Kelly brightened.

"Let me get you an application." Etta began her closure. "Thank you again for working on my bracelet. I owe you for the extra links you've used."

"Don't werrit abart nothen. We yav ter yav extras for the charms we carry anyhoo. They don't inventory these items," Kelly explained.

"Well, back to the desert!" Etta said, carefully looping the bracelet over her right ear. It was heavier than she remembered.

Kelly rolled her curly red head back and laughed, having seen this peculiar bracelet rest before, and then she walked her American friend to the door. When she returned to the cash register, she was aware of the wonderful fragrance of roses. She discovered the flowerpot filled with the petals. She stuck her nose in past the rim of the clay pot and breathed in deeply. She was grateful for the winter treat, but she secretly wished these had been delivered to her. It was a lovely gesture, and she must remember to thank Etta with a note card.

When she broke for tea, Etta sat alone at a table overlooking a panoramic view of the main lawn, which was currently a snowy field. There were several sets of footprints, some human, some animal. With the sun shining and the cold in the air, it was a beautiful sight. The barren cherry trees supported soft lines of white, and the bandstand appeared to be a freshly frosted gingerbread construction.

The orange spice tea warmed from her mouth all the way down her throat. Etta was getting a taste for tea, though she still preferred the fruit variety to the Earl Grey or English teas. Etta reclined in a relaxed position in her chair as she studied the field. She felt a tap on her shoulder and was surprised to find Joseph Colmore standing behind her.

"Good afternoon, Etta," he said rather nervously.

"Hello, Joseph," Etta replied flatly.

"May I join you?"

"All right, then. What brings you to the winter wonderland of the botanicals?"

Joseph conspicuously sat down in the seat next to her instead of opposite her.

"Etta. Did you get the roses I sent?"

"Ah, it was you! A young boy brought them in throughout the day, but he told me that Larkin sent them. How do you know Larkin?"

"We played rugby some years past. That blackie bloodied my nose, and I broke his little toe. We've been pals for a good many years. Now I only see him at the pub on occasion." Joseph reported the bit about rugby with great, manly pride.

Only brave men played the sport, and many of his friends would never set foot on a field, for fear of injury.

It was Etta's turn to clarify. "Joseph, it was a really pleasant gesture for you to send the flowers. I really enjoyed them. But you must know I am seeing someone."

"Oh. So did Arthur beat me to the invitation?" Joseph asked with a hint of disappointment.

"Arthur? No, no, no. I met a man who lives between here and Barcelona named Robert."

Immediately Etta was ashamed for intentionally Americanizing his name. Why? She didn't know. It just seemed Joseph would ask fewer questions of a more common name.

"Well, it's not serious or anything is it? I mean, can I still accompany you to dinner some evening?"

"Yes and no. I'm afraid it is serious, Joseph. We are seeing each other exclusively, so it would not be right to join you for dinner."

Etta was pleased her words did not come out in the rude and harsh tone she had rehearsed in her mind.

"Well, how about tea, then? Do you mind if we have tea, then?"

Etta was evaluating the level of pathetic desperation in this man who so vehemently accosted her with his drunken stupor at their first introduction.

"As you wish."

Etta slowly sipped the bottom half of the cup's contents.

Joseph was not one to be turned down, and he sat there thinking up plan B in the silence, sipping tea with this beautiful foreign woman. He could think of nothing clever or interesting to say. Being in Etta's presence simply stupefied him.

Etta was content to let Joseph stew in the shocking realization that he never had a chance with her anyhow. But the company, even if just this warm, silent, breathing, body next to her, was nice. So they sipped tea together. Quietly. They finished their tea together. Silently. They put up their cups together, speechlessly. And then Joseph said the most humble words to Etta that he could muster.

"Thank you, Etta, for your lovely company today. If you and Robert ever decide that mutual exclusiveness is not necessary, please allow me to be the first to escort you out as a friend. All right?"

Joseph took her hand, which in itself startled Etta. She was expecting a kiss on her hand when he suddenly leaned in toward her, making lip contact with her cheek. He kissed her cheek, and Etta flushed deeply with embarrassment and shame. She had not initiated this contact, and she was also quite unaccustomed to accepting this unsolicited behavior.

"Good afternoon, then. And thank you for the flowers. They were a delightful surprise."

Etta had regained her manners, but not her composure.

Joseph read the blushing to be a positive sign. Perhaps there was hope for him after all. He would be patient and keep showing up occasionally so Etta would not count him out.

Thomas was always such a good judge of character. He told Joseph to call her the day after they met Etta at his mum's dinner. Thomas was correct as always. Etta was a beautiful, smart, kind woman, just as he had said. Joseph would just have to wait his turn as the consequence of his delay in contacting her. Meanwhile, he would entertain himself with one of several other women he enjoyed the company of. Regrettably, they were gals he would not bring home to meet his mum.

Before she left work, Etta remembered the bracelet slung over her ear. She couldn't believe Joseph had not commented on that. She supposed he did not notice since he never really broke eye contact until he sat in silence with his tea next to her. *That* had felt very awkward.

When Etta stepped in the door, she heard the phone ring and ring and ring. She was not one to answer the phone unless Geraldine did not pick up the call. The calls were all for her, anyhow. In her absence, Etta picked up the receiver.

"Good evening?" Etta spoke into the phone.

"Miss Etta Johnson, please," the woman requested.

"This is she. How may I help you?" Etta asked, quite surprised that this was a telephone call for *her*.

"Good evening, this is Mary of HP of E," the proper English speaker began on the line. "Binny Colmore wishes to schedule you in London for the weekend of the twelfth. She requests your arrival Thursday evening, through Sunday evening's departure. If your schedule permits. I will arrange for your transport and accommodations from this end, to co-ordinate with Miss Colmore's."

Etta was speechless. She knew darn well she didn't have enough money to spend even one night in any choice hotel that Binny might select. How could she possibly explain this without humiliating her position with this entertaining friend?

"Ah, Mary, is it?" Etta began.

"Yes, this is Mary."

"Would you please have Binny phone to discuss the itinerary personally?" Etta requested out on a limb.

"Certainly. I will deliver the message to her at once," Mary replied before offering a farewell. "Thank you, Miss Johnson. Good-bye." With that, she hung up the phone.

Etta listened to the dial tone for a few seconds after Mary hung up. She glared at the receiver, wondering how to respond to this interesting invitation. No sooner had she walked back to her bedroom than the phone rang again.

"Hey, wench! What is this? You want me to talk to you *personally* about the weekend? You show up, we have fun, you go home. What's to that?" Binny ranted.

"I don't know how to say this…," Etta began on unsure footing.

"Out with it Etta. I don't have time to be on the social ear tonight," Binny cut her off.

"Binny, I don't make a fraction of the money you do, and I don't think I can afford to take you up on this trip just yet," Etta confessed as directly as possible.

"Oh, nonsense! Consider this one of my business expenses, and the tab's on me. You just bring some shopping money for your Christmas presents, and I will cover the rest. Savvy?"

"Really?"

"Oh, Etta, get off your knees and call Mary back to discuss the details. I have to get back to work. And you! Quit worrying about it! It'll be a gas!" Binny barely allowed a good-bye before she hung up abruptly.

Though Etta had Lana's home number, she never dared to use it. She considered this to be a valid emergency. She dialed her home, and a bellowing voice answered with a deep, "What?"

"Lana Ingle, please. This is Etta," she requested.

Within earshot of the phone the man roared, "Lana! It's the American lass on the line. Pick up!"

Etta heard the pickup, but she knew the man had not hung up the receiver. She could hear his shallow, suspicious breath under the short conversation.

"Lana, this is Etta. Have I earned any vacation time as yet?"

"Well technically, no. Since you are on a consultant status, you have no official time off. But Etta, I recognize how much you have enhanced your glasshouse and improved our winter field trip attendance, so if you plan a day when there are no school groups, we can cover you. You have certainly earned it."

"Thank you, Lana. I will provide the date tomorrow to your desk. Sorry to interrupt you at home," Etta added, in hopes it would at least help this evening's intimate prospects. "I know how much you treasure your nights alone with your husband. Forgive me for calling you."

"No problem," Lana replied and hung up the phone. Etta waited a few seconds, and sure enough, she heard her husband attempt to quietly hang up his phone after hearing the whole line of conversation.

The walk to work seemed easier to bear as Etta prepared more for the chill and endured it with less complaint. She removed her coat and walked the corridor toward the office. But before Etta could deliver the slip of paper to Lana's desk, she met Etta halfway, pulling her into the hall with her hands gripping both of Etta's shoulders. Lana sported a wild eye, coupled with a smile. She spoke intently, but also with the reservation to be as quiet as possible. She did not want others to hear an update of the private discussions they frequently *shared*—at least, that was Mrs. Ingle's take on their conversations.

"Etta, I know my husband spied on our call because, when I got off the phone, he made me a cup of coffee and put on his best pajamas. He cozied up to me like he hasn't in months! It was like erasing years off our courtship, and I was glad! We spent a wild night."

Oh, Etta hated the thought of enduring Lana's graphic details. She was wishing that someone would come around the corner so she would not have to hear the retelling of last night's adventures. Thankfully, Lana dropped her arms, collected a stack of papers, and returned to her office sporting a Cheshire cat grin. Lana was, at least today, a fulfilled woman.

Chapter 17
KING GEORGE IV DIADEM

Morning break was exhausted by a lengthy phone conversation with Mary. She would take care of arranging Etta's shopping excursion with Binny in London. Mary was a pro with the arrangements, treating this as just another of Binny's business trips. With such short notice, they were not able to get the ideal departure time immediately after Etta's work day, though Mary managed to book her into London City Airport, where a driver could fetch her more easily.

Etta would go to the Elmdon Airport terminal directly after work, anyhow. She enjoyed the people-watching opportunities. Etta realized she had little time to spare. She must get some clothes! Etta approached Kelly, pleading for confidentiality in the delicate nature of her request.

"Where can I get good, cheap clothes? I am going to London for a weekend, but I don't have much money to purchase clothes with. I have to look hip, but I can't spend my paycheck either."

"If it were spren, you'd yav be'ah luck. If I moight be so bold, noo yoo yav ter goo indoors. A tough find. Yav yoo considered the benevolence shops?" Kelly offered.

"Are there many in our neck of the woods?" Etta inquired.

"No, but yoo can tek the metro over ter the yowniversitoy areas. Many of the snot noses rid their tenderly used clobber an' get noo ones frum daddy an' mummy."

Of all the people Etta knew, Kelly was the best shot to offer expertise on how to scrounge a deal.

"Thanks, Kelly, I sure appreciate it." Etta turned over the thought of how to get to these areas, find the shops, and the adventure of using the subway with the variety of fees required of her. This information was filed under "important for later." This weekend she would have to stay near home to restock groceries. Besides, she could get away with purchasing only two outfits if she wore her uniform on the flight and her jeans one day. Yow! What would she pack them in? She had moved her worldly possessions in grocery store boxes after the loss of her bags. Boxes just would not do.

"Larkin? You busy?" Etta asked the man buried behind a massive quantity of paper stacks.

"No, Etta. Come in. What bizarre tool do you require today?" Larkin laughed, expecting one of Etta's brilliant, yet harebrained solutions.

"Actually, I have a very personal request. I am flying to London, and I don't have a suitcase *small* enough to carry for the weekend. I just hate to buy one with Christmas coming up. I just wondered if you had a small case I might borrow?"

"Well, Etta, I do own a weekend trunk that may work for you, but if you'd rather, we received our printed brochure samples in the case over there. Not real leather, but I fancy it's good enough for a carry-on." Larkin gestured to a corner pile of papers and booklets covering a box on the floor.

Etta removed the samples, careful to keep them in the order they were stacked. She opened the box and unwrapped a smart-looking carrier that appeared functionally too thick to be a briefcase, yet too slender to be a suitcase. The exterior had a lovely texture punched in, giving it the appearance of animal skin.

"You may have it if you like. We are bidding a whole new line of adverts. The vendors frequently dress up their shipments to coax us their way." Larkin smiled, recognizing the gleam of enthusiasm in Etta's eyes. It was this similar joy that endeared her wild project ideas to him, and besides, her ideas were always successful. She really would appreciate this tote. It was a small perk for Larkin to give up. He could sense Etta would get much more use from it than he would.

"Smashing!" Etta replied in an intentionally bad English accent.

Larkin rolled with laughter. Etta replaced the empty shipping box back in its place with the brochures in their original position. Larkin made note of this simple act of courtesy, so rare from the women in his circle of friends. He was frequently impressed by her acts, wondering if all Americans behaved in this manner. Etta dramatically snatched the bag and sashayed out the door, but she popped her head back in to remark, "Au revoir!" Larkin shook his head from side to side, tilted his head forward to the vision of his paper piles, and chuckled.

Etta returned to the gift shop and waited patiently while Kelly helped the three customers in line. When all had cleared her shop, Etta said quietly, "Kelly, I am going to ask you something really, really tacky, so don't be angry, all right?"

Well, if that was not enough to interest her! Kelly leaned over the counter very close to Etta's face and asked quietly, "What yoo got?"

Etta asked her straight up, "Can I just borrow a few outfits from you for next weekend? I know we aren't the same size, but that doesn't matter. As long as I have something decent, I would be ever so grateful!"

"Well, I'll be. I yam genuinely flattered yoo ood aks. Of couss!" Kelly responded. "I fink yoo should cum over an' try them on, though. Cost cum um with me after werk tomorrer?" Kelly generously offered.

"You bet. Thanks oodles. I really owe you for this!" Etta flew out of the shop clutching her fancy "wannabe" suitcase.

Kelly repeated to herself, "Oodles?"

After a bitterly cold but clear day, Etta dashed out of work with the commercial bag. It looked very nice and would easily pass as a travel case. She dropped it off at the house just inside the door and rushed off to the corner grocer. She bought a few pounds' worth of staple foods, mostly in the form of cans and cereal boxes. Etta was not very motivated to cook for one, and there had never been an arrangement with Geraldine about sharing meals. Etta stocked her own goods in one cupboard and used but half of one shelf in the refrigerator for her cold goods. She also kept a box of Weetabix in her room to snack on. This wasn't very sanitary, keeping food in her room, but she did find herself enjoying the dry cereal more than Geraldine's company some nights.

Etta drove home with Kelly the following day in a little clunker of a car. It may not have been much to look at, but it was more than Etta had. Kelly was a safe driver with good reaction in the snowy streets. She lived in the Handsworth section, quite off the path that Etta knew. These modest homes were stacked side by side with common walls touching. When they pulled up, Etta was disappointed to witness a house in gross disrepair. The impression of it was not like the Kelly she knew.

Though roughly Etta's age, Kelly was still living at home. It didn't appear to be a good situation from Kelly's change in behavior once entering this space. The house's stench resulted from a combination of cigarette smoke and strange food items. Kelly ignored the surroundings and led Etta up the poorly aged wooden stairs. Kelly's room was tiny, smaller than the room that Etta let. The contents, though, were significantly more abundant. Etta noticed immediately how tidy the room was compared to the rest of the house. This room was indicative of the Kelly that Etta knew. She felt the sudden urge to rescue her friend from all this by securing her a job with Binny.

"Don't forget, I need your résumé Thursday," Etta announced quite out of the blue.

"Why then?" Kelly responded with a quizzical look about her eye. Kelly rummaged through a small closet.

"I want to take it to London with me to put in a good word for you to hire as a smithy. Remember, I told you about that? You'd be so good at a smithing job!"

"That would be fine," Kelly remarked with a flat, nearly disinterested tone. She whirled about with four blouses on her arm. With the uniforms, there really was no telling what Kelly wore on her own time. If the four samples were an indication of her taste, Etta was quite impressed.

"I don't have many hobbies, but I do like a good shop," Kelly admitted, pulling out several pairs of pants to coordinate with the blouses.

Etta was unsure if the pants would fit since the two were built so differently. Etta was tall and slender, and Kelly was curvy and the shorter of the two. Etta tried on the pants first. Only one pair was long enough for Etta. Though they rode lower on her hips, Etta believed she could get away with wearing them. She tried the miscellaneous plaids, designed much like old garage sale patchwork quilts, and passed on. Etta selected a wavy, vertically striped blouse that might not be warm enough, but it looked ravishing on her frame.

Etta was most appreciative for the loan of these clothes that would buy her more time. She treated Kelly to a takeaway dinner. They gossiped in Kelly's car, sharing their needs, wishes, and dreams. Kelly promised to prepare a résumé. Trouble was, it was very short. She had little experience or adventure to advertise of herself. Etta promised she would try to help "sell" Kelly for at least a screening interview.

When Etta returned home, she was set to wait out the days before her trip. She had her bag, clothes, and itinerary. She was going to London! Regrettably, on this trip, Etta would not be able to play tourist, but she was hoping to finally see the city where A. J. Bayless had intended to send her for winning the Lucky London contest.

The phone rang. Geraldine answered it on the second ring. Etta could hear her compact frame approaching across the creaking wood floors.

"The call is for you, Etta," Geraldine announced, and she returned to the kitchen phone to wait for Etta to pick up the line. Etta rarely talked on the phone, but when she did, she preferred the parlor. It somehow enhanced the feeling of being treated to a special call.

Etta picked up the phone and heard the other phone click down, assuring her privacy. "Hello? This is Etta."

The rich voice on the other line gave her such a warm feeling of affection that she immediately sat down in the comfortable reading chair and smiled to herself.

"My dear Etta. *Buenas noches, mi amor.*"

Etta was always intrigued that when Roberto spoke English, she could slightly detect the accent of a Brit.

"Well good evening, handsome."

The pause was not uncomfortable. It was clearly evidence of the longing on both ends of the telephone wire.

"I can't wait until next weekend to see you, Etta."

"Whoa! No! That weekend I will be in London with a friend for the big Christmas shop. Can you come the weekend after?" Etta pleaded, feeling desperate to see him, but also not wanting to ditch the wonderful opportunity to finally reach London.

"No, that's too close to Christmas. Can I see you this weekend?"

"You realize that tomorrow is Friday, right?"

Etta hesitated. How different his life was. That he had the liberty to jump on an airplane for the weekend was such a foreign concept to her. But her upper torso burned with the anticipation that she might get to see her boyfriend again so soon.

"I'll meet you after work."

"Roberto, I can't wait to see you. I miss you terribly."

"Etta, there is something...I want a commitment from you. I can't function without your loyalty. My heart aches without you. My work has suffered in this separation from you. If I knew you were mine, I could sleep with anticipation instead of jealous want for you." Roberto sounded serious and ended on the hanging note of serious hope.

"Roberto, if you mean, "Are we exclusive?" then the answer is yes. I finally learned who the mysterious flower giver was, and we had a talk about the nature of the relationship you and I share. I have never felt the way I feel with you. The first night I saw you, I just knew..."

"I knew too. We were supposed to meet. It was not the right time, or place, or even under the right circumstances, but it was going to happen. I can't be without you now, Etta."

Etta let a tear escape down her cheek, realizing that he wanted her and her alone. She was surprised that she too was ready to commit to him so soon. It did not make sense, but she knew it was the right thing to do. How would she ever explain this to her family? How could she ever chronicle the time warp of meeting her soul mate?

"How lucky I was. It was supposed to be Lucky London, but I know it's really lucky in love. I can't wait to see you!"

"I have a serious question for you to consider, Etta. Will you stay with me this weekend?"

"Will you let me think on that one?"

Etta experienced excitement and reservation wrapped into one thought. She was unsure she could rein in the passion she felt for him if she stayed at the Holiday Hotel.

"I have to return to work. Wait for me. I'll be there."

After the warm exchanges of affectionate love, the line went dead. Etta held the phone for a moment, thinking over the less obvious predicament about staying with him. She didn't have clothes. He couldn't find out now that she had nothing, spare a few outfits and her dinner party ensemble. She imagined staying the night with Roberto and knew it would give them quality, private time to get to know one another. And surely, the temptation would be difficult to endure. They could be strong. She must bridle her passions, for it was the only appropriate thing to do.

She packed all casual clothes and her black dress for the weekend. She would do it. Why not? She had found the man of her dreams, and she would just have to work with what she had. He had fallen for *her*, not her possessions or position in this small world.

As a courtesy, Etta explained the schedule to Geraldine, who was suspicious only of the plan to meet up with Roberto this weekend. She seemed fine with the holiday outing with Binny the following weekend.

Work was challenging with a preholiday tour group of very ill-behaved children. Children damaged several succulents by breaking off stems. Etta did not perform a floor show, choosing instead to attempt to regulate the mass of tots. She spontaneously performed an informative ditty about how plants have little souls and are hurt by people who intentionally cause them harm. The adults realized she was delivering this message especially to their little ones. They were a bit put off that she would be so brazen as to lecture their children like this.

Etta was grateful for a quiet afternoon spent trimming off drying parts of her collection. They looked wonderful and had splendidly fared the change in weather, if she could say so herself. The new box was standing ready at the door where Henry would pick her up. This time, the employees would likely discover just whom the limousine was there to pick up.

Etta took one last look around her glasshouse and left for the weekend. She exited out the front along with the other employees. But there was no car waiting. Not knowing quite what to do, she returned to the lobby and collected a newspaper. She read the first section in the cold, sitting on the bench near the entry. She then set the box on the first section so it would not be watermarked by the thin layer of snow at her feet.

She read the second section and even the sports. By this time, only the security guards were left at the garden. They walked their first rounds and returned to the heated office only to see Etta through the glass, still sitting out there on the bench.

"Wozapanin?" the young guard asked his elder.

"Gunnyarta ask the duck," the experienced guard responded.

"Ploise no! You get er palaver," the younger pleaded. "Find out s'up an if shewanna buzz or a cab."

The elder guard approached the patient woman on the bench, quite uncomfortable about having to draw this task.

"Ooroyt there. Parky are you?"

"No. I'm OK. My fingers are still warm."

"Bin ere lung time, missy," he added.

"Yes. I was supposed to wait for a ride, though. Truth is, I didn't expect for them to be," she checked her watch, "over two hours late."

Only now, Etta began to be irritated and impatient at having drawn attention to herself.

"Mizzly out. Warrn't yer off the wikend?" he asked. "Not like a New Street Station round here on a Friday. Allow me to muck in with you. Es noyse en the office."

"I'll take you up on that," Etta responded, not knowing how much longer she would have to wait in the cold.

She occupied herself in the office with lobby brochures trying to stay out from the security officers' underfoot. Her box still waited anxiously by the door in hopes of a journey this evening.

Finally, the car pulled to the curb, just shy of three hours late, and Etta was famished by now!

"Thanks so much guys. See you later!"

The guards waved to Etta as she bundled up and started outside to the curb, purse and bag in hand. Roberto jumped out of the car and took them from her. He grabbed Etta tightly and pressed his cheek against hers, whispering, "I'm so sorry. I got here as fast as I could. Thank you for waiting. Thank you so much for waiting. Does this mean you are staying with me?" he asked, pulling away from Etta to watch her eyes.

"Yes, I will stay with you, but we have to establish some ground rules, Roberto. I'm so glad to see you. I was so worried you wouldn't make it."

"And yet, you waited?" he asked, amazed at her loyalty.

"Of course."

Henry opened the door for the both of them and closed out the cold. He was pleased at Etta's remark, knowing he had no way to coach her today with Roberto in tow, directly from a flight that ran late at the airport.

She will be good for this man, Henry thought.

The window was closed between them, and Henry treated himself to soft music on the radio.

Inside the car, Etta and Roberto greeted each other more intimately with a long embrace and deep kisses. They were gazing into each other's eyes when Etta startled him with a less than obvious comment.

"I'm starving! Can we get a takeaway before we head to your place? I missed lunch today," Etta explained.

Roberto knocked, the radio shut off, the window opened, and that was that. They pulled into a pub, and Henry picked up sandwiches and chipped potatoes for the couple. They would order dessert back at the Holiday. By the time they finished their dinner, the dessert and coffee would arrive at their suite.

Once back upstairs with their food in tow, Roberto removed Etta's coat and his own. He reached into his pockets, fishing for something, and leaned in to kiss her cheek. Roberto handed Etta a small gift box with a charm fashioned as the George IV diadem crown, similar to the one worn by the queen on occasions of the state. Etta admired the metallurgist's attention to detail, wondering if she would ever see the real crown housed in the Tower of London. Etta thanked Roberto and positioned the crown near where it would likely be installed on the lovely charm bracelet.

"Before your dinner, Etta, may I offer some entertainment?" Roberto pulled out a slip of paper from his breast pocket. He read silently and then recited, "You are a queen, my wonderful woman. With eyes of green and love so sudden. You captured my heart in November. With just a glance across forever." He kissed her hand. He looked at her eyes. Clearly, he could see she appreciated his efforts at making this moment romantic.

She clutched the crown in her hand and rested her arm over the arm of the chair. Roberto opened the food service and set the table for them.

As Henry's duty was excused for the night, he drove home, hoping that Etta could teach the man patience.

Chapter 18
IMPERIAL STATE

The Holiday Hotel in Birmingham may as well have been one of Roberto's residences. It was a smaller establishment than Etta had anticipated. The room itself was a standard size, not the lap of luxury that she expected from the particular tastes of this man. Roberto explained that the frequency of his stays here afforded him the same suite, with mostly the same staff serving him. They used "Mr. Fernandez's room" only in the event of a rare, sold-out evening.

The dinner-in-a-box went down without much flavor, Etta was that hungry. The tea and coffee service and a plate of almond sugar cookies adorned with red and green sparkles arrived on a white linen-covered kitchen cart. The white cup and plate presentation was served with a matching vase, filled with small, hothouse flowers. The vision of the tray was a real treat for Etta, who had not been instructed on the lessons of kitchen detail. She studied the layout, memorizing the overall appearance for future replication.

Cookies would not have been Etta's first choice for dessert. Roberto raved about how these confections rivaled the finest *"almendrados"* of his neighborhood baker in Barcelona. They partook of these delicacies at their little table, both feeling the tense freedom of unrestricted privacy. Delicious. Tempting.

Kicking off their shoes, the two retired the conversation to the bed, where Roberto propped three pillows against the headboard and cradled Etta in his lap. He stroked her hair, he kissed her ears and neck, and she took it in, basking in the tenderness of her steady man.

Roberto enjoyed the conversation game Etta played with him. She would ask him a series of five questions with only two answer options. Then it was his turn.

Etta started with the safe ground. "Chicken or beef?"

"Beef," Roberto started off this round.

"Pie or cake?"

"Cake."

"Red or blue?"

"Blue."

"Golf or tennis?"

"Tennis."

"Europe or Scandinavia?"

"Definitely Scandinavia," replied Roberto assuredly.

"Really..." Etta eyed him closely. "Why?"

Roberto gave the logistical answer about not having moved into their business market and that although it would be timely, he did not want to be spread too thin with Etta, his new diversion.

Etta understood with pride that she was the distraction that he occasionally referred to as his *recent diversion*, for he stated it with an obvious tone. Sure, he would pay for the indulgence over the long haul with the lost negotiations and such, but he willingly paid the price for securing his interest in the woman who had changed his life these past few weeks. He was electrically charged, feeling complete with an affection that new love can't conceal. It was Roberto's turn. Etta turned to tousle his hair, and then she kissed him. Etta removed his tie and unbuttoned the top button of his crisp white shirt.

"Flowers or fruit?"

"Fruit," Etta replied, noticing his right eyebrow raise in surprise.

"Antique or contemporary?"

"Antique."

"Coffee or tea?"

"*Fruit* tea."

"Honey or Marmite?"

"Honey! I hate that other stuff," Etta replied referring to the pungent, brown toast condiment.

"Sons or daughters?"

"Both."

"Hey, wait a minute," Roberto turned and laughed. "You broke your own rules! You have to choose one."

"But that's already done for you. It's not a fair question! You can't choose gender because that's already chosen for you. Roberto, it's like you and me, really. Don't you believe in your heart that fate chose for *us* to meet? He didn't let me choose the best pick of my suitors. He chose *you* for me. I can't deny that fact any more than I could deny that I need to be with you."

"Will you make love to me, Etta?" Roberto asked suddenly, taking Etta by complete surprise.

"Not without a church's blessing," she said matter-of-factly, though Etta did realize there was a hesitation in her response. "Roberto, I feel very strongly that the mutual respect we share will make it worth the wait until we are married. You know I love you with all my heart."

Roberto looked down and absentmindedly pulled off his socks and shoes. Etta saw his naked feet for the first time. Like his hands, these were feet that were pampered and tender, unlike her own desert feet, which were healing beautifully in this friendly climate.

She had said she would not make love to him, but the chemistry was undeniable in the room. Roberto was rarely unsure of himself, but he clearly was not calling the shots at the moment. Etta moved in close and stared. Roberto stood, and Etta followed. She reached for his neck and hugged him softly.

Her hair tickled the side of Roberto's neck, and he attempted to understand this unfamiliar dance. They remained there, holding each other for a long while before either spoke.

After removing her own stockings and shoes, she faced him with a tougher set of questions.

"Private or public wedding?" Etta asked brazenly.

"Private. It would be more intimate."

"England or Spain?"

"England. You can't speak Spanish, *mi armor*!"

"Planned or spontaneous children?"

"Both! Lots and lots of children."

"I honestly don't want more than a couple, Roberto." Etta eyed him severely, noting he was pulling her leg once again.

"Till death do us part or for time and eternity?"

"The latter."

"More of the question game or sleep?"

"I think I'm worn out," replied Roberto, who was worn more from his personal restraint than from sleep deprivation.

It was early in the morning, and Etta was feeling sleepy from the long day and especially the hours waiting in the cold for Roberto to arrive. "Do you mind if I use the shower first?" Etta asked, genuine in complying with either refusal or approval.

"No. You go on."

His anticipation was excruciating. Roberto knew she would not make love to him yet. Etta's hair pulled behind her ears, she lingered, locking eyes before releasing his hand. She turned back to look at his eyes again, pausing to memorize the feeling when they looked through time.

Roberto watched Etta walk to the bathroom in her work pants and embroidered shirt. The leather bag she brought into the bathroom seemed more a curious briefcase than a cosmetic bag. But who was he to question this unique American.

She closed the door behind herself, and when Roberto heard the water run, he picked up the receiver on the nightstand. He sat back into the guest chair and spoke quietly to the hotel operator, detailing his schedule and his current business requirements, and this time he included his personal requirements as well. Roberto exhaled deeply, realizing that sweat beads had formed on his hairline.

Etta turned off the water just minutes later and emerged in the oversized king towel, having forgotten her bed clothing in the room. Roberto recognized that his mind was not feeling lust for her but rather a burning, deep affection.

"Your turn," Etta said, quickly turning away from his stare.

There was not a line of makeup, not a dry hair on her head. Not a fingernail painted, nor a spray of perfume. What Etta realized at that moment was that *this* was his last opportunity to bail out. Standing in front of this man, she was as plain as day, exposed as the way she came into the world, flaws and all.

Roberto stood stunned. She was not at all a woman he recognized. Her arms had more muscle than he expected, her shoulders were tanner, and her forearms were covered with blonde hair. Her long toes were unadorned, and yet they were not marred like those of other women her age from the excruciating shoe styles of the time. Her lanky wet hair was darker than when it was dry, and it hung down flat alongside her head. It framed her freshly washed face. The natural beauty of the angel in his room was breathtaking.

Never in Roberto's life had anyone risked total exposure for him. She was as striking as the paintings he fell in love with as a child touring through the Museu Nacional d'Art de Catalunya with his mother. His mother had taught his own sisters the custom of never being seen without makeup. That is why women retire after and rise earlier than men. Mother fervently coached Roberto's sisters at age eleven how to walk appropriately in spiked heels, making the young women appear taller than their Spanish roots might afford.

Roberto appreciated the statuesque vision in front of his eyes, in her bare feet, with only a towel to challenge his imagination. Walking toward her, Roberto fell under some spell, and he hugged her hard from behind, allowing an unexpected tear to drop onto her bare shoulder. He fought hard to maintain composure and whispered in a fragile voice, "I love you."

In the bathroom, Roberto couldn't contain his joy. He sat on top of the toilet with his face in his hands, wondering what guardian angel had fallen from the sky to afford him such a relationship.

Inside the room, Etta was elated that he felt such deep emotion to tear up at her sight. She pulled out her pajamas from the case and looked them over. They were simple, warm, tea-length flannels. This was just not the appropriate look for this special night.

She looked through his effects, noticing the details of his dress code. The cufflinks, tie tacks, and watch rested on the wooden suit butler. She searched the closet for other prospects. Desperate, she phoned the hotel front desk.

"Excuse me, I have spilled coffee on my nightgown. Do you have a gown or robe I can purchase? Quickly?" she asked quietly into the phone.

The front desk staff had seen the lovely new visitor with the suitcase escort Roberto to his private room. In fact, they got a good look at her. So within minutes, and before Roberto even stepped into the running water from his contemplative throne, a bellman arrived with two appropriately sized items folded into white tissue paper. She read the young man's nametag, realizing she had no money to tip him at the moment. She thanked him and signed for the bill. She would pay Roberto back before he checked out. "Oh no!" She realized what she just signed for. She forgot that hotels did not charge the discounted the prices she was accustomed to. These two items alone would amount to everything left of her next paycheck after she surrendered room and board. Bad call, but perhaps necessary for this occasion.

She slid into the emerald green, floor-length gown. It was lovely and showed off her figure and the color of her eyes, yet it maintained modesty. She could layer this with the hotel's white cotton robe as she walked around the room. Etta was alerted by the toilet flushing, and she slid down into the bed, placed the robe by her side, and fashioned the pillows down for sleeping. Roberto briefly left the foggy bathroom to retrieve his bedclothes, modeling his own hotel towel.

Etta's snapshot recall was able to take it all in. She studied the image even after he returned to the bathroom, allowing the steam to escape. His bare back curved up into strong, broad shoulders, dismissing Etta's fear he would conceal a hairy back. Roberto's wet hair was longer than she realized with the curl weighed down by water. That chiseled chest was decorated with a wonderfully conservative T-line of dark, curly hair. His belly button was an outie, which seemed rare to Etta. He had a lovely physique. Even though she had not seen his whole body, she felt comfortable she could fill in the lines below the rim of the towel with pretty close accuracy.

He stepped out of the bathroom wearing satin paisley bedclothes. Etta closed her eyes and mentally started a short, intense mantra: "Keep control. Stay in control. Keep control. Stay in control."

He strode over to the bed slowly and asked an unusual question. "Do you mind switching sides? I would like to hold you while you sleep."

Sides? she thought. Etta had never heard of such a thing. He could hold her from either side. She wondered if she would learn about more little idiosyncrasies. For now, she was content to pull the robe off the chair and walk around the bed self-consciously before replacing her cover on the other side, where she slid into bed.

Roberto lay on his side, watching her move around and resituate herself. He looked into her eyes and kissed her softly. "Would you roll over?" he asked with a matter-of-fact tone that irritated Etta.

She rolled over without kissing him again. But when she faced away from him, she understood what he wanted from her. Resting on his right shoulder, he wrapped his left arm around Etta and clasped her left hand, resting it on the mattress. She could feel his shallow breath on the back of her neck while he folded his body into a Z position to cradle her body in a protective gesture. She felt his lap rest against her rear cheeks, but he kept any excitement in check.

Sleep came quickly, and when the sunlight came visibly through the curtains, the couple woke in the same position they had retired in. With eyes open to greet the day, their heads remained on the pillow. Each was aware the other was awake, though.

"Are you awake, Etta?"

"Good morning to you too, Roberto," Etta said, easing into full consciousness.

"I want you to share a house with me," he remarked.

Etta rolled over, now that he had her attention. "You are serious!" she exclaimed, studying his eyes.

"Yes, love. You pick out a home, we'll get your church blessing, and I suppose we'll need a driver," Roberto continued as if he had spent years designing this succinct invitation.

"Oh my gosh, Roberto!" Etta could not believe her ears. "Of course!" she exclaimed, with tears suddenly flowing freely down her face. Although she knew that this relationship would evolve into marriage, she was somewhat relieved he would not make her wait through a lengthy engagement, laden with this intense, recurring temptation.

"Let's get breakfast, and we can discuss the matter of the house. I think I have nearly paid for this wing of the hotel. They will miss my contributions. I rather like Henry, though. Do you suppose he would work for me?" Roberto rambled on, now aware of the weight of new decisions his plan would require.

Roberto rose out of bed with the left side of his scalp wild and curly and the right side smashed flat. It struck a funny bone with Etta, and she laughed behind her hand to guard any escape of morning breath into Roberto's innocent face.

Etta headed for the bathroom door in her robe, replying, "Henry has a good job here. He may not want to work for you unless you sweeten the deal." Etta brushed her teeth, showered, and changed into Kelly's clothes. She applied her "daily face," although Roberto didn't see it anymore. He saw through the colors she applied onto the perfect face of the Etta he saw last night. *His* Etta.

When Etta went into the bathroom, Roberto began to wonder about her birth name. Was Etta short for Glorietta, Loretta, Alietta, or what? He rehearsed other possibilities like Marietta, Annetta, Claretta, Odetta, and Inetta. He would have to remember to ask her about that.

He showered and dressed to the nines during his routine, hour-long preparation. It was as he always did. Etta felt underdressed, but she could do little about it. Her big worry was how to pay for the nightclothes. When the elevator opened on the lower floor, Etta spotted Charles just coming off his night shift.

"Roberto, do you have some money to tip this gentleman? He was a help to me last night, and I did not have any money to tip him."

"Of course."

Etta sincerely thanked Charles and gave him the tip with a wink and a smile. Charles was very appreciative that she remembered his service and her oversight.

Roberto wondered what service Charles might have provided since they were together all evening. Women were a curious species.

The front desk staff looked baffled with Roberto. He had presented them with a new situation they were not previously advised of. In truth, the night staff had recorded the details of Roberto's check-in, but they had failed to deliver the briefing at the end of their shift. What should they do? The front desk phoned to the back kitchen, where they advised the morning chef of this potential change of routine details. The chef responded by cloaking himself in a fresh, white jacket and directly approaching Roberto and Etta.

"Good morning, Mr. Fernandez, madam. May I show you to a table?" he offered.

Etta responded first, with a polite, "Thank you, yes." And forgetting all the instructions Henry had given her, Etta captured the chef's direct eye contact. He was startled at her behavior and impressed with the deep beauty of her eyes, but he genuinely hoped she was not a local "bind" or professional "scrubba." Etta recognized her mistake after reading suspicion in his interested eyes.

There was a lovely brunch buffet spread out in the center of the dining room with all the foods Etta had hoped to try. Yes, this traditional British breakfast was what she had always wanted to order. She admitted this to Roberto, who was not as enthused, but he also chose to sample the traditional English breakfast feast.

The waiter had not been clued in on how to treat this new situation, either. Generally, Mr. Fernandez and the chef worked together without his service. Today he'd better be on the ball. Something was up.

The waiter brought coffee to the table with cream, just in case. He looked only at his pad of paper and asked simply, "What may I order for you and the lady?"

Roberto responded, "We will both have the traditional, and the lady will require your herbal tea chest. Thank you."

Etta watched, and there was no eye contact at all. She really had to practice this new behavior in order to be accepted as Roberto's wife and companion in his circle. She must increase her public confidence.

The chef personally filled their plates with a boiled egg on the toasted English muffin, set next to the rashers of smoked bacon. He served Roberto sausage, and Etta chose the grilled tomatoes. They both selected sautéed mushrooms and hash browns. Etta requested a scant serving of Heinz beans since this was a common food in her diet lately. She knew them by color and smell. It was one of her strange comfort foods, these beans. Roberto made a face and shook his head to demonstrate his distaste for the item. The chef set their plates at the table and returned to his kitchen.

The waiter had promptly set the toast on the table before returning with a full tea service. Roberto had never seen a woman eat so much. He reacted by asking, "Etta, how can you possibly eat all that when you did not work up an appetite last night?" The glint in his sensual brown eyes told Etta he was chiding her about making him wait, for now.

She felt compelled to sincerely explain the obvious question underlying his teasing. "I eat a large breakfast, but I don't eat lunch. Mostly, I have quite a small dinner."

"I am the opposite. I eat a small breakfast and lunch but a large dinner," Roberto shared.

"We may have a few issues, Roberto. I am a morning person, and I don't like to eat late," Etta said, wondering how he would react to this complaint.

"I will just have to take you out for a late lunch, then. We will compromise. I will only be here a few days a week, anyhow," Roberto remarked.

For some reason, Etta thought by getting married he would be living here full-time now. She had assumed too much. She would need to ask more direct questions.

"Then where will you live the rest of the time?" Etta asked.

"When business is good in Barcelona at the manufacturing plant, I am here negotiating, consulting, and selling. When business is good in Birmingham, I must be in Barcelona. Same thing, only I have to watch my markets. I have only a few, uninterrupted weeks a year that I have to be gone. But of course, I will make it up to you when we get our holidays."

Etta was trying to envision the concept that was crossing the table. They were buying a home here, but he still had to hop back and forth?

Etta laid out her cards. "You don't expect me to go with you all the time, do you? I mean, I don't speak Spanish, and I really like my job here." Etta waited hopefully in the long pause.

Roberto, meanwhile, was relieved at Etta's questions. Her desire to keep the house and the job here solved many issues he was not prepared to discuss with her. Rather, they worked themselves out. How blessed he was. This would work splendidly for the both of them.

"You will manage the house here, and I will staff it for you. I have an idea about what to do for Henry that I will discuss with Steve Ellis, the GM here. You should keep your job, but remember that I will not always be home on the weekends. I could be home in the middle of the week, also. How will you manage that?" asked Roberto with an undertone of sacrificial request on her part.

"Let me work on that," Etta said, not wanting to chew on this detail just yet.

Roberto smeared dark brown Marmite across a toast half. He offered it to Etta, daring her, "If you love me, *mi amor*, you will partake of the rich, healthy benefits of Marmite." Etta broke into laughter with his fairly good rendition of the product's television commercial that was geared toward adults.

She rose to his dare and chomped a huge bite off the end of the foul-smelling, condiment-covered toast. She wrinkled her nose, chewed three or four times, and then washed it down with juice. It was the "love it or hate it" national product of England, and Etta was with the "hate it" group. So was Roberto. Rising to his own gentlemanly dare, he too bit a chunk off the same piece of toast to be a good sport. He had to work to get it down. They toasted each other's health with an orange juice before completing their breakfast.

During the final cup of tea, Henry was summoned to take Etta and Roberto to town. Etta was amazed that even with gigantic gaps in her knowledge of Roberto's life, she just knew she was doing the right thing. She would have to remember to ask about his family, though.

The night clerk woke from her morning slumber with a start. *I'll be fired, for sure!* she thought as she swung her long coat over her nightgown and raced back to work to recover the undelivered briefing in her work cubby. By the time she arrived to deliver the detailed instructions, a chain of employees had miraculously attended to all the requirements Mr. Fernandez had left her. While not fired, she was docked an hour's wage for her gross error.

The sun was fierce for December, and the snow had melted back a good measure, making it safe to walk and less cold than the previous weekend mornings. Henry dropped them off at the Jewellery Quarter train station. As they stepped out of the limousine, several shop vendors came out of their stores to invite the couple in.

"We are just strolling, thank you," Roberto explained, and they walked a few blocks, hand in hand, with their coats unbuttoned. Roberto had not so much as looked in a window on this street. Etta was chomping at the bit, wondering what charms these famous jewelers carried. Roberto sensed her urgency and sat her down on a bench, damp from melted snow.

"Etta, Jewellery Quarter is a few hundred years old. While a few of the structures are rather derelict, there are blocks and blocks of stores. Don't be in a hurry. There are plenty to choose from."

Etta took off her gloves and rested them in her lap, feeling silly for wanting to hunt down a charm so eagerly. He was a man. He would not understand how she or any woman shopped. She was just thrilled he brought her here at all, so she intentionally slowed, relaxed, and settled back on the bench. She looked directly at the bright sun and squinted. Then she looked at a small patch of snow, still seeing the sun's image there.

Roberto started their game again.

"Fountain or stream?" he asked.

"Stream."

"Snow skiing or water skiing?"

"Water skiing."

Then Roberto intentionally set her up. "Watches or rings?"

"Rings."

"Pearls or diamonds?"

"Diamonds," Etta replied innocently, engaged in the game mode.

They stood up and kissed. She started on him in such a way that Roberto was certain she did not pick up his cue.

"Train or bus?" she wondered.

"Train."

"Cotton or silk?"

"Oh, that's tough. Silk?" Roberto answered, knowing the real answer was "both," depending on who was wearing the item in question.

"Marmite or mustard?"

"Mustard."

"Neck or ears?"

"Neck," Roberto responded, reaching over and nuzzling in to plant a soft, warm kiss on Etta's exposed neck.

Etta giggled as Roberto's magical lips again provoked her entire body into immediate attention. She asked one last question as they entered the store. "Town or country?"

"Town."

Etta silently kissed away the deep-rooted childhood hope of ever owning her own equestrian riding stable.

They strolled through many stores and past several public houses before Etta found her beautiful gold imperial state crown. The clerk explained the authentic queen's crown was worn each year at the opening of Parliament. She was kind enough to solder the two crowns on opposite ends of the bracelet, creating a better weight distribution.

While Etta hunted for other charms, Roberto was otherwise distracted in his own hunt. After a small lunch at a pub, they were refreshed and back at the hunt. Etta didn't know why they continued to roam through the stores, but she immensely enjoyed surveying the various metalwork. The stones and gems used in the stores varied, but they revealed not at all the quality that one would suppose under such competition.

After a few more blocks, they both grew weary of seeing jewelry. They phoned Henry from a pub, and Roberto enjoyed a glass of Spanish wine while waiting for the car to arrive. He was only one glass away, and Roberto paid the tip and bill with money left on the beautiful, dark wood bar.

Saturday's ride to the hotel was totally different than the previous night. Roberto's lead conversation took an alarming twist, discussing mostly business instead of familiarity or intimacy.

"Etta, when you find a house in the area, go on and buy it. I know real estate here goes fast, so I will deposit two hundred thousand pounds at work in the event you need my secretary to release it as a deposit before I get back."

"But don't you want to pick it out together?" Etta asked, stunned at the amount of money he had reserved for the down payment on what would be their home.

"No, Etta. You will be the one to live there. I will need to be more involved in the staffing of the house for security issues and my business needs," Roberto replied, shedding his coat in the warm car.

"I don't have a bank account here," Etta admitted, sounding concerned.

"Aw, an illegal, are you?" Roberto chuckled. "No matter. You just select the house under my name, and my secretary will send the remaining money for a cash purchase, providing you don't go over budget!"

"That'll never happen," said Etta, knowing his deposit alone would buy more than four nice dwellings back home. "Do you have furnishings you would like to use?" Etta asked, embarrassed she had nothing to bring into the home to call her own.

"No. I'm afraid that's not my best work. Holiday Hotel furniture is all I have here." This was the truth, but he committed a sin of omission by not revealing the wonderful décor and art currently housed in his Barcelona residence. There were ample furnishings he might choose from. Nevertheless, it would be Etta's home, and she should decorate it in the way she felt most comfortable. Right then, Roberto felt most comfortable in the company of Etta. He had so hoped to find her a nice ring today. It was not meant to be. He would have to contact Mr. Thorne, at Collingwood of Bond Street in London, to select an appropriate platinum piece to present to her.

"You will need your passport. We won't be able to travel without it."

For once, he released Henry early, with a nice tip, and the couple retired for their last evening together before Christmas.

The ease of solutions she was afforded finally relaxed Etta. She was grateful to Kelly for allowing her to pick up the loaner clothes early. She was also grateful to the prompt hotel staff who provided the right sized nightgown, in a flattering color, for the weekend.

Roberto listened politely while Etta shared the exciting anticipation of her trip with Binny to London the next weekend. She detailed some of the stores they would surely visit. Roberto asked how she knew this Binny character, described as a really lively social companion. Etta simply explained they met at Greta Colmore's dinner party. Roberto did not disclose to Etta that he already knew Binny. Greta was a legend in these parts for being a shrewd, sharp, businesswoman. Her only daughter had been a successful understudy. He hoped the negotiations with Binny's company would come to fruition. Roberto decided to outfit Etta for a good shop.

Etta knew which side of the bed to enter this time. She still felt self-conscious in her nightgown when he eyed her striding across the room to the bed. He played as close to a gentleman as he possibly could.

Etta couldn't sleep. She actually wished he understood the dilemma of her family either participating in or being excluded from the wedding. Etta was feeling like a genuine fraud. How could she ever come clean with her story? She breathed in long and slow, exhaling smoothly into the night. He fell asleep spooning to the right. A sleepless Etta weighed her options, trying to swallow the angst in the pit of her stomach.

When Henry dropped her home Sunday afternoon, he carried an envelope Roberto instructed he leave with Etta at her home. Etta was studying her bracelet, which was getting heavier by the week. It had become a trademark item that people recognized in her community. They referred to her at the chemist or post office as the "American with the bracelet of gold bits." This fashion had not caught on in her community so much as in the larger cities in the UK.

Henry and Etta discussed the romantic weekend, and Henry cheered that this brave young lady had stood her ground, insisting on a church wedding before their intimacy. He was also pleased that Etta was improving greatly in her disposition with the hotel employees and servants. She would be fine, Etta told him, if only she could continue to take lessons with him on occasion. There was still so much she didn't understand. He agreed. But she showed great promise, too.

Inside Etta's front door, she curiously opened the padded envelope to determine its contents. The note said, "Have a fun shop, my queen. Love, Roberto." She counted twice, not believing the first effort. Yes, she *was* correct! Roberto gifted her with two thousand pounds to shop in London!

"Merry Christmas to me!"

Chapter 19
TOWER BRIDGE

Etta woke up in her tiny room on her stomach, an unusual sleeping position. She felt something close to her fingertips under the pillow she clutched. Ah yes, it was the money envelope. Etta had never had this much cash in her life! She left it in its hiding place and dressed for work. She checked Kelly's clothes to be sure they were adequately dry. She neatly wrapped them in brown grocer paper and headed out to work. The snow had all melted now, but Etta was advised about the forecast for Thursday, which included heavy snow. She sure hoped her flight would get out on time. At last report, London would not get this portion of the storm.

Etta returned the clothing with sincere gratitude to Kelly, who wondered why Etta did not need the clothing for the weekend in the city, after all. Etta did not elaborate for fear of sounding vain. She explained only that her boyfriend had left her money to shop with over the weekend. She couldn't even call him a fiancé yet since she did not have a ring from him. But she knew in her heart that the blessing of their wedding was right around the corner.

Etta left promptly to hunt clothing at the thrift store. If she hurried, she could shop for just over an hour before the shop closed. She was meticulous with her purchases, checking every seam, zipper, and all sides of the garments for stains. She also asked the helpful stockers their opinions on the various outfits she selected.

What a cache Etta hit! Someone had dropped a ton of clothing there, many close to her size. She had several personal marathon sessions trying on blouses, pants, dresses, and night clothing. She found several funky shirts she could wear if she ever went back to a disco with Binny.

When the shop announced the last call, Etta had narrowed her series of try-on sessions to eighteen articles of clothing. The bill came to just shy of eighty pounds since Etta had splurged on a camel-colored evening coat that would match the other half of her wardrobe.

Etta realized her quandary just then. How would she get all the clothing home? It was more than she could ever carry. As she pondered the dilemma, she laughed and realized her eyes were bigger than her back. She laughed and shook her head. The checker asked what was wrong. Etta explained that she was, in fact, on foot and that she didn't expect to find so many items. The checker lived southwest of Etta but offered to give her a lift anyhow. After all, the Samaritan worked in a benevolence store. She was all about helping anyone in need. Nearly home, Etta felt very guilty, for she was not as "needy" as the checker may have thought from their discussion, especially now. So she gave the lady a five spot to fill her car and thanked her profusely for the ride.

Etta was grateful that Thursday rushed to meet her. She was packed and ready to go with her faux leather case waiting again by the door to her glasshouse. Only this time, her ride to the airport was right on time.

As anticipated, Etta waited for a few hours, watching travelers and listening to their accents. When she heard a rare American, she dared not speak for fear of the flood of trouble and new adventures that would spill forth on some unknowing stranger. She pretended to be a Brummie and was left quite alone.

The small airplane took off from Elmdon with little sign of the snowstorm everyone waited for. She had scant time to really enjoy the flight before they arrived in London. An elderly man waited at her gate with his pickup sign announcing, "Welcome, Etta Johnson."

The driver was waiting with a luggage cart and was surprised that his fare had only the small case. No luggage checked at all! He drove up to the curb on Piccadilly across from the beautiful Green Park. Etta studied the hotel's colonnade front. The chateau-style structure of the Ritz caught Etta off guard. She hoped she could check in, dressed in her work clothing. She chose to leave her good coat on in hopes they would not see her street clothes. Unnecessarily, the driver took her case to the check-in, where he went without ever making eye contact or conversation with his passenger.

Etta collected the key to the room Binny had reserved for her, and while a bellman took her box to the room, Etta was drawn to the resonating sounds of the casino. From the expressions she surveyed on faces in the room, most were losing big. She looked out of place with her coat buttoned up in the warm lobby of the hotel and retired to her room to enjoy a long bath filled with the luxurious chemicals the maids had left on the bathroom counter.

The lotions and potions were all the same line of fragrance. In theory, she would emerge with one pampered aroma. Etta thought this to be very clever since she had never layered lotions and colognes, nor combined scented products, either. So much to enjoy living the high life! One thing was sure—the bowl of the toilet was deep and effective. She was so intrigued by the waste of water that Etta flushed it just to observe the water levels. The water was retracted with so much force that Etta expected it would take baked-on peanut butter straightaway with one flush. "Whoooosh!" She tested it again with simple amazement and laughter.

Easing into the deep porcelain tub, she picked up handfuls of bath bubbles, creating a bikini for herself. She rested her head against a rolled towel pillow and soaked with the front section of the *London Times,* which the maid left on the hotel room credenza.

By the time Binny phoned to meet up for dinner, it was getting late. The two decided to call room service to Etta's suite since they had not met up quite yet, but they had spoken on the hotel phone exchange.

When Binny arrived at Etta's room, her greeting was stiff. They exchanged a few pleasantries, and then in her direct manner Binny demanded, "Etta, roll back the left sleeve of your shirt for me."

Etta curiously complied and found a tag in the inner lower sleeve marked BEC.

"That's my shirt! I had a designer create that for *me*," Binny exclaimed. "Did my mother give you that shirt?" she continued in an irritated tone.

Etta was deeply humiliated, and her burning face flushed with shame. "No. Binny, I didn't have time to round up clothing for the weekend, so I shopped at the benevolent shop for 'fill-ins.'"

Binny threw her head back and laughed from deep in her gut. "Why on earth would you do that, Etta? You can borrow clothes any time you wish. What is up with you?"

Etta felt it was the appropriate confession time if this friendship would ever go further. "You were in London, so

I couldn't possibly ask you here..." She found it difficult to know just where to start. She chose to start in the middle.

Inhale, exhale. And then Etta inhaled once more deeply before she began. "When I arrived in London, my clothing and goods were in tow with my passport, money, and all. I was extremely tired from the series of flights, so while I dozed, someone stole all my stuff. To make matters worse, I was delivered to the wrong town with no money. That's how I met Margaret. Her nephew just happened to be in England, and he took me to her home for assistance."

"Man! Your mum must have had a bloomin' fit!" Binny exclaimed.

"Not at all! I messed it up, and I will work it out. I couldn't ever ask her to rescue me. No, she doesn't know any of it. All she knows is that I have a good job, rent a nice place, and I have a serious boyfriend now. I couldn't bear to tell them about the predicament I got myself into."

"I really admire your tenacity, Etta. I believe I would have done the same. Maybe that's why I like you so. You think like a scrapper, and yet you sport grace. I haven't quite got that yet. I have been accused of being too rough around the edges. But just fer grins, show me your other 'new' clothes."

Etta pulled out the small case and revealed the three other outfits and her coat. Of the seven pieces, five of them were formerly Binny's.

"Well, Etta, at least you have good taste, even if it's last year's look. Promise me something. Now we are in shopping Mecca. Please don't ever buy my hand-me-downs! If you want *anything*, I'll hand it over or take you for a shop."

Room service arrived while Binny was busy updating Etta on her successful winter calendar. It was the perfect time to introduce Kelly's résumé. Etta added to the brief details about this prospect. "Kelly is a perfect fit for the type of lifestyle this job offers. She is a cute, curly-top redhead with a lovely smile. too. She seems to be extremely trainable, perhaps with a silversmith."

"Or in forging iron…" Binny considered. "I may give her a shot. She'd have to meet the foreman. He's a burly toughie. He may not want a female to apprentice. Then again…"

The two friends shared a laugh, both knowing someone in their past who had been tamed by a good woman. With the prospect of a long day of shopping, they wrapped up the evening without tea or dessert. Etta had one final thought after her recent dilemma. How would they transport the newly acquired clothing back to the hotel?

"If you don't have the car, how will we be able to shop very long?"

Binny announced her shopping strategy. "The driver will do double duty, playing fetch for us. He delivers our packages between departments to the car. That way we shop unencumbered."

Etta thought this was a grand idea. Not having ever been much of a shopper at all, she was excited at the prospect of building a new wardrobe this weekend. She had only a few people to Christmas shop for. That would be the easier task.

"Binny," Etta called down the hall as the two departed to bed, "I want you to know how much I appreciate all that you have done for me. Especially this wonderful trip. How can I thank you?" Though she expected it was a courteous, rhetorical question, Binny answered her.

"You, my dear, will join me at a public house, and *you buy*!" Her chuckles could be heard all the way into her room, disappearing behind the door.

This was Binny, in true, rare form—staying at the Ritz but grabbing a pint of stout at a pub.

Etta was at the mercy of Binny's agenda and was along for the ride. So surprisingly, the driver took the liberty of driving along the Thames in a gesture of tourist hospitality. He didn't narrate the marvelous Victorian engineering feats, but Etta could read on his face that he was extremely proud to have the opportunity to show this American *his* Tower of London and the Tower Bridge.

Binny explained that the walkways that linked the two towers had been closed since 1909 due to prostitute trafficking and the popularity of the spot for countless successful suicides.

Etta recalled the childhood dance, "London Bridge is falling down, my fair lady!"

Another bridge, formerly over the Thames River, was deemed too weak in the sixties. Etta recalled the surprising news that an oil chairman had struck the winning bid with just shy of two and a half million dollars. His intent was to reconstruct it at an Army Air Corps rest camp from World War II in Arizona, of all places. With the lord mayor of London laying the cornerstone, thereby adding validity to the strange project, thousands of spectators in Lake Havasu felt just a tad more connected to the British. Etta was proud to have witnessed this English shrine, dedicated in her home state. It was all she knew of England. Now she was up close and personal.

The bridge looked similar to her London Bridge, but this one was in its natural element. This was a well-recognized source of architectural pride. *It was a true London bridge, and it ain't falling!* Etta thought of the Tower Bridge.

Binny's travels were not marked in any logical touring order; rather, they were scattered by how she wanted to shop. The first store they would visit would be to "clothe the inners." The undies store. Etta was unsure she would feel comfortable with the driver wandering around with them until he could carry their purchases to the car. Etta would just have to give up a few things for this strange opportunity—like modesty.

The driver, Harrison, pulled over on Knightsbridge and announced the first stop on Binny's written instructions to him. "Ladies, may I present Bradley's, so you can shop from the inside out. Have a ball!" Harrison remarked in a teasing tone that he could get away with only because Binny had a history of tormenting him in this special lingerie store. He was not comfortable yet with Binny, who modeled particular items for him, but he was getting better at suppressing the anxious feeling of being one of few men in the store. She paid him well to judge her taste. Good thing Binny had a nice body. He rather enjoyed her company on a good day, also.

Etta remarked that while they were here, she would select some unmentionables for her wedding night, too.

"Wedding night? What did I miss, Etta? Are you engaged to Margaret's nephew? No wait! You *aren't* going to marry Joseph, are you?" Binny's quick-tongue mouth kept up with her alert mind, and it was sometimes hard for Etta to get a word in edgewise.

"No, I met the most amazing man. When we were out last month at Circo, I saw a man who instantly caught my eye. It was as if I knew he was there, waiting for me. He felt exactly the same way that night. In fact, it must have been fate because he showed up at my work the next week. It was love at first sight, I swear! Anyhow, his name is Roberto Luis Fernandez. He lives between here and Barcelona running two technology businesses."

Binny took all this information in, not daring to tell Etta that *fate* was actually her big mouth. His intentions sounded honorable if he intended to marry her, after all. She still had a strange feeling about that original call, though. She just couldn't place the origin of that discomfort in her memory.

"I have to start shopping for a house when I get back. Roberto hoped I would find a suitable one by the end of the year." Etta looked absolutely starry-eyed and distant at the moment.

Popping her back into reality, Binny said, "Harrison, this little lady needs something saucy for the holidays. Can you fetch her a prop or two?"

Harrison's ears grew red, and he complied, turning the other direction to find a few things that the man in question might appreciate.

The sensible nightwear was displayed in the tone of "The Night before Christmas," and the warm flannels looked inviting, also. She set one aside with Binny just rolling her eyes.

"Hey! I'll be living alone when he goes to Barcelona for business. Who's going to keep me warm?" Etta stated defensively.

"You can always call Joseph over. He wouldn't mind if you were married. He's still struck with you," Binny teased.

"Get off that dead bronco! I told him I wasn't interested!" Etta replied.

Binny sang, "There's always hope!"

An exasperated Etta looked the full height of the decorations announcing Father Christmas's arrival very soon. It would be a sad Christmas, all alone. But it would also be one of great anticipation. Roberto had promised they would celebrate Christmas together when he returned from business. The bright red ribbons strewn across the room were a stark contrast to the revealing camisoles Etta was approaching on the next garment rack.

Harrison returned with two pairs of French knickers in white and black. He also found an elegant silk camisole with lovely lace and pearl trim. He did have good taste, even if he wasn't a sporting shopper.

Etta appreciated the items he handed to her, but she felt too shy to model them outside the proper dressing room. It was cold in the store, and Etta took only quick peeks at a camisole and the other selections, quickly covering herself to stay warm. She chose several romantic getups, coupled with a colorful, saucy outfit. The final purchase included two proper slips for her dress attire.

As Etta was approaching the checkout counter, she noticed a swarm of men in the store. *They must have to shop for*

Christmas items, Etta considered. She struck up a pleasant conversation with a beautiful woman surveying more items near the register as she waited to check out. After a friendly discourse and a farewell holiday wish, Etta left the other woman to purchase her wares. A coldness swept across the room as if Etta were being watched.

When Harrison placed her items in the car, he exhaled and said, "Fancy that, you having the nerve to speak directly with Princess Anne."

Etta was stunned. She did not attend to her face and would never have been able to pick the princess out of a crowd, despite having spoken comfortably with her. It had been but a simple conversation between two passersby. But she had conversed with the beloved Princess Anne! It seemed so fortuitous. She just knew the rest of the day would be a fabulous success.

Etta replaced the former Binny thrift finds with a lovely assortment of dresses and sportswear from Benetton on Brompton Road.

Binny was not finding as much as Etta, but she was not involved in the desperate pursuit of constructing an entire wardrobe, either.

The holiday gift selections began at Cartier on New Bond Street. Etta modeled various gold and platinum pieces on Harrison, settling on a stunning pair of platinum cuff links set with rubies. She would tell Roberto that the rubies would remind him of their brilliant love.

Binny treated herself to earrings, but she purchased nothing for the family. She felt a pang of jealousy not having a man in her life to shop for this holiday. The cheerful, shiny spheres and beautifully decorated storefront Christmas trees had an adverse effect on Binny this year. Instead of filling her with good cheer, she felt lonely and sad. It would be another holiday with her folks unless she wanted to be alone—again.

After a few more specialty shops, Binny grew impatient with her gift hunting. She instructed Harrison to take them to the Knightsbridge, Harrods department store. Unlike the other stops of the morning, this store was staffed by thousands of employees serving hundreds of departments. This gigantic shopping experience made the Goldwater's department store at home look like a mere community five-and-dime.

Harrison was on his toes, being careful to stay within two departments of the two women. His task was much like herding chickens. Tough, that! He made three, six, nine trips back to the car before he quit counting. The purchase he did not carry off to the security of the car was Etta's jewelry. She bought an elegant statement necklace that matched her bracelet's triple link pattern constructed of sturdy, thick rings. She added large, ornate earrings, which would make a perfect evening set. Finally, she selected another charm for her bracelet. As she shopped the next few departments over, the jewelers mounted the replica of the Tower Bridge on her bracelet. Etta wore the new necklace and earrings, keeping the receipt in her new purse.

Etta selected five gifts for Roberto and two trademark items to bring home for her mother and sister. She bought a beautiful Wedgwood vase for Margaret and a box of Cuban cigars for Harvey. She excused herself to try on a dress, a ruse to let Etta count her leftover cash. She had put a dent in it, all right. Binny had better luck now, sending Harrison to the car more times than Etta. He was genuinely concerned about the passenger seating with the packages piling high into the cab with a full trunk, to boot! Etta reserved three pounds to buy the round of pints for Harrison and Binny. From the leftover three hundred thirty-one pounds, she would offer a really nice tip.

Etta couldn't say she even liked the aroma of the reddish beer Harrison recommended she try. Binny drank a stout one, and Harrison ordered a lighter brown. Etta enjoyed looking at the various colors of brew against the dim lights as she drank her herbal chamomile tea. She was able to put down only one cup before calling it quits. The others had already downed their pints, with Harrison quickly consuming a second. The sun set behind the treasury of chimney pots, casting a broken glow through the spires. Etta was pleased with her first day in London. She saw more about the styles and cosmopolitan habits of English women than she had in her neighborhood of Edgbaston.

The unpacking went smoothly since Harrison had thought to mark each woman's bags with a designated colored ribbon. The two ladies filled the trunk, the left side of the front seat, and the full middle of the backseat, thereby requiring they scrunch against the doors on the trek back to the hotel.

Once relaxed in her hotel environment, Etta showered the stench of the city pollution off her skin and retired into her cozy, flannel pajamas. She tossed and turned, missing the new experience of what it was like to sleep cradled in Roberto's arms. She put two pillows behind her back and slept in the pretense that Roberto was sleeping next to her tonight.

Saturday did not feel as urgent as the previous day had been. The two women enjoyed a leisurely breakfast in the gold-emblazoned décor of the Palm Court, where guests were fortunate enough to be treated to a fashion parade. Though Binny enjoyed the show immensely, taking note of the designers and new cuts, Etta was not about this type of trendy fashion. She preferred to make her own style. Etta was one step ahead or one step to the left of what was determined to be "in style" this season, according to these samples on this catwalk.

Binny's afternoon plans were interrupted by an urgent business matter. She sent Etta off with Harrison and left in one of the hotel taxicabs for a few hours. Harrison drove Etta the short distance to Regent's Park. She felt funny sitting behind him when there were only two in the car, but it was the appropriate thing to do. She enjoyed his company but gained more from her student-mentor relationship with Henry.

Upon her request, Harrison accompanied her on a cold stroll through the London Zoo. Not many animals were active, but their conversation was enjoyable. They hiked out to an open theatre, which protected a few traces of snow. It would be lovely to return in the spring to this area. The lake was inviting, but these boats were hibernating until spring would bring lovers out once again. When they returned to the hotel, Etta ordered a late afternoon tea. She left a message for Binny that she was back and would meet up with her in the hotel somewhere. Easy for Binny. She could eliminate the salon, casino, lounges, and bars. It wasn't that hard to find Etta, really. She was a unique-looking individual, exotic in these surroundings. Binny described her to the hotel staff and was promptly directed to the tearoom.

Binny was shopped out, a rare condition for her. Etta didn't want to blow the entire wad and graciously agreed to throw in the towel on their gift hunt. They decided on French cuisine for dinner, but it was, again, a matter of Binny suggesting and Etta agreeing.

Once spruced up in her russet-colored finery and fresh jewelry designs, Etta felt like a million bucks and carried herself like a billion. Etta entranced a roomful of male eyes as she gracefully walked across the lobby to meet the taxi-cab assigned to them. Binny looked radiant, too, in more feminine attire than her norm. She sported a soft, brown fox fur. Etta enjoyed the appearance of fur, but she was still not comfortable with the idea of wrapping one around her body.

Le Mercury was at capacity, with parties waiting to be seated. Binny, not accustomed to waiting even for her next breath, slipped the host a twenty pound note and said, "Reservation for Colmore, party of two."

With the knowledge of no seats available, the host replied, "Right this way." He slowly walked the room, shifting his eyes only side to side to survey the tables. He found a couple just standing to leave in the center left of the room. He led them in that direction and remarked, "Would you ladies like to freshen up before seating this table?"

"Why, of course, thank you," Binny stated, understanding the obvious.

When the ladies headed toward the powder room, the host himself hunted a bus boy to rapidly clear the table. By the time the two women had checked their hair and washed their hands, the table was prepared with fresh linen and service.

The plethora of shopping bags took extra time getting to and collecting from the airport. The women took it all in stride patiently and appreciatively accepted help from anyone who offered. Etta wished sincerely that every person would have at least one opportunity to be treated in such a special manner. It seemed that money begets money, and status begets status. While cruel reality was one of life's deck of cards, Etta now possessed a very good hand.

Chapter 20
OPEN COUNTRY CARRIAGE

Etta would work only three days. The two days off were paid holidays despite the terms of her employment. The small desk calendar announced a dinner with Margaret on Wednesday evening and eggnog with Binny Christmas Eve. Christmas Day was entirely blank. Geraldine would leave Wednesday evening to be with family. So the house would be empty, save for Etta and the sparse holiday décor that had been hurriedly arranged, more out of obligation than celebratory spirit.

The workdays were tough on Etta with many staff members covering other people's positions so they could spend the holiday with their families. The snow had fallen for two days straight, blanketing the parking lot each night and luring the potential customers to the cozy seats beside their fireplaces, where most had stockings hung with care. Etta could count on one hand each day the total number of visitors. Even Kelly left on Tuesday for the week. She rode the bus to London to meet with Binny's blacksmith in hopes of securing a job. Kelly paid for an economy hotel, but Binny invested in the bus fare.

Etta missed having children around. In this older section of town, no children played. Only a rare visit to relatives provided her with glimpses of children in the streets. With the school holiday, she didn't have any tot groups at the cactus room.

She installed an unused office chair in the back corner of the glasshouse. It looked comically out of place, but she placed it so she would hear when visitors entered, but she could still enjoy hours of undisturbed solace with the stack of books Larkin had ordered for the central reference. Etta brought her journal to fill the time. She was pleased that poetry and lyrical language patterns of her experience had replaced the touristy notes of her formative transition into local culture.

She understood Roberto was busy this week, but she wished she could have talked to him more. The Tuesday evening call, the only one for this week, was mostly a business update. He was between meetings but wanted to hear her voice before Christmas, anyhow. He couldn't wait to see her next week. Roberto asked how London was and if she had found a house. Etta felt like he must be in some time warp to assume she could find a house with the few hours of daylight she'd had the past two weeks. She didn't admit to him she had not begun to look. She was too depressed. From a two-week high, she crashed hard emotionally. Missing home and missing him, she was feeling very low.

Etta was extremely grateful for Wednesday night. Margaret and Harvey had the homey aura of Christmas seeping through every room; the spicy scents of the holiday were especially apparent in the kitchen and living room.

Holly and ivy trails lined the mantle and the broad oak bookcases. A family-created nativity rested in the foyer with a lone angel perched atop a wire overlooking the papier-mâché crèche. The figures were all formed rather nicely with painted robes and faces.

Harvey reported with excitement that both his daughter, Grace, and son, Harold, would be visiting them for Christmas with their families. This would be a first for all of them. The families were both busy with the children's friends and activities. It was tough to get one family, much less both of them, this time of year! A pang gripped Etta, and she struggled to appear happy for them. She observed the gaily wrapped packages under the tree and wondered what the grandkids would be opening.

The Christmas tree was placed in the outer hall, making passage difficult. A star crowning the tree was apparently fashioned by the family as well. It was a conglomeration of foil stretched over cardboard and covered amply with glitter and beads. The boughs of the tree were draped with large swoops of gold garland in five tiers. Ornaments ranged from crimson velvet diamonds, to colored glass circus animals, to spun icicles. There were a few clove-punctured oranges hanging on the tree that Etta breathed in deeply with her eyes shut. This was one of her favorite Christmas aromas.

They sat in the cozy living room in front of a roaring fire. It made Etta feel a tad bit sleepy and lazy. In a mental sojourn back home, she would have plopped down on the floor to nap right there, dress clothes and all. Etta had changed so much these past months.

Etta offered a long speech of appreciation for everything that they had done to help her. She informed them about her plans to purchase a home in the area now that she was to be married.

This was surprising news to the Kendalls, who expected Etta to get on the first flight back to America that she could afford. They didn't pry, but how could she possibly afford a house on her salary? Etta answered their curiosity, detailing Roberto's businesses and how they would have two homes. She would stay here, though, and keep her job. Etta was pleased he did not expect her to travel back and forth with him every week.

The Kendalls agreed that it would be hard on a new bride to have to live between houses and learn a new language to boot. Margaret loved to travel, but regrettably she was also ignorant of other languages. It was a shame, too. So many languages, so close! In the military, Harvey had learned to speak enough French to know he didn't want to speak it or visit France again. He preferred the sound of the German language. Though he was never schooled in it, he could get by.

When Margaret opened the Wedgwood vase, she gasped and placed her right hand over her heart. "Why, Etta, this is the most beautiful thing. You really are too much!" Margaret carefully set the vase in a predominant place on the mantle. "Oh, Etta, it's just lovely, really lovely! You really shouldn't have!" And unexpectedly she grabbed Etta in a tight hug. It was in this evening that Margaret realized Etta was going to be all right financially. She had wondered from afar how to further help this lost American. She knew now that Etta would be fine.

Harvey was equally pleased with the box of fine cigars. He had enjoyed two cigars of equal quality in his life. One was at his own bachelor's party. The other was when the war ended. He couldn't remember who had bought that box, but since there weren't enough to go around, the men had passed them around, each smoking off whichever one was near his grip. He would share these with his son and son-in-law; neither, to his knowledge, had partaken in the festivity of a really great imported smoke.

Margaret acted almost apologetic for their gift to Etta. They bought her a nice gold charm from the Jewellery Quarter. The detail of the horse was exceptional. He was directed by a miniscule driver seated in front of the airy carriage. It was lovely work, and Etta was clearly pleased to add this to her bracelet.

"I hope you have room on the charm bracelet. You could wear it on a chain if you wish."

"By all means, yes! I still don't have a camera, so every charm I add to the links becomes part of my story. I have people to meet, places to go, and contracts to sign!" Etta stated cheerily. "There is room for perhaps twenty more!"

"Then you really must record how you collected these for your own children," Margaret replied, boldly assuming that she and her fiancé would have children soon.

"That's a wonderful idea!" Etta contemplated the project, and it seemed so obvious. Why hadn't she thought to send this to her family back home?

Etta felt so blessed to have found this family who took her in when she was stranded and lost. It made her contemplate the story of the manger even deeper this year. Etta felt relaxed as her body ingested the homemade eggnog, a specialty of Margaret's. She eased into a content, lazy feeling that made all the decorations more lovely and all the ribbon-tied packages less intimidating. With dark setting in and conversation waning, Harvey offered to drive Etta home.

Etta complied, thinking about the energy she would have to expend to hike back home. She hugged Margaret again, thanking her for rescuing her some months ago and for the lovely charm. Margaret felt better, understanding that it didn't matter the difference in cost of their gifts; Etta was obviously very appreciative of the charm she had carefully selected for the bracelet. *Etta will make a wonderful wife and hostess,* Margaret thought. She wondered just what those children would look like with such a beautiful mother and the dark, handsome father Etta described as her fiancé.

Harvey drove slowly through the empty streets. The car slid at every corner, and it eased into every stop. Etta was not even concerned in her deliriously comfortable state. She hugged Harvey, kissed him on the cheek, and thanked him again for opening his home to her.

From the front door, Etta watched his car disappear into the soft, fresh snowfall. *Sigh*. Etta went out the back door, still dressed in her evening wear, and plopped down, back first into the snow. She landed with a crunch, making a perfect body outline. Etta swept her arms and legs back and forth with some restriction from her dress. Standing up, Etta was pleased with herself. She had completed her first snow angel in the backyard. It decorated nearly the entire yard, being a small plot of land. She wondered how long her own Christmas angel would stand watch over the house.

Christmas Eve morning, Etta awoke to observe the continuation of the softly falling snowflakes. She checked the back of her coat, and it had dried just fine. Etta went out back in just her flannel nightgown to check on the angel. Though the outline was still visible, all the details were buried under a fresh layer of snow. Etta felt a little silly for dropping down into the snow last night. But it was perfect timing since no one witnessed her spontaneity.

Sleeping in was a real luxury for Etta, and she accentuated the restful feeling with a hearty breakfast. She found only Typhoo tea in the cupboard. She would pass on the tea, instead adding lemon to hot water to make it taste more along the lines of a fruit flavor she enjoyed most. She served up the last portion (and a half) of Farley's Rusks with milk. Truthfully, she had not eaten cereal with milk in many years. She generally didn't care for milk and instead ate cereal a handful at a time as a snack, rather than as a meal. Planning to eat at the table, Etta worked hard passing the time. She set the table with full silverware, folding a napkin neatly for the side of the bowl. There was an unopened carton of orange juice. She poured a glass and stood with her hands on her hips, wondering what else she could do to the table. Just then, the phone rang. She left the kitchen and picked up the phone in the next room.

"*Feliz Navidad!* Etta, *mi amor*. I wanted to call you before I went to my parents' home. I miss you desperately. I feel only half myself. It's so hard being away from you at Christmas. I miss you terribly, Etta."

Etta had desperately tried to distance herself from the intense feelings she had for Roberto. The call entirely broke the effort. "Roberto, I want you here today. Can't you just come for Christmas? I miss you too, so much."

"I can't come for Christmas, but I can meet you in Italy next week. I have to go there on Wednesday. Can you fly in on Friday, and we will celebrate the holiday and us?"

"Post-Christmas in Italy. Let me check my busy schedule, dear…Oh, I'm not sure I can make it…," Etta teased.

"Did you pack your documents?"

"Yes, I did, but I'm not sure…"

"But Et—"

"Until the afternoon flight." She giggled.

"Thank you, God. I thought you would not want to come. I know how you feel about not knowing Spanish. But I know enough Italian that I can show you a nice weekend."

"Ciao! That's the only word I know so far."

"Call my secretary, Bernadette, on Monday with your documents in hand. Tell her you need to be in Venice by eight Friday evening. I'll let you know next week where I will be working and how I will hook up with you."

"I can't wait to see you. The house is empty here, Roberto. Maybe it will be easier when we have our own home together," Etta said, envisioning a home in spring, not in the cold winter months of her present reality.

"A home together…that has a nice sound. I wish you were here right now! But I need hang up now and attend to my family. Know that I love you forever. I can't wait to see you next week. Merry Christmas, my love."

"Merry Christmas I love you more," Etta challenged.

"Not possible. I am older, so I have waited longer. I have to go." The phone disconnected abruptly.

While Etta did not wait for his phone calls, she sure needed them. She didn't know how to take the hang up. It was similar to the same ill-mannered tone when he phoned her from a work meeting. Cultural? Men in general? Whom to blame? She chose to forgive and forget it.

She returned to the kitchen to celebrate her breakfast alone. She put the orange juice back in the refrigerator and enjoyed her cereal with a background of English Christmas carols coming from the BBC through the portable radio unit in the windowsill.

After breakfast, Etta entertained herself for a few hours making a wreath out of newspaper-wrapped metal coat hangers covered with tin foil. She formed leaves with the quill pen and marked the veins with ink. She attached these foil leaves to hangers with sufficient thickness to cover the newsprint on the circular form.

Removing the picture over her bed, Etta placed the wreath on the wall. She stepped back off the bed and admired it. From a few feet away, it did not look altogether bad. She returned to the kitchen and borrowed a few cranberries from the grocer's pint. Securing the berries with toothpicks, she positioned them on any weight-bearing ledges of the wreath. That did the trick. Now it really looked smart. It was the only cheerful focal point in the room, save for the wrapping paper beneath the box the Kendalls had presented Etta with.

Etta determined that now she could ready herself for the evening activities. She bathed and lathered herself in the multitude of chemicals left over from the London hotel. Freshly groomed and in a new dress, Etta felt much better about the evening. This was definitely a traverse too long for a snowy walk in heels, so Etta phoned a taxicab to take her to the Colmore Manor.

From the looks of the cars at the entry, all the kids were home. The estate was brightly lit against the snow by white holiday lights. Lovely, long strands of garland topped with fresh snow adorned the ironwork on the estate.

Etta thanked the taxi driver, offering a large tip for the season. She unbuttoned her coat and smoothed her wool dress before ringing the bell. Thomas and Molly answered the door, exposing the winter wonderland inside. Thomas grabbed Etta right in front of Molly and kissed her on the lips under the mistletoe above the doorway. Etta appeared stunned; Molly just giggled and took her hand. While Thomas took her coat (as if he owned the place), Molly led Etta into the library where their friends had congregated, sharing stories of Christmas past.

Arthur rose first, greeting Etta with a kiss on the cheek and offering his, "Merry Christmas!"

After which, Greta rose from the best chair in the room to take both of Etta's hands. "So glad you can join us tonight, Etta. Happy holidays." Greta offered Etta a weak but sincere hug.

Binny was dressed in her new black satin dress pants with her legs curled underneath her on the coach. She wore no shoes or socks, which Etta thought odd, for this house was chilly, even with the fires roaring in several rooms. "Merry Christmas, Etta," Binny said, revealing that she had already downed a few drinks and something was on her mind. Etta could pick that much up.

The brothers were all in attendance, but it was Joseph who rose from the couch, and armed with his best manners of the year, he grasped Etta's unwilling hands and kissed her on the cheek. "Merry Christmas, Etta," he said hopefully. He stood while Etta found her seat. There were only two spots available on perpendicular sofas. When she sat down on the one nearest Binny's younger brother, Jeremy, Joseph moved to the seat next to her. A surprised Etta looked Binny's way, just in time to see her roll her eyes and turn her head up slightly in dismay.

Josiah called to the wait staff to bring Etta a glass, and a man in a black suit arrived with a silver tray offering cognac, brandy, or scotch. Having not sampled any of these liquors before, Etta declined, while Binny selected brandy only because it was the bottle in the center. He poured only a few splashes and swirled it in the glass before offering it to her. Binny carefully took the odd-shaped glass offering without so much as a thank you. Etta understood her role. The house staff did not expect to exchange pleasantries with guests, anyhow. They were not offended because it was just the way things were in Birmingham. Etta attempted to balance kindness and appreciation with protocol.

The family Christmas tree stood in a larger room. In the room in which they sat, a massive carved mantelshelf above the roaring fire was lined with miniature Christmas trees decorated with small, dried fruits. Ribbons encircled the small trees like garland. A series of candles burned at various heights in the center, to set off the festive collection.

The enormous mirror on the west wall was framed with thick red and green plaid ribbons. Fixed to the ribbons with straight pins were assorted Christmas cards. An alcove beside the mirror housed a beautifully sculpted marble angel. Etta wondered whether it was a permanent display or if the angel replaced the regular contents for this time of the year.

While Etta took in the room, she didn't notice Joseph taking her in. He was enjoying watching her eyes. She seldom moved her head, but her eyes were actively taking in the details of the room. Gosh, she had beautiful eyes. Joseph did not know how to engage her in conversation, so he just beheld her, entrapping the lovely vision of her in his mind's eye.

The conversation roamed around the room in collections and in whole group political discussions, which Etta had difficulty with, being a foreigner. Thomas announced to the group that he and Molly would celebrate their wedding in February and wanted to be sure all would attend. Josiah applauded first, shaking his head and saying, "Of course we will, of course!"

Arthur offered the toast, "To *one* lucky of us," and then he surprised the group by adding, "Mum." The group howled and jibed Molly, saying they were glad to be rid of Thomas. She was a great sport about it, offering her preliminary apology that she would be keeping him too busy for visits with the boys. Why, with all the yard work, dishwashing, and the rambling list of chores...! Her discourse broke off with sounds of "Oh no!" from all the men.

Greta interrupted the group by announcing they should have a bite to eat. She led the way down the grand hall decorated with floorboard stands of berry-covered holly sprigs and intermittent white-sprayed pinecones. It was so simple, but so elegant. Etta was taking visual notes as usual. She lagged in the group with Binny, who took her by the arm.

"Sorry about Joseph. He thinks there is still time to recover you since you've not announced your engagement and you aren't wearing a noose yet."

"Are you all right, Binny? I can see something is up with you," Etta said, ignoring the comments and choosing to focus on the subtle cues the rest of the group missed.

"Let's talk later," Binny ended right in the doorway.

The tree in the room seemed to catapult up toward the vaulted ceiling. Etta could not even see what topped it. Instead, she saw a collection of fragile, blown-glass ornaments covering a candlelit tree. She couldn't believe the fire hazard or how someone had ever lit the candles in the first place. It was an enchanting spectacle. The flickering candlelight danced off the shiny, painted glass, bouncing along the deep wood panels. When Etta's eyes moved down the walls, she found the table set with china Christmas plates. Green and red candlesticks filled the spectacular candelabra on either end of the table.

Before anyone settled on a seat, the doorbell rang. Jeremy excused himself and escorted three of the cousins in. Jeremy introduced them to Etta, Thomas, and Molly and reintroduced them to Arthur.

They all took their seats, and the plates began to arrive in waves. Though all were bite-sized samples, the group filled their stomachs in feast. The crystal punchbowl was only half emptied, but the dessert trays were bare by the time conversation began to wane.

They collectively rose from the table and followed conversation in all directions. Binny took the opportunity to sweep Etta back into the library. She closed the door and gate to the fireplace to cool the room some.

"Etta, you are different than anyone I know. When I got your sweet note card this week, it made me treasure your friendship all the more. Do you realize that you are the first friend I have had since the sixth grade who has not wanted something from me? Even my best friends expect something of me. I have learned not to trust friends, but I feel I can really talk to you because you vest no interest in me. Isn't that right?" Binny asked with pleading eyes.

"Of course Binny. You can talk to me. What's happening?" Etta asked, with her naturally empathetic tone.

Binny started to cry silently. Her shoulders rocked, and her head went down on her hands. The tears came in a solid stream down her face, and she collected great effort to speak as quietly as possible. "I just don't know if I want all this. I have worked so hard for so long, and for what? To prove I can be my mother? I'm not like her at all. She has it naturally, and I have worked and worked, and I am just tired of it all. All I want to do is settle down and be somebody's mum. I am thinking about adoption, Etta," Binny said, looking directly at Etta now. Her eye makeup had run down her forlorn face, and the desperation in her brow line suggested that this was not an alcohol revelation, but a long contemplation Binny had concealed so deeply that it had festered.

Etta was not sure how to go about this delicate line of questioning. "Do you want a relationship or a child?" Etta began.

"I would love a relationship, but I have no one to trust. I can't follow instincts because I have too much to lose."

"Wait a second. You implied that the business and your money are not what you wanted. If that's true, why aren't you willing to wager it to find a nice guy?" Etta challenged respectfully.

Binny contemplated this. "I really want kids before my clock stops, Etta."

Etta laughed quietly. "Binny, I know women in their forties who had their first child. You are only in your twenties. Why do you worry about that? I don't know about your acquaintances, but I know a whole lot of people who didn't find love until well after school. Maybe what you want is safe companionship, Binny, not a baby. The way I see it, a baby is the product of a loving relationship. I just don't see you adopting a child. Would you consider adopting a small dog that could travel with you?" Etta countered.

"But, Etta, I have never owned a dog," Binny chuckled.

"But, Binny, you haven't adopted a baby, either," Etta replied.

"You know, you're right. I guess I am just really hard up for some affection. The idea of a pup may be a rather good one. Is it possible to meet some nice male without being stung?" Binny asked, cheering up some.

"You could walk the dog. Or...yes. I think I know someone who can entertain you for a date or two. You game?" Etta asked.

"Sure," answered Binny who trusted that even if Etta had never fixed anyone up before, she would recommend only good people. Her circle of friends did not really overlap Binny's, so it was possible to find someone who didn't know her family history and was not out for her money.

Binny's eyes dried, and Etta sighed. Etta offered her friend an uncharacteristic hug before phoning for a taxicab. Binny was sobering as evidenced by the clarity of conversation. She saw the line of logic Etta freely offered with such ease. Etta was a wise one. Binny would take her counsel.

Greta entered the library, startled at the sight of her daughter in such a raw heap of emotion. "Oh dear! What did I interrupt?" she said in her matriarchal tone.

Etta responded, "Binny is going to start the New Year off by adopting a puppy companion." Leave it to Etta to reduce a thirty-minute therapy session to the significant words Matron Colmore honed in on: adopt and pup.

Greta instantly understood the root of the issue and let it go. She offered a small Christmas package to Etta. "I'm sorry you missed the entertainment. Joseph, Josiah, and Jeremy performed a re-creation of the wise men; they sang 'We Three Kings' with beards, wigs, and all. It was a hoot!"

"Thank you so much for inviting me, Greta. Do you mind if I save this for tomorrow? I want to enjoy it on Christmas morning."

"Fine, Etta, I'm just so glad to have another woman in our company. We are now far too many men in the clan."

"Not that any are respectable prospects, mind you...," Binny said, rolling her eyes.

Greta stayed and talked for a few more minutes before the cab arrived. The three women had such different dispositions and outlooks they were guaranteed never to run out of interesting conversation in this lifetime.

Chapter 21
ITALIAN HORN

Etta would have liked to forget that long, lonely Christmas Day, only there were shreds of physical evidence left in her room. The sole Christmas card from her sister and mother. The Christmas Eve invitation from Greta. The only package she opened Christmas morning was from Greta. It was a darling Spode milk pitcher. Etta loved the pitcher's blue pattern, but she contemplated what she would use it for.

Etta had written a nice thank you letter to Greta, including a request for her expertise in search of a home. She was open with the matriarch, detailing how much was in the account and that her fiancé would be taking care of the staffing. She explained that there was no furniture to be moved, which made the matter more difficult as she would need to acquire at least two rooms of furniture and a basic kitchen setup prior to moving in.

Upon receipt of the letter of gratitude, Greta responded to the detailed questionnaire as any loving mum would. She asked Etta to tea. She met Etta at work in the pavilion on Tuesday afternoon. Etta described their requirements and hopes for additional perks. The fact that Etta had resolved to stay in this community would help immensely. Greta was flattered that Etta sought her counsel on a matter of such personal importance. Greta's idea was to locate a furnished home. She gave Etta the cards of her personal banker and lawyer, instructing Etta to introduce herself and announce her intentions prior to working with real estate brokerages. If she could locate a home in legal probate or one that was available through an estate, she might be able to combine the two tasks. Although Greta did not have a property agent to refer Etta to, the banker would be sure to advise her further.

Etta was very encouraged by the wealth of information Greta provided. In an act of courtesy, Etta paid the tab before offering a farewell. Greta was impressed with Etta's mannerly, pleasant demeanor. How she wished that Joseph had cleaned up his act before meeting this wonderful young woman. She would have made a stellar daughter-in-law. For now, she was pleased with her occasional company as Binny's close confidant.

Etta returned to task, but not until after poking her head into the gift shop for Kelly. She was still not back. Etta wondered if it had been a good idea at all to try to find a place in London for her.

Wednesday afternoon she met with the banker, and Thursday afternoon she met with the lawyer. In both cases, she changed into her professional clothing hoping to be taken more seriously. No trouble there. Greta had phoned ahead introducing her as a personal family friend. Both meetings went splendidly and she felt confident they would keep an ear out for the Fernandez's interest.

Geraldine returned from visiting the family and Etta felt the urge to have a sit-down talk with her. She had been a great landlord. Etta explained the engagement situation and that they would be searching for a home in the area. Etta requested she keep an eye open for anyone who may wish to move and settle out of the community.

No reason for Mrs. Bonneville to be surprised there. She had watched this young lady evolve so quickly into a rising star. She was surprised Etta stayed the month of December. Etta had respected her house rules in every minute detail. While she could not understand why a young lady would accept such a short engagement, that was her business. Geraldine had enjoyed a slightly higher status on the block with the more regular arrival and departure of limousines and taxicabs at her home. Etta would stay here until she was married and agreed to pay week to week until she knew for certain when she could pack her room.

Friday welcomed the greatly anticipated flight to Italy. She distracted herself by writing her family about the engagement and Christmas holiday, skating over the sad parts, while strapped onto a turbulent flight to the Aeroporto Marco Polo.

A driver welcomed Etta to the airport with a sign announcing Luna Hotel Baglioni. He was a cheerful chap with a demeanor altogether different from those in Britain. First, he welcomed her in Italian. When he recognized she didn't understand, he tried French and Spanish.

"I speak English. Do you speak English?"

The driver appeared surprised. "English little bit. You speak. Not British."

"No, I am American," She wondered how a man who could speak at least four languages could not find a better-paying position in life. She learned quickly when generously provided with a brief story of the driver's life. He was a third-generation driver; it was his destiny to drive. His joy was infectious, and he enjoyed his work so much that

Etta thought he might persuade others to join the driving profession.

When they pulled up to the fourteenth-century hotel overlooking the Canale de San Marco, Etta wondered just where she and Roberto could honeymoon to top this. She had luggage this time and was pleased to have money to tip the bellman for delivering them to her room. She had changed after work in hopes of arriving to make a grand entry, but this time it was not meant to be. Etta arrived first and was exhausted from the day. She fell asleep on the sofa with her shoes still on.

When Roberto arrived, he entered the hotel room and saw his princess asleep. He motioned the bellman to be quiet. He set the luggage down and carefully closed the door behind. He pulled up a chair and studied Etta sleeping. Her angelic face was at rest with no thought, trouble, or ulterior motive. Roberto resisted grabbing Etta into his anxious arms. It was comical, really, that she had lain on the couch fully dressed in her evening suit. She breathed softly, and her eyelids fluttered in a shallow dream state. He waited for a few more minutes, and then he leaned over and kissed her ever so softly on the lips.

Without even opening her eyes, Etta sleepily remarked, "I know that kiss. Welcome home, Roberto." She opened her right eye and peered a moment. She opened both eyes, stretched, and remarked, "I am awake; you really are here!" Running her fingers through the back of her hair to prop it back up, she reached out to Roberto with both arms and closed her eyes again. "I'm so glad you are here. I missed you something awful."

Roberto was content to stay in this evening with their post-Christmas festivities.

From the balcony, they could see the moonlight reflect on the grand canal. The cold wind whipped at Etta's hair, making it full and fresh again. They stepped out without coats, and Etta wrapped herself in Roberto's arms. Though neither was warm, they enjoyed a few moments of solitude, just soaking in feelings and the lovely view.

Roberto ordered room service and a nightcap at once, expecting the couple would not appreciate interruptions. He stuck with a common menu since Etta had no say in ordering.

Etta removed her shoes and sat on top of her legs on the couch. She asked him how he felt about locating a furnished house.

"Furnished would be wonderful, but don't you want to put our home together? I mean, don't you like to shop for furnishings and that?" Roberto quizzed her.

"Not especially. I enjoy looking at art, but furniture shopping could take much time, Roberto. I have limited time after work, and I'd prefer to spend that time with you. When do you hope to move into our home?" Etta asked.

"However long it takes. I want to find a home that suits you even if we have to live at the hotel for a while," Roberto replied honestly. "Have you asked your work about a floating schedule yet? I don't know which days I will be home, but it would be two or three days a week at this point."

"No. I haven't addressed that yet. There are so many details to attend to set us up together," Etta said, feeling anxious about all she would need to achieve once she returned home to begin this peculiar arrangement. She coached herself silently, *I'm on vacation! I'm on vacation!*

"Tell me more about the company, Roberto. How are you soliciting work?" Etta asked, not clear as yet what her fiancé did when he was in meetings.

"Companies do well in industrial areas such as Birmingham, but they stay pretty isolated. We approach large companies to patch their computers together with other industries outside their communities. By expanding their ability to purchase supplies at a lower cost, we assist them in offering goods or services to other markets and customers at a more competitive rate. The selling point is if you invest a few million lire or a few thousand francs or pounds for the computer system, you get lower production costs and higher sales outside your 'comfort' market. The concept is catching on. It's a novel idea, so I am fully aware I must keep up with demand. If I can set up a large enough network in the two countries I am in, I will add a maintenance group to work those while I explore another market. That comes down the road though. I have many cobblestones and bricks to work yet."

Etta was intrigued by the notion. She knew little about the computers developed after the punch card systems she studied in college. She had never actually used one. Her admiration of this work increased the more Roberto detailed it for her.

After dinner and dessert, Etta showered, readying herself for bed. How comforting to have her man-pillow once again. Stepping out of the shower, Etta dried as much water from her hair as possible before sliding into the emerald green nightgown. Emerging from the bathroom in the hotel-provided bathrobe, she realized she needed another accessory—a bedroom robe. Add that to the ever-expanding list of items Etta would need to build a proper wedding trousseau. Her thoughts were abruptly interrupted by an amazing scene. There was a small, live Christmas tree decorated with tiny crystal ornaments. There was a fresh wreath on the door and a red envelope below a few packages near the tree. The room was dark, except for the fifty some-odd candles lit around the room. It was magical. Etta was greatly impressed and rewarded his thoughtful efforts with an elated expression that caught his watchful eye.

She grabbed him and exclaimed, "Merry Christmas, Roberto," planting an appreciative kiss on his lips.

Roberto excused himself into the bathroom, allowing Etta to bask in the candlelight while he showered. He returned wearing bright red pajamas and a terribly fake-looking white beard. "Ho, ho, ho, little lady. Tell Father Christmas what you dreamed of this year."

Etta was overheating with the candles, or perhaps the excitement of it all. "I'm not dreaming of a white Christmas. I'm not even dreaming of Italy. I am dreaming about being with Roberto. I'm dreaming of the day I was drawn to him across a room, without words. I dream of the surprise that he found me against a million odds. He found me again. And I dream that he is here with me right now."

Etta kissed the bearded man.

"May your Christmas wishes come true!" Roberto sang out. After throwing the beard onto the chair, he exclaimed, "I'm here, your Christmas wish!"

All silliness aside, they embraced and held each other for nearly an hour with little talk exchanged. They relished the company of one another, hoping that it would never end. Etta broke the trance with her invitation, "Would you like your Christmas presents?"

"Presents? I have gifts for *you*!" Roberto replied with cheerful anticipation.

"Be nice now, sir," Etta said, picking up the wicked edge of wolf in his voice.

Roberto opened the package containing a book about succulents. Etta hoped he would appreciate why she loved being in the glasshouse. Etta opened a box with a camera to record her travels with Binny and Roberto. Roberto opened the box of silk handkerchiefs to remind him of her touch and scent when he was away. Etta opened a box with an Italian horn charm that would bring her increased good luck. (Etta reflected again on the polar opposite types of luck. Indeed, she had experienced the extremes of both.)

Saving the best for last, both opened their gifts together. Roberto's eyes moistened at the vision of the ruby cuff links, just before Etta squealed over the beautiful band of diamonds and rubies in the Collingwood box. She tried it on while Roberto watched her light up right through the top of her head. The size seven fit perfectly. How extraordinary. They both selected rubies! They were both prepared to explain the choice, but nothing needed to be said. Etta felt less self-conscious in her robe, and Roberto took great liberty to drink in the beautiful vision of her. Roberto removed his hotel robe and blew out the candles, one by one, until only the bedside candle flickered. They kissed and cuddled, expressing hopes and dreams for a half hour before the final candle burnt itself out on in the jar.

"I guess that's our cue," Etta stated matter-of-factly.

"All right then. Merry Christmas *mi amor*." Roberto kissed Etta's nose in the dark.

"Goodnight, prince charming." She rolled onto her side and met his expectant arm, which awaited the company of his precious Etta.

Morning came quite quickly, and the two lazily made their way into fresh clothing to head out for the day. Roberto dressed up his shirt with the addition of the cherished cuff links. He felt "finished" with these touching pieces resting so close to the hands that held her.

Etta bundled up and wore comfortable shoes to enjoy the day. She brought her camera to record the sights of Central Venice. An employee who had conducted business negotiations in Venice had coached Roberto, advising him where to take Etta. To start the day, they walked through the Piazza San Marco into the luxury of Caffee Florian, where Roberto enjoyed a cappuccino while Etta drank black currant juice. Etta tore a bite off the fresh pastry, exposing the sparkling diamond and ruby band on her slender finger. It was an elegant choice. Roberto congratulated himself.

Tuxedoed ensembles strolled by, drinking in the fresh, passionate love of the patrons. They played several songs Roberto could sing to. Etta understood none of the language, but she clearly understood the emotion of the ballads. They intentionally prolonged their breakfast until nearly midday. They walked, hand in hand, through the courtyards facing the landmark church bell tower. They waited in the chill outside to hear its lovely announcement of noon. They walked toward St. Mark's Basilica at a leisurely pace.

As they approached the eleventh-century sanctuary of the Byzantine treasure, Etta was struck by how effective this architectural treasure must have been in converting people to the goodness of the Lord's hand over the centuries it had been in service. Entering from a striking exterior, Etta felt as though they had entered a palace. The mosaics spilled from wall to wall, backed by gold. They covered the atriums, domes, and ceilings. Etta lost herself and let her eyes freely explore the entire ceiling and walls surrounding them. They mutually paused for a sacred moment in time. Etta and Roberto heard nothing and saw nobody around them. They were aware only of each other as they studied this holy place, both feeling very small. They stepped carefully on the sturdy marble, afraid to mar the surface in any manner.

Roberto turned to Etta and took her hand. With his vision locked on her green eyes, he kissed her hand. "I think we should seek a blessing here. This is a holy place, Etta."

"Right here? Right now? But we have no witnesses. We have no family," Etta said with her logical mind. Then she paused and studied his pleading eyes. She was not prepared. She recalled she had not been prepared for him entering her life, either. It just happened. He was right. This was a holy place. "Sure Roberto. Why not *this* place, today?" She felt the ring on the hand that Roberto held in his sleep.

Roberto fought through the crowds with an anxious mind. He found a man clothed in a dark robe, wearing a rope belt. "Padre?" he asked, seeking audience with the man.

The man turned to face Roberto and noticed an urgency in his mannerism.

Roberto bowed his head and respectfully inquired, "*Questa signora chiede un blessing della chiesa. Potete certificare il blessing per la signora?*"

The man rested his hand under Roberto's chin and raised it to meet his eyes in a serious expression. "*Naturalmente. E malata?*"

"No, padre," Roberto replied with reverence.

Roberto took Etta's hand, and the father walked ahead to a quiet corner near an alcove containing an impressive carved baptismal font.

Roberto held Etta's hand, and the father offered a prayer as indicated by his solemn tone and bowed head. Etta bowed her head in prayer, wishing she understood Italian but enjoying the romance of being wed in a foreign tongue.

The father continued directly, looking at Etta, "*In nome del dio, benedico il thee con fede, resistenza, saggezza ed amor. Amen.*" He bowed to Etta and told Roberto to wait there for the certificate. While he was away, Roberto and Etta kissed and embraced with great excitement. For a fleeting moment, Etta regretted not being surrounded by family for this remarkable event. Etta finally felt she was not dreaming, but rather fulfilling an amazing journey of destiny. She would not disappoint her new husband. Mrs. Fernandez sounded so good!

The father returned minutes later, holding a rolled parchment for the couple. It was ornately created on fine composite paper, which was thick enough to stand up to a few generations, at least. Roberto thanked the man immensely and inquired what he owed the church. He responded back that Roberto owed what was in his heart this day, referring to Roberto as "my son."

Roberto offered his hand and thanks stating, "*Grazie. Avete reso noi molto felice questo giorno.*"

The father departed back into the crowd, and Roberto held Etta tightly with both arms and then gripped the certificate, hoping he had, in fact, done the right thing. Roberto crossed himself and offered his own prayer silently in his native language. "My God, I loved this woman before, today, and tomorrow. Please God, I beseech thee, allow me to care for her until my death. Bless this woman richly, oh my

God. Amen." He crossed himself again. Roberto then let the emotion of his earnest plea grip him, and in front of Etta, the tourists, the worshipers, God, and everyone else, his eyes filled with tears of joy that spilled down his cheeks.

Etta was touched by the depth of his emotion for her. She held him tightly while Roberto let go his reservations and replaced them with hope for a rich life with this beautiful woman. His beloved, cherished Etta.

Roberto required a nap that afternoon as he was so emotionally drained from the exciting day. They returned to the hotel early, and Etta prepared during his slumber for their wedding night. She realized, once again, she had the wrong wardrobe. Etta slipped out the executive door and quietly roamed through the Luna Hotel Baglioni.

The front desk manager regretfully explained to Etta in English that most of the nearby stores were closed for the winter. She might ask the hotel shop if they could assist her. Etta wandered that direction and found nothing close to a wedding night ensemble. She struck on a better idea.

Etta snuck back into the room and quietly showered and dressed. She wrapped herself in the shower robe and rearranged the candles in three long tiers. As she lit them, Roberto awoke from his stone-hard sleep. She told him to wash up while she readied the room. He didn't argue, needing a refresher.

When Roberto emerged from the bathroom with the clouds of steam, his skin was reddened and still damp. Etta was propped in a chair, wearing his stark white, pressed shirt. He imagined she was naked beneath the Egyptian cotton. As Etta stood up, Roberto saw her legs rise to their full height and the shirt rested at the top of Etta's legs. He was clothed in the red pajamas, with no guise anymore of being Father Christmas. Roberto was Etta's, tonight and forever.

The familiar fantasy—now turned reality—filled him with anticipation. Roberto approached his beloved Etta and pressed his anxious body against hers. She sensed his earnest want for her, and she instinctively wrapped her right leg around his back to entice him closer. Roberto suddenly picked her up, and Etta's other leg wrapped around his torso. Roberto dropped Etta onto the bed, where her hair landed in a wild design across the bedspread. He pulled back the sheets on half of the bed, lifting Etta into a position to rest her head on the pillow. Roberto stroked Etta's hair, caressed her cheek, and gazed deeply into her eyes.

Yesterday. Today. Forever.

They held each other late into the night without words. Both were afraid to break the spell in the room. They watched the candles expiring, darkening the room with each fatality. They kissed and held on tight. Both were desperately afraid this was a vision that would soon pass. They wanted so earnestly to prolong the deep feeling of their private eternity. It was a long, delightful night. It was the way it had always been. Roberto was with *her*. His lovely Etta was before, in every new breath, and for evermore, his *destino*!

Chapter 22
HAMMERED URN

There was a mutual urgency with the home hunt after the couple's weeklong adventure in Italy. When work called, Roberto left Etta an additional fifty thousand pounds for furnishings that would be required for their comfort. The buzz of Etta eloping with a man she barely met spread like wildfire.

Etta was grateful she was able to meet with Larkin and Lana before word spread to them. "I have so much to tell you," Etta began. "First off, I really appreciate the opportunities you afforded me under your employ. This has been a wonderful position. I met a man last month who changed my life, and we eloped this weekend."

Larkin and Lana both tensed, expecting her resignation.

"We have an agreement about my interests," Etta explained. "I want to continue to work here, but my husband's schedule will provide only floating days in Birmingham. I want to be off when he is home. So what I would like to request is if I might stay on as a four-day employee, with floating days off? Likely, it will be one weekend day and two weekdays off per week. I believe the glasshouse is stable enough now that you will not require additional staff to work there. Of course, there are two downsides I foresee at this point. Someone would need to check the room on my second off day, in the event of a temperature or humidity change. The other issue would be school groups generally plan their field trips far into the school calendar, while I would need to make a schedule just a week in advance."

Lana and Larkin eased back, understanding now there would be no need to replace Etta. For this, they were both relieved. While she desired to stay on, these issues were something to consider carefully.

Lana posed the first obstacle. "Etta, how would you be able to manage the school groups if you don't know when you will be off?"

"I considered two solutions there. First, if we can schedule all school groups for Monday and Tuesday, it's not likely I would require those days off. If I need the day, I will either come in solely for that appointment, or I will personally see to it that they receive a priority reschedule. I just don't see that happening."

Larkin then posed a question. "Who will cover you with our visitors in the glasshouse when you're gone?"

"I have an idea for laminated information flip cards on meter-length wood posts. I will take the strangest and most interesting data from the room and create information sheets that can be posted throughout the room. These would offer tidbits I generally discuss with patrons."

"That's a great idea! We should consider this for all the glasshouses to save personnel hours," Larkin said directly to Lana.

"Splendid! I see that...," agreed Lana.

"I realize I'm asking a lot, but since kids are out of school right now, we had hoped to take a honeymoon next week. Is it possible to take off the week?" Etta implored once again, proving she had no cards to hide—they were all on the table.

"Who would cover your duties then?" Lana asked, anticipating Etta already had one solution and two contingency plans.

"I was thinking that a volunteer would fill in. I know a great lady who would come in as a favor for me. She knows much about my work, and if that doesn't fly, I can have Larkin fill in." Etta stared at Larkin, and he jolted a moment until he saw her teasing expression.

"Of course I would be exuberant to lie with the cacti!" replied Larkin, yanking on her right back.

Lana suggested, "Go ahead with your honeymoon plans, and let us know how you will arrange coverage. And just when will you introduce us to your new husband?"

"With his schedule, it will be a few weeks yet. He travels a great deal for his company, Horizon-Tech, and I'm more of a homebody. Roberto will be here a few days a week, and the rest of the time he will be in Barcelona or courting other vendor prospects. Say, if either of you knows of anyone wanting to sell their home, let me know. We urgently need to find a home in the area and would sure like to find a furnished one."

"That'll be nearly impossible, Etta. People here aren't transient. They're born, live, and die in Birmingham," Larkin advised.

"Well, I'm optimistic. I think there is a home for us here."

Kelly came in later in the day. Etta was sitting in the dirt, a customary position when groups weren't announced.

"Tar so much for setten me up with the touren group intervioo," Kelly stated simply.

"Kelly! How did it go?" Etta asked with great anticipation.

"Well, the iron geezer was really mane. Ee wanted naaa part of trainen me. But I met a brass geezer who was interested in chancen me. Ee already 'ad a wet-eared kid under him, though. So ee let me knoo I cud be anunst in lion," Kelly said happily.

Etta couldn't contain her disappointment. "I am sorry, Kelly. I had really hoped it would work out now."

"It 'ad, really," Kelly continued. "This was the fust toyme I was awoy frum me folks. I 'ad a smashen toyme an' I fink it's toyme ter move ert. Bostin chops too abart the brass geezer, wull, ee fancoys me!" Kelly beamed and blushed at the same time.

"So...?" Etta prodded for more details.

"So we am guin ter date sum an' see oo it guz. Ee travels the curcuit so we wull yav ter start ert sloo. But he's a roight nyc felloo with bostin arms."

"I have an idea, Kelly. I need to find a house, and you need to let a room. I have a terrific widow landlord that I think you'd get along fine with," Etta said, extending an invitation. "Come on over tonight, and I will show you around and introduce you."

"That'll be bostin!"

Etta waited in the parking lot near Kelly's car. She swept the loose snow off the windshield. When Kelly came out the gate, she appeared to be hopping mad.

"Why didn't you tell me yoo miskin married? I was the last one to hear. That should've come from you, Etta!" Kelly said, feeling very hurt.

"I thought I had told you we were engaged. Oh, wait, no! You were in London. I was going to tell you first, but you extended your vacation. You really are out of the loop, Kelly. Boy, do I have to catch you up on the nitty-gritty," Etta said, realizing her gross error.

Kelly softened some and drove Etta home. She was surprised at how close it was to the gardens.

When they pulled in, they noticed two neighbors peeking through their windows, not recognizing the car. Etta explained that until recently she was on foot, so the neighbors were very interested in the comings and goings of the household. Geraldine was not in when they arrived, so Etta showed Kelly into the public area of the house.

Kelly remarked, "It's so clane!"

"No kidding! The house rules are: no men, no cigarettes, no drugs or drunks, and be tidy. That's what sold me. I wanted to live in a tidy home. My room's back here."

When they walked into the room, Kelly's eyes lit up. "It's a nice place, Etta. But, where's yaw stuff. Yav yoo moved already?"

Etta confessed, "This is all I have. When you met me at the garden, I had only three changes of clothing. The uniforms were a huge benefit for me. When I arrived in England, everything I had was stolen, so you can say I started from the street up."

"My Lord, girl! I never ood yav dreamed! I thought yoo were alrooight off. I was surprised when yoo wanted ter lend me clobber. I understan' noo."

"Kind of embarrassing, being a foreigner, stuck without clothes, you know?" Etta reminisced about the first tough weeks. "I was so fortunate to get this job. It suits me like you have no idea!"

"Wow, Etta, If yaw room is up fer let, I wull move in tonoight if I yav ter! This is crackin!"

Just then the door opened, and in walked Geraldine. She eyed Kelly with suspicion.

Etta asked, "Mrs. Bonneville, can you come in the kitchen for a talk?"

"Why of course," she replied, turning to put coffee on.

"Wait, Mrs. Bonneville, this is my friend from work, Kelly. Kelly, this is my landlord, Mrs. Bonneville."

"Hello then," the little robust woman replied on her heel as she turned to the kitchen.

Etta couldn't figure it. Though she had never brought friends over, Geraldine was always pleasant to her. She brought Kelly into the kitchen and sat down for the undoubtedly bitter coffee that would soon be ready.

Geraldine sat down at the sterile table in the immaculate kitchen and eyed Kelly with distrust. She let out an unexpected, "You aren't one of those swing-one-way types, are you?"

Etta and Kelly rolled in laughter, realizing that Geraldine thought they were closer than just friends.

Etta tried to stop laughing long enough to check her tone. "Mrs. Bonneville, this weekend when I went away, I was in Italy."

"What were you doing there?" she asked, appearing puzzled.

"I was eloping. I got married. I'll need to find a house pretty soon. But in the meantime, I am going to stay in a hotel with my new husband. Roberto and I will be moving in the next few days. Kelly here is real tidy. I have seen her room. I thought if you didn't mind, I would try to find you a tenant so you would not lose any rent money."

Geraldine's smile contorted her face into a thousand wrinkles as she responded, "Why, Etta, that is the sweetest chops! You have been wonderful here. I am sorry to see you leave, but I am happy for you two. Kelly, I'm sorry to be so abrupt, but you know I *do* read the papers, and I know that *that* type of thing does go on here, too. If Etta can vouch for you, then that'd be all right by me—if you like the place."

"Mrs. Bonneville, I *love* this place. Yoo keep a natty um, an' it's so close ter me job. If yoo don't mind, consider it taken when Etta moves ert."

Etta knew she would really appreciate this move. She was a neat freak living in her folk's dump. That would have to strain any relationship. Amazingly, she never had picked up the smoking habit, though. One more reason she would like Geraldine's home.

Onto her own task at hand.

"Geraldine," Etta said, slipping out of formal manners. "I have to find a house in the area. I would love to find a furnished home, but I definitely want to move into this area. Do you have any friends who may be selling their homes? We are looking at homes this size or slightly larger for a family."

Etta was shocked that a remark like that had escaped from her brain without being examined. An extended family option, humm.

"I'll have a look about," Geraldine remarked.

The rest of Kelly and Geraldine's coffee was simply exchanging information and pleasantries. They might get along better than Etta and she had. They had much to talk about. Kelly was a lovely person, and Geraldine took to her instantly.

When Etta walked Kelly out to the car, she clarified, "You are serious about moving in any day I move out? I hope to move by Friday. As you can see, it will only take one trip with *all* my stuff." Etta laughed.

Kelly confessed, "Etta, I was so yampy at yoo for not letten on abart yaw beau, I cud yav never talked ter yoo. I'm sorry I misunderstood yoo. Tar so much for hooken me up eya. This wull be so bostin ter get ert of me parents' owse. An' I brought this for yoo frum London, but I was too angry ter gid it ter yoo. Forgiv' me?"

"Of course," Etta said. Etta knew the contents of the box would be a charm. Kelly knew her charm bracelet as well as Etta did since she had worked on it a few times. She anticipated correctly. It was a lovely, hammered coffee pot.

"It reminded me of the forgers an' metal workers, Etta. Remember when yoo told me that yaw bracelet was loike yaw camera? Well, this charm looks loike the pounded art werk these blokes mek at werk. Since yoo hooked me up with the job openen, it ood remind yoo of me. Only I thought when I bought it, I 'ad the job."

"But you met this nice man, and you are next in line for a job, and...? And what?"

Etta hoped to cheer the brief, down moment.

"That's true. Ee is the nicest geezer, an' ee really does wanna see me. Wonder 'oo much it ood cost ter get the train the'er when they am at the shap? Wull said they only travel less than fawer months roight noo."

"If he comes here to visit you, I know a real nice hotel..."

"Etta! Oo bold of you!" Kelly said, half joking.

"Well, you know Geraldine's rule..." Etta trailed off.

Kelly considered being in an orderly home for the first time in her life. It would be rather nice for a change. "Of course."

Etta got the call only an hour after Kelly left the house. Geraldine yelled at Etta to pick up quickly. A hysterical voice screamed though the phone.

"Etta, I need ter get ert of eya. Can I cum over noo?" she sobbed into the phone.

"Absolutely, Kelly. What's going on?" Etta asked to the dial tone of the dead phone connection. She looked at the receiver and contemplated what might have happened to make Kelly so distraught.

Kelly's car came screeching up the drive, and Kelly burst out of the car, crying hysterically. Her wild hair only partially concealed a rapidly swelling eye and bruised cheek. Her bloody nose spilled onto her shirt unchecked.

Etta ran toward her, but seeing her condition, she ran back into the house for a kitchen towel. She ran back out, meeting Kelly at the door.

"What on earth happened to you?"

"My dad. Ee went yampy when I told him about this place. Ee said I can't move ert until I marry. Ee called me a 'scrubba' an' laid into me face with his fists. An' then ee bunted me roight ert the door. I fink I've hurt me back. Me mum stood the'er watchen an' said nothen! Oh, I hate 'er! She said nothen!"

Geraldine ran to the sounds of the commotion and responded, "Oh my Lord!" She ran to phone a local bobby, who arrived in two minutes.

Kelly looked from Etta to the bobby and to Geraldine. She was in unfamiliar territory here. Kelly released the officer, saying it was no more than an accident and she was sorry that he was bothered. He looked suspiciously at her, not sure whether to do as she instructed, or wait to investigate what had caused these three women such commotion.

Geraldine shared a long look with Etta, not knowing what to do. They coerced her inside and shut the door so the neighbors would have less to talk about at tea the next day.

Geraldine instinctively ran a bath for her. Etta surveyed Kelly's face close up, wiping blood away to assess the damage. She took Kelly's shirt clear over her head and swung her around. Kelly had a horrid bruise developing alongside her backbone on the right.

"What did you hit?" Etta asked, wondering if she had broken anything.

"I bellile the step when Dad bunted me ert the door."

"Do you feel any breaks, or do you think it's bruised?" Etta asked with grave concern.

"I don't know; I hurt in every bone frum me knees up, at the jiffy." Kelly stopped crying, but she was now shaking uncontrollably.

Geraldine helped Kelly into the bathtub and called her doctor at home. "Dr. Gornik? This is Geraldine Bonneville... Yes, I'm fine...No they haven't come back yet...Say, I have a lass who got beat up right bad. She hit her back and maybe broke her nose. Can I trouble you to see her straightaway?"

Dr. Larry Gornik did *not* make house calls, but he had held an affection for Geraldine from the moment they met in their school years. She had not felt the same toward him. So they had both married and moved on in the community with their families. But he never forgot her. Larry would do anything she asked of him.

Dr. Gornik arrived not a half hour after Geraldine's desperate call. His thoughts vacillated between his ill-fated love for Geraldine and his call to attend to the broken young lady. When he arrived at the home, his physician's calling took over. He didn't even knock, bursting thought the door with only an emergency kit. Geraldine called from the bathroom and gave Kelly a towel to cover her front. By now, Kelly's wavy red hair was pulled back from her contorting, swollen face. Dr. Gornik carefully leaned her forward, inquiring, "What happened to your back?"

Kelly answered the same as she had to Etta. "I was bunted ert a door an' landed on the front step."

Dr. Gornik studied her face, touching it only gently in critical points. "I have bad news and good news, lass. You'll need to come in for X-rays first thing in the morning. But you were lucky to miss your vertebrae during the fall. You'll be awfully sore for a few weeks. Your nose is broken, for sure. Your cheek is fine, though."

"Didn't yaouw soy the'er was good news?" asked Kelly, who was in desperate pain, but she was attempting to be both modest and brave.

"Your nose broke just off the side, so when the bruising is gone, you'll have the original nose, only it'll be a tad weaker. You can't take another blow to it, or you'll have a new nose, and that won't be pretty. Have you had the perpetrator picked up for questioning?" the doctor inquired.

"I...I can't," Kelly said, bursting into tears again.

Turning to Geraldine and seeing her lovely face once again, he instructed, "I will leave sturdy pain chemicals for the young lady to take every four hours for the next three days. I want to see her first thing in the morning, and I hope to see you sometime soon, too," he remarked hopefully.

Larry was dreadfully optimistic. Why, his wife was still alive! Geraldine knew he was honest and loyal. She knew him well enough to recognize Larry would never leave his wife.

Payback was easy, though. Geraldine walked out the door with Larry, and Etta just happened to catch sight of her kissing Dr. Gornik sweetly on the cheek and thanking him genuinely. He returned from his car to deliver the pain medicine for Kelly.

Kelly was concerned about how this would appear at work. She did not want to lose the job she enjoyed. How could she explain this?

Etta devised a plan. "I'll cover you tomorrow until they get someone to cover you through the weekend. I'll let them know you were in a car accident and that your car is in the shop. You are mending the break and bruising. No one would suspect otherwise."

That was true. Everyone believed Etta. She was frank and honest to a fault. Kelly was very appreciative, extremely sore, and quite tired. Etta lent her warm flannels and her bed. The pain medicine kicked in after a short while, allowing Kelly much-needed rest.

Etta slept on the couch and woke up two minutes before her alarm was set to go off. She snuck into her bedroom where Kelly slept, disarmed the alarm clock, and pulled the drapes tight.

Chapter 23
GONDOLA OF LOVE

Etta stood at the gift shop counter creating a simple sign. AT LUNCH BACK AT NOON. She wouldn't actually eat; instead, she would attend to the duties at hand. Arriving early, Etta took a quick survey about and left notes about Kelly's accident with details of volunteer coverage in both Larkin's and Lana's offices.

Meanwhile, a heater fuse blew in her precious room. It was dangerously cold in the glasshouse. She immediately installed the portable heaters until the main fuse could be repaired or replaced. The portables tended to be tricky to judge. She would have to check these every so often and pray that the main unit could be repaired before she left on her honeymoon.

There was only rare time with customers, but a host of employees did come in inquiring about Kelly and her accident. "The car was not too bad off, but it'll be in repair." Etta didn't think this bald-faced lie was out of order under the circumstances. "She hit her face on the steering wheel, and it is pretty bruised. Her nose was slightly broken. She would have returned to work, only she bruised her back upon the rebound from the impact." Etta genuinely hoped that the newspapers didn't cover all the crashes in the area, or the goodly people who inquired could become suspicious.

After work, Etta braved driving Kelly's car, approaching the door to her parents' home. Thankfully, Kelly's mother answered the door. "May I help you?" she asked as if nothing had transpired.

"I am here to pick up a load of Kelly's belongings. She is too *injured* to pick them up herself," Etta started, fishing for information. None was offered. She followed Kelly's mother up the narrow stairs into Kelly's room, and she left Etta in full charge of the big job ahead. "Thank you!" Etta called back down the empty hallway, checking her tone but feeling immense contempt.

Etta took three trips up and down the stairs, collecting clothes bundles on hangers. She returned for two more trips, filling empty garden boxes with drawer goods. Etta was not surprised to find that even Kelly's drawers were neatly organized. It made for a quick pack. Her personal treasures would have to wait. Etta heard Kelly's father in the house and wanted nothing more than to clear out before she could provoke him to further violence. It was a good call, after all. Kelly's little car was filled to the gills.

Taking some liberty with the car, Etta slowly drove into town. She cased the streets of Jewellery Quarter, trying to recognize the street front of the store in which she found the nicest men's rings. She found the shop on Vyse Street. Yes! This was it, Weston-Shield Jewellery Services. She recalled only that "shield" was in the name somewhere, and her memory had visualized an armor shield.

She peered through the glass case in the small shop. Their selection of styles was excellent, but the range of sizes was extremely limited. She estimated his size to be a nine and a half, but she would take what she could find that suited her.

Etta settled on a thick, stovepipe band of brushed gold. Years of wear would not be as apparent as would be with a shiny band. Underneath, she had three words engraved. They were words that Larkin offered to translate for her, having taken a few classes in Spanish some years ago. *Antes, Ahora, Siempre:* Before, Now, and Forever. The engraving would be under half of the ring, in the event it needed sizing.

Etta drove slowly back to the house for fear of getting a ticket for not possessing a license to drive. That fear coupled with the terror of the visual distortion driving on the wrong side still plagued her.

Geraldine met Etta in the driveway and carried an ample load for a small woman. They placed the clothing directly into the closet and drawers. Etta moved her scant collection to the coat closet. While Kelly slept under her wild red rings of hair, the two women filled the drawers with the best intentions, knowing she would want to arrange these articles in her own orderly fashion later.

Etta answered the only call back of the evening on the first ring so Kelly could sleep soundly. At Etta's request, the caller replied simply, "I'll be there," and hung up.

Etta met Binny at the gate before work. Binny gave her a big hug, congratulating her on her elopement, and then she punched her on the upper left arm. "You could have called! I would have flown right over!"

"I know, I know. We really did not know until we were in that amazing, spiritual place," Etta defended.

"Yeah. Uh huh! And that's why you already had the wedding ring?" Binny challenged. "I will absolutely never forgive you," Binny teased, and then she gave Etta another hug. She studied the channel diamond and dark red ruby ring and then whistled. "The boy has good taste…in women!"

Etta smiled. "Thanks so much for coming. I owe you big for this one. Now please don't tell anyone your last name or the game is off. Understand?"

"All right, then. Let the game begin!"

It was not too much of a sacrifice for her. This was a slower time for her company, and Binny trusted most of Etta's instincts with people. She had not done anything so trite since—well, she had *never* worked at any post this far beneath her. It would be a good character challenge. She would have to try especially hard not to be so bossy with Etta's patrons.

Etta introduced Binny to the coworkers, explaining she was covering for Kelly for the day. She led the way to the gift shop. Etta demonstrated the register and showed her the magazine stack behind the counter to help curb boredom. Etta left her to peruse the inventory of souvenirs and checked on her own landscaped region. She cranked up the heaters more, feeling the temperature was still too chilly, and then she worked her way toward Lana's office. Lana was now in on the prank, so the two women waited for the opportune moment when Larkin was situated within earshot of their conversation.

"Yes, she's here as a favor to me, so you don't have to assign her, really."

"She sure is a looker. Do you think I could set her up with my brother Arnold?" Lana asked on cue.

"No, she gets enough attention without blind dates. She always draws a crowd when we go clubbing. Besides, she'll only be here for the week. Then she'll return to London for a spell." Etta sealed the bait.

Larkin took the bait—hook, line, and sinker. He wondered who this curious woman was that she would come from

London to help Etta. A friend of Etta's huh? He was certainly up for an adventure challenge, and this sounded like one.

Later that morning Larkin innocently wandered into the gift shop for some chewing gum. He introduced himself by title in the hopes of improving that first impression. Larkin was not disappointed with the vision of this lovely lass. "Mrs. Ingle and I want to thank you for your service to the Birmingham Botanical Gardens during Kelly's unforeseen accident. Can we make it up to you in any way?" Larkin invited.

What Binny wanted to say was, "Smashing! Take me to dinner, love." That was not in the predetermined playbook. "Would you be ever so kind as to arrange for my lunch at the pavilion? That would be nice," Binny inquired with a charming smile that even she did not know she was so comfortable to flaunt.

"Done!" Larkin remarked, and he left to inform the cafeteria staff to send her bill to his office.

Binny thoroughly enjoyed the anticipation of being entertained by this handsome, dark stud with the deep, brown eyes. She had never dated a black man before.

Just before noon, Etta came into the shop to check on Binny. The two exchanged no words, only looks—that and an audible purring sound Binny offered as a clue to the preliminary introduction to Larkin.

It was at tea when Binny saw Larkin again. Etta had let her Black Currant London Herb tea steep for nearly five minutes when she saw Larkin approaching through the corridor. She quickly emptied most of the contents of her teacup into the bus tub, and when he arrived, she stood with the posture of wrapping up her break.

Act two. Etta innocently called Larkin over to the table. "Larkin, I want to introduce you to my friend Binny. Binny this is Larkin Ladimore He's one of the two superiors here. A fine gentleman to work for if you ever need anything permanent."

"Actually, Etta, we met just this morning. Nice to see you again, Mr. Ladimore," Binny offered with a straight, cool demeanor.

Larkin was pleased that Etta offered some positive tidbit for her to consider. Binny was pleased Etta suggested she may need a job like this sometime. Etta was pleased that this charade was transpiring so smoothly.

"Nice talking with you, Binny. I have to get back to my heaters if I'm ever going to get out of here on our honeymoon." With that, Etta departed, turning only once to suggest, "Larkin, why don't you join Binny for tea?" She didn't wait for an answer that she predicted with certainty. Instead, she left and sat behind the gift shop counter relaxing with a magazine detailing the winter ski accessories of the year.

By the next afternoon, Larkin had invited Binny to dinner. She requested they meet at an obscure little place in Digbeth knowing that most people in the community knew her family by sight. Larkin might even know her mother's home if she had him pick her up. Certainly he would discover Binny was not the person she professed to be. She also opted for a cab over her C-type Jaguar. Binny reversed her customarily dominant role by asking Larkin dozens of questions. She wanted to be sure that he was not a money digger before she enjoyed this too, too much.

Etta drove Kelly's car back into Birmingham to the Weston-Shield store to retrieve the ring. It was a strong, fine band, and Etta couldn't wait to present it to Roberto.

Next, Etta made an attempt to pick up the rest of Kelly's effects. This time Kelly's father opened the door.

Smelling of alcohol, sweat, and smoke, he bellowed, "What do you want?" into the cold.

Etta tried hard to conceal the shaking that immediately occurred just below her knees. She replied, "I am here to pick up some of Kelly's things."

No response, no emotion spent. Just a slammed door.

Etta bravely rang the doorbell again. This time Kelly's mother opened the door. "What?" was all she said.

Etta repeated herself and then followed the woman up the stairs with two boxes in tow. She worked quickly, trying to collect the most time-relevant items Kelly might want. She bypassed childhood treasures and books on this trip.

Seeing herself out the front door, Etta hesitantly thanked Kelly's mother, but the gratitude was unacknowledged. Kelly's father emerged from the kitchen with another drink in his hand. "Be gone with you. Goo awoy!" he bellowed. With that, Etta closed the door.

Safely back at Mrs. Bonneville's home, Etta placed the boxes in the room where Kelly rested. She looked better today—more colorful, certainly, and less swollen. Etta gave her the work update, the inventory of items left at her parents' home, and inquired about her well-being.

"It's better this way," was all Kelly offered, and she lay back on her pillow in either a chemical or depression-induced daze.

When Roberto called, Etta was spry enough to grab it midway through the second ring. She was relieved to hear that he too still did not know what to pack for the last-minute honeymoon.

"Etta, *mi amor*, this is not a terrific time to travel. I am having difficulty locating anything romantic. I have two ideas. Would you like to go to a ski chalet, or would you like to go to a secluded cabin?"

"I have never skied before, but I have enjoyed seclusion," Etta said with a short laugh. "How about you teach me how to ski?"

"So be it! I'll let you know tomorrow where we can meet up. I'll arrange for your flight," Roberto said before he engaged in romantic small talk with the spark in his life. Etta hung up the phone smiling until she realized she forgot to ask her husband where he was calling from.

The sofa was not all that bad to sleep on. Etta didn't even need an alarm. She woke to the sound of silence and peered out the front door. It was snowing lightly. She dressed and hiked through the snow to work. Halfway there, a black car pulled up alongside her. Joseph was at the wheel.

"Hey there, Mrs. what's yer new name! Would you like me to carry you to work, then?" Joseph called at Etta in between the flakes.

"That would be nice. It's Mrs. Fernandez, actually," Etta responded before seeing with relief that Binny was in the car, also. She climbed in, and being a good sport, she offered, "How are you, Joseph? Pleasant day to chauffeur a couple of pretty ladies, wouldn't you say?"

"One pretty lady and one hussy," he replied, poking fun at Binny for coming home in the wee hours after the big night out with Larkin.

Etta waited to hear the update until after Joseph dropped them off at work. As luck would have it, Larkin was already walking in from the parking lot, so updates would have to wait for another opportunity. The day passed without the repair of the heater, without the opportunity to talk to Binny, and without the conclusion of the soft snowfall.

When Roberto phoned back that evening, he had the trip set. She would fly into the Unique Zurich Airport, and he would fly into the Geneva-Cointrin. Since he would arrive first, the driver would take Roberto to pick her up. She may have to wait a short while, but he would meet her at luggage retrieval.

The plan included a ski trip to Gornergrat-Stockhorn. They would stay at a hotel named Zermatterhof, which reportedly had a wonderful in-house Italian restaurant. Etta was not sure what to bring for this trip. It was an outdoors trip, and she was ill equipped for this cold sport. She was eager, though. She loved to hike and be outdoors. She just was unsure how much fun it would be until she grew accustomed to the cold weather.

On Binny's last day, Etta lunched with her. "I can't tell you how much I appreciate your filling in. Not the most exciting job, but I have to say that it had good *exposure* for you!"

"Absolutely, Etta. I not only met Larkin, who appears to be an entertaining prospect, but I collected a few other numbers to entertain myself with as well. Only two customers recognized me, and when they did, it was not a big deal. Larkin may have some potential. He has been the most refreshing company I have had in a very long time. We'll keep in touch, this one."

"I'll miss having the luxury to pop in to see you again. I hope you know how much I genuinely value your friendship, Binny. I hope Kelly is ready to come back. She still feels pretty sore and justifiably angry."

"That bastard!" Binny considered her own loving father and wondered how anyone could be so cruel with such a lovely daughter. She was instantly taken with Kelly. They had two lengthy conversations, and Binny could read that she had a true, pure heart. For fear that any slip of her lip might color Binny's incipient relationship with Larkin, she never did fill Kelly in on just what was brewing.

Etta was relieved when the main fuse was replaced. She no longer had cause for worry. It would be fine for her to take this holiday. The new information posts had been erected with well-researched information and illustrations about the unique treasures in her fabulous cactus room. And there would be a little help from her friends. In the flurry of recent activity, Etta realized she had not informed her family that she and Roberto had eloped. She had sent a postcard from Italy, but that was before the magical day. She could call them now too, only she knew hearing their voices would create a weakness she could not tolerate right now. No, she would write them. It would be a good time-killing activity during the flight.

Kelly helped Etta pack for the trip. She was extremely grateful for the assistance at work. Kelly would be able to show her face—literally and comfortably now—with the help of a heavy layer of foundation to cover the various irregular shades of skin. Etta had paid for another week's let, but she expected to move into the hotel the following week. Perhaps a house would fall from the sky. Everyone was correct. People did not leave this community.

Etta phoned a taxicab early, blaming the snow accumulation. Etta was anxious about this week despite the fact that she already committed to love, honor, and cherish Roberto in Venice, in Italian. She arrived with time to spare, a routine occasion in Etta's life.

When the flight took off, Etta began to write a detailed letter to her family chronicling the issues at work with Kelly and Binny. As she was getting to the good part on the fifth page of stationery, they landed at Unique Zurich Airport. She hoped that the wait would not be too long. When she disembarked, Etta was in no hurry to get to the luggage collection turnstiles.

Instead, Etta wandered past the airport shops, finding a few postcards of Switzerland in snow and a jewelry shop with gold charms in the window dressing. Sorting through the various trinkets and bits representing Swiss life, she narrowed her focus to winter themes only. She studied a Saint Bernard, a ski tram, a bear, and a sleigh. Etta bought a gondola with the number six on the side but did not wait to have it mounted.

At baggage claim, Etta was right on time for the luggage to regurgitate out of the chute and onto the claim belt. She carried two pieces of new luggage on this trip, and both were near the middle of the lot. She collected these and searched the crowds. She witnessed the long-separated families, hugging at their reunions. She listened to airport personnel, but her ears struggled with the French and German language surrounding her. Seeing no sign of Roberto yet, she settled onto a plastic molded airport chair and propped her feet on top of the suitcases. She wrote another three pages, taking great care to explain every detail she could so as to ward off the impending bad feelings they would have about being left out of the nuptials.

During the first hour of patiently waiting, passengers from a few other flights arrived and claimed their luggage while she chronicled her recent adventures in the letter and in her own journal record. After the next antsy hour, Etta succumbed to weariness. She lost track of time, her head falling off to one side in light slumber. Etta felt somewhat secure with her feet protecting the luggage and her purse buttoned within her warm coat.

Roberto ran into the airport, urgent to find Etta. He muscled and fought his way through the incoming passengers to the luggage belt. His eyes frantically searched the room. Close to desperation, Roberto exhaled once he spotted the sleeping beauty. Roberto attempted to rein in the heaving of his chest, approaching her as quietly as possible. It was difficult to recognize Etta asleep in that chair with the collar of her coat pulled up framing her visibly chilled face. He squatted in front of Etta and softly kissed her folded hands.

Before Etta opened her eyes, she said through a yawn, "I know those lips. Where have you been? I have been waiting a long time." There was sadness in Etta's voice.

"Oh, Etta, it was awful! My flight was late, and the snow came down hard. We were not sure the air traffic control would allow us to leave. I didn't know how I would get a message to you. I'm so glad you waited, Etta." Roberto gave Etta a stifling hug and kissed her hard on the lips. He kissed her eyelids and her nose too before embracing her once again. "Let's get you out of here," Roberto stated, taking both of her bags to the car waiting outside.

When they arrived early in the morning, the grand Hotel Zermatterhof added to the difficulties of the past twelve hours. They had given out Roberto's reserved suite since he was apparently a no-show. Roberto blew his top, raising his arms in frustration. He proceeded to utter a lengthy discourse in Spanish, which he knew well they would only partially understand. He let off an incoherent stream of frustration for a few minutes longer and then asked point-blank, "What *can* you do for us? Our limousine has left, and there are no other lodges available. We are tired, we are cold, and we are hungry. What do you intend to do to amend this gross blunder?"

The front desk clerk could not respond to this error. She brought out the night manager to answer to Roberto. The manager was briefed and then introduced to the two haggard-looking guests, who were waiting with their arms resting up on the counter. "Mr. Fernandez, I understand you had a reservation for a holiday suite? We have filled our suites for the evening, but if you will accept a standard single room for now, we will waive the charge and buy your dinner tomorrow evening in your choice of our restaurants. The bellman will move your belongings to an available suite tomorrow afternoon. Would that be acceptable?"

Roberto was frustrated that so many things had gone wrong. He wondered if he was the reason for the bad karma. "Yes, we will take the single, but I want to be moved as soon as a suite becomes available. This is a special holiday, and we do not intend to waste it in substandard accommodations. Do you understand me, sir?"

"Of course," the manager replied. "We will put you in right away."

The bellman led the couple to a remote area of the complex, which apparently was not part of the official hotel. Although it appeared to be a hotel room, its location suggested that perhaps it was a room the manager might use for business or family guests. It had a small double bed, and yet they were grateful for it. The two were so exhausted they did not change into bed clothing. They collapsed, fully clothed, under the sheets, facing opposite walls. Slumber fell upon the room within seconds as the exhausted couple rested, without making any physical contact whatsoever.

Chapter 24
SWISS SKATE

T he short, roundish servant wearing a traditional black uniform delivered the son's letter on a silver tray with an assortment of other nondescript envelopes to the madam of the estate in Barcelona.

"Senora Fernandez," the woman announced herself, presenting the tray to Luciana with a short curtsy.

"Gracias," Luciana replied rather flatly as she waddled past the kitchen staff on knees prematurely stiffening from excess weight and the perceived luxury of inactivity.

Luciana took the postal stack into the privacy of the library, where she sat down into the burgundy leather chair facing her French renaissance desk. She began to systematically shear into the envelopes with the gem-encrusted letter opener. She then placed them in careful piles for work, correspondence, investments, bills, and advertisements. She worked through the investments, bills, and ads, saving the business contents for her Maximiliano to attend to.

Finally, she allowed herself to savor the correspondence from friends and family. Luciana was well respected for her role as family communicator. Her letters were articulate and well rounded, offering recipients a timely picture of the events in both their community and family.

Smiling to herself, she opened the letter from her son Roberto, the successful one. The one she enjoyed bragging about when she penned news of his two computer divisions in Spain and Britain to friends and family. Her smile contorted a third of the way down the first page into rage, and she stood straight up out of her chair.

Luciana screamed at the top of her lungs, "Maximiliano! *Dios mio*! Maxi!"

The angry tone echoed through the chambers of the well-appointed stone estate. Yet only the servants heard. Most scattered to the far depths of the larger rooms to avoid her tirade. Only one was brave enough to fetch the master of the house and report that his wife was in need of him.

Maximiliano strode rapidly to the aid of his wife, who was hysterically firing off a Spanish rant.

"Luciana, what has happened?" Maximiliano asked, mustering the gentlest disposition he could, knowing the full wrath of his wife could be deadly.

"This woman! This woman will ruin everything he has worked toward! How could our precious risk it all? Doesn't he realize what is at stake?" Her nostrils flared, and her breathing was labored, deep, and wheezy.

Maximiliano would not be able to side with his wife this time, for he genuinely understood Roberto's predicament. He had entertained the same burden in the folly of youth. In his days, Maxi was quite a catch. His own family had discouraged him from love, steering him instead toward an elite university opportunity. Yes, he understood his son's decision. But how could he possibly comfort his wife? He approached her carefully from a distance. He explained casually that these things happen, and that he might grow out of it. Since she was unable to accept the comfort of his words or physical presence, he backed away slowly until he passed through the door of the library and into the hall.

Turning on his heel, Maximiliano stopped. His head dropped, and he studied his feet, dreaming of the young love and passion he had let get away. A long sigh escaped his lungs. With Luciana still yelling to nobody now, Maximiliano walked away, shaking his head. There was no reckoning when it came to the cruel realities of true love.

⁓

Across the Atlantic Ocean, another mother collected her mail after walking through the Phoenix dust in bare feet. She tugged at the rusted mailbox several times before the lid popped open. The contents were few—the phone bill, a K-Mart ad, a wrong address (belonging to Pete up the road), and a letter.

The excitement of another letter from Etta caused Martha to run to the phone and call Abigail right then and there. She plopped down on the shag carpet in the living room, with the long phone cord stretched painfully from the kitchen wall.

"Abby! We got a letter from your sister!" Martha yelled into the phone. The sound of the envelope being ripped open by her index finger was audible over the phone connection. So was the expletive when Martha sliced open her finger on the paper.

"Damn!"

"Mama, please don't say that! What? What does she say?" Abigail asked, anxious to hear when her sister would return. Although they understood and respected that her interesting job would keep her there long enough for a fun adventure, it was approaching five months now, and Etta's small family missed her dearly.

The phone suddenly became very quiet. The former joy traversing through the phone line quickly became a sad, lonely silence. Martha hung up the phone without a word. Abigail looked directly at the receiver of the phone, which now emitted a mere dial tone. She hesitated for just a moment to collect her thoughts, picked up her keys and purse, and signed out on a "family emergency."

"I don't understand. How could she do this? How could she give up her home, her family? How could she?" Martha demanded of the gods she did not believe in. Martha wept. This strong rock of the family had finally been dealt a card too painful to suck the tears back.

When Abby arrived, Martha was slumped on the floor with the letter crumpled in a ball. She sobbed through swollen eyes and the primal depth of pain in her cries made Abby reach for the crumpled letter. She sat on the couch to read what terrible news the letter contained.

News of a wedding would normally bring joy to the recipients, but this was not an announcement. No. She had eloped with a foreigner with no plans of returning to the desert. The only things Martha had in this awful place were her beloved daughters. Perhaps they did not realize they comprised her entire life's reward.

"Oh no," was all Abby said before joining in the unnatural sound of wailing, deep from the belly of women's sorrow.

Etta sat alone in the Holiday Hotel room back in Birmingham. The table was covered with a barrage of paper. Etta enjoyed the task of sifting through the souvenir books and newly developed film. Photos from the Swiss holiday were nothing short of spectacular. Her otherworldly love was apparent in every pose.

Roberto cherished the ring Etta had selected. During the vacation, he had recited over and over those precious words that Etta had so thoughtfully engraved on his ring, "*Antes, Ahora, Siempre:* Before, Now, and Forever. *Antes, Ahora, Siempre:* Before, Now, and Forever." As if to memorize the moment forever, she had also traced the words on his back as they waited for the lift line, offering them up to the next tram.

The scenery had been breathtakingly majestic. Roberto held true to his promise to teach Etta to snow ski, which she found quite exhilarating. She was a quick athletic study, keeping up with him on most Alpine trails and slopes by the second day.

The suite had been worth the wait, and the magnificent European décor accentuated the romance of that rare moment in eternity. The cool marble floors of the sitting room and enormous tiled bath made the return to the hotel a visual treat. The deep burgundy and gold hues of the bedroom were rich, and silk-covered armchairs welcomed long conversations about home furnishings for the couple's own future home back in the Harborne section of Birmingham.

Indeed, the two were insatiably romantic. Well-suited as a couple on multiple levels of intellect, interest, and intimacy, they began to settle into the realization that their gut suspicions were correct; they were meant to be together.

Etta was surprised how easy it was to travel abroad, despite her foreign language deficit. It seemed with a few courtesy words, she could acquire much help. She kept a phrase book of five languages in her purse. Though her pronunciation butchered any words she used, people seemed appreciative of her effort. Roberto was always a grand help with conversing, though many people seemed uncomfortable with the couple. It had never occurred to Etta that she was not suitable for him because of her family heritage. Roberto felt this tension on several occasions as well, though he willingly disregarded it as rude demeanor.

Shopping in Switzerland had been entertaining. With his impeccable taste and panache, Roberto could place a dent in the vacation budget equal to Etta's. The ornate Swiss figure skate installed on Etta's bracelet bore record that Roberto might be a better skier, but Etta was a wonderful skater. She had shown him up by twirling and skating backward on the outdoor ice, while poor Roberto could barely keep the skates beneath his awkwardly rigid frame. They would return chilled to the bone, to a hot shower and warm companionship.

Time did not seem to pass too rapidly or too slowly. It was right in sync with the universal clock. Days were filled with entertainment and the evenings even more so. The athletic adventures were invigorating and the scenery remarkable. The camera Roberto bought had special lenses that helped Etta record close-up views and far-away scenery that she formerly believed impossible for amateur photographers.

They had both written letters to their families. Roberto knew that karma may turn on him at any moment, but he was genuinely excited to show off this poised, beautiful woman to his employees and parents. Etta anticipated the thrill of being able to introduce him to her modest family. She didn't feel nervous anymore over their lack of means. Though she did not disclose the specifics of her mother's lot in life, she knew Roberto would accept any situation out of respect for her. Etta was committed to helping provide for the necessities of her family back home.

Neither Etta nor Roberto anticipated the resentment and contention their relationship would cause both families, but for very different reasons. The common thread binding the receipt of both letters was that it created sorrow for the people they dearly loved.

⁌

Etta organized the documents, feeling a new sense of longing. She appreciated her independence, but she missed the close companionship of her husband. It would be a long, lonely night, spent wondering if he missed her. Could he feel her?

Roberto's mind was a tornado of activity. The work had suffered with his ill attention during the holiday. And the woman in his bed was warm, but she gave him no pleasure. He longed for his Etta and wondered if she missed him tonight. Could she feel him? His thoughts were broken by a loud snore coming from the raven-haired woman lying beside him.

Chapter 25
CASTLE HAREWOOD

After Etta secured a few groceries at Tesco, Henry chauffeured her back to the hotel. He had pondered how to approach this awkward conversation with Etta.

"Madam, Mr. Fernandez approached me abart worken as yaw family driver. Ee says I ood be at cha beck an' call. I cud werk on staff at cha noo um as a sort of butler. I want yoo ter knoo as I explained ter Mr. Fernandez, that I doe yav experience in that area. But it's important ter me ter knoo just what yoo thought of such an arrangement."

"Wow. I had not thought that far ahead, Henry. But I have to say, you would be spending more time with me than Roberto. How do *you* feel about that?"

"Miss Johnson... I'm sorry, Madam, I ood be delighted ter serve yoo, but I does yav me own family ter fink abart."

"Please, Henry, it's still Etta. You're like family to me. I think heaven sent you as part of the grand rescue plan for the stranded American in England." Both laughed, understanding the "other demeanor" required of Henry while in the company of Roberto.

"What troubles you, dear friend?" Etta asked, searching earnestly for unguarded candor.

"As it is with the Holiday job, I miss much toyme at um with the family. It ood require mower hours been on owse staff than me missis is accustomed to; however, Mr. Fernandez did offer a, well, 'generous' salary." Henry was careful with his words, but he still spoke from an honest heart.

"Does your wife have skills? Does she work outside your home?" Etta asked what under other circumstances would be a very rude line of questioning.

"No. Elizabeth tends garding an' cooks for whatever family cums in. She makes me uniforms an' the grandchildren's clobber. Me missis is quite skilled in many areas, but she does not werk."

"Doesn't work? My Lord, Henry! She is working all the time! I have an idea. If we were to find a home with servant quarters, would Elizabeth consider being on staff as well? Between the two of you, I would not need another soul!" Etta proposed, anticipating each prospective reservation he might have.

"Who ood care for ar um if we were ter care for yourn?" Henry countered, not in a rude manner, but with matter-of-fact, sincere curiosity.

"I can't imagine that caring for a home with one person in it would be much more than for your home of two. Besides, with the additional income, your wife would work less by hiring services of her own. It would be possible to live in our home part-time and in your own home part-time. Will you at least consider this?"

"I wull yav ter terk ter Elizabeth. This is a big change for us, an' it wull affect all ar family."

"We understand, Henry. I hope you two will come to an agreement."

The limousine approached the hotel. Etta needed a few hours to upgrade to professional attire. She carried her own grocery bag. A solo bag was a nuisance to ask for help with. She turned the key and set the food down. Behind the door of the hotel room was a screaming sense of loneliness. She did not really notice the beautiful room, which had become, in her eyes, common and uncomfortable. By now, she was ready to locate a place that they could both inhabit and participate in assembling decor. She placed her hands on her hips in frustration.

She wished the vision of this hotel room on her first visit would return magically with its former beauty. It wasn't lovely in these minutes as she paused in the room alone, in bare feet.

She surveyed the closet in hopes of finding the appropriate attire for such an important introduction to the banking agents and for the negotiations to locate a proper home. She carefully selected the clothing and then assembled it on the bed. The top was exchanged and the outfit reexamined. She chewed the corner of her index finger with nervous energy. She scrapped the entire ensemble, selecting instead a warm auburn dress with a camel-colored wrap. She studied the leather pumps, conservative and pretty. But what was missing? The ring, of course. She didn't always wear the ring as it remained such a cold and foreign object on her customarily naked hand. She recalled removing it and placing it on a small tray next to the sink near the bar. She slid the diamonds and rubies back on her ring finger, imagining the warmth of Roberto's hand and the cool sensation of the gold band. The image was so vivid in her mind that, for a moment, Etta thought she could feel him approach her and caress her from behind.

She looked out the window to the street and viewed the skyline with appreciation for the variety of artistic chimney tops. She noted several broken roof tiles since the last wave of storms. Etta poured herself some juice and realized that she was too stir crazy to wait for the Colmore phone call. Instead, she took action into her own hands.

Bath, hair, nails, makeup, jewelry, nylons, suit, heels. It was still new to her, this grand preparatory ceremony. But it was time. Perhaps the bank would have a connection with a prospective seller in need of relocating. Was there a home that would balance Roberto's discriminating tastes with Etta's simple upbringing? She inspected herself with severe scrutiny and approved of the reflection before picking up the telephone.

Etta phoned the Colmore residence only to find the servants. She left a detailed message with their housemaid.

Henry drove her unquestioningly to the important meeting. Etta took great liberty and risk in the gross oversight of a proper introduction in such a crucial matter. She brazenly walked into the office, searching for the chief executive officer at the bank. Through two of the financial staff, Etta located the referral and requested time in his presence. Etta approached the gentleman with the gesture of an extended hand before beginning her string of discourse.

"Hello, Mr. Volworth. I am Etta Johnson Fernandez. Mrs. Greta Colmore referred me to you for assistance in locating an estate. We would like to find a partially furnished property and perhaps something with a space for the wait staff. We hope to locate a proper agent who can help us locate a home with a reserve of two hundred thousand pounds."

Mr. J. B. Volworth was sincerely taken aback with the American, partially for her boldness, and partially that this young woman would keep company with the elder women he considered to be of a particular social standing in the community. Of course he would help her; she had the declared funds in hand.

Before many words were exchanged, Mr. Volworth was interrupted by an urgent phone call, which was none other than Greta Colmore. She detailed Etta's social history, as she knew it, and apologized for not arriving to make the introduction herself.

With this voucher, Mr. Volworth responded with a much more cooperative, helpful response to Etta's lengthy list of questions regarding this process of purchasing a home in the Harborne area. Privately, though, he wondered why a woman would make such an important decision alone. Why would her husband not accompany her on this house hunt? This was no business of Mr. Volworth's and he was usually more proficient at squelching such curiosities from his mind.

Mr. J. B. Volworth extended the hospitality of setting Etta up in an unused office with ample reading materials while he made a chain of phone inquiries on her behalf. Etta enjoyed not only the unexpected break, but also the lovely British homes and gardens magazines left by other women who had the luxury of a free afternoon. She looked at more styles of homes in the first twenty minutes than she had studied in her entire stay in England. Surveying the landscape was one thing, but looking for a private abode was quite another! The interior magazines proved helpful in that Etta was now entirely convinced that she would require an interior designer. She had not the training, patience, or disposition to take on such a lofty project as making an estate into a pleasurable multisensory experience.

Approaching the magazine-shielded face on the leather sofa, Mr. Volworth cleared his throat to break her literary spell.

"Ah, Mr. Volworth. Have you learned anything?" Etta asked, standing up out of courtesy at his approach.

"As a matter of fact, yes. You are in luck on several levels, Mrs. Fernandez. I have telephoned an associate of the bank, Aloysius Louden, who helps manage estates of the recently departed. Mr. Louden should arrive shortly to meet with you. I also took the liberty of arranging a second meeting thereafter in the early evening with Ponsonby Jordison who has a few offerings in the Harborne area to discuss with you as well. Both were pleased you and Mr. Fernandez have your sights set on Harborne."

"Thank you so much, Mr. Volworth. Greta Colmore was accurate in her prediction that you could find the correct network within hours of our meeting."

"Why, thank you. It's an honor to be of service to friends of Mrs. Colmore, our special client. Why don't you enjoy lunch and meet me back here in an hour. I'm sure Mr. Louden will arrive by then."

Etta departed the bank feeling extraordinarily satisfied with the quick progress made thus far. She strolled across the street from Greta's bank and phoned her from the privacy of the red phone booth.

"Etta! I apologize for not being there for your introduction. I can't elaborate on this morning, but suffice it to say I am out the tail end of it, only slightly scathed," Greta reported.

"Would you like to come along on a house hunt?" Etta inquired innocently.

"No, dear. That is a highly personal endeavor, reserved for old friends and family."

Etta was surprised and hurt by Greta's reply. Apparently, Etta's vision of the relationship between the two women was not reciprocal. She hoped that this had not been too forward an invitation to ruin what authentic *acquaintanceship* they had established.

"Well, thank you again for the referrals, Mrs. Colmore," Etta returned with more humility in her tone.

"Have a lovely home tour," were the last words on the line.

Etta ate fish and chips alone, pondering who her real friends were. Pondering who her adopted family members in England might be. Suddenly, the prospect of finding a home seemed less important than clarifying the interpersonal issues in her circle of Birmingham people. Between work and home, neighbors and friends, who was authentic and who was perceived? This gave Etta cause for a great burden in her heart.

Etta finished the unsavory ingestion, distracted by recent events. In the ladies' powder room at the bank, she squeezed a small amount of toothpaste onto her tongue and swished away the fish and chips from her breath. Repairing her lipstick and inspecting her appearance, she attempted to adjust the hardened look about her. She looked as though she was poised to instigate an argument, not receive help finding a domicile. Etta breathed deeply in and exhaled numerous times, trying to flush color back in her face.

As Mrs. Fernandez approached Mr. Volworth's office, a particularly unusual-looking man in a navy suit interrupted her. The man's face appeared to have been damaged by fire or explosives of some kind. It was difficult to maintain eye contact, but Etta focused intently on the task of courtesy.

"Excuse me, madam. Are you Etta Fernandez?"

"Why, yes, I am. And you are…"

"Aloysius Louden, at your service. Forgive me, I was expecting a Spaniard."

"I'm American, actually," Etta responded without any irritation over the assumption. "Pleased to meet you, Mr. Louden. Mr. Volworth thought you may be of some service to my husband and me."

"Please call me Aloysius."

Etta thought on either account it would be difficult to form the sounds on her lips, as both the man's names were foreign to her ears and tongue.

"I was told that you have a meeting with an estate manager soon, so may I take the next two hours of your time?"

"Of course," Etta replied, feeling more comfortable with his damaged face after the initial shock. She continued to focus on his bright blue eyes and blur out the rest.

For the next twenty minutes over tea in an adjoining office, Etta detailed the circumstances of the relationship, the need for staff housing, and the practical hope of finding a furnished home. She was not honest enough to detail her rapid rise from homelessness to wealth.

Aloysius Louden was a gracious guide, opening Etta's door for her and narrating the sections of Harborne they passed through.

"You will find that Harborne or Edgbaston are equally sought after for location from Birmingham and for availability of their fine estates. Hagley and Bristol are the two main roads for daily commute, but in the evening, you need to enjoy the clock tower and shops along High Street. Junction Pub offers a nice lunch. You'll find the library over there on High Street. The schools are well respected. St. Peters and St. Mary's are wonderful primary schools. There is Station Road as well, though I don't know much about that one."

He hardly gave her room to ask questions about the community she toured. Mr. Louden turned off the road and onto a tree-lined drive with a stately bachelor's estate in the near distance.

Etta and Aloysius toured the home of a recently deceased client who had no surviving relatives residing in all of the UK. It was an informative and spectacular tour, but the property proved over double what she would ever consider managing on her own.

The next property was indeed far more modest, but it was historically well maintained. This property was under a nasty legal dispute between the original and subsequent wives and their resulting families. Perhaps both sets of people could be satisfied with funds derived from simply ridding this home of either family's ownership. As the two surveyed the various rooms and furnishings, Etta felt a warm sensation overcome her, and she could envision raising children here.

"Are the furnishings being offered with the home?" Etta inquired.

"I think it would be generous and reasonable of you to offer such an arrangement, considering the tangle of legal issues surrounding the possessions. Without an option such as this, the families would have to wait years to sort out the estate feud."

"Interesting prospect," Etta commented partially to herself. Her eyes followed the long walls up to the ornate molding along the ceiling perimeter. The master bedroom was drenched in wood from the enormous floor planks to the floor-to-ceiling wood paneling, which sported paintings of the Irish countryside. There were servant quarters with a private entry, measuring nearly as large as her mother's simple tract home. The guest quarters were somewhat larger and offered many amenities for long, seasonal stays. The furniture was all in good condition, save for the children's playroom, which perhaps had seen the result of ill-mannered, unsupervised tots. The grade of the furnishings was directly commensurate with the function of each room. The main areas housed high-end, sturdy, ornate pieces, while the secondary bedrooms had common bureaus that would last for years to come, though they were not intended so much to please the eye.

Etta requested a moment alone before locking up the home. She walked every room slowly, in silence, to hear the walls and floor. Envisioning the sounds of a life here, Etta attended to the transition from room to room through the various levels. Yes, she determined that they could make a fine life here.

Aloysius Louden was nonetheless equally interesting on the return to the bank as he detailed additional history of the area and its role in the Second World War. The train station was close by, as were the Birmingham Botanical Gardens. Etta's ears perked up, not realizing the route had taken a circular tour. She was, indeed, very close to her work. Another plus.

Etta offered polite thank-yous upon their return to the bank, and she collected business cards for future contact. While readying herself for the property manager, she enjoyed a conversation with one of the bank employees on break. Their comments and questions helped Etta define with better clarity what requirements she should shop for. She had never projected into the future on any level, living instead in "real time" with whatever resources were currently available to her. A new mindset would be required to go with the new home.

Ponsonby Jordison was an extremely large man who dominated the lobby upon his arrival. He appeared more like a Viking than an Englishman. Ponsonby located his target and offered a hand to Etta with a thunderous personal introduction. His massive paw could have surrounded a stack of half a dozen of Etta's feminine hands.

In the privacy of the office once again, Etta explained the circumstances by which she and Roberto were attempting to locate a suitable home. When quizzed on the design or architecture of the other home in Barcelona, Etta suddenly felt very ignorant of her husband's life away from her.

"Never mind!" Ponsonby bellowed. "This home will be yours to enjoy most of the time, anyhow. Let's see what we can muster up."

And off they went, back into Harborne, though this ride was far different than the last. There was silence the entire way. No conversation, no tourist assistance. Just the sound of the powerful engine, engaging all eight cylinders. The first three stops were uneventful, and Etta was not impressed by any of the estates they toured.

At the third property viewing, Etta and Ponsonby were welcomed by homeowners who persuaded Etta that their home could be prospect number two. They generously shared the history of the home and service structures on the estate. They detailed their participation in the Harborne Cricket Club and the Football Club, both of which were established in the latter 1800s. The couple was moving to Durban, South Africa, to rejoin family who had established a network of businesses over the last decade. It was now or never for them to join in the family's prosperity. When asked if they would leave their furnishings, the couple responded, "Maybe," and searched each other's eyes for joint confirmation.

Ponsonby Jordison drove Etta to five other homes that evening. None matched the charm or facilities of the select two seen that day. The second tour was scheduled for the following afternoon, and Ponsonby was kind enough to drop Etta at the Holiday Hotel, saving Henry a trip to fetch her.

Etta phoned Roberto at work to report the preliminary findings. Bernadette was curt with Etta. How strange it was, as Etta had never met the woman, nor given her cause to be so rude. She would inquire about this later with Roberto.

"I was just heading out the door tonight, Etta. It was a wonderful *dia de negocios*!" Roberto reported with a celebratory tone. He detailed how he acquired two other contracts, which all but made up for his time off in Switzerland.

Etta reported the house-hunting news, describing the two prospects of the day. Roberto inquired about the architectural details necessary for his own work and comfort. He listened generously to Etta's interpretation of her own work and leisure space. Roberto would phone again the following evening after the second round of tours. With the ample budget Roberto was willing to spend, there were limited luxury homes available to view, making the decision far easier than Etta had anticipated.

After an excruciatingly long morning, filled with anticipation and many design magazines to study, Etta saw nothing the second day to convince her there was a better prospect than ones shown by Aloysius and Ponsonby the prior day.

Roberto could not take the opportunity to fly in to view the properties, which Etta found absolutely absurd, considering the sizable investment he proposed to spend on this home. But he did give Etta his full support on whichever estate she would secure, and he placed funds on reserve, awaiting her decision for release. Etta was unsure of her comfort level with his apathetic regard over the transfer of such a huge sum of money.

Etta pondered the lofty decision while escaping to West Yorkshire for the day. She found solitude in a castle tour. Within the echoing stone walls inside the restored Harewood Estate, Etta made peace with her decision. The gift shop offered books illustrating the extensive renovation process this particular castle had undergone. Etta overlooked these in favor of a charm of the castle. It was the perfect reproduction of the estate with the name *Harewood* engraved on the side. As with all her charms, this one held a special memory for Etta. Today was the day she chose her own castle.

Despite the finality of her decision on which home to purchase, Etta once again slept fitfully, and alone, in the hotel room.

Chapter 26

GERMAN CROSS

Etta met Aloysius Louden at his personal office. She waited in a comfortable leather armchair and gazed out the eight-pane window. Surveying the garden, she imagined it in the full glory of spring with explosions of color and cascades of rich, English hues. The new manor (could she even call it a *castlette* without giggling?) surely held much potential for spring as well. She could barely make out an abandoned bird's nest in the brush outside the window of the waiting area.

Despite being in the eye of a hurricane, Etta felt comfort in her resolve to negotiate the estate of the recently deceased Judge Ryle. Roberto seemed comfortable with her decision-making ability and gave her much financial room with which to negotiate the deal. Although she had the legal authority to secure funds for the contract, Etta would not be able to sign the final deed.

Aloysius made the initial phone call to the judge's original wife, Clara, explaining the terms of Etta and Roberto's offer to acquire the residence with its furnishings. He presented a persuasive case in the oration of why it would be easier to divide the money, rather than the possessions. Clara agreed to consider it with the family.

Wife number two, Beth, took more convincing. She had loved the estate and very much preferred buying out the others, using her current husband's financial holdings. It was doubtful that he could raise the commensurate value of the estate and would require financing. Nevertheless, Beth would also discuss the offer with her family.

Wife number three, the true love of His Honor's life, Sarah, was deep in mourning and eager to part with it all. Their children were still young enough to begin a new life elsewhere, should she ever be blessed to find new love. Being too tired to care for such a sizable house, Sarah was ready to sign it all away and begin anew in another part of England. Sarah had cheerfully endured the emotional burdens of the other wives in exchange for his undeniable favor. Once the judge passed away, the exes' true selfish natures surfaced over the contention of the will. The initial cat-scratching mood left her physically ill, and Sarah fiercely protected her children from it. Yes, sadly, but willingly, she would sign most of it away to protect her children and attempt to mend her broken heart. If she agreed to be more flexible with the estate, she wondered if she could persuade the other wives to settle this. Maybe then, she could move on with her life.

Aloysius phoned Clara and Beth again, explaining the position Sarah had taken in her desire to part with it all. He bravely invited them all to his office to iron out details. Surprisingly, neither put up a fuss. They both agreed to meet with Sarah, Etta, and Aloysius. Aloysius and Etta would be prepared for the worst.

Sarah's requests had been modest and simple. Of course, her and the children's remaining personal effects would be packed and moved. She wanted the paintings in the children's rooms and her bedroom armoire. The few furnishings and china service Sarah brought to the marriage would be returned as well. During the Honorable Judge Ryle's final months of suffering, Sarah had let an apartment close to the hospital so she could be with him nearly every moment. Nanny Rachel tended to the children, protecting them through the ordeal. Neither Sarah nor the children had returned to the house. It was too painful.

Etta prepared Roberto over the phone for the altercation she anticipated in acquiring their future home. She dressed to the nines and took the entire day off work for the big event.

Aloysius reserved the largest conference room with the massive plank oak table for this event. His assistant had prepared for a long parley by preparing a tea and biscuit service for these clients. Thankfully, the various children and spouses did not show, allowing the negotiations to be exclusively among the three widows and Etta.

Aloysius discussed the many levels by which the sale of the property and contents would expedite the settlement of the judge's final will. The terms he left had been vague enough to deliberate for many years, despite his brilliant personal record in the legal arena. One beautiful woman can steer a rational man's disposition away from common sense, but what about three?

Etta was relieved that Aloysius was able to convince the women that it was in their best interest to join Sarah's lead in splitting the proceeds lock, stock, and barrel. An appraiser would be called in to calculate the furnishings' worth. The home's original treasures and historic pieces had mostly been stripped with each passing marriage, anyhow. Neither of the first wives desired anything else formerly left in the house. All of the women had been persuaded to accept their shares of the settlement to preclude legal fees.

The surprisingly successful negotiation was put to rest until the appraisal could be presented. Clara and Beth would not need to be present for that. They needed only to report to pick up their settlement checks, which Aloysius assured them would be before the beginning of March. Sarah would sign over the property once the final sum was established.

Etta had respected Aloysius's request to remain silent throughout the negotiation. After she wished the women well, Etta sat down in the chair for a moment, feeling lightheaded and giddy. Aloysius placed both hands on the table and collected her attention with the question, "Etta, are you feeling all right?"

In answer, she slowly rose from her chair and embraced the slight man with a tight bear hug. Aloysius was taken aback by the American's brazen display of affection, blushing deep red.

"Thank you," was all Etta could choke out. Within the month, they could move out of the Holiday Hotel and into their new Harborne home on 3 Metchley Lane.

Etta needed a stroll to take it all in. She walked a few blocks, blind to the lovely window dressings of the downtown shops. Her feet did not take notice of the swelling and tightening within the fitted dress shoes. Her scalp tingled from the tension of the session as she continued to walk stiffly with her pocketbook in hand.

Etta's mental image of the remaining furnishings was sheer splendor. It made her wonder what had been removed, if these were indeed the leftover, undesirable pieces of the judge's décor.

As if magnetic, the town jewelry storefront pulled to Etta's stiff frame, offering a momentary reprieve from the shock of purchasing her first home with no family input. The cases sported diamonds, precious stones, watches, and fobs. Etta had always been drawn to the selection of fobs, wondering if she could ever persuade Roberto to wear a watch chain with an ornamental fob dangling from beneath it. He was, after all, a cuff link man, with a collection close to that of her collection of bracelet bits.

"Oh, there they are." Etta popped out of deep thought, observing a narrow, velvet-lined tray of charms in silver and gold.

The clerk approached Etta, greeted her, and inquired regarding her wants. She was surprised at how Lim (as his nametag read) spoke with such a thick British accent. His Chinese features were entirely symmetrical, having movie-star-like qualities. She just expected him to have an Asian accent. She also wondered if he was Lim or Mr. Lim. Feeling more ignorant of international cultures, she thought to herself, *Billy would feel uncomfortable hiring someone at A. J. Bayless with Lim's sharp appearance, coupled with such a funny accent.*

"Well now, is there something that caught your eye?" Lim's wide smile replaced nearly a quarter of his face with stark white, perfectly straight teeth.

Etta exercised great restraint from laughing at the comical mix of the clerk's sight and sound. She tried to avoid looking him in the eye, choosing instead to focus on the items beneath the glass in the jewelry case.

Lim's trimmed and clean nails showed no sign of ever having experienced manual labor. Etta quickly learned why Lim held his head so high with confidence as he offered a lengthy, unsolicited discourse on the grades of gold and the markings of the regulatory system used for fine jewelry in England. The more the clerk educated Etta on the jewelry in his care, the less she was entertained by the thought of a Chinese Brit.

Feeling celebratory, Etta bought a broach inlaid with a spray of multicolored stones. She also recorded the event of purchasing their home with a German cross charm. The house was a blessing, but truthfully, Etta would not have guessed this filigree design to be a cross at all. It resembled perpendicular pairs of triangular shaped ribbon, encircled by a fine filigree rope. Etta was partially German. This was supposedly a cross, and she really was blessed this day. So, the filigree cross was linked to the bracelet of memories.

An elegantly dressed woman entered the store with a uniformed servant in tow. The young woman in uniform boldly approached the clerk directly, not even gaining eye contact as she blurted out, "Mate! The Ryle estate sold ter am American! Cost imagine at?"

"Amanda! No gossiping!" the woman sternly corrected.

The clerk turned directly toward Etta, bypassing the servant's fixed gaze. "Would that be all for you then, madam?"

Etta was surprised by the interjection of the relaxed Brummie dialect and the swiftness by which her negotiations swept the community. Etta's face flushed, anticipating the uninvited attention she would surely soon be given.

"Amanda! Wait in the car!" the woman sharply snapped. She then turned and offered her glove-covered hand to Etta. "Terribly sorry dear. This community rarely witnesses a change in family demesne, and I venture to admit we have never heard of a foreigner interested in this section, either. I assume you are the buyer? I am Mrs. Percy Blunkett, apparently one of your new neighbors?"

"Yes. Etta John…Fernandez. Pleased to meet you. I am genuinely surprised that news travels so fast. I have not purchased the home yet. In fact, I just came from the negotiations with the judge's family."

"You mean families? The 'wives club' was the talk of the town for the last two decades. Etta-John is an interesting name. Is it a family name?"

"No, Etta Fernandez. I was formerly Johnson, and it still rolls off my tongue more easily than my married name."

"Etta Fernandez then. Where is your husband from? What is his business?"

Etta began to feel extremely uncomfortable providing all their personal information to a stranger. Her out was the fact that the charm was now affixed to her bracelet.

"Excuse me, Mrs. Blunkett, I have another appointment to attend to. I hope to see you again very soon," Etta remarked, hoping she sounded sincere and polite.

Bracelet fastened and bill paid, Etta walked quickly out and down High Street with what felt like a block full of eyes following her. There was no appointment and no car waiting. Etta dodged into the nearest red telephone booth and called Henry to rescue her from her social discomfort.

༄

"Mom?" Etta spoke over the crackling, overseas connection.

"Etta, is that really you? Abby, get on the bedroom phone! Etta's calling! Honey, where are you?"

"I'm at a hotel right now. I have so much to tell you, and I couldn't wait to hear your voice."

"Hey, punk!" Abby announced into the receiver. "How is your prince charming?"

"We are doing really well. We bought a home and will be moving in very soon. I had hoped you two could come for a visit." Etta did not get too far into the master plan.

"Honey, we can't possibly afford a flight over there," her mother replied.

Abby offered, "Etta, we might be able to swing it in the fall if we pick up an extra job for a few months."

"Whoa, Nellie! Hey, you two, since I am not coming home this spring, I was planning to fly you both here. We'll pay for your flight, and you'll have a place to stay. What more could you want? You absolutely must bring spending money, though," Etta elaborated, feeling especially pleased to present the offer to her own precious, but tiny family.

"Mom, Roberto's company is doing very well, and it is no problem to have you here for as long as you like. The flights are covered, and you will stay in our home." The sound of "home" rolling off Etta's tongue caused an emotional tear to escape her eye.

"I can't wait for you to meet him."

"Does he have any good-looking, rich brothers?" Abigail wondered.

"I suppose we could work on that while you are here too, sis. Gosh, I have missed you both. So much has happened." Etta trailed off.

How could she explain the low point of being stranded? What could she possibly report about her fortune in finding a job at the gardens? How could she retrace the amazing relationship she found with Roberto? She chose not to. Instead, she wanted them to witness, and evaluate, firsthand. The arrangements would be made for late summer or early fall. Etta would attempt to send photos. Abby and Mom would attempt to write more news from home.

All parties hung up feeling unsatisfied with how much could *not* be discussed on the phone. The once inseparable women were all keeping recent, pertinent news under wraps.

Chapter 27
EDELWEISS

The brown, masculine hands fingered the gold edelweiss flower on the bracelet attached to her slender wrist. His hands moved up her arms, and Roberto caressed her satin-covered shoulders. "My, you are beautiful. *You* will be the best furnishing at the new house."

Their recent trip to Switzerland landed a professional tip, and the negotiation had paid off with a modest test contract for Horizon-Tech. The flower charm seemed inconsequential to Roberto, but he knew that Etta would appreciate this more than if he brought her home flowers. What was it she once said? Charms in life, roses in death.

Roberto was being especially attentive to Etta after the separation had left them both longing for each other's companionship. His lips traced and kissed the line of her neck. The moment was ruined by the sudden sound of furniture knocking against the wall in the adjacent room.

Wham! Bang, bang, bang!

Suddenly, the origin of the sound slapped the couple with embarrassment. Their privacy was at the mercy of the hotel guests surrounding them. It would be such an improvement to move into a more private, generous space than this hotel room. Silently, Roberto reached for Etta's hand.

With the mood ruined, Etta kissed Roberto's hand, and she escaped to the quietest space in the room. Etta sat on the toilet top while the water was adjusting to her preferred temperature. Sliding deep into the water, Etta relaxed for nearly a half an hour while Roberto watched rugby with the volume turned up high.

When Etta emerged from the bathroom, she plopped down next to the feet of the armchair. Roberto studied the top of her head, wondering just what thoughts rolled through her mind.

༺༻

The appraiser had proved to be extremely generous to Roberto and Etta by estimating the contents of the judge's home at a pittance of what the replacement cost would authentically be. The balance of the property was paid in full by Roberto's reserve. During the transaction at Greta Colmore's bank, he had also deposited another sum into a new account for Etta to use for additional furnishings and shopping, though he grossly overestimated what Etta required in sustenance.

Henry picked up Roberto from the Holiday and then Etta from the gardens. Henry navigated the streets through both Edgbaston and Harborne, as Etta had previously instructed.

Pulling into the circular drive in front of 3 Metchley Lane, Roberto was surprised by the presence of the mailbox already adorned with "Fernandez" spelled out in colorful Italian tiles. This rather public announcement of the occupants took him quite by surprise.

With keys in hand, Etta practically dragged Roberto out onto the drive, excited to allow him to finally survey their new house, or rather, his investment. The restored estate was originally constructed on thickly forested acreage as a hunting lodge with a façade fashioned in Tudor architecture. The low, weathered-timber doorway was even more pronounced as the top of Roberto's tall frame tentatively approached close to the keystone above the door. These doorways would require all guests over six feet to duck their heads slightly, or risk a crack on the noggin.

The grand salon was tread with solid English oak board planks spanning thirty-five feet with a thirty-inch width. The ornamental wood trim traced every line of the room, causing a visibly warming effect.

Etta led Roberto to the enormous statuary marble fireplace, graced with a tablet of dancing cherubs and Grecian figures playing musical instruments. The interior opening sported an egg and dart molding. Opposite the wall of the fireplace was an electric radiator that the couple would locate in various sizes throughout the home for more regular usage.

Roberto's soft eyes approvingly surveyed the tasteful, though sparse, décor of the main floor. Up the walls his eyes traveled and down to the feet of every piece of furniture. Etta watched him observe her "work in progress." He said few words as they navigated the bedrooms hand in hand. Etta had condensed the remaining furniture from five of the bedrooms into four, leaving the former children's room bare.

Roberto's hand moved down, relaxing around Etta's waist. "What room is this?" Roberto wondered of the noticeably less maintained and sparsely regarded detail of this virtually blank canvas.

"This may be your Harborne office…or an art room…or just maybe, the baby's room."

Roberto began to chuckle. "The baby's room. That's a far cry off."

Etta was stunned. Carefully weighing her every word, she replied, "It was not intended to be funny. We are going to have a child." Then she waited for what could be called a genuinely pregnant pause before his reaction. "Dear, we're going to have a baby."

Roberto paused for a few moments, studying her serious expression and drinking in the news. He picked up Etta and swung her around so that her loose hair flew parallel to the ground.

"Does that mean you *are* ready to be a father, Roberto?" Etta inquired with noticeable concern in her voice.

"Oh, yes, Etta. I am just really surprised, that's all. I've been distracted by travel and the demands of the company."

Yes, he was happy. Thrilled? No. But happy nevertheless.

They discussed preliminary baby plans while negotiating the bathroom suite. It had marble shelves that housed clear apothecary jars Etta had already filled with bathing products. The deep, freestanding tub encased in dark wood was too tempting for Roberto, and a rare silly side kicked in. He jumped down into the tub and welcomed Etta to join him with the gesture of his open arms.

"A son should be named Roberto. A daughter, Roberta. That would be appropriate for our first child."

"There is absolutely no way we will name our daughter Roberta. We have eight months to discuss better options than that."

Etta laughed and joined him in the tub, fully clothed. She rested her back against his chest as they tested the size of the large tub. Oh yes, this would be large enough for two! Suddenly all the reservations she had over the surprising pregnancy were over. As they silently shared a few minutes in the tub, she knew Roberto would be a wonderful father, though she worried about the additional responsibilities while he was away.

The master bedroom was inviting to the couple who roamed their new place arm in arm, in a heightened level of "couple-dom." The massive carved headboard depicted a fox-hunting scene, which was a lovely complement to the Irish countryside paintings on the paneled walls. Roberto found his dresser. It was a Batavia seven-drawer tallboy with glass pulls. Next to it stood a refined, and highly collectible, uniform butler. The tog stove stood between his furniture and Etta's more elaborate, roomy pieces. It now occurred to Etta that the delegation of bedroom furniture seemed ridiculous since Etta's wardrobe was a mere fraction of her husband's.

Both Etta and Roberto appreciated the carefully selected radiator ventilation grills and covers, which complemented the design or tone in each room. These and the details of the ornate locks, latches, and handles gave the home a step up from the others Etta had considered.

The tour continued into the gentlemen's smoking room. The Victorian button chairs of Hessian fabric were fashioned in dark, heavy shades of brown and burgundy. The vintage sofa had proportioned cushions against a high back.

The ladies' tearoom, by contrast, was a light blue sitting space with French hand-woven linens throughout. The floor had been updated with a more contemporary tile that was light and cool to the eye. The white marble mantle above the fireplace would be a wonderful place to display travel treasures or bric-a-brac.

Roberto wandered curiously ahead of Etta now past the beautifully gilded library and the unified wood colors of the upper rooms.

"Hello...?" an unfamiliar voice echoed through the chambers to Roberto's ear.

"Love, there is someone calling from downstairs," Roberto reported the obvious with disinterest in attending to the intrusion of his tour. He continued with his exploration of the home's countless details as Etta descended the wide stairs to meet Mr. Louden in the entry.

"The bell's broken," he said matter-of-factly as he handed Etta a massive arrangement of flowers vaulting up and outward with the breadth of a large sitting chair.

Etta nearly dropped the weight of the arrangement, so Aloysius jumped to aid her grip from underneath. Together, they positioned it in the center of the entry table square in the middle of the foyer. It was an explosion of colorful flowers and sturdy greens that was befitting a lovely home such as this.

"Thank you so much! This is quite a surprise! Let me get Roberto and introduce you…"

Roberto descended unannounced and was visually grimacing at the sight of Aloysius's disfigured face. Etta had grown accustomed to it and had failed to prepare her husband for the cosmetic defect.

"Hello, Mr. Fernandez. It's a pleasure to meet you; after all, I have heard of your prosperous Horizon-Tech in this area. I'm sorry to startle you. I was burned in the war. But the upside is that I never have to shave again!" He chuckled.

Roberto chuckled too, though not as genuinely or comfortably as Etta did.

"How do you like the little hunting cottage your wife selected? She has a good sense of what she likes and doesn't like, then, doesn't she?" Aloysius continued, refusing to give in to Roberto's tension.

For some reason, Roberto paused at this remark and slowly articulated, "I love what I have seen so far. Etta has not shown me the garden or garage yet."

"Please, join us! I was going to take Roberto to the outer grounds next." Etta took her husband's hand and led him through the back of the house and across a stone-lined path to the old carriage house. It had been lovingly preserved with vaulting rafters and strong timbers amid the brick. The stabling partitions had long since been removed, but there were still a few remnants of equestrian artifacts hanging from various walls. These items had instantly charmed Etta, and she imagined her own children's horses corralled behind the conservatory someday.

As the men were exchanging small talk, Etta led the way to the adjacent terrace garden and sitting area. There were specks of green everywhere as spring threatened to awaken the sleeping gardens very soon. Inside the hardwood conservatory with the white flagstone floors, Etta motioned the men to peer through the glass to where the cuttings garden would be planted. Teak bench seats surrounding two large trunks invited afternoon conversations, and a Chelsea lounger and steamer chairs had recently been moved outside to add a visual measure of comfort to the late winter appearance of the property.

Their final trek was through the servant's quarters off the back of the kitchen. The local stone and wood floors complemented the fabric-covered walls. The condition made one suspicious that servants had lived here anytime recently. Visible past the marble worktops of the kitchen was the eighteenth-century solid mahogany dining table. It was set with seven chairs of generous elbow room posted on either side, with two curved table heads.

The men wrapped up their conversation, and Roberto admired the floral arrangement now dominating the front reception hall. The antique bird's eye maple pieces in the front of the house had been lovingly preserved and now appeared to glean more interesting hues under the competition of the colorful floral arrangements.

Etta shook Mr. Louden's hand and thanked him earnestly for all his help. Roberto offered his appreciation for helping Etta locate a fitting estate for the couple. When the door closed, Roberto was shocked back to reality, recalling the news that they would soon not be just a couple anymore.

Etta saw the silly look in Roberto's eyes, the teasing bend of his chin, and the animal-like crouch into which he placed himself. She shrieked and ran up the broad oak stairway as Roberto raced after her, growling. He caught her in one fell swoop, six steps from the top, and threw her over his shoulder. Roberto carried her up the remaining distance to the top of the stairs, where Etta slid back down to the weight of her own feet. Etta kicked the bedroom door closed with her foot. Etta giggled a moment and said simply, "Welcome home."

Chapter 28
GARDEN BOOT

The deep trance spilled thousands of words onto pages of Etta's precious journal. This "other world" was interrupted by a startling ring. Binny didn't announce herself, instead opting to go straight to the point.

"Good God, I can't keep up with you! I just finalized plans for your wedding reception, and now you have a new home to celebrate. Christ, Etta!"

"I know, I know. It all happened awfully fast. How's your luck with Larkin these days?"

"Dead in the water. He has the looks, personality, and self-sustenance, but he has the wrong goals."

"What do you mean? He is always looking to improve himself. I know he goes to training all the time to keep himself poised for whatever opportunity may present itself."

"No, no, girl. For me! He wants a stay-at-home wife. His entire master plan for companionship is servitude and childbearing."

"Really! I would never have thought…"

"He was fun while he lasted, and actually my brother Thomas is getting married to Molly quite soon, so there will be another social gathering. Perhaps I can find a bloke to hook up with there."

"How great! They're finally closer to the wedding date. Such a nice couple. Have they found a home yet?"

"No. They were hoping to settle wherever Thomas establishes his new company. He hit on something, Etta. He is working on telephones that don't have cords. Say you are in one room and the phone rings. You pick it up and walk back to what you were doing. He's using some type of radio wiring configuration that the Royal Army used in the last war for ground communication. Mum is helping him get a start at it."

"And what of Joseph?"

"Don't ask! So! Can we celebrate your nuptials the first week of March? I know you are working that day, and I am hosting a surprise party with Larkin's help. We will have it in the tearoom at closing. What do you say?"

"Binny! If it's supposed to be a surprise, why are you asking me?"

"I have learned my lesson in parties past. All you need to do is have that husband of yours in town to pick you up for 'dinner' from work. If you just put on your best stage face, act authentically surprised, and graciously accept the loving kindness of your Brummie friends, I'll do the rest."

Etta laughed and shook her head. That's Binny for you.

"I have to be in London this week to oversee the blacksmith we just brought on tour. By the way, I am sending over Mum's interior designers to meet with you this Thursday afternoon."

"Isn't that a little bold, Binny?"

"Aren't you a little pathetic in that area?"

Etta laughed. "I know, I know, don't rub it in!" Etta knew that Binny struggled in this area also. The courtesy was extended to prepare her for guests, who would begin intruding on their privacy very soon.

⁂

Kelly checked her shop till, which was entirely unnecessary. In the years she worked there, she had never been off by even so much as a pence. Etta waited patiently at the book rack, studying the new selections for spring. She was anxious to watch the outer grounds come to life as winter expired. There were already signs of the sleeping flora awakening, and Etta was keen on watching their progression.

⁂

"Ready!" Kelly's perky voice announced.

Henry drove the two ladies to the Garden House pub for dinner. Etta was extremely pleased Henry was able to split jobs serving both the Holiday and the Fernandez home. Someday she would be comfortable enough to regularly drive herself.

"It's such a fancy chops ter be driven by a felloo, even if it is an older geezer. Am ya still looken for owse help?"

"Yes, no luck there. I can't wait till you see the house. It's a dream, Kelly! I never thought in my wildest dreams I would need a person to help me clean and manage my own house."

"Well I knoo sum really bostin ladoys that ood be honest an' werk sound for yam. Yam interested in their papers?" Kelly tested, not knowing how much to push Etta into considering her school chums for employment.

"I trust your recommendations, Kelly. You are an outstanding worker, and I wish you'd think about us. But if you won't, I will certainly consider anyone you deem worthy of the job."

"I was hopeen yam ood soy that. I yav them roight eya." With that, Kelly produced a folded legal envelope from her purse. She carefully pulled out four, no five applications for Etta. Kelly thought that using the Birmingham Botanical Gardens and Glasshouses official forms would give the impression to her friends that this was serious business, working for Etta. And besides, Mrs. Ingle wouldn't miss these application copies anyhow.

Etta laughed and looked over the applications briefly. One trend she noticed right away with all the carefully completed forms was the longevity of employment. None of her friends had worked at more than two establishments or residences.

While Etta was surveying the information, Kelly reached over and studied her bracelet. She noticed several new charms installed on the triple links since they had a proper visit. Though they always had a chat at work, it wasn't enough focused time to enjoy a good catch-me-up, especially now that Etta was working only a few days a week.

"I yav just the chops for yam Etta. We yav a noo garding boot in gold. I knoo yam miskin watchen for spren."

Etta knew that Kelly would not offer if she didn't think the boot charm would balance, match, or announce some important element of Etta's journey. "It's a deal!" Etta declared, agreeing to purchase the charm sight unseen. She knew Kelly would install it, plus polish the bracelet up, just as she did for all the customers.

When they arrived at the Garden House Pub, Henry left his home number with the waiter so they could phone him once the waiter cleared their dessert.

Etta ordered the bangers and mash, and Kelly ordered the kidney pie. Kelly finished a pint and progressed to her second even before Etta had downed half of her herbal tea. Etta already started to relax. Witnessing Kelly become increasingly tipsy, Etta remembered why she would not drink beer. Kelly, on the other hand, had been practicing tolerance for ale since her twelfth birthday party when her dad made her down a pint as a prank. Not wanting to be shown up, Kelly had kept her feet and tongue rather steady. Her father was most proud of Kelly that night. No future accolades outdid that one in his eyes. Quite a sad thing, really.

Kelly pulled out more paper from her large purse, only this time it was from the Sunday funnies. The cartoon of Asterix and Son depicted a door-to-door house hunt. "I crack this in the news, an' it seemed loike yam tryen ter buy an owse." Indeed, the door-to-door hunt for Asterix's house was reminiscent of a childhood book of Etta's named *Are You My Mother?*

"Is this her house? Is this her house? Is this her house?" Etta mimicked, and the ladies shared a laugh. "I'll put this on the icebox at home. Thanks for thinking of me. How is Geraldine these days? You will greet her for me, won't you? I want to include her when we have our open house."

"Ers as feisty as ever! Yam were roight. We mek crackin roomantes we does. Ers well natty."

Etta could read the comfort level in Kelly's eyes. She knew that this was a brilliant place for Kelly to live. She was pleased the living arrangement was beneficial for both ladies.

"I accidentally met one of my neighbors, Mrs. Percy Blunkett. She seemed so much like another busybody I knew back home named Mrs. Edwin Earl Busch. It was pretty funny, really. Her house girl blurted out to a shopkeeper about us buying the house, and Mrs. Blunkett made the connection through him. From her demeanor, I expect everyone in the neighborhood knows three things about us. First, I am American. Second, Roberto is Spanish. Third, we are not 'old blood' in the community. So with three strikes, I hope that we will be accepted at all by our neighbors."

"So stroike 'em if they doy loike yam!" The third beer was beginning to speak for Kelly, and Etta realized that dinner should soon be wrapped up for the evening.

☙

Thursday morning promptly at ten o'clock, a knock at the door startled Etta from preparing a three-course dinner for Roberto's arrival home. It was only the second time people had braved the walk to the door. The other had been Aloysius when he delivered the flowers, which were now beginning to wilt in the entry.

As Etta opened the heavy door, two well-dressed women were standing expectantly on the step.

"Good morning. I am Katrina from Essex, Grain, and Felbrigg Interior Design. May I see Etta Fernandez, please?"

"Oh dear. Ladies, I *am* Etta Fernandez! I forgot you were coming. Please come in." Etta instantly realized she stumbled on the lack of an appropriate door greeting, the lack of house help, and her casual attire for a business appointment. Her ears burned with shame as she led the ladies through to the sitting room and excused herself, bringing back a tray of beverages that should have been brought by the house help. Cognizant of these gross oversights, Etta was grateful the women did not seem affected by this.

"Etta, as I said, I am Katrina, and this is another associate, Margaret. Our company was founded in 1945, and we cater only to distinctive homes in the Birmingham area. When Binny Colmore phoned for your appointment, she was enthusiastic about the terms under which you purchased most of the furnishings with the estate." Katrina removed her glove and offered her hand to Etta, whose hand was available after setting the tray down on the buffet.

Etta shook the women's hands less assertively than usual, following their limp lead. "May I ask what services you offer?" Etta asked innocently, realizing this sounded pathetic once the words escaped her lips.

"We study the architectural style and elements of your home or renovation project and determine how to create a flow of furnishings that will be pleasing to the eye as well as functional for the household."

Simple enough, Etta thought, understanding now that Binny's idea to prepare the home, even before she visited, was a really good one.

"Please follow me this way."

Etta stood and invited the ladies to tour the home. She chose the carriage house and the conservatory first, explaining her personal vision and memories of her brown childhood in the desert and her love of horses.

"Does your husband want input in the selections, or is he allowing you to decorate?" Katrina asked.

"Roberto is leaving it all up to me because I will inhabit the house on a regular basis, and he travels much of the time." Etta thought that being frank with these women would be in her best interest so that the dwelling would be less showcase and more *home.*

The two women began making notes and comments regarding the exterior spaces. None of their comments resembled a negative slant. Instead, they had many positive interjections, suggesting very little change to these work areas.

Moving into the home, Etta knew they would not be so kind, and she was thus mentally bracing herself for the worst kind of British bashing. On the contrary, the comments presented were all remarkably painless, and the ladies pointed out many lovely details in the home that Etta had not noticed with her untrained eye. The EG&F ladies seemed to feel that this would be a quick enhancement project, with few changes to the styles or layout of the furnishings. They wanted the most restyling for the window dressings, which Etta admitted to knowing nothing about. Here falling on Etta's lap was the opportunity to learn about contemporary fabrics, style, and color flow.

Margaret was noticeably impressed with the range of fixtures, decorative moldings, and wood trim throughout the main house, which normally would be her specialty and contribution. Katrina was surveying furniture and color to enhance the layout of the rooms. She also considered privacy of window dressings, balanced with the lush view of the acreage about the estate.

When they entered what Etta jokingly referred to as the "blank room," they both looked to Etta, not asking, but expecting a plan to spew forth from the creative mind of the lady of the estate. Though not as eloquently detailed as most of their customers would have offered, the American attempted to share her vision, articulating ideas for the nursery.

"This room should be sacred. My husband and I seem to have been chosen to be together, and it was love at first sight." Etta further explained. "We have this inseparable bond that transcends the distance between us. Although Roberto does not live here most of the time, his spirit is always present. His heart reaches home, and his mind reaches home, calling me. I know this sounds very strange, but this is the man of my dreams. This man is the father of the child I am carrying. I want this room to celebrate our life together and our first child together. It's a sacred place. Yes. Sacred, that's what this place is."

"Well then! Congratulations on expecting," Katrina offered first. Margaret and Katrina both seemed to understand Etta's unusual rambling and responded as positively as they had with the other upgrades noted.

They would return after lunch with the sample books of furniture selections. The window dressing and wall finishes would take the most time. But it seemed that with only minor work to be done, the entire project could be completed within the month. The ladies had also referred Etta to a crystal and china shop near Jewellery Quarter to select some fresh place settings for the newlyweds.

Etta had chuckled when Margaret said "newlyweds" because she felt as though she had known Roberto always and that they had been married for years. Only months? Could it have only been months?

Chapter 29
STORK

Etta led each candidate into the kitchen, where Roberto was enjoying a glass of German wine and writing notes on papers beside each application. Staffing was a chore he was quite good at, and he was thrilled that Etta had included him in the selection of the house help.

Eileen Aplin was skilled in childcare, but she was not much of a cook. She did well cleaning, but she was allergic to some household chemicals. Sophie Kelly was a very sociable lass with a chatty manner and cheerful disposition (almost too cheerful). Elsie Bodfish was quiet but thorough. Elsie was adventurous in the kitchen and attended to details of cleaning duties, but as a youngest child, she had little experience with children. Her years of geriatric experience had not afforded interaction with small children. Doreen Knibbs offered award-winning creations in the kitchen and wonderful experience with small children, but she admitted that her cleaning skills left something to be desired.

Etta mainly stood by observing the notes that Roberto took as he drew out information from each candidate. He had a smooth way of relaxing each applicant and putting them so at ease that even incriminating questions were answered honestly, without ruffling even so much as an eyebrow of Roberto's steady face. Etta was fascinated, witnessing this new side of her husband. For with her, he demonstrated a wide range of emotions, in fact, quite broader than most men she had ever met. But with business, he was even, almost too steady in his demeanor. Etta was certain that this professional profile attributed to the contract success he enjoyed in several cultures and countries. Business was good, and life was good for this couple.

Etta's private thoughts were interrupted by Roberto's introduction of yet another candidate. "I asked Steve Ellis from the Holiday to send over another prospect for us. I don't have any papers for her, though."

Etta sat back as the elderly woman spoke with pride of her seamstress and tailoring talents. She was not very literate, but she was wonderful with children. She had a strong back for gardening and was polite enough to tend to visitors. Yes, Elizabeth had much to offer the Fernandez estate, despite her age.

As each applicant completed her questions, she was led back to the sitting area to wait for the others. Roberto then led the entire group through the nearly completed décor of the warm home. For only one primary inhabitant, this home had a wonderful feel of family and life. Happiness and a radiance of joy permeated the walls. All would have been happy to work here. After the tour, Roberto returned to the kitchen and re-interviewed the lot, making a second round of notes before excusing them all to talk privately with his beloved companion.

There were two standouts in the group—Elsie Bodfish and Elizabeth Deeley. Etta and Roberto discussed the various options, and Etta agreed that it would be best to hire a staff of one and a half instead of the two they had planned for. After all, they would not need that much help once the routine was established. That, they agreed on.

The announcement was made to the group with a gesture of gratitude for their interest in helping the family. Henry was called to discreetly return the women to their various places of employ. When Henry entered the sitting room to collect the ladies, he lagged behind.

All of a sudden, Elizabeth grabbed Henry around the neck and shrieked, "I did it, love! I got me fust job, I did! I pail ert the youn ones too!" Henry was flushed with embarrassment, yet he maintained his formal stance despite the woman's approach.

Etta's face showed unguarded shock as she watched the woman carry on. She was comforted only after Roberto quietly clarified for her, "Elizabeth is Henry's wife." Henry had been the ultimate professional in not responding to his wife's enthusiasm.

With Henry and Elizabeth on half time, all of Henry's private concerns vanished in Etta's mind. He would have his family time. They would have a better income, and after such rich patronage from Roberto's stay at the Holiday, Steve Ellis was more than happy to allow Henry to continue to serve the Fernandezes part time, using the hotel's limousine.

Elsie was happy with her position as well. She would manage the entire household, a very rare opportunity for a lady of her young age. She would begin straight away and move into the maid's quarters, which proved to be more lovely and spacious than any place she had lived. Elsie had really hit the jackpot!

The couple reclined in their comfortable bed. The becoming antiques, coupled with the spruced-up window dressings and accent pieces, now felt like a real home. Etta rested well in the comfort of knowing that Elsie was settled into the servant's quarters now and available at a "beck and call." Roberto was also more relaxed knowing that the burden of it all did not rest solely on his precious Etta. Lost in his own thoughts, Roberto reached into his nightstand and dangled the charm bracelet in front of Etta's face as he rested his other hand on the soft rise of her belly.

"I wondered where I left that!" Etta exclaimed, pointing out the new spring garden boot she had added from Kelly's shop. But then, Etta noticed another charm that she had not seen before. "Oh, Roberto," was all she could offer before she sobbed into his shoulder with tears of joy, a sign of the hormonal swings of a woman with child. The stork charm dangled a wrapped babe from its bill. With the meticulous detail, it could not have been a common charm. Roberto must have commissioned this one to mark the anticipation of their first child.

⁌⁍

It was a rare stroke of luck that Roberto was able to spend the entire week at home while his business was tended to by associates. Etta let Roberto assist in the glasshouse one afternoon. The equipment ran well. Her school groups were pretty easy to accommodate. She loved her job, and Roberto could see in her eyes that this was her way of connecting with her roots, her own family and home back in the desert. He would not have wanted her to work, but it brought her immeasurable joy while he was away.

The clock neared closing time, and Roberto helped Etta put away her things. Kelly popped her head in the glass door. "Hello. When yam tewthree finish up eya why doy yam cum yav toy with me for a tewthree minutes. I yav sum really bostin news."

"OK, we'll see you in about five minutes," Etta remarked off the cuff.

"How do you understand anything Kelly says?" Roberto wondered.

"When we first met, I had so few people to talk to that I spent a great deal of time watching her and listening to her. I learned much of her dialect as it was translated through her subtle body language. You understand much of what Henry says, don't you?" Etta wondered aloud for the first time.

"Half maybe," Roberto leveled with her.

"Well, you have three Brummies in the house now, so you had better start listening more and learn how to communicate with your staff!" Etta said with a hint of authority in her tone.

"Why bother? That's what I have you for!" Roberto teased and picked up a smudge of dirt and smeared it on her nose.

"You want war?" Etta invited, and then she stopped herself short of what would normally be a romp around the room. "Let's get going; I don't want Kelly to wait too long."

Etta washed her face and checked her makeup. She smoothed her uniform shirt and then met Roberto, who patiently waited just outside the ladies' room door. He took her hand and looked through her. His soft brown eyes lovingly gazed into her pools of green. They walked to the noisy pavilion room overlooking the gardens, and Etta wondered aloud, "Gosh, it's crowded today. I wonder how long the wait will be."

As the couple entered, the thundering, "*Surprise!*" resonated through the room. A crudely painted banner read, "To the Bride and Groom." It was stationed near a professionally imprinted banner that read, "Mr. Roberto and Mrs. Etta Fernandez," with horseshoes and bells on each side.

Etta played the scene to the hilt with tears of joy (that could have been tears of surprise had she not already known about Binny's gala). Roberto though...what was that look?

It was an original expression that Etta could not decipher. Was it shock, anger, embarrassment? What was that expression? Etta refused to let his unsettling behavior ruin this tender moment between them and this surrogate family in Birmingham.

Harvey approached Roberto and introduced himself, pumping his hand enthusiastically while Etta was collecting hugs from Binny's brothers. A gift table positioned near the coffee service was overflowing with gifts of every size and covering. This was an exciting time for Etta, and she wished Roberto appeared even half as overjoyed as she felt in this moment. This was even bigger than the bon voyage her family had thrown for her before she left for London!

Champagne flowed, and the couple received numerous toasts and well wishes. Etta sipped sparkling cider hoping alcohol would settle Roberto's nerves. Instead, he appeared even more dark and brooding.

Lana was the first to offer up a gift for the couple to open while Geraldine and Kelly staffed the recording table. Many of the gifts were handmade, and Binny knew just what she was doing, mixing the social classes. No one felt upped when Greta's gift was a cut crystal punch service. None of the local friends was looked down upon for their handiwork and modest offerings to the couple. Etta would not have had it any other way.

When the gifts were all open and careful snippets of paper had been collected by Geraldine, Binny announced one last gift.

"Etta, in the short time I have known you, you have proved to be the most loyal friend I have ever had. It means more than anything else in the world to have you stumble upon such wonderful love in your life. So, my gift is more for *you* so you can enjoy more freedom to get yourself about without always having to telephone Henry. Now, Henry, I know you are irreplaceable, but Etta just has to get over her fear of traffic!" Binny hugged Etta and dropped a keychain into her hand.

Etta turned white, as though she might faint. Binny led her out front to where a sleek, light brown Jaguar announced itself with a four-foot white ribbon.

"You can drive it, too," Binny quietly informed Roberto as she elbowed him in the side. Binny also recognized the odd reaction Roberto had to her surprise party. It really stung her. It took a lot of work to fashion this party, and he didn't seem appreciative. Nope, not at all. She comforted herself thinking that with all his money and all his professional prowess, this fuss was beneath him. She hugged and kissed him anyhow.

Etta's whole body shook, and everyone "oohed" and "ahed" at the leather interior of the luxurious car. Etta climbed into the driver's seat, tears streaming down her face. "Oh, Binny..." was all that came out.

To Binny, Etta's expression more than made up for Roberto's lack of emotion over her "surprise" wedding reception.

As the party wound down, Henry loaded the gifts into his car and the new Jaguar. Both vehicles were filled to the brim, and Binny rode with Etta back to the house to help with the unloading. Etta was unsettled, driving without a driver's license. They arrived twenty-five minutes after Henry. Etta wanted to drive very safely and felt quite unsure of the powerful engine under the hood that she would someday have to let loose. Binny would want it that way.

Roberto and Etta waved to Henry and Elizabeth as they pulled out of the drive with Binny. Roberto's arm was around Etta, but it felt stiff and unnatural.

"Don't you like surprises?" Etta asked, anticipating that he would really be upset if he learned she had prior knowledge of the event.

"It's not that. It's just so much fuss. I don't know, Etta. I just thought we could have a quiet, happy life here. I didn't appreciate all the attention." Roberto stammered around his words.

"But friendship is part of a happy life. Our friends were celebrating because we eloped, and they wanted to share part of our joy as a couple."

"*Our* friends? Is that what you really think, Etta?" Roberto said, with a flush concealed beneath those brown eyes.

Chapter 30
LEPRECHAUN LUCK

Binny was determined to help Etta break in the new XJ12C. She was quite pleased to find this vinyl top, leather seat, 12 cylinder, 5.4 liter cat. It was the last Jag that bore the influence of Jaguar's founder, Sir William Lyons, and it represented his vision wonderfully. For Binny personally, this car represented adventure, prestige, and presence, all of which Etta should command.

Despite not having her driver's license yet, Etta was willing to give it a go, under Binny's direction. She still could not believe this generous gift Binny bestowed on her, and she did not fully appreciate the history or mechanics of the light caramel car. Roberto had taken no interest in the car nor in driving in England—none whatsoever. He had not so much as thanked Binny. She was unfazed at his grossly defective manners. After all, her efforts were for Etta, and Etta was extremely appreciative.

Binny decided the best way to break in the Jag was to kidnap Etta for a road trip. She and Etta aligned their days off work, and planned to hit the road to Ireland, a trek laden with long stretches of road to cut loose the power under the lovely, sleek hood.

"How do you propose we go on a road trip to Ireland?" Etta thought there was some mistake over the journey's summit.

"We'll just ferry her over!"

Roberto would be tied up for two weeks. Etta would have been alone with Elsie anyhow, and she was eager to see more of the UK.

Roberto's recent work schedule seemed a good tradeoff. If she sacrificed time with him for longer stretches, then she was also assured longer stretches when he could be home with her.

The various travel bags barely fit in the trunk of the spotless car. Binny drove first, navigating the twisting streets and freeway exchanges out of town. Etta was grateful for the scarf-adorned driver, who was so determined to promote Etta's independence. The hours and hours of greenery were nearly as relaxing as the radio station Binny found to lull them through miles of rich farmlands.

The brewing tension between them finally came to a head as they approached Liverpool. Binny inquired, "What's the deal with your husband? He seemed to be such a different man the last few times I have seen him socially."

"Truthfully? I don't think he likes the attention. He is absolutely wonderful privately or in small groups, but in large situations, such as your party turned out to be, he is a different creature. I don't even know that man."

"Etta, dear friend, you know that can't be true. Like me, he has to hustle for business, and I know how keen you have to be to keep on top of clients. Why, Roberto's business is twice the size of mine!"

"That's a good point. But perhaps he's out of his cultural element here, and that may play a part in his comfort…"

"Poppycock! Comfort nothing. If he wasn't comfortable with the Brits, he would not have added the second division to Horizon-Tech. Have you ever toured his operation in Barcelona?"

"No. Truthfully, I have no interest in his business. I can't speak Spanish, either, so what would I benefit from spying on his operation there?"

"*Your,* operation Etta. You two are partners now. It's not his; it belongs to you both," Binny corrected. "Perhaps you better attend more to your business, Etta. It's not good to leave it all to him."

"I suppose you're right. Maybe I should join him on the next long trip."

"I have a gut feeling that you really need to do that to understand the other dark side of your husband, my friend. You know…I thought I saw a conference coming up in Spain on my calendar. Maybe you could come along with me and meet up with Roberto in Barcelona."

"That would be entertaining, Binny. Let me know when it is, and I'll see if I can join you."

The car hugged the curves of the left lane as the ladies rode in silence for several dozen minutes. Each was lost in her relaxation mode, mutually enjoying the company of a friend who was respectful of occasional, and necessary, silence.

༄

In the heart of Barcelona, Horizon-Tech had recently lost three clients. Roberto seemed distracted in his office and missed his original secretary, Marie. She had always done his bidding without question. Bernadette, while efficient in office management, was a devoted and persecuting Catholic who believed Roberto would go to hell for his every little infraction. He was not fond of confession, and Bernadette was even more disgusted by his unwillingness to set himself right with her God each week at church.

Marie had elongated her maternity leave and decided to stay home to raise even more children than the recent newborn. This left Bernadette in charge of Marie's old office and managing Roberto's complex affairs. Roberto could not bring himself to fire Marie's replacement over religious fervor, but it did make working with her most uncomfortable at times.

Roberto gazed out the window, his lap filled with reports from the recent quarter profits. He fingered his right cuff link with nervous energy and seemed lost in thought for a moment until Bernadette barged in, breaking the spell.

"Sir, here are the messages from the Birmingham division, the western sales director, and someone named Etta who says she's your wife." She held the messages just out of his reach so he had to lean forward to retrieve them.

"Thank you, Bernadette. Please have Jose Luis sign the new employee confidentiality agreement, and send him in to me for the rest of the processing. Might I remind you that when you took over Marie's position, you also signed this agreement." His eyes pierced her "holier than thou" aura, and she audibly huffed as she departed his stately office.

His eyes slowly tracked the lush furnishings he surrounded himself with, so unlike the English décor of his new home. It was a brief and intense pause that gave Roberto little comfort. He missed Etta terribly. It had become an unwanted addiction, one that distracted him from the rational, day-to-day affairs of his business. It became increasingly difficult to be apart from her without physical signs of withdrawal that hung heavy from his very heart. Roberto sighed, imagining her bending deep at the waist to hunt desperately in the garden for new spring life.

Roberto's heart raced more powerfully now as frustration raced through his competitive veins and snapped him temporarily back into type-A corporate mode. He had hired this high-demand marketing manager when they secured the two new contracts, quite oblivious to the emerging clues that the company would also be losing three of his primary clients to a new startup firm. Perhaps he should move Bernadette into the mailroom where she would be less troublesome and irritating to him. Yes, that was it. Roberto personally strode down the hallway to announce his intention of promoting the highest qualified employee to the coveted, glamorous job as his right hand. The highly esteemed slot of Mr. Fernandez's personal secretary was up for grabs.

Several strong candidates provided Roberto with their references the following day. Anahi was selected with everyone's confidence, and Bernadette was mortified to learn she had been moved to the mailroom with no pay decrease, but an increase in shame. That lasted approximately the same amount of time it took to thoroughly train Anahi, who was gentler and more humble as Marie had been with Mr. Fernandez.

Bernadette handed Anahi her resignation and requested her final check be mailed. Her final remark hung in the air: "Don't you let that awful man drag you down!"

Anahi watched her broad shoulders force the door and her sturdy frame exit the building for good. "I've always thought he's a very nice man," Anahi offered to nobody, in defense of Mr. Fernandez, from her fancy new office.

The ladies debarked the Jag from the ferry in Ireland and then gassed up with petrol in Dublin. They were off into the countryside toward Mullingar. With street snacks and pub sandwiches in tow, Etta let the pistons flare and pushed the metal closer to the floor with a new sense of excitement. She recognized a correlation to racing horses back home. The thunderous sound of the pounding hooves easily compared to the rage of the powerful engine. The vibration of the car traveled up her spine, providing an exciting sensation.

Binny enjoyed Etta's enthusiasm as well. It was money well spent to see her pal cut loose on the open road with her new toy. They decided to stop in Mullingar for the night. After cleaning up in their respective rooms, the ladies met in the lobby to window shop in the center of town. There were two important shops they decided to return to in the morning. One was a terrific shoe store with heels that stood out as works of art.

"Me mum used to tell us a story about this little Irish town, Mullingar," Binny began as the ladies strolled through the town's colorful cobble streets.

"An elderly shoemaker was losing his vision and the steadiness of his hands. His business suffered, and once down to his last piece of leather, he pleaded to a rainbow out the window of his shop. 'Please, oh please! Someone help me tonight!'

"He and his wife retired to bed hungry. But he awoke to find a finely crafted pair of shoes left on his workbench, and he sold them for double his customary price. The next morning, there were twenty pairs of the finely crafted shoes. He sold these for a fine price as well. But curiosity got the best of him, and he was determined to spy on the blessed culprits. Around midnight, he witnessed six naked leprechauns sneaking into the shop. Poor fellows! It was an unseasonably cold winter. The man and his wife sold their leprechaun shoes quickly and set into town to find the finest material to make six finely crafted outfits.

"They used all the money from the shoes to buy the finest green silk, the warmest green wool, and the fanciest green tweed. They barely finished the six sets *of clothing before midnight. At the bottom of the pile of leather the leprechauns used to fashion this night's shoes, they found a thank-you note with the elegant green clothes. They fit perfectly! Because of that thoughtful gift, they helped the old man every time he was in need, and they offered the same favor to every shoemaker in Mullingar. That's why Mullingar shoe wearers and their shoemakers are the luckiest people in the world!"*

"What a cute story!" Etta responded. "I'll have to buy some Mullingar shoes for myself. When I got the airline ticket for the Lucky London contest, it didn't turn out all that lucky at first. Now, I *know* it was. All of it. Finding my friends and husband too. Yes, I should have lucky Mullingar shoes, don't you think?"

Binny laughed. "Why, of course! Why else would we come to this little place?"

The ladies retired and slept reasonably late after their long road trip and ferry ride. Once they awoke, breakfast went down with little attention paid. Both were eager to shop for their new shoes.

Before they made it back for the shoes, Etta found a jewelry shop and pleaded with Binny to give her just fifteen minutes. With an exaggerated sigh, Binny complied. It didn't take all that long to find the real souvenir of the trip. The ladies shopped for shoes while the leprechaun charm was being secured onto the bracelet. It was the perfect lucky charm for a lucky shoe shop. Neither could decide which pair to get, so they each filled the backseat with several pairs of the wonderfully crafted, lucky shoes from Ireland.

༄

At the post office counter back in Harborne, Etta surrendered her United States driver's license for their inspection.

"I'm sorry, miss. We cannot exchange this for a full UK license. You will need form D100. It details what you need to know about driving licenses. Once you apply for a provisional license, you must take the theory and practical tests. You also have to pass a driving test with your own vehicle. You do have access to a vehicle, don't you?"

"Yes, sir, I have my own car." Etta attempted to memorize the various steps required in securing her license.

"Where do I get all the papers or document forms?"

"You can go to the DVLA in Birmingham. They will give you the D1 form and the D750 form for the provisional. It's quite expensive, so don't mislay your papers."

"Thank you, sir. I'll keep that in mind." Etta was still unaccustomed to not having to worry about money or the practices of thriftiness.

Across town she drove, careful not to draw traffic tickets or attention to herself as she negotiated the licensing process. At the DVLA, Etta was given a number behind seventeen others for service. After a short wait, the efficient woman at the counter greeted Etta warmly and asked for her papers. Etta explained she was here to pick up the papers to fill out. She was given the provisional papers and another number behind a dozen people. The wait was brief again as Etta was distracted by the various questions required on her provisional application.

At the counter, the forms and US license surrendered, Etta was given another minor obstacle. Her license was in her maiden name, and she had recorded her married name on all the forms. Now they would need her marriage license, also. She pondered the predicament while studying her replacement passport. The current photo was much improved from the one taken in Arizona. Etta was instructed to collect the necessary documents and return with the fees.

Etta searched the entire house, to no avail. She simply could not find the beautifully crafted certificate they got when they eloped. So Etta phoned Roberto at work.

"*Bueno?*" Anahi answered in the mostly monolingual Spanish office.

Etta did not even attempt her flat accent greeting, favoring instead the rude English request, "Do you speak English?"

"*Si.* Yes. How can I help?" Anahi responded.

"This is Etta. Is Roberto available? It's kind of urgent I speak with him."

"Who? Etta?"

Etta could faintly hear the message being scrawled down by hand.

"Etta, his wife."

There was a very long pause on the phone before Anahi finally said, "One moment, I will see." He was not in.

Etta was impressed that the new secretary took such careful notes during her requested message to Roberto. She would not have time to return the forms today, as the DVLA closed earlier on Friday. She wondered if Monday would come soon enough. She wondered where the marriage license could be. She wondered why Roberto could not come to the phone.

༄

Roberto phoned late Friday night. "What is it you need, my love?"

"I need the marriage license from Italy, so I can get my driver's license."

"The license…"

"Roberto, remember the man in the church put it into the white tube when the calligraphy ink dried."

"You need *that* for a driver's license?" Roberto sounded confused.

"Even with the replacement passport and US license, they can't process it without our marriage license."

"The tube is in the smoking room in the lower cabinet where the company letterhead is. But I don't know if that will work." There was a curious hesitation in his voice. "Why do you need a license when you have Henry?"

"Quit teasing! After the trip with Binny, I feel very comfortable driving my new car, and I want to be able to legally use it here. The insurance company needs my license on file, too. I really didn't want to have to get it all done with my maiden name. Hey! When are you coming home?"

"I can't come home now. Etta...Oh, Etta! I want to come home, but I am swamped trying to recover lost business. How is my little belly?" Roberto smoothly changed the subject.

"I am having a little morning sickness, but overall, I feel pretty good. I keep Weetabix in my purse for when I feel nauseous. I had to get a new size of pants for work, too. I'm not mentally ready to enter real maternity pants just yet."

There was a long pause as Etta waited for him to probe further about her pregnancy. He didn't. "Can you meet me in Switzerland next week? I am going to attempt to expand the original contracts we signed there. I'll be there for a week. Can you fly in?"

"A week! I'd love to fly in. What do you want me to bring?" Etta's mind switched channels easily when distracted by a fresh opportunity to travel and to hook up with her husband.

Chapter 31
SWISS COWBELL

"It would be a great opportunity for Elizabeth and Elsie to get to know us and each other. Plus, they would be wonderful travel companions and shopping company for me while you attend to your presentations in Bern."

"Etta, Etta. Why do you feel the need to make *compadres* of our staff? Have you met our neighbors yet? I'm sure there are a few ladies you could shop with."

"They'll have their own room, and they can dine separately…"

"Oh, all right. You make the arrangements. Reserve coach transportation and a standard room. No, let my secretary do that. She already completed part of our reservations."

"Perfect! I'll tell the ladies to pack their bags. Thank you, dear. Don't work so hard. Things will work out, I can feel it!"

"Anahi will phone you later today."

Roberto signed off the call wishing he had more of her contagious optimism.

Anahi's call arrived sooner rather than later, as Roberto had forgotten Elsie's last name and Etta's passport number. She was efficient and courteous. Etta made sure to acknowledge her skills at the closure of their phone call.

"Anahi, Mr. Fernandez had already told me you were extraordinary in your new position. That was an understatement. Congratulations on the promotion! And thank you for everything you do to take care of him and the business. Can you please book my travel reservations under Etta Johnson since I have not worked out the identification papers as yet for Fernandez?"

There was a long pause on the other end of the phone as Anahi desperately held her tongue at the seemingly well-meaning American. She was stunned at the day-by-day activity in this new position of privy. She was beginning to understand just why Bernadette had tweaked so on Mr. Fernandez's last nerve during the final week of her employment.

When Etta phoned Elizabeth to propose the trip, she worked her way through several family members before finally reaching her hand.

"Hello, Elizabeth, I have a special job for you next week. Do you have a good babysitter?" Etta attempted to restrain her excitement.

"What does yo yav in mind, Miss Etta?"

Etta could hear the several ages and octaves of conversation in the background of the call.

"Mr. Fernandez and I would like you and Elsie to get to know each other. So we thought it would be nice to take the two of you with us to Zurich, Switzerland."

Etta was able to offer no more. The phone dropped from Elizabeth's hand to the floor with a thud, and a scream raced through the phone line with sufficient loudness to blow an eardrum.

"Elizabeth, Elizabeth?" Etta decided that she would wait patiently to allow Elizabeth to regain her telephone composure.

"Oh, miss! I yav never miskin ert of Englan'. I yav never even miskin on a train! Be sure I wull get a babysitter fer the young ones. I ood not miss this fer the world! Wait till I tell me Henry!" Elizabeth labored with a shortness of breath caused by her celebratory kitchen jig and hollering.

The ladies agreed to meet that afternoon for planning, despite it being Elizabeth's day off. Elsie had been far more reserved during the invitation. She attempted not to reveal too much emotion at the exciting news of her first trip out of the country. Perhaps she had mastered a courteous manner, graciously accepting on the phone that afternoon, but Etta could read the genuine excitement in the sparkle of her eyes and the upward tilt of her pencil-thin eyebrows upon the invitation.

As the functioning manager of the household, Elsie preferred a starched black uniform, despite Etta's invitation to wear more comfortable clothing. This formal black and white uniform represented that all of Elsie's hard work had been worth it. She had *earned* this dress and the spotless, bright white apron. Elsie wore it with great pride, creating a vision of formality in the otherwise casual routine of the manor.

Although it took only three extended days to map out the maintenance and culinary schedules for the interior of the Fernandez home, Elsie still had not been given a chance to practice door greeting. As head of the house staff, she instinctively knew how critical a guest's first impression of her would be for the family. Elizabeth's ring of the recently repaired bell was therefore a disappointment to Elsie.

Elizabeth preferred her own clothing to that of a uniform. Besides, Etta loved her wide, colorful skirts and puffy blouses that she embroidered herself. Etta was amazed Elizabeth could work in the soil and never muss her clothing. Her hands were telling, though. Elizabeth sported strong, tan hands with short nails that were still accustomed to hard work.

Elsie led Elizabeth into the ladies' tearoom, where Etta's new blue floral Limoges tea service complemented the delicate French linens. Elsie enjoyed the deviled shrimp and Camembert cheese sandwiches of her own creation. Etta had started with the treacle scones slathered with clotted cream. While Elizabeth enjoyed the upper tier of the high tea delicacies, Etta laid out their plans.

Since it was still rather cold, in the five- to ten-degree Celsius range, all would require amply warm and proper casual clothing. Much of the travel the women would enjoy would be on foot and outdoors.

Roberto generously recommended gifting them with envelopes with bonus money up front, so the women could enjoy a good shop. The two squealed with delight, peering into their envelopes, not counting as such, but each noting that there was a good sum of money contained therein. A good sum more than a regular payday!

The plan was to bus to London, fly to Bern, rail to Zurich, and meet up with Roberto, who would be flying in from the office in Barcelona. The bus ride was inconsequential. But it would be the first airline flight for Elizabeth and Elsie. Elsie was surprisingly the less adventurous of the pair, feeling rather nervous at the prospect of being above a deep body of water, connecting on another craft in Paris, and crossing half the distance across France in a winged vehicle that, reportedly, sometimes crashes.

Elizabeth was gleeful at the prospect of sharing detailed stories of her adventures with cherished family. A wonderful storyteller, Elizabeth had always lived vicariously through pictures in the papers, being unable to read well herself. Her joyful disposition and sacrifices over the years of washing, cleaning, cooking, and bearing children were being rewarded with an opportunity of a lifetime! How she wished Henry could accompany her. But then, he had been afforded experiences over the years that she had not been included in, either.

Elsie moved the teacart out of the way, just off the Indian rug, while the three discussed a travel itinerary. They would have a free night when Etta and Roberto would attend *Don Giovanni* at the Zurich Opera House.

Etta suddenly excused herself as a wave of nausea flowed over her. She became weak in the knees and made it to the lavatory only in time to collapse on the floor in front of the commode. When she came to, Etta felt a solid lump on the left side of her head where she had hit the floor from a sitting position. She stood on shaky legs and observed her appearance in the mirror. The ghostly reflection and dreadful feeling gave her solid cause to worry, and she mustered enough energy to call Elizabeth, who, with Elsie, was flittering away with conversation about their prospective journey.

Elizabeth's motherly instinct knew what the appropriate call to action was. Within minutes, Henry was diverted from an airport pickup, bringing the guest along for the speedy ride to the Fernandez estate. The client was more understanding once he witnessed Etta's deplorable state in person. Elsie stayed at the house while Elizabeth accompanied Etta to the hospital.

An enthusiastic young nurse, who was in her first year of practice, tenderly cared for Etta. They had thankfully given Etta pain chemicals to ward off the intense discomfort. The physical pain was no match for the emotional pain Etta was experiencing. It was good being numb at the moment, for Etta's sorrow caused an insufferable ache above her barren womb.

The doctor was gentle with Roberto as well. Roberto had flown immediately to Birmingham during Etta's drug-induced sleep.

"Your wife lost the baby due to an ectopic pregnancy. For whatever reason, the fetus was located in an abnormal position. It appears the tissue and blood work revealed some abnormal sites. So, we would like to keep her and further examine the lab samples before we release her home." Dr. Robson waited for further questions.

With an uncustomary waver in his voice Roberto asked, "Will she be able to have children?"

"Certainly, certainly. Miscarriages are not all that uncommon in first pregnancies. If the fetus is not viable, it will not make a full-term pregnancy in anyone. She is a healthy woman, though. We will want to clear her uterus to prevent any resulting infection. She will be fine, chap," Dr. Robson assured.

When Etta was deemed healthy enough to return home, Roberto knew she was devastated. "There will be more children, my dear," Roberto said to Etta, be he was also trying to convince himself.

༄

Dr. Robson approved Etta's vacation with prescribed activity limitations. Reviewing these cautions in her mind once again, Etta unpacked her belongings into the large hotel room at the Schweizerhof Hotel. Roberto opted out of the Renaissance Zurich Hotel, favoring a more central location for Etta to limit her activity somewhat.

Elizabeth and Elsie were thrilled with their spacious room, which was significantly smaller than Etta's, though it was no different in the luxurious furnishings and high-quality textiles spilling throughout the room. Elsie dropped her bag first, leaping onto her personal, queen-sized bed for the stay. A broad smile spread from ear to ear across her joyous face.

Elizabeth enjoyed the bathroom, reporting with delight that the maid had left them smelly soap and hand lubricant. Some potions she did not recognize, but she was determined to figure out how to use them and put them right to work. Elsie came to the rescue, reading the labels on each of the bottles for her.

The Schweizerhof Hotel was but a stone's throw from the railway station they arrived from. In fact, it was right on the renowned Bahnhofstrasse strip of luxury commerce. The Swiss proclaimed their Bahnhofstrasse to be the finest shopping street in the world, spanning from the main train station to Lake Zurich. There, the threesome could peruse the opulent fare, elbow to elbow with wives of wealthy oil sheiks or heads of government. They would admire the same furs, watches, silks, and jewelry as movie stars and barons. This realization made both Elizabeth and Elsie begin to giggle with excitement in anticipation of the following day.

⁌

The mammoth Alpine glaciers were a wonderful backdrop to the stately hotel in the crossroad of Europe. Elsie had already been sensitive to the cleanliness and efficiency of her surroundings. From the transportation to the method by which people communicated, nothing was wasted or in excess.

The linden trees lined Bahnhofstrasse, and waves of the German language floated through the air as the vendors began to unlock and ungate their shops. The local trams, nicknamed "Holy Cows," had been bustling people to work now for several hours.

Two members of the trio of women walked more slowly than usual, causing a stir with the third.

"Come on! I'm not lame. I'm fine, really. I will let you know if I need to slow down. If we go at this pace, we won't see half the stores this week." Etta's tone was tainted more with frustration than anger.

By midday, Etta had spent over thirteen hundred pounds on high-end whatnots. Elizabeth and Elsie resolved to look twice and purchase once. If they found something they liked,

Elsie wrote down the name of the store, the item, and the price. Elizabeth dictated her share of potential purchases for Elsie to record also. The ladies made a pact to buy on the stroll back to the hotel.

Etta was struck with a flashback of having nothing. She remembered that only recently had she been gifted with this position of wealth. Having so much more money to spend than her companions all of a sudden felt deeply awkward.

At Bucherer, the ladies were wowed with Swiss watches that were as much works of art as fine timekeeping pieces of jewelry. Elsie found a beautiful Rolex watch that she carefully wrote onto this day's wish list. Elizabeth was focused on a gentleman's Patek Philippe with a heavy band, sufficient for her large husband. Etta decided to buy it as a gift for Henry before Elsie could finish writing it down on Elizabeth's list. In a flash of an eye, the watch was paid for and hanging from Etta's arm.

"Elizabeth, I bought this one for Henry as a gift from Roberto and me. He has served Roberto so well during his work in Birmingham. I think Henry will like this one."

"Oo kind of yam! He's a big geezer, an' ee needs a big wetch. Ta bab so much fer thinken of him. Than yam so much! Ee wull luv it!" Elizabeth responded through wet eyes. She was touched with how thoughtful the couple was. They treated Henry and her very, very well. Why, she found herself here in Switzerland! My, oh my!

For lunch, the ladies went into a sandwich shop, which was more occupied by gentlemen than ladies. While sitting at their booth, they observed a boisterous table of men who were toasting an apparent new hire.

In broken English, one man bellowed, "When you drink with the Swiss, toast us each with the eyes. If yer forget and drink first, you have seven years bad sex!" to which the table erupted in thunderous laughter and a German chant of "to good sex."

"*Zum guten geschlecht! Zum guten geschlecht!*" The men toasted one another in German or English, being sure to exaggerate the eye contact before swigging down their lager.

The ladies were not offended. The men, meaning no harm, were entertaining in their jovial demeanor.

༄

Etta's toe exposed itself just above the surface of the rich blanket of fragrant bubbles in the large hotel tub. She was pleased with the shopping of the day. Both Elizabeth and Elsie had spread their money around with plenty to spare for a few more days and evenings of fun.

The floor-length, black velvet theater dress was slit several inches up the left side. The rhinestones visibly shimmered across the room, where it hung expectantly for a special evening at the opera. Etta had selected a long ebony fur just for this event.

In Etta's relaxed mind, she recalled the remarkable circumstances in which she met Roberto and the incredible intimate familiarity they shared. She desperately hoped she would become pregnant again before next Christmas. For now, she would respect Dr. Robson's recommendation to give her body a proper heal. She would give Roberto cause to anticipate their next opportunity through this evening's elegant getup.

Etta's fresh manicure and pedicure from the hotel spa boasted a deep, seductive red. Dramatic makeup accentuated Etta's features beautifully. The dress was clearly a knockout. She couldn't wait until he arrived to find her primped and smelling of new French perfume from Bahnhofstrasse Street. But tears began to fall without warning, and Etta cried long and hard.

When Roberto finally arrived, Etta rose carefully from the chair where she was reading a magazine. The vision of the dress burned through his retinas and engraved itself onto Roberto's memory neurons. Stunning!

How did this ever happen to me? Roberto wondered silently as Etta approached him in what appeared to be slow motion. *I can't believe how lucky I was to work this out. It will all work out.* Roberto congratulated himself on landing not only a soul mate, but one encased inside such a body and face. Had it been fate or luck?

Roberto's hands ran along the sides of the soft dress, and he inhaled the sweet perfume that encircled her. Kissing her neck, Roberto imagined showing her off on his arm this evening. He kissed her, told her he loved her, and excused himself to the shower. Roberto expended extra care in preparation for the performance of *Don Giovanni* at the Zurich Opera.

While her husband was in the shower, Etta fastened the charm bracelet with the day's new gold Swiss bell around her wrist. The links and charms were becoming quite heavy. The artifact had already become quite a testament of Etta's adventures in Europe.

Chapter 32
FORK IN THE ROAD

By May, the Fernandez household was running smoothly, and the women worked splendidly in sync after the grand introduction party in Zurich. The ladies got along just fine, despite Roberto's overt gestures to exclude Elizabeth and Elsie at every opportunity.

Not far from 3 Metchley Lane in Harborne, the Birmingham Botanical Gardens emulated Etta's own lovely gardens on a grand scale, with Mother Nature phasing out spring's daffodils, cherry blossoms, magnolias, and camellias. Etta had a vision that Mother Nature would appear much like Geraldine, elfish though much taller in stature. In her mind's eye, she must also utilize a golden twig as a magic wand. The spring bedding with its rhododendrons and azaleas was quite a competition for her Fantastic Cactus Room now.

Etta greatly appreciated her artificial desert home, though the explosion of color on the garden grounds and in the other glasshouses created a grand diversion. Even the roses were starting to wake with enormous buds. This made it difficult for Etta to spend extended time with the succulents in her care.

Etta was convinced she was living in a dream. In less than a month, her mother and sister would visit. What a wonderful time that would be. She was unable to express to her modest family the opulence she enjoyed. Where would they start? Her work? Their home? Her new husband?

Soon she would be introduced to Roberto's parents. Etta was concerned about what could become lost in translation. She knew fewer than a dozen courtesy words to communicate with them. How she longed to have tea with Luciana. The language barrier would definitely prevent any private visits.

Etta and Roberto were unable to locate the scroll containing their marriage license, so Etta could not get a driver's license. Only seldom did she drive her precious Jaguar. When she dared, Etta was extremely careful, resolving not to take chances until she was deemed legal.

Binny had been persistent in her plans for the Canberra cruise to Naples. Etta thought the timing would be perfect to meet the Fernandez family and surprise Roberto with a visit to the Barcelona facility, which recently appreciated a sales surge, courtesy of Italy. Most of the manufacturing continued to be centered in Spain, the largest facility. Etta planned to fly into El Prat de Llobregat and spend a week with Roberto before meeting Binny for their cruise on the grand Canberra ship.

Binny had also been anxious to break for a holiday after a surge of business with her own company, the Historical Preservation of England. Etta had prodded Binny with a plethora of ideas in which to bring the HP of E reenactments and services on a smaller scale to schools. The government had agreed it was a splendid idea, thus awarding generous funding for her proposals. The execution of the outreach project would require Binny to hire an entirely new staff and train them to demonstrate and explain their craft to various student levels. Binny's success was founded on her drive to preserve the old trades that built the United Kingdom.

The new program was a smashing hit, just as Etta had envisioned it would be. In this manner, helping Binny expand this novel business endeavor made Etta felt less guilty about driving the expensive wedding gift.

Roberto had been kept entirely in the dark, and it became excruciatingly difficult for Etta not to spill the beans about the nautical adventure the two friends were planning. Elsie agreed to care for Bernard, the tri-color, Pembroke corgi pup Etta had given Binny for her birthday. Binny already spoiled her beloved pup much like a child. It had filled a void in her life for now, allowing her to relax more in the social pressures of her job. Even Etta loved to puppysit Bernard when Binny was required for longer stints in London.

Kelly no longer lived with Geraldine. She was hired as half of the fine metal duo of Binny's schooling staff. The children were delighted with her rich Brummie accent, and she thrived in the public's eye.

Etta had preordered a custom Canberra cruise charm since she had already been advised that they cast their souvenir charms only in sterling. She would collect it when they sailed. This would be Etta's first cruise. She had prepared for the exciting adventure by shopping for designer sportswear suitable for on board, on land, and to meet the parents.

༄

As a prank, Etta phoned Roberto both from the airport and from the Museu Picasso. He was unable to entertain her call with sufficient time for Etta to read his obligations of the day. The cabbies had nearly all been proficient enough in English to navigate Etta to her desired destination.

"Hello, Anahi, is Roberto available yet?" This new secretary had a fine demeanor, and she was always courteous, even when the multiple lines of her PBX phone were audibly ringing off the hook while she prioritized the incoming calls. Roberto was slow to pick up the line once again.

"Hi, dear! How goes it?" Etta posed, attempting to squelch the excitement of knowing she was already within ten miles of the office.

"Quite good, actually. It looks like I will be free to come home tomorrow night instead of having to wait until Saturday. Etta, the new marketing manager has revolutionized my job. He's bringing in twice the interest in our products, and I will have much more time now to enjoy you and our spring garden."

"I'm so glad to hear that! What do you have lined up today?" Etta felt him out, attempting to assemble the spontaneous plan for the afternoon.

"Nothing much. A little bit of this, a little bit of that. I'll have Anahi make my reservation this afternoon also," Roberto responded with nothing remotely resembling business in his tone.

"I was thinking about going shopping for some gardening equipment. I don't have adequate—" Etta was abruptly cut off.

"I have to go. I'll catch you up in a few hours," Roberto interrupted before hanging up the line without a final goodbye.

Etta could wait in the lobby if necessary. Whatever he was experiencing on this stressful day, she resolved to cheer him up. Etta brought a book along to entertain herself during any wait time she might be dealt. She decided on immediacy, hailing a taxi driver on Via Laietana. Etta successfully directed him to Carrer de Balmes via La Rambla due to the driver's proficiency in English.

The sophisticated seaboard city was not difficult to navigate, but architecturally it moved in waves of Gothic, modernist, and *nou urbanisme*. Fashion appeared to be three clicks up from her Harborne community, as well. "Brave," "confident," and "self-assured" were all terms Etta came up with to describe her vision of the local style in Barcelona.

Upon arriving at the Horizon-Tech building just off Carrer de Balmes, Etta exhaled with disappointment. In her brief impressions of building design, this factory and office were plain and lifeless from the street. Even the sign announcing the business impressed her as being merely an afterthought. Maybe it *was* the size that mattered? Etta tipped the driver well, and he let loose a toothy grin.

Smoothing out her lovely (though conservative) dress, she approached the front desk just within the unattractive heavy doors. "Hello, do you speak English?" Etta inquired.

"Yes," the girl returned without so much as raising her eyes in hospitality.

"Can you direct me to Mr. Fernandez's office?" Etta attempted again.

"Do you have an appointment?" Clara asked, being introduced by nametag only.

"No, but I wanted my visit to be a surprise. Can you direct me there?" Etta responded, attempting to remain even-tempered as her frustration and anticipation began to rise.

"He is with another visitor who did not have an appointment. You will have to wait. Go down this hall and up the elevator to the fifth floor. His secretary, Anahi will greet you," Clara offered with a half-hearted gesture of eye contact that resembled boredom.

Etta's heart beat more wildly now as she paced the hall. The elevator ride was slow, and when the doors finally parted, she was offered a vision of elegance at last. The reception area was magnificent! Serene paintings lined the walls, and a wood wrap-around desk enveloped a stunning secretary in a dress with large polka-dots. A huge arrangement of flowers stood off the left side of the desk, and Anahi greeted Etta warmly with a smile and full eye contact.

"Hello, Anahi. I'm Mrs. Fernandez. It's such a pleasure to finally meet you. Roberto thinks so highly of you." Etta warmly offered her hand.

Anahi's demeanor changed in an instant as her eyebrows raised and her eyes became large. The lovely secretary offered her hand, but no salutation. Before a word could escape her crimson red mouth, a highly coiffed, portly woman exited the office with a little boy in tow. A little girl, lassoed around Roberto's neck, was retrieved by the mother after a farewell kiss was planted directly on Roberto's lips.

Etta was unable to contain herself. "Who is this?" her voice escaped in a shriek.

Roberto's face paled. The woman's eyes became fire. The children looked at Roberto. Etta repeated lower and slower in the event she was not understood, "Who...is...this?"

Anahi reported, "Mrs. Fernandez."

In one instant, the plump little Spanish woman read the situation like a book. She exploded with a loud rant of harsh screams and beat on Roberto's chest with her fists. Etta understood nothing except there was something awful happening here. A slap ripped the side of Roberto's face, and the woman turned on her heel toward the elevator, yelling from behind her back, "¡Maldígale al infierno! ¡Usted cerdo de engaño!"

Etta was not as quick to understand what she was seeing, and she caught Roberto's eye momentarily before he turned away in a posture of shame. The elevator door closed for the children and the woman, and Anahi quickly left the scene of the tragedy.

Roberto was left alone with Etta. "I didn't expect...," Roberto stammered.

"You're damn right. Who the *hell* is that woman? *Those* kids?" Etta punctuated.

"Come in, Etta. Please come in." Roberto led her into a luxurious, window-filled office that Etta could not appreciate at the moment. "Etta, I never meant to hurt you..."

"What are you saying...?" Etta's voice dropped a few octaves.

"My wife, and those are my children," Roberto stated. Finally, Etta understood.

The adrenaline in Etta's body ripped through her scalp and into the air, joining the shrieks of her desperate inquisition. "How can you have two wives? This has got to be illegal! How could you hide this from me? You told me over and over that *I* was the love of your life..."

Roberto cut her off right there. "Etta, you have to believe me. You *are* the love of my life. You must know this. You must *never* forget this. I couldn't tell you because you assumed so much, and I did not want to break your heart."

"Break...my...heart?! You commit this heinous deception? *You* created this monster. What in the name of hell were you doing?" Etta began to sob between the shrieking. Her body could physically take no more of this deep-seated torture, and she fled away from arms that reached out to comfort her. She heard his pleading as the elevator door closed.

"Etta! I do love you. Etta, please let me ex..."

The meticulously applied makeup washed down her face as she hailed a taxi back to the airport. Roberto watched from the corner window, screaming to the glass, "Don't go! No! Don't go!"

When Etta returned to the airport, she collected her baggage from the locker. She closed herself into the handicapped stall of the ladies' room and fell apart into sobs. What had happened here? How could she have been so wrong about her husband? He was not her husband after all. What was he? Who was he? Etta's head swirled in confusion, heartbreak, and sorrow. Instead of going home, she resolved to get to the bottom of this.

Etta emerged from the restroom and headed to a telephone booth, where she called St. Mark's Basilica in Italy. No, there had been no Fernandez wedding that cursed day.

Blessings? Yes, perhaps. Tourist blessings were offered daily for a fee. A lovely parchment accompanied each blessing. That was it. She was not married, she was *blessed*. Somehow, she didn't feel blessed at all. She felt betrayed.

Etta resolved to hide in the city for the week to sort things out. She had to find a place where no one could find her should anyone be searching. *Is it possible for someone so young to have a heart attack, over a heartbreak?* her body demanded of her through its pounding fury. Another call, this one to a detective agency. Etta arranged to collect everything she could on this ruin of a man. Yes, she would drop off a payment right then, on her way to locate housing for the week.

༄

Roberto was crushed. He genuinely thought he had a handle on this arrangement. Silly man. He phoned Greta for help. Binny was on holiday. He phoned Kelly for help. She reported Etta was on holiday. He phoned Elsie, who cheerfully inquired about how the surprise had come off. He was surprised, all right. Roberto gave her a private number, instructing she phone him confidentially and immediately with Etta's whereabouts once she phoned home to check in. All he could offer in explanation to Elsie was that they'd had an argument, and it had been a bad one.

Nobody knew anything of importance at this crushing moment in his life. He knew that though he did not love his wife, the church would not accept his divorce from her. Nor would her well-attached network of family, who had positioned Roberto in his company. Finances aside, what of his own happiness? He could never return to what was. It was a Pandora's box. It was the disastrous "happiness machine." Now that he *knew* love, he could not have it. The loss of his Etta would torment him, *eternally*.

༄

Etta spent the week holed up in a room that would be let on a more permanent basis as soon as a tenant could be secured. It was across the street from the office, where Etta could watch Roberto arrive and depart Horizon-Tech through the lace-covered windows. Though her heart was broken, she could not believe the obvious. And Etta would never be able to say good-bye to him. So she spied, unbeknownst to the visibly broken man she observed. She watched him arrive early and leave late for six straight days. Little did Etta know that Roberto was slowly going mad, consumed in his search for her.

∽

Binny immediately recognized the numb fog in which Etta boarded the ship. She knew not why, but she knew well enough she would have it out when she was ready. Etta was never ready. Binny wouldn't ask, and Etta wouldn't offer. Nevertheless, Binny and Etta attempted to enjoy their girls' cruise with relish.

Alone on deck the third night, Etta realized that on this cruise, she could disappear forever. As she carefully studied the water, she contemplated jumping ship and deeply inhaling the sea. The end. It was too simple. Instead, she planned. Etta would clear out of Dodge and leave no trace. She certainly could not bear the humiliation of it all with her dear, adopted Birmingham family. She simply could not endure being shamed publicly and socially in such a dreadful way.

Not even Elsie was in on her plan. Etta became friends with the communications officer on board. He assisted her in reserving passage of only one moving crate and one car. Etta understood there could be no good-byes. The bank was alerted that she would be picking up the funds and closing the account upon her return home. All was set for a quiet escape from an unlucky sojourn in England.

For the last two days of the cruise, Binny was certain that the air had done Etta good. She seemed calmer and more relaxed. Not quite normal, mind you, but closer to her old chum.

⁓

At the airport, Etta hugged Binny extra hard with a delayed embrace and a sing-song, *"Thank you, Thank you, Thank you!"* followed by a kiss on the cheek. Binny's driver was there to greet her. Etta pretended to wait for Henry, whom she had not phoned. Instead, she rode a cab directly to the bank, leaving the meter running. With luggage still in tow, the balance of money was drawn into a small sum of cash and a large wire transfer to her mother's bank account in Phoenix. Etta graciously thanked the bank for their services to her family. This caused another wave of sorrow. *Family?* Etta sobbed all the way to the lovely home she must leave behind.

Etta phoned her mother about Roberto's "tragic and fatal accident" and announced she was returning home with the estate money. Perhaps she and Abby could exchange their England vacation for Hawaii so Etta could join them in her time of mourning.

The moving truck was visibly posted in the turnabout waiting for her arrival, just as she had instructed. Elsie was in the back garden and never saw the swift evacuation coming.

The movers packed the master bed with the inlayed wood. The table in the entry was wrapped carefully. The radiator was disengaged from the master bath and packed without question by the movers. Several paintings were carried with a solitary box of clothing. Only a few selections would she take from the cursed home. Etta had taken Roberto's favorite suit and best cuff links from the bureau. She didn't know why. The car was backed onto the truck last. Within the hour, things both precious and quirky were tucked away and rolling across the country to be shipped back home to the USA. Home. It had taken on a very different connotation these past two weeks.

The final ritual prior to Etta's departure began with the methodical arrangement of her largest mixing bowl on the cobblestone entry just below the brick doorstep. Inhaling the familiar British aromas deep down into her lungs, Etta then fell to her knees. In the bowl, she placed three journals, borne of her innocent soul and spilled with ink onto paper pages. The ritual was crudely drawn from Etta's memory and was reminiscent of tribal offerings witnessed in her youth on the reservation. After two misses, the third strike against the matchbox set fire to the record of her life in Birmingham.

⁌

Trucks, ships, and many flights later, Etta was encircled in the comfort of desert-brown hues. She was deeply traumatized. Fingering the cruise ship on her charm bracelet, she reviewed happier times of perceived innocence.

Chuck knocked and then let himself in. His large frame gathered her wilted spirit into his arms, and he silently hugged her long and hard. She sobbed into his broad chest, and the healing slowly began.

⁌

For two years, Roberto searched for his beloved Etta. Without knowledge of her complete birth name, the search was complicated. Alietta? Odetta? Glorietta? Doretta? Loretta? What was her birth name? The name on the blessing parchment had been recorded simply as "Etta." Her surname, Johnson, was far too common.

Over time, Roberto became disinterested in his progeny when they developed into spoiled, rude children under his wife's direction, or lack thereof. *Work has always been my real love anyhow,* Roberto reflected unconvincingly.

Etta Johnson had simply dropped off the face of the earth, offering no farewells to her employer or her closest friends. There would be no healing for Roberto's fractured heart.

Chapter 33
Equestrian Luck

Grace asked only to borrow *some* of her mother's jewelry for her friend Lilly's wedding in Madrid. Fingering the charms on the bracelet just then, Grace knew she deliberately pulled a fast one on her mom. She remembered this wondrous, curious item from her childhood, having spied it longingly in her mother's top drawer. The no-brainer accessory of choice! This bracelet was a storybook of visions she could not read. The language of these artifacts was dead, and her mom never translated or visited the thirty-three charming records. Etta would never approve of lending Grace the mysterious bracelet.

Grace was thrilled to be a bridesmaid in her college roommate's wedding. Spain proved an excellent choice, both as a viable place to validate the union between Lilly and Harold, and as a vacation excuse for the wedding party and select guests.

Grace's copper brown, tea-length dress fit beautifully on her perfect size eight frame. She was taller and tanner than her mother, but she was the same vision of athletic prowess. Grace's father, Colonel Ezra Klydunn, was a practical man who would not have understood why Lilly wanted a wedding so far from her family.

He had died just over a year ago after being thrown from his saddle during an encounter with a rattlesnake. Ezra's favorite mount, Suerte (Lucky, in English), had never balked at snakes before. But this was a terrible intrusion on two mating diamondbacks, infuriated to be so rudely interrupted. It wasn't a rattler that killed Colonel Klydunn, it was the impact of a rock against his skull as he was thrown off the back of the saddle.

Floating away, above his own lifeless body, the last vision Ezra had of this earth was his mortal figure being embraced angrily by two rattlesnakes, and his faithful horse running back to the stable to signal for help.

Grace missed her dad. He was old school military and a loving father. Though called out for duty many times over the years, the army had left him home much of her childhood. He rarely missed her horse shows or volleyball games. He actually camped out the night before her college graduation, in uniform, to get front row seats to watch Grace receive her Spanish degree from the University of Arizona. Etta met up with him the following day driving from the ranch by herself. Etta was delighted that Ezra secured the choice seats. They both took so much film of the ceremony it filled an album and a DVD.

Etta missed her husband terribly. Ezra had brought her stability as a husband and success as her business partner. He had been a model father. Grace was overcome by sorrow and tears, realizing that he would be absent from her own wedding some day.

The arranged tour of Madrid was less memorable than the actual wedding ceremony. Grace could feel the love and spiritual nature of the union between these two people, desperately in love for the right reasons. Lilly and Harold's love was absolutely contagious.

In her room with a picturesque view of the city, Grace zipped the digital photos to her mom, who was eager for the nuptials report. Grace called under a wicked time discrepancy. Regardless of her customary sleep schedule, Etta was anxious to entertain her daughter's call. She opened the photos online while Grace reported details and events that happened at the Gothic cathedral that day. Grace's gift for gab made Etta so well informed with specifics and photo narration that Etta almost felt as though she had been in attendance.

Hanging up the cell, Etta marveled at the blessings of communications and technology. Donning her mucking shoes while still in her pajamas, Etta headed out to the barn to review the details of Grace's report with the horses.

Etta greatly appreciated the remarkable surge in equestrian breeding options over the past decade, enabling their insemination program to be greatly enhanced. Any afternoon a mare was ready, Etta could remove the prospective stallion's semen from its frozen liquid nitrogen state and thaw it in the barn. Within six hours of the mare's ovulation, the batch was artificially implanted.

At a whim, Etta could fire up the laptop in the barn office and search worldwide for a good sire. She'd receive a little package in a day or so. Since the semen had an indefinite storage life in its frozen state, babies were a twinkle in Etta's eye years prior to plan. The ranch had thrown one fine colt and some nice fillies this way. Suerte had been one of them.

Ezra loved that horse, and so did Etta. They sometimes rode together bareback on Suerte, through the cleared trail backing the mountain. Though she didn't blame the horse for the tragic accident, Etta was unable to ride her just yet. She had been grateful for Suerte's thundering gallop and demanding whinny, enabling them to recover Ezra's body before the buzzards or vultures swooped in to rip apart his flesh.

Etta was also appreciative that Grace chose to move back home during her professional transition of pursuing her master's degree. Comforted in the fact that Grace would be on the plane back home the next day, Etta let her tears spill onto Suerte's coat for nearly an hour before putting up her boots and returning to the solitary quiet of her bed.

Etta tuned into public radio after a solid night's rest. The news had reported the Al-Qaeda strike was in retaliation for Tony Blair and the world leaders' G-8 Summit on poverty and environmental issues. What had the world come to? Terrorists around the world had orchestrated so many attacks against the innocent. They had no respect for innocent life. Spain offered unconditional help to England to bring the culprits to justice. Etta was extremely grateful that Grace was just hours from boarding her flight home.

Grace waited impatiently in line, clutching the carry-on with both hands. Her proximal awareness was heightened with news of the terrorist attacks in London. The hair on the back of Grace's neck was on alert as her eyes swept the other shocked people around her waiting to check onto various flights. Was Al-Qaeda in Madrid? Of course they were. They were everywhere. Grace just wanted to get home—quickly.

She shifted the bag onto her left arm while collecting her documents from the international flight desk. The clicking sound of the boarding pass being printed distracted her for only a moment, when a hand firmly grasped her left wrist, causing her to drop the carry-on. In that moment of terror, Grace whirled around to view the culprit, wanting to scream with fright. Instead, she was silenced by the vision of a middle-aged man with fire in his eyes.

"Where did you get this?" the man demanded with a wheezy restraint in his voice.

"I borrowed...I...It's my mother's."

The resemblance was unmistakable. She was cut from this same stalk. Why didn't her mother ever tell her? She always thought that the colonel was her father. But as she stepped back from the counter with her wrist still imprisoned, she saw her own reflection in the features of this stranger.

Roberto's eyes moistened as he too recognized that she was his own. He couldn't understand it. But his paternity was undeniable both in her face and in the familiar jingle of that haunting artifact.

Instinct advised Grace it was crucial that this man come with her. Common sense would have told her otherwise. A few "propinas" to the right officials at the airlines, and Roberto secured his urgent passage with Grace back to America. Several stops through security were necessary because Roberto was suspiciously unaccompanied by luggage. Boarding the flight, a pair of businessman took interest in Roberto's remarkable fortune, and they offered their seats so Grace and he could journey together.

Together. Untangling lies. Erasing and rerecording history. Learning that his beloved Etta was *Henrietta Klydunn.* No wonder he could not find her. The formal birth name of *Henri*etta never occurred to him. The detectives assigned to hunt for her whereabouts years ago hadn't found the unlisted resident, either.

Knowing nothing of her mother's privileged life in England, Grace fought sleep in exchange for historical clarity. Roberto detailed explicitly how each bit had come to be fused to the marvelous record. He and Grace surmised that when Etta returned from her devastation in England, she came in contact with her childhood buddy Chuck, who promptly fixed her up with his serviceman friend Ezra. Grace recalled when Ezra and her mother met, he had not had time with his military career to date or settle down. Etta must have been a breath of fresh air with her sunny disposition and her ability to provide him with a home base.

Roberto shared that another soldier, George Lockley, had been the one to play hero when Etta was stranded in Birmingham. George set her up with accommodations with his Aunt Margaret. It was then Etta became the caretaker of the wonderful cactus room at the Birmingham Botanical Gardens.

Grace said her parents' engagement had been short because of the army. Ezra was assigned to Fort Huachuca where Etta was thrilled to remain close to her mother and sister.

Grace learned she had two step-siblings. Roberto was not close to either of them, but he shared the photos in his wallet. They must resemble their mother, for Roberto was attractive and muscular, while both of the children were fairly peculiar in both physique and features.

Max was an accountant who desperately, but unsuccessfully, wanted to take over Roberto's company. Marie was a housewife as her mother had been, with a brood of seven children already. From the photo, Grace couldn't help but think she was not *that* much younger than Marie but, boy, were her aspirations different!

Sleep finally came, and Roberto was touched that Grace fell asleep with her head on his shoulder. He could tell from her demeanor that Grace had inherited Etta's kind heart and loving soul. How he had wasted those years, poured into his precious company! It was all unrecoverable.

༺༻

After feeding the horses for the night, Etta cleaned up and drove the truck into town to meet the plane. She was pleased Grace was finally able to get a taste of Europe, and she was anxious for her customarily vivid stories of uncommon adventures.

The flight was predictably late with the heightened security levels in all the major airports. Etta went into town shopping for tack for the new colt while phoning the airport every half hour or so for updates on the changed arrival time.

Etta walked from the outer edge of the nearly filled airport lot. The Arizona sun had set in its colorful glory, and now there was sufficient breeze to make her hike fairly comfortable. Once in the air-conditioned airport, Etta searched unsuccessfully for a seat to await Grace's arrival. None was available or offered, so she plopped down, parking herself on the floor. Sitting cross-legged against a post, and deep into an article on natural horse training, Etta didn't notice Grace's arrival through security.

"Hey, Mom! You couldn't find a bench somewhere?" Grace broke the spell of the interesting article.

"Naw, couldn't find one, and nobody let one, so I figured I didn't need one," Etta replied, earmarking the corner of the article for later reading. She stood up and hugged her precious Grace, offering a quick prayer of thanks for her safety.

"Mom, I have a confession. Don't blow a circuit when I tell you, OK?"

"This doesn't sound good." Etta eyed Grace sideways.

"Mom, I borrowed your charm bracelet. And now, I don't have it."

Etta's eyes went down, and she just shook her head. No words would come. She could think of absolutely nothing to say in response to this heartbreaking news. So she just hugged her daughter in the spirit of attempted forgiveness. Over Grace's shoulder through tear-blurred vision, through the passage of time, she recognized that man's undeniable gait. That unmistakable locomotion. Smooth, like a jaguar.

Approaching the two women, holding the bracelet in Etta's view, Roberto said simply, "I have it, and I will *not* let it go."

"Oh my," Etta said breathlessly. "It's *you*."

It was striking how much Grace looked like her biological father. Etta didn't notice that through the growing years, attempting to force those dreams and visions of him from her broken spirit. Besides, Ezra had been a willing and wonderful father.

Pulling into the circular drive instead of the garage, Etta left the truck outside the door, anxious to bring her surprise guest through the front arched entry of the Casa de Klydunn. It had not occurred to Etta until just then that only Grace carried luggage. The story really burst to life as Roberto admitted his desperate phone calls to abandon a business flight and his luggage service, in exchange for following the sound of the enchanted charm bracelet on Grace's arm. The resonating sound of that jingle was unmistakable then and now.

"Well, I've done enough damage for the day," Grace said, excusing herself to the guest room.

"Etta, I never meant to hurt you. You have been the only love of my life. You could say my marriage was a social arrangement by my mother's creation to help me get the business started. It was never about affection. When I met you, all I could think about was this foreign discovery of real love."

Etta looked away for a moment, cutting straight through the pain he caused her years ago. "How could you let me believe I was married to you? That was an unforgivable hoax!" The hurt was still there. "I had to tell everyone here you *died* in a tragic accident. When I fled for home, I lost all my friends there. Those were the best people I have ever known." Remembering and reliving this painful reality of her past brought tears and a furrow on Etta's angry brow.

"Why didn't you let me know you were with child?"

"Was that relevant with your real children exposed?"

"Wow. This is harder than I thought. I need to explain what I did after our last meeting, Etta. Listen carefully." Roberto stood up now, placing his hands on her shoulders and forcing her to look at him squarely. "Etta, when I saw you in my office, I knew the act I was playing for my wife and children was increasingly poor. I became estranged from them, selling off part of the company to one of the partners in exchange for my freedom. And that's all she wanted, anyhow. She just wanted the money. Our relationship was for procreation only, and it brought no pleasure to either of us."

Etta still felt salt in the old wounds and was unsympathetic about his perceived troubles. "And *you* were not divorced. I know that the church would not grant you that." Etta's tone was surprisingly harsh.

"That is true."

"Then why the hell did you come here, into *my* life, when everything was forgotten?" It was a pathetic lie, and he could see straight through it.

"May I shower before we continue this?" Roberto requested with a level tone.

Suddenly, Etta broke the grip Roberto had on her shoulders with her wrists and marched back through the airy hallway to the guest room.

Etta realized her daughter set her up. Grace had taken the guest room. She shook her head and turned on her heel. Roberto followed Etta into the spacious bedroom shrine of all things Colonel Klydunn and the army.

"Oh..." escaped from Roberto's throat as he was presented with a view of Etta's husband and their life through photos and effects in the bedroom. So many questions; so much time had passed. Maybe this was a tragic mistake. She had been happy in all those family photos. He had spent those same years feeling terribly alone.

Etta offered Roberto the towels and toiletries in the marble bathroom. "Do you need replacement clothing or a nightshirt?" Etta asked, using her best hostess manners while struggling to keep the tone of her voice in check.

"A nightshirt would be fine." Roberto made efforts at cheerfulness, but he feared the worst...deportation in the morning.

Etta left and stood with one foot propped up on the wall of the hallway, right outside her bedroom. She listened for the sound of the shower running and then the patter of his feet onto the enclosure. Only then did she allow herself a peek. Though distorted through the cubical glass, she could tell he still had that sleek line. How badly she wanted to be in that shower right now! "Ugh!" She scolded herself and instead put on a pot of tea, a decaf, western, Lipton tea. She banged on Grace's door.

"Yes?" Grace answered innocently.

"I need the shower. That was just wrong, Grace. I don't even know this man!"

"You must have known him *pretty well*, Mom. He's obviously my father, so you better get to know him all over again."

Etta showered slowly in the guest bath and put another set of clothing on, determined not to allow him back in her bed. But the ache for him was different than what she felt for her beloved Ezra. Though she loved and dearly missed Ezra, Etta was still physically and emotionally—but illogically— Roberto's. Etta was still in love.

Roberto had wandered around the cocina, locating the teapot and cups. He helped himself to a teabag. The vision of this attractive man sitting in the kitchen, in her nightshirt, brought Etta to instant laughter.

"This is the worst tea I have ever tasted!" Roberto remarked with a wrinkled nose. Roberto offered a comical appearance with his hairy calves protruding from the bottom of the paisley nightshirt, and an exaggerated pinkie stuck out from the cup as he criticized her decaffeinated tea.

"Cowboy up, Roberto!" He was right. Nearly any English tea selection put her Arizona sun tea to shame. "They say it'll put hair on your knuckles."

Roberto grabbed her hand and teasingly inspected her knuckles. He found that even the touch of her skin stirred him once again. That longing he buried so many years ago when she disappeared was now a present and familiar comfort. Etta pulled her hand back.

"Etta, I did not get a divorce. I couldn't, that is true. But I never lied to you about my feelings. I have never loved another. My wife died several years ago, so I have been buried in work. I don't deny I have since been with other women, and maybe that was wrong. Now it's all different. You are here. You are alive. And Etta, you have to believe me, I love you and *only* you!"

Roberto studied her reaction. She was clearly not convinced. The pain had been deeper for her than he anticipated. So, in an unexpected gesture of hope, he dropped to his knees and kissed her hand.

"My dear, Etta. Will you marry me?" Roberto asked with such anticipation—and at the same time, so much fear—that his emotions burst. He heaved great sobs of remorse and longing, love and hope, and recovery. It was all too much, and he collapsed on the floor with her hand still in his. He feared the worst now, awaiting her answer.

Etta collected him off the floor and held Roberto in her arms. She breathed the familiar scent of his skin. She let him exhaust all the pent-up years of longing. But no certain answer would come to her. She was unable to think rationally with the shock of this evening's events. Silently, Etta led him to her bed and held his eyes while pulling up the covers and making him comfortable. She kissed him tenderly and then silently left him.

In bare feet, Etta trudged out to the tack room and collected the cleanest horse blanket she could find. She wrapped it around herself and unlatched Suerte's stall. It was the closest she could feel to Ezra, being with his favorite mount. She and Suerte exchanged thoughts, whinnies, and words. All their efforts at communication made no sense, except each enjoyed the company of the other. Etta lay down in a shallow straw bed in the corner of Suerte's stall and slept soundly.

Etta slept through the first feeding, and the restless horses alerted her to the oversight. Suerte had slept in with Etta, enjoying the company of her second-favorite human in the whole wide world. Etta shook off the straw the best she could and offered hay to the demanding equine gods and goddesses in the barn. When she finished with their round of pellets, she walked back to the house.

Grace was at the sliding kitchen door, laughing her head off. "What on earth were you doing out there?"

Etta was quite a sight, with pieces of straw still protruding at different angles from her hair. Black makeup streaked horizontally from her eyes, across the bridge of her nose, and toward her right ear. It was comical even for Roberto, who just entered the room in some of Ezra's ill-fitting old clothes.

"What happened to you?" he remarked to the barefoot stranger before him.

"You ever heard of someone being in the dog house? Well, this is kinda like that, sleeping in the horse house. I'll be back." Etta wandered into her bedroom where, indeed, she agreed with the pair. The mirror revealed quite a fright!

Once showered, clothed, and even perfumed, Etta returned. Grace had prepared the good Starbucks coffee, reserved for company, and poured Roberto a hefty mug.

With eyes locked straight with Roberto's, Etta addressed Grace. "Well, honey, this old man wants to know if I will marry him. What do you think?"

Grace followed suit by looking him over sternly. "Humm, he has good teeth. His hooves seem healthy. The coat is good. Can't tell how toned he is. I don't know, Mom. We'll need to give him a test run. Did you get a good deal?"

"What *is* the deal, Roberto? You have a life in England; I have a life here."

Roberto shifted uncomfortably. "If you will have me, I will retire and rent out the Harborne home…"

Etta was stunned by the news. "You still own it?"

"Of course, Etta. That was the home you chose for us. I would have never sold it. Elsie and her family live in the rear quarters and care for the house and gardens."

So much news. So much catching up. Her family would be confounded with news of Roberto resurfacing and her admission that Grace's father was not, in fact, buried.

"Roberto, I have thought about it so much my head hurts. We have both built complex lives and have to compromise on the details of any arrangement. I would appreciate it if you would just slow down. Grab your cup. We have mucking to do."

Ignorant to the terms of the given task, Roberto compliantly followed Etta out the backdoor. Grace was spellbound for a moment, witnessing her actual parents begin a surprising new chapter in life. She shook her head, laughed, and offered them under her breath, *"Buena suerte, padres!"*

Epilogue

"Perhaps Kelly could forgive me," she thought as she carefully packed the bracelet into the shipping box. She set the emotional letter on top and sealed it tightly. If Etta could muster the courage to rekindle their friendship, then it was also time to seek forgiveness from Binny.

The package made its way through customs to Kelly's doorstep. Intercepted by her wayward son, the precious artifact was thoughtlessly pawned in Jewellery Quarter for just enough to keep him high for the next three weeks. What of the letter? It had fallen from the box just inside Kelly's front door...

Afterword

You have witnessed a fictional account of a mysterious woman's life. Thirty-three chapters for thirty-three bits. It is my challenge and calling to locate the family to whom this extraordinary charm bracelet belongs.

I have, therefore, intentionally excluded a few of the charms so the bracelet can be appropriately identified and claimed. Readers will note these omissions through the illustrations, as David brilliantly drew the replacement charms without links.

We aren't sure if she is alive, having successfully researched and dated many of these charms, but the story of her journeys will forever live through this charming bracelet. God bless us in locating its rightful heirs.

To the mysterious woman, I thank you deeply for the loan of this touching bit of your estate. I have thoroughly treasured the time your charms spent with my family, to enjoy and share speculation of your adventures.

Finally, I ood loike ter offer un final bit ter Burminum. Yam brought *me* luck, an' I aspire ter share it. Ta bab ever so much! Cheers!

Our team members are driven in the pursuit of the woman who faithfully chronicled the events of her life in metal. Please log on: **www.Claim33Bits.co.uk** or **www.Claim33Bits.com**

Made in the USA